P9-DTQ-661

Blues for a Black Cat   & Other Stories

Blues for a Black Cat & Other Stories

Boris Vian

Edited and translated by Julia Older

With a foreword by Louis Malle

The University of Nebraska Press

Lincoln and London

Acknowledgments for the use of previously published
material appear on page vi.

The paper in this book meets the minimum require-
ments of American National Standard for Information
Sciences — Permanence of Paper for Printed Library
Materials, ANSI Z39.48-1984.

Library of Congress Cataloging in Publication Data
Vian, Boris, 1920–1959.
[Fourmis. English]   Blues for a black cat and other
stories / by Boris Vian ; edited and translated by Julia
Older ; with a foreword by Louis Malle.
p.   cm. — (French modernist library)   Translation
of: Les fourmis. Includes bibliographical references.
ISBN 0-8032-4661-7
I. Older, Julia, 1941–.   II. Title.   III. Series.
PQ2643.I152F613 1992 843'.914-dc20 91-34866 CIP

Publication of this translation was assisted by a grant
from the French Ministry of Culture.

CONTENTS

ACKNOWLEDGMENTS

The English translation of "Blues for a Black Cat" appeared in *New Directions* 38 (1979). "Good Students" originally was published in translation by *New Letters* 51, no.4 (Summer 1985): 153–59.

The translator is grateful for resources and assistance from the Columbia University Translation Center in New York; Alliance Française in São Paulo, Brazil; the French Library in Boston; and the Keene State College Mason Library in Keene, New Hampshire.

FOREWORD

In Paris in the 1950s Boris Vian was everything – poet, fiction writer, singer, subversive, actor, musician, and jazz critic. He was my friend, and I admired him passionately for his eclecticism, devastating irony, and taste for provocation.

At the beginning of 1958 when I was finishing my first film, *Elevator to the Gallows* (Ascenseur pour l'échafaud), Miles Davis was playing in a Parisian club, and Boris helped me convince the renowned jazz trumpeter to do the music for the film. It all took place in a single evening, Miles improvising magnificently with enthusiastic encouragement from Boris, who also wrote great liner notes for the record jacket.

I'd been seeing Boris from time to time when I received the dreadful news of his death from a heart attack while in a projection room. Boris had been watching the film that had just been made from his novel *I Shall Spit on Your Graves* – a really bad film. I've always thought that Boris died of shame from having seen what they'd done to his book. Like anything else, the cinema can kill.

Fortunately, in France since his death Boris Vian has become the object of a veritable cult, and his work constantly is being reprinted.

LOUIS MALLE

INTRODUCING BORIS VIAN

Boris Vian (1920–59) grew up in an ordinary family of ordinary middle-class means in the ordinary setting of Ville-d'Avray. But he himself was extraordinary. In early adolescence he threw over convention for invention, social stodginess for amusing life experiment. In his midtwenties Vian decided to be a writer. From then on publishers didn't quite know what to make of him, and critics thought they could make or break him. Later, the French government even got into the act.

It scarcely fazed Vian. He simply played a trumpet fanfare, doffed a ringmaster's top hat to announce his next escapade, climbed on a platform for a few literary somersaults, and ushered out his life as a Pataphysical clown.

During the fourteen years Vian was under the Paris Big Top, he produced at least 10 novels, 42 short stories, 7 theater pieces, 400 songs, 4 poetry collections, 6 opera libretti, 20 short story and novel translations; sang on records; acted in films; and wrote about 50 articles on as many subjects.

FAMILY AND FRIENDS

Boris was born March 10, 1920, to Paul and Yvonne Vian. He had no Russian background; his parents simply liked the name. He was a second child and his two brothers and a sister (Lélio, Alain, Ninon) were playmates. At first tutored at home, Vian then attended the Lycée Hoche in Versailles. But his education abruptly came to a halt because of rheumatic fever when he was twelve. A few years later, he also suffered from typhoid. Unfortunately, these two serious illnesses weakened his heart. By the time he was ready to enter prep school at the Lycée Condorcet in Paris, Vian already had spent a good deal of time convalescing at home.

Some critics have speculated that Vian's novel *Heartsnatcher* (L'Arrache-coeur), which portrays an overprotective mother who builds a wall around the house and puts her children in a cage, depicts his own sheltered childhood. Reductive analysis of this kind seems to ignore completely Vian's fertile imagination. Any author who has an eel slipping out the bathroom tap to snitch the toothpaste, or a piano that mixes a certain cocktail when "Mood Indigo" is played, can't be counted on for true-to-life personal disclosures.

Nevertheless, all of the poems in the collection *Cantilènes en gelée* are dedicated to family members and friends. Vian playfully inserted some of his best friends in his novels and stories, satirizing their endearing traits and salient characteristics.

His first novel, *Vercoquin et le Plancton,* nostalgically looks back on a series of carefree youthful surprise parties. Although Boris's father was facing financial problems, he built the teenagers a dance pavillion. By then, the Vians had moved to a smaller house and were renting their villa to the biologist Jean Rostand. Rostand's son François, nicknamed "Mon Prince," was one of Vian's closest friends, and figures prominently in the novel. So does his friend Jacques Loustalot, referred to as "Le Major" throughout Vian's other work. The Major plays a minor role in two stories collected here,

"Blue Fairy Tale" and "One-Way Street." Vian's brother-in-law, Dr. Peter Gna, also makes frequent guest appearances in "Blue Fairy Tale" and "Blues for a Black Cat."

Which leads to the question (seldom the answer) of women in Vian's life. In 1941 when he was twenty-one Boris married Michelle Léglise, and a year later their son Patrick was born. Meanwhile, Vian had earned an engineering degree from the École Centrale in Paris, and signed over life and limb to AFNOR (Association Française de Normalisation) as an engineer. In the four years he was thus employed, Vian wrote two novels, *Trouble dans les Andains* and *Vercoquin et le Plancton,* and played regularly in Claude Abadie's jazz orchestra. It's difficult to say when he found time to carry out his role as father.

Vian left AFNOR in 1946 to write a romantic fantasy, *Froth on the Daydream* (*L'Écume des jours*), which since has become his most widely-read novel. It centers on two young couples, Colin and Chloë, Chick and Alise. Colin is independently wealthy and deliriously in love. However, a slow dissolution sets in when his new bride discovers a water lily growing in her lung. Their large airy flat starts to shrink, and their pet mice sicken and fade as Chloë does. Chick fares no better. Consumed by a passion to find rare editions by Jean Sol Partre, he completely neglects Alise. The objects of desire take control, leaving both couples hopelessly destitute.

Romantic love and organized religion aren't far apart for Vian because of the conventional assumption that they render those who engage in them happy. His books alert us to beware of the objects of affection – whether people or things. Sooner or later they're bound to take over if we let them – and often when we don't. Grand churches, baptismal fonts, ornate chasubles, and silver chalices have a lot in common with insubordinate houses, wandering water pipes, throttling neckties, and churlish flutes.

The tone of this novel approximates that of "One-Way Street" in the present collection. In this story Naomi is engaged to Faithful, a student tombstone-engraver. Like most of Vian's romantic muses, she is pretty, and as with many of them, she dies. There's a sad tenderness about these romantic fantasies. Vian's friend and colleague Raymond Queneau called *Froth on the Daydream* "the most poignant romance of modern time," and Jean Paul Sartre, who had excerpted a few chapters in his journal *Les Temps modernes,* nominated it for the coveted Prix de la Pléiade.

When Vian isn't in a White Goddess frame of mind about women, he delights in sexual innuendo and women of questionable (seldom answerable) character. In the story "Cancer," the landlady's "half-opened housedress gaped on mossy shadows . . . and Jacques smelled the strong pleasant odor of her bearded mystery."

His blasé, virtuous heroines aren't half as intriguing as, say, Garamuche, who in "Voyage to Khonostrov" enjoys showing off her nickle-plated garters, or the good-natured whore in "Blues for a Black Cat," who generously treats everyone to a cognac. Sex à la Vian almost always is lively and droll. He offers biting crudités fresh from a constantly active imagination, and sexual wordplay for him is as important as foreplay. Let's face it. Vian was a tall, handsome cuss. Women were attracted to him, and vice versa.

In 1949, a year after the birth of his daughter, Carole, he moved in with Ursula Kübler, a ravishing dancer from Zurich whom he'd met at a publisher's party. They fast became an item, frequenting Parisian night spots, gala openings, and literary gatherings. Five years later they were married, and lived in a flat over the famous Moulin Rouge cabaret.

Vian collaborated on translations with his first wife, Michelle Léglise, and wrote a few poems for Ursula. But one is left with a niggling impression that in Vian's short, crowded life, writing and music took top priority, and that intimate personal relationships received whatever time and energy remained.

WAR AND JAZZ

The Nazi occupation of Paris was brutal. The Vichy government instigated a police action called "Spring Wind." The Jewish population was rounded up and taken to the Vélodrome d'Hiver, where they were issued gold stars and ordered to keep out of public places. In addition, the gestapo introduced obligatory work service, drafting men of eighteen to fifty years of age not otherwise employed.

Mandatory curfews were in effect. Blackouts and bombings were frequent. In the story "Fog" ("Le Brouillard") Vian writes about the terror of war: "The evening of the bombing, André had seen the clock through the lawyer's open door. It said six o'clock, half an eternity, and at that moment the bomb surprised him — showing him a menacing door, and blowing death into his face." It was a time of austerity, repression, and malaise. In an underground publication poet Paul Eluard, alias François Colère (Angry François), wrote: "Paris is cold / Paris is hungry / Paris no longer eats chestnuts in the streets."

Food was rationed and bread coupons were scarce. By the third year of the German occupation, starving Parisians were skinning alley cats for dinner. The Vians' son, Patrick, was a toddler, and these hardships must have deeply affected the family.

Time was not ripe for an emerging writer. Most established French authors, in fact, had submerged from public view and were contributing to underground Resistance newspapers such as *Combat*. The sale of paper was prohibited, and publications were banned. Liberal teachers at the Lycée Condorcet, which Vian had attended and where Jean Paul

Sartre taught, were dismissed. Intellectuals disappeared. Saboteurs were being executed.

At last, in a triumphant release from this oppression, Paris was liberated by the Allied troops on August 26, 1944. Boris Vian was given a new lease on life to become a writer, and one of the primary topics he had to get off his chest was the idiocy of war.

His story "Pins and Needles" ("Les fourmis") is based on the landing of the Allied forces on the beaches of Normandy. The narrator, who is a soldier, graphically describes the mud and blood, the lead and dead, in lively burlesque style. For, to Vian, war was the greatest farce of all. This story precedes his first play, *Knackery for All* (*L'Équarrissage pour tous*) by a year.

The play (unproduced until 1950) also deals with war and is set on D-Day, June 6, 1944. Of this "paramilitary vaude-ville" and other satires on military exploits, Vian wrote in the preface: "There is nothing scandalous in provoking hilarity by evoking war. I must confess to being among those in whom war inspires neither patriotic reflexes, nor murderous enthusiasm, nor poignant and emotional good-fellowship, nor sudden piety – nothing but a desperate, all-consuming anger against the absurdity of battles of words, but which kill men of flesh and blood."

Unmitigated anger of this kind seldom enhances creativity. However, Vian found a harmless and entertaining way to counteract his desperation. When he was seventeen he had heard Duke Ellington in concert, and the experience so overwhelmed him that he purchased a trumpet and immediately set about mastering jazz riffs. By the time he was with Michelle in Paris, Vian was a trumpeter in Claude Abadie's jazz orchestra.

Black jazz musicians had been in France since World War I with small jazz combos that played in Parisian hotels and night spots. Now, Vian jammed with these musicians, practicing American slang, and making friends. His first publication was an article for the magazine *Jazz Hot*. He became a regular contributor.

After the Liberation, writers and artists moved from literary cafés into the dark cellars of Saint-Germain-des-Prés. It was as if they'd been underground so long, they decided to stay – bebopping and drinking from dusk to dawn in the dank existentialist caves.

Vian had attended Sartre's famous lectures on existentialism, and no doubt had rubbed shoulders with the celebrated philosopher in the crowded jazz cellars of the Left Bank. But not until 1946 were the Vians formally introduced to Jean Paul Sartre and Simone de Beauvoir. Though a classical musician himself, Sartre had written a few pop lyrics, liked jazz, and had sought out Charlie "The Bird" Parker and Coleman Hawkins on 52nd Street in New York.

The two jazz enthusiasts hit it off, and soon Sartre invited Vian to write a column for his new, widely acclaimed magazine *Les Temps modernes*. In postwar France writers were coming out of the woodwork, and Sartre's new avant-garde protegé annoyed not a few of his more staid literary colleagues.

Suffice it to say, music was Vian's livelihood at times, and his life. When he was forced to give up the trumpet because of his heart condition, he started to sing and record some of the four hundred songs he'd written. In tune with the times, he acquainted listeners with rock and roll. Vian also was one of the first to start a ground-swell protest against the Algerian war with his song "The Deserter" ("Le Deserteur"). The record sold thousands of copies before it was banned.

Allusions to jazz tunes and musicians are scattered throughout Vian's work, including this collection. In the story "Cancer" ("L'Écrevisse") the American jazz artist Jack Teagarden is a down-and-out flutist, and in "Pins and Needles" the Colonel is playing "Jada" when a grenade accidently hits his piano. The narrator in "The Plumber" ("Le Plombier") retires to his room to play the "Deep South Suite," and the police cadets in "Good Students" ("Les Bons Élèves") whistle marches and swing their billy clubs to violin quadrilles. "Blues for a Black Cat" ("Blues pour un chat noir") is a title with a double meaning that relates to black musicians known in the jazz world as "wailing cats" when they're really swinging.

AMERICAN POTBOILERS

In the forties hardboiled detective novels with sex, violence, and macho prose were selling in the United States like Coca-Cola. Jean Paul Sartre had returned from New York City with a roster of best-selling novelists he'd signed on for French editions by Gallimard. Both Michelle and Boris Vian, proficient in English, apparently were recommended by Sartre as translators.

In the interim, Vian had quit his job and was hatching some schemes of his own. His friend Jean D'Haullin owned Èditions du Scorpions and was looking for ways to bolster sales. He asked Vian if he had connections with any American pop-pulp writers. Vian didn't, but he knew where he could find one. A few weeks later Vian slapped the finished manuscript of *I Shall Spit on Your Graves* (J'irai cracher sur vos tombes) on D'Haullin's desk. The book was by Vernon Sullivan, a.k.a. Boris Vian.

The rest is history, if not legend. The novel, about a mulatto who murders two wealthy white women in revenge for the lynching of his brother, appeared in 1946 to rave reviews. French critics compared Vernon Sullivan to William Faulkner and Ernest Hemingway – that is, until their dig for details drew blanks from reliable sources. The press suspected they'd been conned, and praise turned to accusation.

But Vian was busy, now working on *real* translations. Gallimard had commissioned him to translate *The Big Clock* by Kenneth Fearing and both *The Lady in the Lake* and *The Big Sleep* by Raymond Chandler. Translating this genre of American fiction helped Vian to polish his own writing style for the Vernon Sullivan series. Good press or bad, Vian's American potboilers were turning out to be a great success.

In 1948 sales hit the ceiling when *I Shall Spit on Your Graves* was found in a hotel room beside a murder victim. Vian was dragged into court and he admitted to his authorship of the book. In 1949 the notorious Vernon Sullivan novel was banned by the French government, but not before Vian, with the help of the American Milton Rosenthal, had translated his own French version into English and published it. In 1951 the court sentenced Vian with a fine of 100,000 francs. Nevertheless, the three subsequent Vernon Sullivan titles continued to keep baguettes and bordeaux on Vian's table.

The French father of science fiction, Jules Verne (1828–1905), had given Americans a taste for future worlds, and half a century later author A. E. van Vogt reciprocated by giving France its first taste of future-fiction American-style. *The World of Null-A,* van Vogt's tale about a non-Aristotelian thinker and a Games Machine of electronic brains, landed on Vian's desk for translation. The book was based on the ideas of semanticist Count Alfred Korzybski, who believed that as observers we are limited by our perceptions and even scientists can never be totally objective.

In Korzybski, Vian recognized a soul mate, and the Count's favorite maxim, "The map is not the territory," quickly became his own. However, much prior to his *Null-A* translation, Vian had unloaded Cartesian logic for unfettered creative spontaneity and imagination. In fact, he had a run-in with Cartesians from the *Temps modernes* review board, who had censored a few of his zanier "Chronicles of a Liar" columns. As the jacket copy of the now collected "Chronicles" puts it, the censors obviously "confused banter and the lack of gravity with the laws of Newton."

In any case, *The World of Null-A* caused quite a stir. The first edition published by Gallimard sold 25,000 copies, and Vian was touted as a champion of modern science fiction in France.

Boris and his wife, Michelle, had collaborated on translations as well as individual commissions. When they separated, she continued as a translator, often while in the company of Jean Paul Sartre. In the engrossing biography, *Sartre: A Life,* Annie Cohen-Solal writes: "Michelle with her golden hair, her sweetness and precision, was always ready to lend her proficiency in English to such and such a translation, such and such a meeting. Always present, always fragile, she never broke with Sartre." Indeed, when film and stage director John Huston asked the existentialist playwright of *No Exit* to do a screenplay on Freud, Sartre urgently turned to Michelle Vian for a French translation of Ernest Jones's long biography on Freud.

Boris also took on increasingly challenging projects. The year of his divorce in 1952, Gallimard asked Vian to translate General Omar N. Bradley's voluminous *History of a Soldier.* The publisher wanted it in a hurry and suggested he find a collaborator. The indefatigable Vian promised he'd do it alone, and by the deadline. According to David Noakes's biography (*Boris Vian,* Classiques du XXe Siècle 69), Vian shut himself in a room, and with only a few pauses now and then for Ursula Kübler to massage his cramped hand, he finished translating the 552-page opus in a record two weeks. Clearly, this must have been a doubly difficult undertaking for a man who despised war as much as Vian. But no doubt he used it later as cannon fodder for his parodies on jingoism and military brass.

In a "superliminal note" to a special issue of the *Evergreen Review* in 1960, Roger Shattuck writes, "Pataphysics is the science of imaginary solutions," adding, "The idea of truth is the most imaginary of solutions." At this point the reader might want to cry, "Help! Is there a pataphysician in the house?"

We owe pataphysical science (or the lack thereof) to French playwright Alfred Jarry (1873–1907), whose life curiously paralleled Vian's. Specifically, it was short. While young, he wrote playlets with his older brother and performed *en famille*. (Vian wrote skits with his brothers for the Vian surprise parties.) And like Vian, when he was twenty he moved to Paris to live and work. They both share the versatility of writing poetry, plays, novels, journalistic articles, and criticism. Jarry died of chronic illness and poverty stricken. In keeping with the Vian phenomenon, his posthumerous fame exceeded humerous infamy.

Alfred Jarry created the character Dr. Faustroll to expound on the ever-spiraling, ever-lively contrasts of language, life, and ever-ything. Jarry's other exponentially inventive creation was the *Ubu* cycle, which started out as a series of schoolboy sketches lampooning a physics teacher, and turned into a fullscale farce based (loosely) on *Macbeth*.

In unreality, Alfred Jarry was a Laughing Buddha. His satires pointed out the folly of taking oneself too seriously, of believing whole-headedly in one's pretensions and conventions. Ubu epitomized the bungling idiot who points up the absurdities of human failings and flailings.

Cartesian *cogito ergo sum* logic had been around for almost three centuries and was a crumbling safehouse when Jarry appeared *en scène*. Like a Zen master, he beat his disciples over the head with their own outrageous egos. The slapstick worked, and Charlie Chaplin took over where Jarry left off.

Nearly fifty years after Dr. Faustroll bumbled on stage, the mysterious Collège de 'Pataphysique was inaugurated in Paris with a speech by his Magnificence, Dr. I. L. Sandomir, reacting as vice-curator and Founder. Exceptions and opposites made up the core curriculum. Members were called "Transcendent Satraps" (petty princes who exceed their rank). The Pataphysicians chose the spiral as their insignia, since Father Ubu's pot-belly symbolized consciousness ever-circling around the umbilicus of the unconscious — or something to that effect. (For a complete discussion of spirals and their significance in the second, third, and fourth dimensions, take a look at *Hamlet's Mill* by Georgio de Santillana and Hertha von Dechend.)

In 1952 Vian's friends Raymond Queneau, Jacques Prèvert, Eugène Ionesco, and other Pataphysicians named him "Knacker, 1st Class" in recognition of the obvious pataphysical qualities of Boris's play *Knackery for All.* In 1953 Vian became a Satrap and one of the College's most zealous members, contributing numerous essays and letters to their published notebooks and dossiers. The ex-engineer also presided over the subcommittee in charge of "Licities and Harmonies." His function, as defined in the College history by F. Lachenal, was "to provide an infinity (at least three) of lineaments or semi-virtualities for any subject."

But, of course, Vian always had been a Pataphysician — contriving words, playfully creating new rhymes, inventing musical instruments, improvising on the trumpet, and fabricating amusing stories – all with brio and panache. Now, however, the coterie of Marcel Duchamp, Joan Miró, René Clair, Michel Leiris, Maurice Saillet, Jean Mollet, and other estimable talents, reinforced Vian's creative productivity and provided a new outlet. With exquisite grace and an Astaire-like lightness, he slipped into Jarry's ratapataphysical shoes.

In 1897 Jarry had published his first novel *Days and Nights:*

Story of a Deserter (Les Jours et les nuits: Roman d'un Déserteur). Analogously, in January 1955, Vian launched his song "The Deserter" ("Le Déserteur"), which was broadcast by several interpreters over French radio. In 1911 Jarry wrote a chapter in the Dr. Faustroll book titled "The Surface of God" – a geometrical speculation concluding: "God is the tangential point between zero and infinity." In the same vein, Vian wrote a monograph published in the Pataphysical notebooks titled, "Memoire Concerning the Numerical Calculation of God by Simple (and False) Methods."

A year after Vian's death, Raymond Queneau, who had been at the forefront of French Surrealism in the 1920s and of the Collège de 'Pataphysique in the 1950s, introduced an experimental Workshop (Ouvrier) on Literary Potential called "OuLiPo." The inimitable collection of Queneau's *Pataphysical Poems* translated by Teo Savory (Unicorn Press, 1985) alludes to OuLiPo as a continuing group meeting in Paris. *Vowel Movement: A Pataphysical Journal* recently advertised in the American publication *Poets & Writers*. These are a few indications that the spirit of 'Pataphysique continues to attract readers and adherents.

THE OUTWARD SPIRAL

Vian himself often predicted he would die before he reached the age of forty, and made the deadline by a year. He was attending a private showing of a film based on his screenplay for *I Shall Spit on Your Graves*. Some say the film, which Boris contracted to direct but didn't, was enough to cause anyone heart failure. Moreover, the morning of June 23, 1959, Vian hadn't taken his heart medication.

Until then, a few small publishers such as Toutain, Le Terrain Vague, and Éditions du Scorpions had published most of his novels. They had sold a few thousand copies each. His collected short stories, poems, and two plays had sold even less. At one poetry reading, Vian autographed seven books (including two for the French Ministry and one for the publisher). He couldn't make a living as a serious (that is, seriocomic) writer, and lived primarily from translations and the Vernon Sullivan detective novels.

Today, Vian has been exhumed and pronounced Literary. (Capital C for French publishers currently living off the *corpse d'esprit*.) His works are being dredged up and recycled at an amazing rate – sixty-eight titles, and still counting. They include obscure essays, juvenilia, and collections of unedited manuscripts. We're talking about a writer who, when his ticker still beat a weak tattoo in his over-six-foot-body, pointedly was snubbed by critics and compromised by publishers.

Vian's literary predecessors were formidable. Stéphane Mallarmé had revolutionized poetry with original language and syntax, and Proust had written the precursor to the interior modern novel. Sartre was astounding audiences with his avant-garde existential plays, later transformed into the Theater of the Absurd by playwrights Ionesco and Beckett. Vian's play *The Empire Builders* (Les Batisseurs d'empire; ou, le schmürz) which he never saw performed, now often is included in Theater of the Absurd anthologies.

In any case, many of these elements remarkably coalesced in Vian's writing with few traces of derivation. By the time he drafted his early stories in 1945–46, he had assimilated some of Proust's narrative technique, Mallarmé's wordplay, Sartre's existential perspectives, and in the process, created a voice of his own.

The short story form came naturally for Vian, and he published these and other stories in journals and tabloids. In the preface to *Le Ratichon baigneur,* a posthumous collection of miscellaneous stories, editor Noël Arnaud writes: "Boris Vian no doubt conceived of the story as short, fast-paced, never stuck, turning on hubcaps, stopping dead at the finish line – and assuredly, he wrote it that way."

I first was introduced to Boris Vian while living in Tellaro, a small fishing village on the Ligurian coast of Italy. Marie Geneviève, a French friend from student days, arrived for a visit and brought Vian's poems and the story collection *Les Fourmis*. She was a songwriter, worked as a script girl in the Paris cinema and naturally was attracted to Vian's versatility. For hours we sat on the rocks below Villa Isoela overlooking the Mediterranean and took turns reading Vian out loud. I was hooked. But it wasn't until several years later, while I was employed as a musician in Brazil, that I started to translate these stories.

This is the only collection of Vian's short fiction published during his lifetime (by Éditions du Scorpions in 1949). It was reissued by Le Terrain Vague under the original title in 1966. Oddly, three stories collected as *Les Lourettes Fourées* are appended to Vian's novel *L'Herbe rouge*, published post-humously in 1962 by Jacques Pauvert. In addition, two other collections have appeared: *Le Loup garou* and *Le Ratichon Baigneur.* In all, a total of forty-two stories are in print in France.

Blues for a Black Cat and Other Stories provides a perfect introduction to Vian for readers of English. These stories contain the pivotal characters and absurdist qualities germinal to his later novels and plays. Some of the stories, such as the title tale, pave the way for Vian's blacker humor, which surfaces in "Voyage to Khonostrov" and "Dead Fish." Though boldly defiant, Vian always disguises social protest in vertiginous flights of fancy, quirky sexual encounters, and doomed romantic affairs. But his unique parody tends to heighten the masked terrors of war, poverty, ill health, and unemployment that hound the bizarre protagonists of these fablelike narratives.

Although this collection originally was titled *Les Fourmis,* after the lead war story "Pins and Needles," I couldn't resist renaming it after "Blues for a Black Cat." My reason has no raison d'être, only a sense that this story best underlines Vian's colorful wordplay, jazzy overtones, delightful innuendo, and amusing observations of Parisian night life.

I hope readers will not be dismayed in learning that one story "The Walkon" ("Le Figurant") has been omitted. Perhaps in placing it at the end of his collection, Vian himself realized that this novella-length work failed to live up to the spontaneity and vigor of his other stories.

Finally, the order of these stories has been slightly altered to accommodate English-speaking readers, showcase Vian's masterful pacing, and highlight his first-class knack as a writer.

JULIA OLDER

Blues for a Black Cat   & Other Stories

THE PLUMBER

I

It wasn't Jasmine knocking because she was in a seedy district shopping with her lover. It wasn't my uncle. He'd died two years ago. The dog always knocked twice, and I had my key. So it had to be someone else. It was a distinguished knock – heavy, perhaps ponderous, no, rather dense, a slow costly knock. So it had to be the plumber.

He entered fortified with a shoulder strap on which hung a degenerate tool box of herbivorous leather filled with jingling scrap metal. "The bathroom's that way," he told me with a Sagittarian gesture. He didn't ask, and because of the directness of his short statement, finally I'd discovered where the bathroom was. It might have been a long time before I'd found it.

At this time of day, since Jasmine was gone, my uncle dead, and the dog knocked twice (and most often), only my eleven nephews and nieces were home busy playing with the kitchen gas range. I couldn't hear a single sound.

After a roundabout detour, the plumber came back to the living room. Annoyed by his error, I put him back on the right track and guided him to the bathroom. I was going in with him when he pushed me out, not rudely, but with a finality common to specialists. "I don't need you," he said. "Besides, you'll get your beautiful *new* suit all dirty."

I said nothing because he sneered, and moreover, with cunning, so I left to unstitch a tag hanging from my suit. This was another of Jasmine's oversights. But after all, you couldn't expect a woman who didn't know you, who'd never heard your name, who didn't even know you existed, who perhaps herself existed only partially, or in truth not at all, to render the services of an English governess such as Alice Marshall, who was born in Bridgeport in the Wilshires. And I scolded Alice for her chronic carelessness. She pointed out that one can't neglect looking after nephews and nieces and remove suit labels at the same time.

I had to lower my head, because at that moment I passed through the door leading from the sitting room to the dining room, a door notoriously too low, although many times I'd pointed it out to the deaf architect employed by my landlord.

The disorder of my dress accounted for, warily so as not to cause alarm, I directed myself toward Jasmine's mother's room. I'd reserved the most beautiful room of the apartment for her – one of those that face the street and continues on the other side when no one's looking to conserve its symmetry.

Perhaps it's time for me to describe Jasmine to you, but in the dark (we never open the window shades because Jasmine doesn't exist and consequently couldn't have a mother, an incontestable fact that eventually I'll prove in this story) – in the dark, therefore, the description would be inaccurate.

I crossed Jasmine's mother's room and with caution I opened the door that leads to the billiard room adjoining one wall of the bathroom. In anticipation of the plumber, a long time ago I'd made an opening in this wall, and from this angle at my leisure I could observe his acts and gestures while he busied about his work. Raising his head, he saw me and signaled for me to join him.

I hurried, retracing my steps in the inverse direction. In passing, I noticed that my nephews continued to move about near the gas stove and conceived (though briefly, because the plumber was waiting, and I didn't want my delay to be misconstrued as the arrogance to which some people attribute my serious demeanor) a complete and irrational scorn in respect to those imperfect appliances called gas stoves. Quickly, I reached the hall and opened the door onto a landing with four choices, one which would have served as a billiard room if it weren't condemned, the other also condemned, Jasmine's mother's room, and the fourth – the bathroom. I closed the door of the third and finally entered the bathroom.

Seated on the edge of the tub, the plumber melancholically contemplated the planks protecting the dismantled pipes. He'd just made them jump with the point of a soldering pen.

"I've never seen such an installation," he assured me.

"It's old," I commented.

"You can see that," he said.

"That's why I said it," I told him. I'm incapable of determining the age of an installation when no one else can either.

"There are some who are always yakking, and where does it get them?" he observed. "Whoever installed this wasn't a plumber."

"Your company did the installation," I said. "I remember, distinctly."

"I wasn't with them then. Otherwise, I'd have left."

"So it comes back to the same thing since you'd have left. It's as if you were there from the moment you weren't there," I said.

"In any case, if I could get my hands on the dirty son of a bitch with his fat kangaroo ass, who botched this goddamn whorehouse of a shit installation – well, as they say, I wouldn't be paying him compliments." As he swore, the veins in his neck swelled like ropes. He shifted positions, directing his voice toward the bottom of the tub to obtain a lower resonance, and he kept it up for a good hour.

"Right," he concluded out of breath. "Well, I'll set to the task at hand."

When he took a large soldering iron from his leather case, I'd already positioned myself comfortably to watch him work. Pulling a flask from his pocket, he poured its contents into the hole designed by an industrious manufacturer at the foot of the gas adductor tube. A match caused a large flame to leap toward the ceiling.

In the blue light, the plumber leaned over and dubiously considered the two pipes for hot and cold water, the gas pipe, the central heating duct, and a few other pipes I didn't recognize. "The best thing to do," he said, "is to cut everything flush and start from scratch. But you're going to feel it die."

"If you must," I said. Not wishing to participate in the massacre, I left on tiptoe. He turned the point of the soldering iron the moment I closed the door, and the roar of the volatile gas covered the slight clacking noise of the ball-bearing spring coming to rest in its housing.

I passed the door of Jasmine's room, initially condemned, but whose execution had been stayed, and crossing the living room, I forked toward the dining room to get to my room. I'd already been lost in the apartment more than once. Jasmine would like us to change flats. She has trouble finding it herself, and persists in coming back without my asking her to. Besides, I myself persist talking with you about Jasmine, and it's simply because I love her. She doesn't play a single role in this story and probably never will – at least unless I change my mind, but no one can foresee that. As the outcome will soon be revealed, it's useless to dwell on such an uninteresting subject – even less so than others. In particular, I'm thinking of the propagation of Tyrolean gnats or the treatment of laniferous green flies.

Once in my room, I positioned myself near a waxed oak piece of furniture which a long time ago (without exaggerating) I'd transformed into an electrophone. And, maneuvering the circuit breaker allowing the apparatus to function, I triggered the turntable on which a record was deposited in preparation for the extirpation of the contained melody by the intermediary of a sharp point.

The black accents of the "Deep South Suite" soon plunged me into my favorite lethargy, and the acceleration of the movement of the pendulums transported the solar system into reinforced gyration, curtailing the duration of the world by nearly a day – so much and so well that it was eight-thirty in the morning and I got up. I was anxious not to intertwine my legs with Jasmine's tempting legs. Alas, Jasmine wasn't even aware of me.

I constantly am waiting for her. She has hair like water in the sun and I'd like to encircle her waist with my strong arms and make her expire with my *sang-chaud* kisses (except on those days she resembles Claude Farrère).

"Eight-thirty," I said to myself. "The plumber must be dying of hunger!" I dressed quickly and oriented myself, then set out for the bathroom. The surroundings seemed profoundly altered as if in the wake of fundamental disasters. I soon realized that the only difference was the absence of customary pipes, and resigned myself.

Stretched out beside the bathtub, the plumber was still breathing. I injected some bouillon through his nostrils because his teeth were closed on a bead of solder. Reanimated, he again set to work. "I've found that I've finished most of the job. Everything's cut flush to the walls and I'm starting from scratch. Now it's your decision," he said.

"Do your best," I told him. "I trust your expertise as a specialist. For nothing in the world would I want the least of my suggestions to conflict with your initiative, which I admit is an exclusive attribute of the Corporation of Plumbers."

"Don't exaggerate," he advised me. "In principle I understand, but I'm a long way from my certificate, and if you bullshit me, I won't talk with you. It's funny how people who think they're educated feel they have to shit on everyone!"

"I assure you that I honor the least of your acts highly," I told him. "Don't doubt my humility."

"Right," he said. "I'm not a bad guy. So what I'm going to do is, I'm going to reassemble it exactly as it was because a colleague installed it and a plumber always has his reasons. Often he says to himself, 'There's a pipe that's not straight.' And he asks himself why, and naturally he accuses another plumber. But if he really wanted to get to the bottom of it, more often than not it's some unknown reason and he prefers to believe it's the pipe when really it's the wall. To come back to our situation – I'm redoing everything exactly as it was, and afterward I'm sure it'll work."

I held back one crucial comment. It had worked before he arrived. But maybe I knew nothing about it. I remembered the parable of the straight pipe and kept my mouth shut. Once more I located my bed. The noise of impatient footsteps reverberated from the story above. People are infuriating. Can't they go to bed nervously instead of pacing the floor nervously? I surrendered to the truth – no.

Jasmine's image haunted me to distraction, and I cursed her mother for taking her from me with the bad conscience that nothing's justified. Jasmine is nineteen years old and I know that she's known other men besides me, more the reason for her to allow me into her intimacy. It's her mother and jealousy. I forced myself to think of some gratuitous wickedness and had such trouble understanding its exact

6

form, materialized in skimpy red and white cotton threads, that for a long time I lost consciousness. In the bathroom, the humming of the soldering iron turned the edge of my dream blue with rough oxidized fringes.

II

The plumber stayed with me for forty-nine hours at a stretch. The work was far from finished. I was passing by the entrance to the kitchen when I heard someone knocking. "Open up!" they cried. "It's urgent!"

I opened the door and the neighbor from above stood before me in great bereavement. Her face bore the marks of a recent affliction and she dripped on my carpet. She looked like she'd been dragged from the Seine.

"Did you fall in the water?" I asked with interest.

"Excuse me for disturbing you, sir," she said. "It's just that I have a leak at my place. I called the plumber and he should have arrived three days ago."

"There's a plumber here," I said. "Maybe he's yours."

"My seven children have drowned. The two oldest still are breathing because the water's only up to their chins. But if the plumber still has work to do here, I don't want to disturb you – "

"I suppose he made a mistake. I'll ask him so it's not on my conscience," I said. "Actually, my bathroom was in good working order."

III

When I entered the bathroom he was just putting a final touch on a soldered joint in the form of an iris which covered a bare spot on the wall. "It'll work like this," he told me. "I redid everything exactly as it was. I added a few welds because it's what I do best, and I like work well done."

"A woman's asking for you," I told him. "Weren't you supposed to go to the story above me?"

"Is this the fourth story?" he asked.

"The third," I said.

"Then I made a mistake," he concluded. "I'll go see this woman. My company'll send you the bill. But don't feel badly – there's always work in the bathroom for a plumber."

PINS AND NEEDLES

I

We arrived this morning and weren't well received. No one was on the beach but a lot of dead guys (or pieces of dead guys), tanks, and demolished trucks. Bullets flew from almost everywhere. As entertainment I don't like this chaos. We jumped in the water, but it was deeper than it looked and I slipped on a tin can, keeping it as a souvenir. The boy just behind me had had three-quarters of his face removed by a whizzing bullet. I put the pieces in my helmet and gave them to him. He ran off to get help but it looks like he took a wrong turn because he walked over his head into the water and I don't think he could see well enough at the bottom to find his way.

Then I ran the right direction and got there just in time for a kick in the face. I tried to insult the guy, but a mine had left only a few inconvenient pieces, so I ignored his gesture and went on.

Ten meters farther, I rejoined three other guys behind a concrete bunker. In a sweat and water-soaked, they fired at the corner of a high wall. So I could be like them, I knelt and fired too. The lieutenant came back holding his head in both hands, and red flowed from his mouth. He didn't look too happy, and he quickly went and stretched out on the sand, mouth open and arms in front. He must have really messed up the sand. This was one of the only spots that had stayed clean.

From there, our stranded boat at first looked completely idiotic, and then it no longer even looked like a boat when the two shells fell on it. I wasn't overjoyed, because two buddies still were inside riddled with bullets that had hit them when they tried to jump out. I tapped the shoulders of the three guys with me and said, "Come on, let's go." Of course I made them go first. Intuition served me well because the first two were felled by two enemy soldiers. Only an unlucky poor chap remained ahead of me. As soon as he extricated himself from the worst of the two, the other one had just enough time to kill him before I took over.

The two bastards behind the corner of the wall had had a machine gun and cartridges. I turned it in the other direction and fired, but stopped short because it broke my eardrums. Besides, it had slowed down. I guess they've regulated it not to fire in the opposite direction.

Now I was nearly calm. From above the beach I could take advantage of the view. Smoke billowed from every part of the sea and the water rose very high. I also could see salvos from large battleships. Their shells passed overhead with a strange muted sound, like a low-resonance cylinder rocket in the air.

The captain arrived. We were only eleven. He said we weren't many but we'd manage. (Later they brought us up to strength.) Momentarily, he ordered us to dig holes. I thought they were to sleep in. But no, we had to get in and keep firing.

Fortunately, it got lighter. Now large contingents of boats disembarked, but most of the crews fell in the water. They surfaced flailing as if lost, and the fish trailed between their legs to avenge themselves for the confusion. Many didn't surface, but departed beneath the waves. The captain soon told us to wipe out a machine-gun nest that had recommenced progressive firing behind the tank.

We got behind the tank. I went last because I don't have much confidence in the brakes of those contraptions. Anyway, it's easier to walk behind a tank because you don't get tangled in barbed wire, and the stakes fall automatically. But I don't like the tank's manner of reducing corpses to a pulp with the sort of noise that's hard to remember – at the time you hear it, though, it's pretty unmistakable.

After three minutes, the tank jumped over a mine and started to burn. Two of the guys were unable to get out. The third managed, but one of his feet didn't clear the tank. I don't know if he realized this before he died. Finally, two of the shells fell on the machine-gun nest, crushing the eggs and also the guys in it.

Those who got out discovered a change for the better. But then an anti-tank unit began to spit fire in turn, and at least twenty men fell into the water. As for me, I lay flat on my belly. From my position, by leaning a little, I could see them fire. The flaming tank body protected me somewhat and I aimed carefully. The gun-loader fell, writhing a lot. I must have hit him too low, and I wasn't able to polish him off. First, I had to blast the other three, but I had trouble. Fortunately, the noise from the burning tank drowned out their screams. I didn't really polish off the third one completely, either.

The flames continued to jump and smoke from all sides. Sweat poured into my eyes, and I rubbed them well so I could see better. "Can you bandage my right arm tightly against my body?" he asked. I told him yes, and started to bandage him with the dressing. Suddenly, both of his feet left the ground at once, and he toppled onto me. A grenade exploded behind him and he stiffened immediately. (This seems to happen when you die tired.) Anyhow, it was easier to lift him off me. And then I had to sleep and when I awoke the noise was in the distance, and one of those guys with red crosses all around his helmet poured me some coffee.

II

Afterward, we left for the interior and tried to practice the training maneuvers we'd learned from the instructors. Mike's jeep returned with Fred driving and Mike in two pieces. They'd run into a wire that had cut him in two. We're equipping the other motor cars with a steel blade in front because it's too hot to ride with the windscreens up. There's still gunfire everywhere, and we make patrol on patrol, I think we've advanced too fast. We're having trouble keeping in contact with the Service Corps.

The enemy destroyed at least nine of our tanks this morning. And a strange thing happened. One guy's bazooka got caught in his rifle strap and went off. He waited until he'd reached forty meters in the air, and then came down by parachute.

I think we're going to have to ask for reinforcements because I've just heard (as distinctly as the loud snapping of scissors) that they had to cut from arrears.

III

It reminds me of six months ago when they cut from arrears. Actually, we must be completely surrounded. Summer's gone. Fortunately, we still have food and ammunition. Guard duty's at two-hour intervals. It's tiring. The enemy's taking our uniforms from prisoners, and they're beginning to dress like us. We have to watch out. As if this weren't enough, we have no electric light. We're experiencing the impact of face-on shelling from four directions at once. For the moment, we're trying to establish contact with the rear. They have to send us some planes. We're short on cigarettes. There's noise

outside. They must be preparing something. We haven't
even got time to take off our helmets.

IV

They sure did prepare something! Four tanks nearly reached
us. I saw the first one leaving. It stopped soon enough because a grenade suddenly demolished one of its caterpillar
bands with a terrible drumming noise. But the cannon on
the tank wasn't so easy to dispose of. We used flame projec-
tiles, but the trouble with them is that you have to force the
tank to open its hatch. Otherwise, the guys inside are roasted
like chestnuts. Three of us forced the hatch open with a
metal saw. But two other tanks bore down on us. We had to
blow up the first one without forcing it open. The second
blew up too, and a third made a half-turn. But this was a ruse,
because it was moving backwards. It startled us slightly to see
it fire on the guys behind it. The tank sent us a birthday
present of a dozen 88 shells. We'll have to rebuild the house
if we want to use it. It would go faster if we took another one.

We got rid of the third tank by loading a bazooka with
snuff. The guys inside the tank knocked their skulls so hard
against the windshield that they came out cadavers. Only the
driver was still alive. But he caught his head in the wheel and
couldn't get it out. So rather than ruin the tank, we cut off
the guy's head.

Motorcyclists with machine guns were making hay behind
the tank. We successfully destroyed them – thanks to an old
reaping machine and sheaf binder.

Meanwhile, a few bombs showered down on us along with
a plane that our DCA had just shot down for the hell of it. To
tell the truth, it was on our side. My company's lost Simon,
Morton, Buck, and P.C. We're left with the others, and Slim's
arm.

V

We're still surrounded. It has rained without letup for two days. The roof has only one tile out of two, but the drops fall just where they will. We aren't really soaked. We don't know for sure how much time it's going to last. Constant patrols. It's difficult to look at a gunsight when enthusiasm's gone, and it's tiring to stay neck-deep in mud more than a quarter of an hour.

Yesterday, we encountered another patrol. We didn't know if it was ours or the enemy's. Under the mud it's safe to fire and you can't injure yourself – the rifles blow up immediately.

We've tried everything to get rid of this mud. We poured gas over it. The burning dried it, but afterward we cooked the soles of our feet walking on it. The real solution is to dig on firm soil. But it's even more difficult to patrol firm soil and we'd end up with a solution as good as it is bad. The trouble is that so much rain has fallen, it's formed pools. Actually that's ok, they're at the barricade. But now the water's risen to the first story, and that's unpleasant.

VI

Something bad happened to me this morning. I was under the hangar behind the barracks preparing a diversion for two guys that we'd seen through the binoculars. They were trying to knock us off. I had a small 81 mortar which I'd placed in a baby carriage. Johnny was going to disguise himself as a peasant and push it. Before we got started, the mortar fell on my foot. That's nothing new nowadays. But then it exploded and I sprawled out holding my foot. With a hellish noise it exploded on one of those wing fans in the second story just over the piano on which our captain was playing "Jada." The piano was demolished. More annoying, however, the captain wasn't even scratched. Anyway, he wasn't wounded enough to stop him from slugging me hard.

Fortunately, right after that an 88 mortar shell struck the same room. He didn't realize they'd taken sighting from the smoke of the first explosion, and he thanked me, saying that I'd saved his life by calling him downstairs. I lost interest in the affair because of my two broken teeth, and also because all of his bottles had been stored just under the piano.

We're surrounded more than ever. It gets worse and doesn't abate. As luck has it, though, the weather's starting to break. It scarcely rains nine hours out of twelve. Between now and a month we can count on relief air drops. Three days of supplies are left.

VII

The planes are starting to drop articles by parachute. I was disappointed when I opened the first package. It was a lot of medication. I exchanged them with the doctor for two nut chocolate bars – good ones, not the junky rations – and half a flask of cognac. But he recouped them while I was taking care of my injured foot. I had to give back the cognac. Without this barter, today I'd only have one foot.

It's starting to roar overhead again. There's a small opening, and they're still sending down parachutes. But this time they look like men.

VIII

They were men. Two of them were jokers. It seems that they'd spent the entire flight playing judo, giving each other goose-eggs, and rolling under the benches. They jumped at the same time and played at cutting each other's parachute rip cords. Unfortunately, the wind separated them, so they continued with gun shots. I'd rarely seen such good shots.

Right now we're interring them because they fell from quite a height.

IX

We're surrounded. Our tanks returned, but the others haven't noticed. Because of my foot, I could no longer fight seriously, but I encouraged my friends. It was exciting. I could see well from the window and the parachutists that arrived yesterday struggled like the devil. I now have a silk scarf from a yellow, green, and brown parachute. It goes well with my beard. Tomorrow I'm going to shave. They gave me permission because of my convalescence. I was so excited that I swung a brick at Johnny's head. He'd just missed an enemy soldier, and now I'm missing two more teeth. This war is good for nothing as far as teeth are concerned.

X

Routine dulls impressions. I told that to Huguette – they have names like that here – while dancing with her at the Red Cross Center and she replied, "You're a hero." But I didn't have time for a good answer because Mac tapped me on the shoulder. So I let him have her. The other girls spoke with an accent and the orchestra played much too fast.

My foot still hurts a little, but in fifteen days it'll be over. We set off again.

I'd limit myself to one of our girls, but the uniform is too thick. It also dulls impressions. There are many girls here but they understand what you tell them and I blush easily. There isn't too much to do with them. I left, and immediately found lots of other girls, not the same, more understanding. But they're five hundred francs minimum – more because I'm wounded. Strange. They have German accents.

Afterward, I lost Mac and drank too much cognac. This morning I have a terrible headache where the MP hit me. I'm broke because toward the end I bought some French cigarettes from an English officer. I smelled them as he walked by. I've just thrown them away. They're disgusting. He had good reason to get rid of them.

XI

When you leave the Red Cross store with a box of cigarettes, soap, candies, and papers, they follow you in the street with their eyes. I don't understand why. Surely they could sell their cognac for enough money to buy some and have their wives remain intact as well.

My foot's nearly better. I don't think I'll be here much longer. I sold the cigarettes to get out a little. And then I touched Mac for some. But he doesn't give them up easily. I'm starting to get bored. Tonight I'm going to the movies with Jacqueline. I met her last night at the club. I don't think she's too intelligent because she takes my hand off all the time. And she doesn't move at all when she's dancing. These soldiers from here give me goose pimples. They're too sloppy, and no two of them wear the same uniform. Well, there's nothing to do but wait for tonight.

XII

Here again. Anyway, I'm much less bored in the village. We advance slowly. Each time we've finished preparing the artillery, we send out a patrol. And each time, one of the patrol comes back shot by an isolated gunman. So we prepare the artillery again. We send planes. They demolish everything, and two minutes later the isolated gunner fires again. At this very moment the planes are returning. I counted seventy-two of them. They aren't very big planes, but the town is small. From here, we can see the bombs spiral down. They make a rather stiffled sound and leave beautiful columns of dust.

We're going to attack again. But first we must send out a patrol. Just my luck, I'm in it. We have to cover more than one-and-a-half kilometers on foot, and I don't like walking such a long time. But in this war they never ask us. We're crowded behind the rubble of the first houses. I think not one house is left standing in the village. It doesn't seem like there are too many inhabitants either. Those that have survived make a strange sight. They have to realize that we can't risk losing our men to save their houses. Three-quarters of the time, they're old uninteresting houses. Besides, it's the only way to get rid of the enemy. Usually they understand that, although some of them believe it's not the only solution. After all, they're in it too, and perhaps they depended on their houses — certainly less so in their present state.

I continue patroling. I'm still last. It's wiser. The first one just fell into a mortar hole full of water. He's come out with a helmet of bloodsuckers. He also caught a large bewildered fish. On our return march, Mac taught the fish to sit up and beg, but it doesn't like chewing gum.

XIII

I just received a letter from Jacqueline. She'd given it to someone else to mail, because it was in one of our envelopes. Really, she's a strange girl. But all girls probably have extraordinary ideas. We've fallen back a little since yesterday. Tomorrow we advance again. Villages completely demolished. It's depressing. We found a new radio. They're trying it, but truthfully, I don't know if we can replace the battery with a piece of candle. I think we can.

I hear "Chattanooga" playing. Just before we left, I danced to it with Jacqueline. I think that I'm going to answer her if I still have time. Now it's Spike Jones. I like that music, too. I really wish all of this were over so I could go buy a civilian tie with blue and yellow stripes.

XIV

We're leaving again soon. Once more we're very near the front and the shells have resumed. It's raining, but not too cold. The jeep's working well. We're going to get out and continue on foot.

It looks like the end. I don't know how they feel about it, but I'd like to get out as comfortably as possible. There are spots where they're still hanging on hard. We can't foresee how it's going to turn out.

In fifteen days I'll be on furlough and I wrote Jacqueline to wait for me. Perhaps I was wrong. You shouldn't let yourself get carried away.

XV

I'm still standing on a mine. We patrolled this morning and I was last as usual. They all passed to one side, but I felt the mechanism underfoot and stopped. Mines only detonate when you take your foot off them. I threw the contents of my pockets to the others and told them to go on.

I'm all alone. I ought to wait until they return, but I told them not to come back. I can try to throw myself flat on my belly, but I'm terror-stricken at the thought of living legless. I kept only this notebook and a pencil. I'm going to throw them aside before I shift my legs. I have to. I've had enough of this war – and I'm getting pins and needles.

BLUES FOR A BLACK CAT

I

Peter Gna left the movie with his sister. He'd been affected by the stuffy room painted Auvergne-blue, and the fresh lemon-scented night air felt good. There'd been a profoundly im-moral animated cartoon and Peter Gna, infuriated, twirled his Canadian coat, enveloping a still untouched old woman. Odors preceded people on the sidewalks. The street lighted by street lamps, and the lights of the cinemas and cars, curled slightly. Things settled down in the cross streets and they turned toward the Folies-Bergère. A bar every two houses, two girls in front of each bar.

"A lot of syphilis," grumbled Gna.

"All of them?" his sister asked.

"Every one. I see them at the hospital and sometimes they offer themselves under the pretext that they're clean bills."

His sister felt a shiver up her spine. "What do you mean by clean?"

"When there's no more Wasserman reaction. But it proves nothing."

"Men aren't particular," his sister said.

They turned to the right and immediately to the left, and something miaowed under the sidewalk, so they stopped to see what it was.

II

At the beginning the cat didn't feel like fighting, but every ten minutes the cock emitted a strident crow. The cock belonged to the woman on the first floor who fattened it to eat on a special occasion. (Jewish people eat a rooster on a certain date. It almost jumps onto the platter, one should say.) The cat had enough of the cock. If only it played, but no, always on two feet instead of four, just to be smart.

"Take that!" The cat landed a good kick on its head.

This took place on the concierge's windowsill. The cock didn't like to fight, but there was his dignity. He crowed loudly and worked at the cat's sides with his beak.

"Louse!" the cat exclaimed. "You take me for a beetle, but you'll change your mind!"

Bam! With his head the cat hit the cock's breastbone. Cocky animal!

The rooster pecked with his beak at the cat's spine and gave a good jab at the thick of the loin.

"We'll see!" the cat said, and he bit the cock's neck, but spit out a mouthful of feathers. Before he could see straight, the cock hit him with two flaps of his wings and the cat rolled onto the sidewalk. A man passed. He stepped on the cat's tail.

The cat jumped into the air, fell back into the street, avoided a bicycle that rushed by, and established that the sewer measured a depth of about one meter by sixty centimeters with an angle to one meter twenty centimeters at the top, but at the bottom extremely narrow and full of rubbish.

III

"It's a cat," Peter Gna said.

It was improbable that another animal could push perfidy to the point of imitating the cry of a cat, usually called miaowing by onomatopation.

"How did he get there?"

"That louse of a cock," the cat responded, "and subsequently, a bicycle."

"Did you start it?" Peter Gna's sister inquired.

"No. He provoked me by crowing all the time. He knows I abhor that."

"You shouldn't be angry with him," Peter Gna said. "They're going to cut his throat soon."

"Well done," the cat commented with a satisfied, derisive laugh.

"It's bad for you to rejoice in the misfortune of another."

"No, it isn't," the cat retorted, "since I myself am in a tight corner." And he cried bitterly.

"A little more courage," Peter Gna's sister scolded. "You aren't the first cat to fall into a sewer."

"But I could care less about the others," grumbled the cat, adding, "You don't want to try and get me out of here?"

"Yes, of course," Peter Gna's sister told him. "But if you're going to start fighting with the cock all over again, it's not worth the trouble."

"Oh, I'll leave the cock alone," the cat promised in a detached tone. He'd had it.

The cock let out a chortle of joy from the upper story. Fortunately, the cat didn't hear.

Peter Gna unwound his scarf and placed himself stomach-down in the street.

All the commotion had attracted the attention of passersby and a group formed around the mouth of the sewer. There was a pedestrian in a fur coat wearing a pleated rose dress you could see through. She smelled terrifically good. There were two American soldiers with her, one on each side. You couldn't see the left hand of the one on the right, or the one on the left either, but he was left-handed. Also, the concierge from the house across the street was there, the maid from the bistro across the street, two pimps in soft hats, another concierge, and an old cat woman.

"It's terrible!" the whore said. "The poor animal. I don't want to look." She hid her face in her hands. One of the pimps compellingly held her a newspaper that read "Dresden reduced to small pieces. At least 120,000 dead."

"Men!" scoffed the old cat woman, who had read the headline. "That makes no difference to me, but I can't stand to see an animal suffer."

"An animal!" the cat protested. "Speak for yourself."

But for the moment, only Peter Gna, his sister, and the Americans understood the cat because of his strong British accent. The Americans were repelled by it. "Shit on this limey cat," the biggest one said. "What about a drink somewhere?"

"Yes, my dearest. They're certainly going to get him out of there," the whore remarked.

"I don't think so." Peter Gna stood up. "My scarf is too short and he can't catch hold of it."

"How awful," moaned a concert of sympathetic voices.

"So shut up and let him think," the cat muttered.

"Has anyone got a string?" asked Peter Gna's sister.

They found a string, but from all evidence the cat couldn't cling to it.

"It's not working. It slips right through my claws and is very disagreeable. If I had that louse of a cock, I'd cram his nose in this rubbish. It smells revoltingly like rat in this hole."

"Poor little thing," simpered the maid from across the way. "His miaows are enough to break one's heart. I'm touched."

"It's more touching to me than a baby. It's too atrocious. I'm leaving," the whore said.

"To hell with that cat. Where can we get a cognac?" the second American asked.

"You've drunk too much cognac," the girl scolded. "You're just as bad. Come on, I don't want to hear that cat."

"Oh, you could help these men and women," the maid protested.

"I'd like to." The whore melted into tears.

"If you'd shut up, up there – " the cat told them. "And hurry. I'm catching cold."

A man crossed the street. He was bare-headed, tieless, and in espadrilles. He was smoking a cigarette before going to bed. "What's going on, Mrs. Grindstone?" he asked, apparently addressing the concierge.

"Some errand boys must have landed a poor cat in the sewer," the cat woman interrupted. "These errand boys! All of them should be put in a house of correction until they're twenty-one."

"They ought to put away roosters," the cat suggested. "The errand boys don't sound off all day under the pretext that the sun's going to rise."

"I'm going back to my place," the man said. "I have something that will be useful in pulling him out of there. Wait a minute."

"I hope this isn't a joke," the cat said. "I'm starting to understand why water never runs out of sewers. It's a cinch getting it in, but the inverse maneuver is a tiny bit delicate."

"I don't see what we can do," Peter Gna said. "You're badly located and nearly inaccessible."

"I know that well enough," said the cat. "If I could, I'd get myself out."

Another American approached. He walked straight ahead. Peter Gna explained the situation to him.

"Can I help you?" the American asked.

"Lend me your flashlight, please," Peter Gna said.

"Oh, yeah!" The American held out his flashlight.

Once more Peter Gna laid down on his stomach and caught sight of a bit of the cat. The cat remarked, "Send down that thing. It looks like it works. It's Yankee, huh?"

"Yes. Now I'm going to hold out my Canadian coat. Try to hold onto it," Peter Gna instructed. He took off his fur-lined coat and let it hang into the sewer, holding it by a sleeve. The people were beginning to understand the cat's accent.

"Try again," the cat prodded, jumping to catch onto the garment. They heard the cat's terrible curse. The coat disappeared into the sewer.

"Is it all right?" Peter Gna asked apprehensively.

"Holy name of God!" the cat swore. "I just bumped my skull on something I hadn't seen. My word, it's throbbing."

"And my Canadian coat?" Peter asked.

"I'll give you my pants." The American started to take off his pants to help in the rescue.

Peter Gna's sister stopped him. "It's impossible with the coat," she said. "It won't be any better with your pants."

"Oh, yeah." The American rebuttoned his pants.

"What's he doing?" asked the whore. "Don't let him take his pants off in the street. What a pig!"

Nondescript individuals continued to congregate in a small group. Under the electric light of the lamp the sewer mouth took on a strange allure. The cat grumbled and his curses reached the ears of latecomers in a strangely amplified echo.

"I really would like to recover my Canadian coat," Peter Gna said.

The man in espadrilles elbowed his way to open a passage. He carried a broomstick.

"Ah-ha. Maybe that's going to work," Peter Gna told him. But before putting it into the sewer the pole stiffened and his elbow, formed by the arch, stopped him from getting it in.

"You should look for the sewer grate and loosen it," Peter Gna's sister suggested, translating her proposition to the American.

"Oh, yeah," he said. Immediately he began to look for the

grate. He stuck his hand into the rectangular opening, pulled, slid, let go, and knocked himself senseless on the wall of the nearest house.

"Take care of him," Peter Gna told two women in the crowd who picked up the American and took him with them to ascertain the contents of his pea-jacket pockets. In particular, they found a small bar of *Lux* and a large *Oh Henry!* bar of creamed chocolate. In return, he gave them a vaginal disease he'd contracted from a ravishing blonde he'd met two days earlier at Pigalle.

The man with the stick tapped his head with the palm of his hand exclaiming, "Eurekat!" and went home.

"He doesn't care about me," the cat said. "Listen, you up there, if you don't hurry, I'm going. I'll be able to find my way out."

"And if it starts raining you'll drown," Peter Gna's sister said.

"It won't rain," the cat told her.

"Then you'll run into rats," she said.

"I don't care."

"Ah well, go then," Peter Gna said. "But you know, there're some rats bigger than you. And they're disgusting. Moreover, don't piss on my Canadian coat."

"If they're dirty it's another story," replied the cat. "In any case, the fact is they stink. No, seriously, manage by yourselves up there. And don't worry about your Canadian. I have my eye on it." He moved out of hearing distance.

The man reappeared. He had a net shopping bag at the end of a long string.

"Marvelous!" Peter Gna said "He's surely going to be able to hold onto this."

"What is it?" the cat asked.

"Here." Peter Gna threw it to him.

"Ah, that's better," the cat approved. "Don't pull immediately. I'm bringing the coat."

A few seconds later the shopping bag reappeared, the cat comfortably curled inside. "At last!" he said, disentangling himself from the net. "As for your Canadian coat, shift for yourself. Find a hook or something. It was too heavy."

"That good-for-nothing!" Peter Gna grunted.

Applause greeted the cat upon his exit from the shopping bag. They passed him from hand to hand.

"What a beautiful cat. Poor thing! He's full of mud."

He smelled awfully bad.

"Dry him with this." The whore held out her lavender blue silk scarf.

"It's going to be ruined," Peter Gna's sister advised.

"Oh, it doesn't matter," said the whore with a burst of generosity. "It's not mine."

The cat shook hands all around and the crowd dispersed. Seeing that everyone was leaving, the cat remarked, "Now that I'm out I'm no longer interesting. By the way, where's the cock?"

"Shut up," Peter Gna warned him. "Come have a drink and don't think about that cock anymore."

The man in espadrilles, Peter Gna, his sister, the whore, and the two Americans stayed with the cat.

"We're going to have a drink," the whore explained, " – in the cat's honor."

"She's not bad," the cat observed. "What a figure she has. For the most part, I'd sleep with her tonight."

"Calm down," Peter Gna's sister said.

The whore shook her two men. "Come. Drink. Cognac," she articulated laboriously.

"Yeah. Cognac!" the two men responded, rousing themselves simultaneously.

Peter Gna walked ahead carrying the cat and the others followed. A bistro remained open on Richer Street.

"Seven cognacs," ordered the whore. "It's my round."

"You're a winner," the cat told her with admiration. "A little valerian in mine, waiter."

The waiter served them and they joyfully clinked glasses.

"This poor cat probably caught cold," the whore said. "What if we made him drink some nice hot beef bouillon?"

Hearing this, the cat nearly choked and spit his cognac all over. "What do they take me for?" he asked Peter Gna. "Am I a cat or not?"

By the light of the fluorescent bulbs, they really saw the type of cat he was. A terrible large cat with yellow eyes and a William II moustache. Lacy ears confirmed his virility and a large white scar, deplete of hair and coquettishly accentuated by a violet border, ran across his back.

"What's that?" the American asked, touching the scar. "Wounded, sir?"

"Yep. FFI," the cat answered, pronouncing *Ef Ef Ai* like he should.

"Great," the other American said, vigorously shaking the cat's paw. "What about another drink?"

"Okey doke," the cat said. "Got a butt?" Without malice toward the cat's atrocious British accent, the American proffered his cigarette case. The cat thought he would repay him by pulling out some American slang. The cat chose the longest cigarette and lighted it with Peter Gna's lighter. Each of them took one.

"Tell us about your wound," the whore said.

Peter Gna found a fishhook in his glass and left soon thereafter to fish out his Canadian coat.

The cat blushed and lowered his head. "I don't like to talk about myself," he said. "Give me another cognac."

"It'll make you sick," Peter Gna's sister said.

"No, it won't," the cat protested. "I have armored guts. A real cat's gut. Also, after that sewer – Bahh! How it smelled of rat." He gulped his cognac.

"My Word! How you toss down that cognac!" the man in espadrilles exclaimed in admiration.

"The next one in a glass of orangeade," the cat ordered.

The second American moved away from the group, sat down on the wall bench, put his head in his hands, and started to throw up between his legs.

"It was in April of '44," the cat began. "I'd come from Lyon where I'd contacted the cat Lion Plouc, who also was with the Resistance. A cat up to snuff, moreover. He was taken by the Cat Gestapo and deported to Buchenkatze."

"What a shame," said the whore.

"I'm not worried about him. He'll get out of it." The cat continued, "So leaving him, I went back up to Paris and in the train I had an unfortunate meeting with another cat. The trollop. The slut!"

"You must watch your language," Peter Gna's sister reprimanded.

"Excuse me," the cat said, and took a large gulp of cognac. His eyes lighted up like two lamps and his moustache bristled. "I passed one of those nights in the train," he said, stretching himself with complacence. "Good Gracious! What a kidney attack. Hup!" he concluded, because he had the hiccups.

"So?" the whore asked.

"So – that's it," the falsely modest cat told her.

"But your wound?" Peter Gna's sister insisted.

"The feline's patron had hobnailed shoes and he saw my tail, but he missed it. Hup!"

"That's all?" the whore asked, disappointed.

"You wanted him to cream me, huh?" the cat mocked sarcastically. "Well, you have a ripping mentality, you do! Do you ever go to the Pax-Vobiscum?" It was a hotel of the district, in short, a house of ill-repute.

"Yes," the whore answered without evasion.

"I'm a pal of the maid's," the cat told her. "Does she knock me up."

"Ah, Germaine?" the whore asked.

"Yes, Ger-hup!-maine," the cat said. He finished his glass in one gulp. "I'd very much like to roll a tri-color."

"A what?" the whore asked.

"A female three-colored cat. Or a small inexperienced cat." He laughed evilly and winked his right eye. "Or the cock. Hup!" The cat rose on four paws, his back arched, tail stiff, and bristled his spine. "Hang it all. That rooster bothers me."

Uneasy, Peter Gna's sister rummaged in her purse.

"Don't you know one?" the cat asked the whore. "Aren't you a friend of pussy cats?"

"You're a pig," the whore said. "Forward ladies and gentlemen."

The guy in espadrilles didn't talk much, but excited by the cat's conversation, he drew near the whore.

"You smell good," he told her. "What is it?"

"Flowers of Sulfur, by Oldpal," she said.

"And that?" he asked, putting his hand there. "What's that?" He placed himself on the side vacated by the sick American.

"Come on, my dear," the whore said. "Be good."

"Waiter! A crème de menthe," the cat ordered.

"Ah, no," Peter Gna's sister protested. "Well, finally," she said, seeing the door open. Peter returned with his Canadian coat soiled by refuse. She accosted her brother. "Stop him from drinking. He's completely soused."

"Wait. First, I must clean my Canadian coat. Waiter, two vacuums!" Peter Gna hung his Canadian coat on the back of a chair and vacuumed it copiously.

"Strange – Waiter – this crème de menthe – Hup! – It's you, my Savior!" the cat exclaimed, clasping Peter Gna. "Come, I'll pay the tab."

"No, old chap," Peter Gna told him. "You're going to catch a cold."

"He saved me!" the cat roared. "He pulled me from a hole full of rats where I would have died."

Moved, the whore let her head fall on the shoulder of the man in espadrilles, who let go of her and went to finish himself off in a corner.

The cat bounded onto the counter and emptied the remaining cognac. "Brrr!" He rapidly shook his head from right to left. "It's going down hard." Then he howled, "I'd be finished without him."

The whore flopped on the counter, her head in her arms. The second American left her and stationed himself near his compatriot. Their vomit synchronized and they designed the American flag on the floor. The second one occupied himself with the forty-eight stars.

"Into my arms. Hup!" the cat beckoned.

The whore dried her tears. "But he's kind."

In order not to vex him, Peter Gna kissed the cat on the forehead. The cat squeezed him between his paws, suddenly let go, and collapsed.

"What's the matter with him?" Peter Gna's sister inquired apprehensively.

Peter Gna pulled a speculum from his pocket and put it in the cat's ear. "He's dead," he said. "The cognac went to his brain." They watched it seep out.

"Oh dear!" Peter Gna's sister began to cry.

"What's the matter with him?" asked the whore uneasily.

"He's dead," Peter Gna repeated.

"Oh no, after all the trouble we went through," she said.

"He was such a good cat and he knew how to chat," the man in espadrilles said.

"Yes," Peter Gna's sister agreed.

The waiter from the bistro still hadn't said anything, but

he appeared to come out of his torpor. "That makes eight hundred francs."

"Ah me," Peter Gna was upset.

"It's my turn." The whore took one thousand francs from her beautiful red leather purse. "Keep the change, waiter."

"Thank you. What should I do with that?" With a look of revulsion the waiter pointed to the cat. A stream of crème de menthe ran over the cat's fur in a complicated pattern.

"Poor little thing," the whore sobbed.

"Don't leave him like that. We must do something," Peter Gna's sister told her brother.

"He drank like a hole," Peter Gna said. "It's stupid. There's nothing to do."

The noise like Niagara, which had been in the background since the Americans left, came to a fresh halt. They got up together and approached the group. "Cognac!" the first ordered.

"Dodo, my big boy. Come." The whore entwined each of them in an arm.

"Excuse me, ladies and gentlemen," she said. "I must go put my babies to bed. Poor little cat, just the same – an evening that started so nicely."

"Good-bye, Madame," Peter Gna's sister said.

The man in espadrilles tapped Peter Gna's shoulder affectionately without saying anything, but with an air of condolence. He shook his head, apparently sorry, and left on tiptoe.

Obviously, the waiter was sleepy.

"What are we going to do?" Peter Gna asked, and his sister didn't reply.

So Peter Gna put the cat in his fur-lined coat and they went out into the night. The air was cold and the stars exploded one by one. Chopin's *Marche Funebre* played by the bells in the churches, announced to the populace that one o'clock had sounded. Slowly, they cleared a path through the sharp night.

They arrived at the corner of the street. Black and greedy, the sewer waited at their feet. Peter Gna opened his Canadian coat. With care he removed the completely stiff cat and his sister silently caressed it. Then, softly, regretfully, the cat disappeared into the hole. It went "Glop" and with a satisfied smile the sewer mouth closed.

CANCER

I

Jacques Teagarden was suffering in bed. He'd caught a cold playing his churlish flute in a bad draft. Because times were hard, the chamber orchestra had agreed to rehearse in an ordinary hall. Although the musicians weathered the inclement times, their health frequently was in jeopardy.

Jacques Teagarden didn't feel well. His head stretched in one direction and his brain in another. In the intervening hollow, foreign bodies slowly introduced themselves – fluid parasitic thoughts, and a sharp invasive pain similar to acid in the throat. From time to time Jacques Teagarden coughed, and the foreign bodies collided sharply against the lining of his skull. They surfaced abruptly like waves in a bathtub and fell back with the grinding sound of trampled grasshoppers. A bubble burst here and there and small white beams, soft as the inside of a spider, starred the bony vault swept away by the backwash. After each attack Jacques Teagarden waited in anguish for the next cough. He counted the seconds by an hourglass on his night table. He was tormented because he couldn't practice his flute. His lips would grow flabby, his fingers round, and he'd have to start all over again.

The churlish flute requires a terrifying willpower because it's learned with difficulty, and what's learned is fast forgotten.

In his head he practiced the cadenza he'd been working on from the Eighteenth Symphonic Movement in B double flat. The trills of measures 56 and 57 heightened the pain. He felt an attack coming and raised his hand to his mouth to hold it back. It mounted, gained volume in his trachea, and issued in large turbulent fountains. Jacques Teagarden's face turned purple and his eyes filled with blood. He dabbed at them with a corner of a red handkerchief chosen expressly to hide the stain.

II

The stairwell hummed. Mounted on metallic rails, the banister vibrated like a gong. Surely it was the landlady bringing him some lime-blossom tea. In time, tea congests the prostate, but Jacque Teagarden didn't drink it often, and doubtless he'd escape the operation. She had only one story to climb. She was a beautiful large woman of thirty-five. Her husband, a German prisoner for many months, had laid barbed wire as soon as he returned, figuring it was his turn to confine others. The entire day he fenced in cattle and rarely showed much sign of life.

She opened the door without knocking and flashed Jacques a big smile. She held a blue faience pot and a bowl, which she placed on the night table. Her half-opened housedress gaped on mossy shadows when she leaned over to arrange the pillows, and Jacques smelled the strong pleasant odor of her bearded mystery. He blinked because the odor struck him, and with a finger he pointed at the transgression.

"Excuse me, but – " He interrupted himself, prey to a violent attack. The landlady, misunderstanding, rubbed her lower belly. "It's your – thing," he concluded.

So that he'd laugh, she seized the hilarious object in both hands and imitated the sound of a duck foraging in the mud. But not wishing Jacques to cough, she quickly closed her dress again. A weak smile relaxed on the boy's face. "Normally, I rather like it," he explained, excusing himself, "but my head's so full of noises, sounds and odors already."

"Should I pour you some lime-blossom tea?" she asked with maternal concern. As she lifted the pot to pour, her dress reopened. Jacques teased the tiny beast with the end of his spoon and suddenly it stuck. He laughed so hard that his chest tore apart. Bent in two and suffocating, he couldn't even feel the soft rapid slaps she made on his back to stop him from coughing.

"I'm just a fool," she upbraided herself for having made him laugh. "I ought to have realized you don't have the heart to play." She gave him back the spoon and held out the bowl. He sipped the fallow-tasting tea, stirring it all the while to mix up the sugar. Then he swallowed two aspirin.

"Thank you. I'm going to try to sleep now," he said.

"I'll bring some more tea later." The landlady folded the empty bowl and faience pot in three.

III

He woke with a start. The aspirin had made him perspire. According to the Archimedes Principle, he'd lost weight equal to that of the displaced sweat, and his body levitated above the mattress, dragging along the sheets and blankets. The draft of air which this produced rippled the pond of sweat on which he floated, and small waves plashed on his hips. He took the plug from his mattress and the sweat poured into the mattress spring. Slowly, his body descended and reposed on the sheet that steamed like horse urine. The sweat left a gummy deposit, and in his effort to get up and lean on the spongy pillow, he slipped.

Once more his head vibrated a hummed accompaniment. Millstones formed behind his brain, and ground the substances that always had bothered him in the void of his skull. He raised his hands gently, examined his head with caution, and felt the buckling. His fingers slid over the occiput to the swollen parietals, touched his forehead, followed the abrupt edge of his eye sockets, reaching his temples, then returned to the malar bones that gave slightly under pressure.

Indeed, Jacques Teagarden wished he could see the exact formation of his skull. Some skulls are so pretty in profile, so well-balanced, so round. They'd taken an X-ray during his sickness last year, and all the women he'd shown it to readily became his mistresses. The back protrusion and inflation of the parietals worried him. The churlish flute, perhaps –

His hands returned to the occiput, lingered at the juncture of his neck where the socket turned soundlessly but with difficulty. Heaving a sigh of helplessness, he let his arms fall to his sides, rapidly moving his buttocks from right to left and making a small comfortable hollow in the soft but hardening crust. He didn't dare move too much. With a single movement, the sweat in the box springs sloshed from left to right. When he propped himself on his right arm, he threw the bed off balance. He was obliged to tie a large strap of unbleached muslin around his back. It barely held him up. When Jacques leaned on the other arm, the bed turned completely around, and the neighbor below tapped on the ceiling with the butt end of a smelly leg of mutton. The odor seeped through floor cracks, causing Jacques to raise his head.

He didn't want to spill the box springs onto the floor. The baker from the corner gave him a good price for the sweat. He poured it into bottles labeled "Sweat from the Front," and people bought it to wash down the 99 percent burnt bread of the Service Corps.

"I'm coughing less," he thought. His chest regularly relaxed and the wheezing in his lungs was barely perceptible. With caution he extended his left arm and seized his flute from the chair, putting it in bed near him. Again, his hands reached for his head, slid along the occiput to the swollen parietals, touched his forehead, and followed the abrupt edge of his eye sockets.

IV

"Eleven liters," the baker said.

"I lost a few liters," Teagarden apologized. "The bedsprings aren't too watertight."

"It isn't pure. To count it as ten liters would be more accurate."

"You'll sell it as eleven anyway."

"Naturally," said the baker. "But I'll feel guilty and that should count for something."

"I need the money," Jacques said. "I haven't played for three days."

"I don't have much money either. A twenty-nine horsepower car costs a lot to keep and the maids ruin me."

"What can you give me?" Jacques asked.

"My God! I'm offering you three francs a liter and eleven count as ten," the baker said.

"Try harder. That isn't much."

"All right," the baker agreed. "I'll go up to thirty-three francs, but it's a swindle."

"I'll take it," Jacques said.

The baker pulled out six denominations of seven francs each from his wallet. "Give me back nine francs."

"I only have ten," Jacques said.

"That will close the deal," said the baker. He pocketed the money, picked up the pail, and walked toward the door. "Try and make me some more," he urged.

"I don't have a fever."

"Too bad," the baker said, and left.

Jacques' hands reached for his head again, and caressed

his deformed bones. He tried to lift up his skull, anxious to know its exact weight, but he'd have to wait until he was completely cured. His neck hurt him too much.

V

Painfully, Jacques threw off the covers. His thin legs, wrinkled from five days of rest, stretched before him. He considered them absentmindedly, attempted to smooth them with the flat of his hand, then sat on the edge of the bed. With effort he got up. Because of his legs, he'd lost five good centimeters. He threw out his torso and his ribs cracked. The cold left a few traces. His nightshirt fell in long flaccid pleats over his furrowed buttocks, and his softened lips and swollen fingers no longer allowed him to play the churlish flute. He knew it right away.

Beaten, he let himself fall onto a chair, head in his hands, fingers mechanically feeling his temples and heavy forehead.

VI

The orchestra conductor climbed the staircase; he stopped a minute in front of the door, read the placard and entered. "Hello," he said. "So you're feeling better?"

"I got up a moment ago," Jacques told him. "I'm weak."

"It smells strange in the stairwell," the conductor said.

"It's the landlady. She never closes her dress."

"It smells good, like wild rabbit."

"Yes," Jacques agreed.

"When are you coming back to play with us?"

"We have to discuss a few things. I don't want to play in the hall anymore. After all, chamber music is played in a chamber."

"You aren't going to say it's my fault that you caught a cold," the conductor said. "After all, we all played in the hall."

"I know. But I was sitting in the draft, and that's why you didn't catch anything."

"That's a lie. Besides, you always had a poor constitution."

"I know. But I don't like being sick. It's my prerogative."

"Then I'll have to find someone else," the conductor told him. "We can't play with someone who's always dissatisfied."

"But I nearly died!"

"You piss me off. I didn't come here to waste my time. When can you play again?"

"I don't know. I'm weak," Jacques said.

"You're exaggerating. It's not professional. I'm going to ask Albert to replace you."

"Pay me the two jobs you owe me. I have to pay the landlady."

"I don't have it on me. I'm going to see Albert. You've got a bad temper."

"When will you pay me?" Jacques asked.

"Oh, I'll pay you! I'm going now."

Jacques' fingers wandered over his forehead and his eyes were half-closed. Four kilos, maybe?

VII

The small alcohol stove hummed valiantly. Provoked by the noise, the water quivered in the aluminum pan. It was too much water for such a little stove, but Jacques had come to the end.

He waited on a chair. To distract himself, he practiced a little on the flute. Constantly, he missed the B flat by two centimeters, but finally caught it and crushed it between two fingers. He was glad that the note had returned. But he stopped because the pain in his head also returned, and the water started to boil.

"Maybe more than four kilos," he said to himself. "We'll see."

He took a large knife and cut off his head, dropping it into the boiling water with a few crystals to clean it without altering its weight. He died before he'd finished, because this was in 1945, and medicine wasn't as advanced as it is today. Jacques Teagarden mounted to heaven in a large round cloud – never having a single reason to go elsewhere.

DEAD FISH

I

The compartment door resisted as usual. At the other end of the train the capped conductor pressed hard on a red button, and compressed air spurted into the pipes. The assistant strained to separate the door panels. He was hot. Drops of gray sweat zigzagged over his face like flies, and you could see the dirty collar of his shirt of danger-proof zephyr.

The train was about to pull out when the conductor let go of the button. The air belched joyously under the train and the assistant nearly lost his balance as the door gave way unexpectedly. He descended, stumbling along, tearing his tote bag on the closing mechanism.

The train departed and the atmospheric displacement flattened the assistant against the foul-smelling latrines where two Arabs talked politics with forceful stabs of a knife.

The assistant shook himself, patting his hair matted on his soft cranium like decayed plants. Steam rose from his half-covered chest. His prominent collarbones and the beginning of one or two pair of poorly positioned ribs jutted out. With a heavy step, he walked the platform tiled in red and green hexagons soiled here and there with long black trails. It had rained octopi that afternoon. But the station employees spent their time on undisclosed duties instead of cleaning the platforms as specified in their monumental charter.

The assistant dug into his pockets and fingered the rough corrugated cardboard ticket he was supposed to hand in at the exit. His knees hurt, and the humidity from the ponds he'd explored during the day made his poorly secured joints creak. True, he carried back more than honorable bounty. He held out his ticket to the nondescript man standing behind the gate. The man took it, looked at it, and smiled ferociously. "Have you got another one?" he asked.

"No," the assistant answered.

"This is counterfeit."

"But my employer gave it to me," the assistant said kindly, with a small childish smile and a little sigh.

The ticket-taker laughed derisively. "Then it doesn't surprise me that it's counterfeit. He bought ten from us this morning."

"Ten what?"

"Ten counterfeit tickets."

"But why?" The assistant's smile dimmed and he leaned to the left.

"To give to you – *primo*, so that you're first for abuse, which I'm in the process of doing, and *secundo*, so that you have to pay the fine."

"Why? I've got very little money."

"Because it's revolting to travel with a counterfeit ticket."

"But you're the one who made them!"

"I have to, because there're characters revolting enough to travel with counterfeit tickets. Do you think it's fun to make counterfeit tickets all day long?"

"Surely you'd do better to clean the platform," the assistant replied.

"No backtalk. Pay the fine. It's thirty francs."

"That's not right. It's twelve francs when you don't have a ticket."

"It's a grave offense to have a counterfeit one. Pay, or I call my dog!"

44

"He won't come."

"No, but you'll get an earache."

The assistant stared at the gloomy, gaunt face of the ticket-taker, who gave him a poisonous look. "I've got very little money," he repeated.

"Me too. Pay."

"He gives me fifty francs a day. And I have to feed myself."

The employee pulled the visor of his cap and a blue veil fell over his face. "Pay!" he ordered, rubbing his index finger with his thumb.

The assistant reached for his shiny restitched wallet. He took out two denominations of scarred ten franc notes and a small denomination of still bleeding five francs. "Twenty-five," he proposed uncertainly.

"Thirty," answered the three extended fingers of the man.

The assistant sighed and the face of his employer appeared between his toes. He spat right in his eye. His heart beat faster. The face melted and blackened. He placed the money in the extended palm and left, hearing the visor snap into its normal position. With measured steps he reached the edge of the steep ramp. The tote bag bruised his thin thighs, and with the random motion of his gait, the bamboo handle of net beat against his frail, poorly formed calves.

II

He pushed the wrought-iron grill and it gave way with a frightful creaking. A large red lamp burned above the steps and a doorbell rang weakly in the vestibule. He entered as quickly as he could and closed the grill again, electrocuting himself in the process because the burglar alarm was on. He went up the path. Just at the middle, his foot struck a hard object and a frigid squirt of water sprang from the earth, penetrating the cuff of his pants and drenching him to the knees.

He began to run. As on all evenings, anger progressively won him over. He scaled the three steps with clenched fists. Arriving upstairs, his net caught in his legs, and in a gesture to avoid falling, he tore his bag a second time on a nail jutting from nowhere. He'd wrenched something inside his body and gasped wordlessly. After a few moments he calmed down, and his chin fell back onto his chest. Then he felt the cold of his damp pants and seized the door handle, letting go in a hurry. A foul-smelling vapor arose, and a fragment of his flesh stuck to the burning porcelain, blackened and shriveled up. The door was open. He went in.

His thin legs carried him ineffectively and he sank down on the cold floor in a corner of the vestibule, which smelt of decaying skin. His heart growled between his ribs and shook him with great, brutal, irregular throbs.

III

"It's skimpy," his employer said, examining the contents of the tote bag. The assistant waited in front of the table. "You've ruined them. The denticulation of this one is completely ruined."

"The net's too old. If you want me to catch young brains in mint condition you have to pay for a proper net."

"Who uses this net? You or me?"

The assistant didn't answer. His burnt hand was hurting.

"Answer," the employer commanded. "If you have the audacity to earn fifty francs a day, at least you can account for it!"

"Minus thirty francs for the ticket," the assistant countered.

"What ticket? I pay your way round-trip."

"With counterfeit tickets."

"All you have to do is pay attention."

"How do I recognize them?"

"It's not difficult. They're obviously false when they're made of corrugated cardboard. The regular tickets are wood."

"Good. Give me back my thirty francs."

"I won't. All of these brains are in poor condition."

"That's not true. I spent two hours fishing for them, and I had to break the ice. I took the greatest care and scarcely two are ruined out of sixty."

"Those aren't the ones I wanted," the employer told him. "I want the two hundred from Guiana, 1855. I'll have nothing to do with the Zanzibar series you caught yesterday."

"I catch what I find — especially with such a net. Besides, it's not the Guiana season. You'll be able to trade the Zanzibars."

"Everyone's finding them this year. They're worthless."

"And the water up my legs, and the fitting on the grill, and the doorbell?" The assistant's thin yellow face hollowed into wrinkles, and he seemed about to cry.

"It toughens you up. What do you want me to do? I'm bored."

"Go look for brains," the assistant said, containing himself at considerable expense.

"I pay you for that. You're a thief. You steal the money you should earn."

With a weary gesture the assistant passed a worn sleeve over his brow. His head was clear as a bell. The table moved slightly away from him and he looked for something to catch hold of. But the fireplace mantle evaded him too, and he collapsed.

"Get up," the employer said. "Not on my carpet."

"I wanted to eat."

"Next time you'll return earlier. Get up. I don't want to see you on my carpet. For God's sake, get up!" His voice trembled with fury and his gnarled hands thrummed the desk.

The assistant made an effort and got onto his knees. His stomach hurt and his hand dripped blood and pus. He twisted a dirty handkerchief around it. The employer made a quick decision and threw three brains in his face. They stuck to his cheek with the sound of a suction cup.

"Go put them back where you caught them." The employer hammered his syllables into sharp points.

The assistant wept. His soft hair fell on his forehead, and the brains stuck out on his left cheek. He lumbered to his feet.

"For the last time, I'm telling you I don't want brains in poor condition. And don't give me any stories about a torn net."

"No, sir."

"Here are your fifty francs." The employer pulled a bill from his pocket, spat on it, tore it in half, and threw it to the ground.

The assistant painfully bent down. His knees cracked in brief dry triplets.

"Your shirt's dirty. You'll sleep outside tonight," the employer said.

The assistant picked up the bill and left the room. Wind whistled worse than ever and agitated the wavy door in front of the wrought-iron grill of the vestibule. He closed the office door, not without glancing at his employer's silhouette. The latter, leaning over his Zanzibar album with a large yellow magnifying glass, started to arrange and evaluate them.

IV

He went back down the flight of steps, pulling around him a long vest that had turned green from prolonged contact with the brain ponds. The wind blew through the holes in the cloth and billowed in back, making him look like a hunchback, and causing coniderable damage to his spine. He suffered internal mimesis. Each day he had to fight to preserve the usual functions and ordinary form of his poor organs.

It was completely dark now, and the earth emitted a cheap and leaden light. The assistant turned to the right and skirted the wall of the house. He directed himself along the black line of the unwound hose that his employer used to drown rats in the cellar. He reached the decrepit hole where he'd slept the night before. The straw inside was humid and smelled of cockroaches. An old fragment of a blanket covered the rounded entrance. When he lifted it to hurry in, there was a blinding light and explosion inside. A large bomb had just gone off inside the hole, filling it with a strong odor of powder.

The assistant jumped and his heart stampeded. He tried to retard the beatings by holding his breath, but his eyes danced, and greedily he swallowed a mouthful of air. The powder odor filled his lungs at the same time, and calmed him down a bit.

He waited until silence returned and listened attentively, then whistled softly. Without turning around, he crawled into the hole and curled up on the unhealthy straw. He whistled again, then pricked up his ears. Slight footsteps. In the pale glow of the earth he noticed his soft and tame living thing which he nourished, after a fashion, with dead fish. She entered the hole and lay against him. All of a sudden he remembered, and brought his hand to his cheeks. The three brains started to suck his blood and viciously he tore them off, restraining himself so he wouldn't cry out. He threw them far from him outside the hole. The humidity of the soil no doubt would preserve them until tomorrow. The living thing began to lick his cheek and he spoke to it to calm down, whispering because his employer had devices for listening in on him when he was alone.

"He upsets me," he said.

The living thing made a sweet murmur and licked him more than ever.

"I think I should do something; not let myself be mistreated, wear clean shirts despite what he says, and have counterfeit tickets of wood, and also repair the net and stop him from filling it with holes. I think I ought to refuse sleeping in this hole and demand a room, and demand a raise because I can't live on fifty francs a day, and also get fat, and become the picture of health and very handsome, and rebel when he doesn't expect it, and throw a brick at his face. I think I'll do it."

He shifted positions, meditating with such intensity that the air in the hole escaped in fits and starts through the round opening so that not enough remained inside to breathe. A little seeped through the crevices under the dirt of the hole and across the straw. And it brought out the cockroach smell in the warmth now blended with the disagreeable aroma of slugs.

"I don't like this hole. It's cold. Fortunately, you're here. There are noises in the cellar; it's the water flowing into the rat holes. No one can sleep with the shrieking of rats in their ears every night the Good Lord turns out the light. Why does he want to kill those rats at all cost, and kill them with water? Rats are killed with blood."

The living thing no longer licked him. He saw her in profile on the gray background of the luminous earth, with her fine snout, pointed ears, and yellow eyes reflecting a few cold glints. She turned over, looking for a comfortable place, and ensconced herself against him, her nose on his thighs.

"I'm cold." He began to sob silently. His tears slipped onto the straw from which arose a slight vapor, and the contour of objects became vague. "Wake me in the morning. I have to carry back those three brains, provided he doesn't give me a counterfeit ticket for the train."

50

There was a din far away, then some sharp hoots and tiny galloping noises.

"There it is. He's at it again with those rats! I wish he were a rat. I'd hold the hose myself. I hope he'll give me my fifty francs tomorrow evening. I'm hungry. I could eat a live rat."

He pressed his stomach with his hands, still crying, and then the rhythm of the sobs subsided little by little like a machine stopping, and his twisted body relaxed. His feet stuck out the hole and he slept, his cheek pressed against the malodorous straw. A gravelly sound came from his empty stomach.

V

From the room where he crawled, the employer heard the melodious phrase that announced the pepper seller's passing. He got to his feet, and, finding that he could walk, ran toward the vestibule door. He opened it with deliberate force. Standing on the steps, he watched the young girl approach.

She wore the usual uniform: a small pleated skirt smooth against her buttocks, short red and blue socks, and a bolero covering the bottom half of her breasts – without forgetting the red and white striped cotton bonnet that pepper sellers from the Isle of Maurice have imposed on the world by sheer will.

The employer signaled her and she came up the path. He came down the steps at the same time and advanced to meet her.

"Hello," he said. "I'd like some pepper."

"How many corns?" she asked with a feigned smile, because she detested him. Her black hair and complexion produced the effect of a cold glass of water on the employer's ass – a very important effect, as a matter of fact.

"Go up the stairs," he said, "and I'll specify the amount."

"You want to stay below and see my thighs, don't you?" she said.

"Yes," the employer slavered. His hands came forward.

"Pay for the pepper first," she said.

"How much?"

"One hundred francs a corn, and you taste it first."

"Will you come up the stairs?" he murmured. "I'll give you a Zanzibar series."

"My brother brought three back to the house yesterday," she said, giving a mellifluous, derisive laugh. "Taste my pepper."

She held out a pepper corn. The employer didn't notice it was a toxic seed corn from a carnation. Trustingly, he put it in his mouth and swallowed it. The pepper seller already moved away.

"What?" wondered the employer. "And the stairs?"

"Ah! Ah! Ah!" said the pepper seller with consummate wickedness.

Meanwhile, the employer started to feel the stimulating effects of the poison and began to run full speed around the house. The pepper seller watched him while she propped herself against the grill. On the third turn she signaled him and waited until he spotted her, which he did the fourth time around, always running faster and faster. Then she lifted her small pleated skirt. From where she was standing she saw the face of the employer turn purple, then black, then commence to burn. And as he kept his eyes fixed on that which she showed him, he tripped on the hose he used to drown the rats. He fell, his face hitting a large rock, and it sunk in between his cheekbones to his nose and jaws. His feet still dragged against the soil and cut a double furrow. Little by little, as his shoes wore away, the five huge toes holding on his socks appeared.

The pepper seller closed the grill and continued on her route, throwing her cotton bonnet aside as a token of scorn.

VI

In vain the assistant tried to open the compartment door. It was purposely very hot on the train so that the passengers would catch cold as they got off. The engineer had a brother who sold handkerchiefs.

The assistant had worked all day for a miserable catch and his heart was swollen with satisfaction because he was going to kill his employer. Finally, he succeeded in separating the two halves of the door by pulling up and down, realizing, of course, that the conductor with the cap had turned it on its side in order to play a wretched trick. Happy at beating him at his prank, he jumped lightly onto the platform and dug into his pocket. Without any trouble, he found the corrugated cardboard he was going to hand over at the exit, and quickly moved toward the booth occupied by a man of sly appearance. He recognized the ticket-taker of the preceding evening.

"I have a counterfeit ticket," he said.

"Ah? Let me see."

He held out his ticket and the man took it, then examined it with such great attention that his hat moved aside to let his ears into the lining.

"It's well done."

"Except that it's not wood, but cardboard," the assistant said.

"Really?" the man said. "I'd swear it was wood. If I didn't know it were cardboard, naturally."

"All the same," the assistant said, "to think my employer gave it to me as the real item."

"A real one only costs twelve francs. He pays much more for these."

"How much?"

"I'll give you thirty francs for it," said the man putting his hand in his pocket. Because of the ease of this gesture, the assistant thought he must have bad intentions, but the man only pulled out three walnut-stained denominations of ten counterfeit francs each. "There!"

"They're counterfeit, of course?" the assistant asked.

"I can't give you good bills for a counterfeit one. Do consider," the ticket-taker said.

"No, you can't, but I'm keeping my ticket." The assistant contracted and sprang. Thanks to this action, his small fist denuded the skin on the right side of the face beneath the cap. The man brought his hand to his visor and fell at attention, which caused him to hit his elbow on the cement of the platform tiled in that particular spot with blue phosphorescent hexagons.

The assistant stepped over the body and passed on. He felt imbibed with hot limpid life, and he hurried to climb the steep ramp. He disengaged his net from the pole and used it to ascend. In passing, he harpooned the tops of the iron posts holding the protective fence along the high-banked route, and pulling on the handle, hoisted himself easily among the rocks cutting the path. After a few meters, the torn pocket fell away. He'd loop the wire ring over his employer's neck.

He arrived quickly at the grill and pushed it without thinking. He'd hoped to intercept the current and intensify his anger, but he felt nothing and stopped. Something moved slightly in front of the steps. He ran along the path. Despite the cold, his skin started to burn and he smelled the neglected odor of his body, an unpleasant smell of straw and cockroaches. He flexed his filiform biceps and his fingers gripped the bamboo handle. No doubt his employer had killed someone.

He stopped, stupified, recognizing the dark suit and shiny starched collar. His employer's head was nothing but a black mass, and his feet had finished digging two deep tracks. A sort of despair took hold of him and all his limbs trembled, agitated by anger and his desire for massacre. He looked around, worried and uncomposed. He'd prepared a lot to say. He must say it.

"Why did you do that, pig?" *Pig* rang through the neutral air with an obsolete and insufficient ring. "Pig! Skunk! Coward! Shit! Dirty coward! Thief! Scoundrel! Coward!" Tears flowed from his eyes because the employer didn't answer. He took the bamboo pole and planted it in the middle of the employer's back. "Answer, old fool. You gave me a counterfeit ticket."

He leaned with all his weight, and the handle pierced the tissues softened by the poison. He turned it to let the worms out, maneuvering the other end of the handle like the spindle of a gyroscope.

"A counterfeit ticket, straw with cockroaches, my thirty francs, and I'm hungry, and my fifty francs today?"

The employer barely moved, and the worms remained.

"I wanted to kill you, dirty coward. It was imperative that I kill you, kill you dead, old fool. Yes, you! My fifty francs, eh?"

He wrenched the handle from the wound and with heavy blows, struck the charred skull. It caved in like the crust of an overcooked soufflé. In place of the employer's head no longer was anything. It terminated at his collar.

The assistant stopped trembling. "You want to leave? Ok. But I must kill someone."

He sat down on the ground, weeping like he did the night before, and his living thing ran with light steps, seeking friendship. The assistant closed his eyes. On his cheek he felt the soft and tender contact, and his fingers closed on the frail neck. The living thing didn't make a move to defend herself, and when the caress turned cold on his cheek, he knew that he'd strangled her. Then, he got up. He staggered along the path and left on the road. He took a right without knowing it, and the employer no longer moved at all.

VII

Straight ahead, he saw the large pond with blue brains. The night fell and the water shone with mysterious and faraway reflections. The pond wasn't deep. Brains were there by the hundreds, but they weren't of great value because they reproduced all year round.

He took two stakes from his tote bag and planted them near the pond, a meter from each other. Between them he stretched a strident steel wire and sounded a sad note on it with his finger. The wire was ten centimeters from the ground, parallel to the edge of the pond.

The assistant withdrew a few steps, then turned, a shape beside the water. He walked straight toward the wire. His eyes were closed and he whistled a tender tune that his living thing had liked. He walked slowly with tiny steps, and his feet caught on the wire. He fell, his head in the water, his body rigid. Under the silent surface the blue brains already stuck to his sunken cheeks.

JOURNEY TO KHONOSTROV

I

The locomotive heaved a strident cry. The engineer realized that he'd applied the brake too hard, and turned the crank in the right direction while a white-capped man whistled to have the last word. The train moved away slowly. The station was humid and somber and the train didn't like staying there.

There were six people in the compartment – four men and two women. Five of them had exchanged a few words, but not the sixth. Starting from the window on the seat opposite and from left to right were Jacques, Raymond, Brice, and Corine, a young, very pretty blonde. Opposite her was a man whose name they didn't know, Saturn Lamiel, and opposite Raymond, a brunette woman who wasn't too pretty – but who showed off her legs. Her name was Garamuche.

"The train's starting," Jacques said.

"It's cold," Garamuche said.

"Shall we play cards?" Raymond asked.

"Damn it, no!" replied Brice.

"You aren't a gentleman," Corine commented.

"What if you were to sit between Raymond and me?" Jacques suggested.

"Of course," Raymond agreed.

"It's a good idea," Brice, who wasn't a gentleman, concurred.

"She'll be opposite me," said Garamuche.

"I'm going to come beside you," Brice told her.

"Don't move," Raymond said.

"Come on then," Jacques said.

"I'm coming," Corine complied.

They all got up at the same time and mixed, and we'll have to start at the beginning again. Only Saturn Lamiel hadn't changed seats and continued to say nothing. As it stood, starting from the window on the other seat and from left to right were Brice, Garamuche, an empty space, and Saturn Lamiel, an empty space across from him, then Jacques, Corine, and Raymond.

"It's better this way," Raymond said. He threw a glance at Saturn Lamiel, who took it straight in the eye and blinked but said nothing.

"We're hardly worse off," Brice said.

Garamuche once more arranged her skirt. They could just see the nickle-plated garters she used to hold up her stockings. She managed so that they could see more from one side than the other.

"Don't you like my legs?" she asked Brice.

"Listen, you aren't behaving yourself. A person doesn't ask those things," Corine told her.

"You're incredible," Jacques said to Corine. "If you had the face she has, you'd show off your legs, too." He looked at Saturn Lamiel, who didn't turn his head but stared at something far away.

"Should we play cards?" Raymond asked.

"Hell! That's no fun for me. I'd rather talk," Corine told them. There was a moment of embarrassed silence and each knew why.

Brice put his foot in his mouth. "There's nothing worse

than a person in a train compartment who doesn't talk when they're addressed."

"Well, I trust you considered me before saying that!" Garamuche replied. "What if I don't answer you?"

"It's not you we're referring to," Jacques said. He had brown hair and blue eyes and a beautiful bass voice. He was closely shaven, but the skin on his cheeks was blue like the back of an uncooked mackerel.

"If it's me that Brice means," Raymond said, "perhaps he should say it outright." He looked at Saturn Lamiel a second time, but Saturn Lamiel seemed absorbed in his thoughts.

"In the past," Corine said, "they had ways to make people talk. During the Inquisition. I've read about it."

The train sped along now, but that didn't stop it from making the same movement with its wheels every half-second. Outside, the night was dirty, and the sand of the steppe reflected a few stars. From time to time a tree slapped the large cold window with its foremost leaves.

"When do we arrive?" Garamuche asked.

"Not before tomorrow morning," Raymond told her.

"We have time to muck around," Brice said.

"If only some people would answer," Jacques persisted.

"You're saying that because of me, aren't you?" Corine said.

"No, it's him we have a grudge against!" Raymond blurted. Suddenly, they were silent. Raymond's pointed finger designated Saturn Lamiel. He didn't move, but the four others jumped.

"He's right," Brice joined in. "No subterfuges. He must talk."

"Are you also going to Khonostrov?" Jacques asked.

"Do you like this journey?" Garamuche inquired. She moved over and occupied the empty space that had been between her and Lamiel, leaving Brice all alone near the window. This movement uncovered the tops of her stockings, and the rose garters of her nickle-plated whatchamacallits also disclosed the skin of her thighs, tanned and smooth in keeping with their desires.

"Do you play cards?" Raymond asked.

"Have you heard about the Inquisition?" Corine queried.

Saturn Lamiel arranged his feet in the green and blue Scotch lap robe over his knees. His face was very young and his blond hair, carefully separated with a part down the middle, fell in even waves on his temples.

"Well, he's provoking us!" Brice exclaimed. These words scarcely echoed, a natural phenomenon considering that the walls of the compartment, constructed as they were, acted as soundproof material. Besides, one had to remember that a certain length of seventeen meters came into play.

The silence was embarrassing.

"Shall we play cards?" Raymond asked next.

"Oh, you and your cards!" Garamuche obviously wanted to do something else.

"Shut up," Jacques ordered.

"Under the Inquisition," Corine offered, "they burned their feet with a branding iron, or whatever, to make them talk. They also tore off their fingernails or punctured their eyes. They – "

"That's enough," Brice said. "That's already sufficient to work on."

Except for Saturn Lamiel, they all got up together. The train passed through a tunnel with a loud raucous howl and the noise of colliding rocks. When it emerged from the tunnel, Corine and Garamuche were near the window opposite each other. Raymond was seated beside Saturn Lamiel. Between him and Corine was an empty space. Opposite Saturn were Jacques, Brice, an empty space, and Garamuche.

On his knees Brice held a small new suitcase of yellow

leather with nickle-plated rings on the handle and the initials of someone else called Brice, but whose name started with double *P*s.

"Are you going to Khonostrov?" Jacques directly addressed Saturn Lamiel, who had closed his eyes and breathed softly so as not to waken himself.

Raymond put his glasses back on. He was a big strong man with large glasses and rather messy hair parted on the side. "What should we do?" he asked.

"The toes," Brice told him. He opened his small yellow leather suitcase.

"We must take off his shoes," Corine directed.

"I prefer the Chinese method," Garamuche said. She blushed because they all looked angrily her way.

"Don't start that again!" Jacques told her.

"In the name of God, the slut!" Brice said.

"You exaggerate," Corine said.

"What's the Chinese method?" Raymond asked.

There was a deathly silence because at that moment the train was moving along the rubber portion of track that just had been built between Considermetrov and Smogogolets. The quietness awakened Saturn Lamiel. His beautiful hazel eyes suddenly opened, and he pulled up the Scotch lap robe that had slid off his knees. And then he closed his eyes and seemed to fall asleep again.

Raymond turned aside during a great crashing of the brakes and didn't insist. Garamuche muttered in her corner and looked to see if she had her lipstick. Stealthily, she took it out and put it back two or three times so that Raymond would understand. He turned even redder. Brice and Jacques leaned over the small suitcase, and Corine looked at Garamuche with disgust.

"The feet. Take off his shoes," Jacques suggested to Raymond. Happy to make himself useful, Raymond kneeled near Saturn Lamiel and tried to undo the shoelaces, which wheezed and writhed upon seeing the passenger approach. Not succeeding, he spat at the laces like an angry cat.

"Come on," Brice said. "You're holding us up."

"I'm doing my best. But we can't undo them," Raymond said.

"Wait a minute!" Brice held out a small pair of very shiny pincers and Raymond cut the shoe leather around the laces so that he wouldn't ruin them. He rolled them up on his fingers after finishing the operation.

"Ok," Brice said. "There's nothing left but to take off his shoes."

Jacques charged himself with this task. Saturn Lamiel still slept. Jacques put the shoes in the luggage rack.

"What if you were to leave on his socks?" Corine proposed. "They'll keep heat and dirt around the wound so that afterward he'll get infected.

"It's a good idea," Jacques complimented her.

"Agreed," Brice said.

Raymond sat down again beside Saturn and played with the laces. Brice took a neat miniature blowtorch and a small bottle from his yellow suitcase, and inserted the gas into the hole. Jacques lighted a match and ignited the gas. A beautiful smoky blue and yellow flame shot up and scorched Brice's eyelashes. He began to swear. At that moment, Saturn Lamiel opened his eyes, but he closed them again. His lovely, long, and manicured hands rested on the Scotch lap robe, interlaced in such a complicated manner that for five minutes Raymond had a headache trying to figure them out.

Corine opened her handbag and took out her comb. She re-did her hair in front of the window. The black background of the night permitted her to see herself. Outside, the wind whistled loudly, and wolves galloped to warm themselves. The train passed a traveler bicycling on the sand with the last of his strength. Briskipotolsk wasn't far. The steppe extended to Cornopoutchik, two-and-a-half versts from Brantchotchar-novnia. In general, no one could pronounce the names of these villages, and they'd taken to calling them Urville, Mâcon, Le Puy, and Sainte Machine.

The blowtorch was spewing wildly and Brice adjusted the nozzle to get a short blue flame. He passed it to Raymond and put the yellow suitcase on the floor.

"Shall we try one last time?" Raymond asked.

Jacques leaned over Saturn. "Are you going to Khono-strov?" Saturn opened one eye and closed it again.

"The bastard!" Brice said angrily. He knelt before Saturn and raised one of the man's feet without being particular about which.

"If you burn the nails first, it hurts more and takes longer to heal," Corine said.

"Pass me the blowtorch," Brice ordered. Raymond gave him the torch and Brice cast the flame on the door of the compartment to see if it was ready. The varnish melted and smelled awful.

Saturn's socks smelled still worse. Garamuche identified the odor as pure wool. Corine didn't look. She'd taken up a book. Raymond and Jacques waited. Smoke, a strong sizzling, and an odor of burnt callus wafted from Saturn's foot, and a few black drops fell onto the floor. Saturn's foot contracted in Brice's clammy hand so that he had trouble holding it. Corine left her book and lowered the window slightly to let out the fumes.

"We're going to try again," Jacques said.

"Do you play cards?" Raymond asked Saturn, turning affa-bly in his direction. Saturn retreated into the corner of the compartment. His mouth was a little uneasy and his fore-head wrinkled. He smiled and closed his eyes tighter.

"It's no use," Jacques said. "He doesn't want to talk."

"What a bastard," Brice repeated.

"He's an ill-bred lout," Raymond said. "When you're six to a compartment, you talk."

"Or you have fun," Garamuche interjected.

"Shut up!" Brice ordered. "We know what you'd like."

"You could try the pincers," Corine suggested. She lifted her pretty face and her eyelashes beat like the elytrons of a butterfly. "In the palms of the hands you'll find some interesting elements to attack."

"Should we stop the blowtorch?" Brice asked her.

"No, continue with both," Corine said. "What's the hurry? Khonostrov is far away."

"He's going to end up talking," Jacques stated.

"Even so, he's a cad," Garamuche added.

A fugitive smile appeared on Saturn Lamiel's oval face. Brice took up the blowtorch and attacked the other foot right in the middle of the sole while Raymond searched in his suitcase. The blue flame of the torch crossed Saturn's foot at the precise moment that Raymond found the nerve. Jacques urged him on.

"Try under the knee next," Corine suggested.

They laid out Saturn's body on one of the two seats so they could work more easily. Saturn's face was all white and his eyes no longer stirred under the lashes. A violent draft filled the compartment because the burnt skin odor had increased, becoming unbearable. Corine didn't like it. Brice turned off the blowtorch. Black tissue fluid flowed from Saturn's feet onto the stained seat.

"Should we stop a minute?" Jacques asked. He swiped his face with the back of his hand. Raymond lifted his hand to his mouth. He felt like singing. Saturn's right hand looked like a split fig. Pieces of flesh and tendons hung from it.

"He's strong," Raymond observed. He jumped when he saw Saturn's hand fall of its own accord onto the seat.

Since all five couldn't sit down on the other seat, after having taken a sheet of sandpaper and a file from his yellow suitcase, Brice went into the corridor to stretch his legs. So from the window to the door were Corine, Garamuche, Jacques, and Raymond.

"What a cad!" Jacques exclaimed.

"He doesn't want to talk," Garamuche said.

"That's what we're going to find out," Raymond said.

"I'm going to suggest something else," Corine contributed.

II

The train continued to roll through the hoary steppe and crossed lines of beggars who had come from the underground market at Goldzine. It was broad daylight now and Corine looked at the countryside. It felt itself being watched and hid modestly in a rabbit hole.

Only one foot and one-and-a-half arms remained on Saturn Lamiel, and as he had gone to sleep they couldn't reasonably wait until he spoke.

They passed Goldzine. Khonostrov was six versts away. Brice, Jacques, and Raymond were exhausted, but their morale still hung by three green threads, one for each.

The theological bell resounded in the corridor and Saturn jumped. Brice dropped his needle and Jacques almost burnt himself with the electric branding iron he was holding. Diligently, Raymond continued to look for the exact position of the liver, but Brice's catapult lacked precision.

Saturn opened his eyelids. With great effort he sat upright. The absence of his left buttock seemed to unbalance him, and he lifted his Scotch lap robe over his shredded leg. Their shoes plashed on the floor and blood sloshed in every corner. Saturn shook out his blond hair and gave them a nice smile. "I'm not too talkative, am I?" he said. At that moment the train pulled into the Khonostrov station. They all got off.

BLUE FAIRY TALE

I

At eighteen kilometers in the afternoon, that is to say nine minutes before the clock strikes twelve, because he was doing 120 kph (and that's in a car), Phaeton Goodfellow stopped on the edge of the shady road, obeying a thumb extending from an attractive body.

Anäis had decided to hitch only as a last resort because of the scarcity of trains, and no less important, the condition of her shoes.

Phaeton Goodfellow really was called Oliver. He opened the door for her and Jacqueline (Anäis was an assumed name) got in.

"Are you going to Carcassonne?" she asked in a vampish voice.

"I'd like to," Oliver told her, "but what road do I take leaving Rouen?"

Actually, they were close to Havre and heading toward Paris. "I'll show you," Jacqueline said.

Three kilomoters later, Oliver, timid by nature, again stopped his car, and fortified with a monkey wrench so that he could adjust the rear-view mirror, he perched on the left fender. This done, if he turned to the left, he could see three-quarters of the woman on his right – which is better than

67

nothing. A naughty smile played on the lips of Oliver's mind, and a simple smile on hers.

Just the Major and the dog were in the back with two suitcases. The Major slept, and the suitcases were too far away to torment the dog. Oliver put the monkey wrench back in the chrome glove compartment under the dash, got back in, and shifted the car into gear.

Like most people who work a lot, he'd wanted to take this vacation since the last one. For eleven months he'd prepared for this cherished moment (even more so with train travel) of escape into the clear of the morning toward the burning solitude of tropical Auvergne stretching as far as Aude and extinguished only at twilight.

He relived his last morning at the office – the effort of placing each foot beside the telephone and throwing envelopes from mail that had just arrived into the wastebasket, the sweetness of air escaping from the elevator with a silky grinding, the ray of sun dancing before him and reflected in his watchband as he returned to his apartment on Dock Street, the cry of the gulls and the black and gray bowling-green birds, the rather lazy animation of the port, and the strong odor emanating from the shop of Mr. Tulip, his pharmacist neighbor below.

A Norwegian freighter had just unloaded a shipment of lost pine cut into three- and four-foot logs. Visions of living freely in a log cabin near Lake Ontario preoccupied Oliver with daydreaming. He tottered on a hawser, and found himself sinking in the oil-slick water, or rather elevated by fuel oil and the flotsam of summer, since he weighed less than the water under the same volume.

That was yesterday. Now reality had passed far beyond his most secret expectations – Oliver at the wheel with Jacqueline, the dog, the two suitcases and the Major. Oliver still didn't know her last name.

II

Leaving Rouen, Jacqueline directed Oliver to the right road. His gracious compliance drew her nearer until her brown hair brushed the young man's cheek. A limpid steam passed before his eyes. He came to his senses five minutes later, and profitted by taking his foot off the accelerator. The pedal returned regretfully, because from its former position it could see most of the road through the little hole in the floorboard.

With great speed, the road wound itself around the wheels. At a Cyclist Counters sale he'd purchased a system similar to the Super Nail Remover that automatically detached the road. It fell behind them in soft waves, drawn out by the rapidly rotating tires. The road crew, forever dedicated to their thankless sport, cut away at periodical protuberances with scissors. The height of these bumps met the car speed in direct proportion, thus conditioning the stretch rate. With the recovered asphalt, each year they constructed new roads so that the roadside livestock in France increased on a regular basis.

The solidly rooted trees on either side didn't participate in the winding road. Sometimes, however, they jumped at the passing car because Oliver had turned on the exhaust. Those branches out of touch with the telephone wires (generally the case because they were pruned on schedule by responsible road agents) weren't warned in time. Nesting birds, familiar with this procedure since 1898, marvelously resisted it with somersaults.

A few small clouds gave the sky an aspect of sky seeded with small clouds. The sun shone, and the wind displaced the air – unless it was the displaced air that produced the wind. This could be discussed at great length because the dictionary defines wind "agitation of air," and agitation can be the act of agitating, or the state of that which is agitated. From time to time a porpoise crossed the road, but this was only a mirage.

Oliver continued to look in the rear-view mirror at three-quarters of Jacqueline. His heart flamed with more or less troubled desires, and surely Max du Veuzit would agree.

A bump more violent than the others (there had been quite a few) suddenly pulled the Major from his torpor. He stretched his arms, rubbed his face with the palm of his hand, pulled his comb from his pocket, and put his mop of hair in order. He removed his glass eye from its socket. Spitting on it, he rubbed it carefully with a corner of his handkerchief and held it out to the dog, who refused to take it. Then, he put it back in, and leaned toward the front seat so that he could hold up the lagging conversation.

He leaned his elbow on the back of the seat between Jacqueline's back and Oliver. "What's your name?" the Major asked.

"Jacqueline," she answered, turning slightly toward the left to present her profile.

Now Oliver saw her from the front in the rear-view mirror. The last fraction of his view having been absorbed by the new fraction Jacqueline presented as she moved toward the Major distracted him from an occurrence on the road. Had he had the right perception at the right time, he could have avoided the upheaval. But he no longer was looking at the road, and he ran over the aforementioned object in the form of a goat.

Because of the ricochet of the goat, he crashed into the cornerstone of a garage door. Permitting the grease monkey to collect himself, the car ended up in the middle of the garage. But speeding by, it left its right fender on the ravenous cornerstone.

The garage mechanic began to repair the car, and Oliver helped Jacqueline out his side. The right door had just been removed by the mechanic. In turn, the Major and the dog got out and began to search for a restaurant, hopefully one fortified with a bar. The Major was thirsty.

As they passed, they saw that the goat and prime mover of the accident carried herself very well, considering that she was in doomsday. Her fur had been painted white by the mechanic who used her to lure people to his garage. Out of sympathy, the dog pissed the length of one of her hooves.

The only hotel, the Crowned Tapir, was an awesome sight. In one corner some men were busy around a sort of stone feeding trough filled with hot coals, and one of them struck violent blows with a hammer on a red-hot iron horseshoe. More curious yet, a horse with a nosebag of unbleached linen around its neck bent his back foot, waiting his turn as he ground out the blues on robust teeth. They were forced to face facts – the hotel must be on the opposite side.

At the hotel, they were served empty plates on a white tablecloth, knives, forks, glasses, and a salt-pepper-mustard holder in the middle, then napkins, and to finish it all off, something to eat. The Major drank a small glass of bladder, and with the dog, steered in the direction of an alfalfa field.

Oliver and Jacqueline remained under the arbor. "So did you know that I was going to Carcassonne?" he asked with a burning heart.

"No," Jacqueline answered. "But I'm happy that you were going there, too."

Oppressed by happiness, Oliver lost his breath and began to breathe like a man being strangled – with one exception, the laugh of the hangman was missing. With time on his side, he got ahold of himself and again overcame his shyness. To this degree, he grew a good half a head taller, and slightly moved his hand close to that of Jacqueline, who was seated opposite him.

The birds under the arbor brayed like donkeys and bombarded each other with bread crumbs and small green pebbles, and the joyous ambiance slowly intoxicated Oliver. "Will you be there a few days?" he asked.

"I intend to spend my vacation there," Jacqueline assured him with a rather overwhelming smile.

Oliver continued to move his hand forward a little. The beating blood in his arteries caused the golden wine in one of the glasses to tremble slightly, setting up such a resonance that suddenly it shattered. Time again to gather courage. He continued, "Are you going to your parents?"

"No, I'm at the Albigensian and United Station Hotel," Jacqueline said. She really didn't have brown hair, especially when the sun traversed it like that – and the tiny freckles on her arms tanned in the open air. She must have others, and thinking of them Oliver blushed.

Then, taking his courage in both hands, he placed it entirely in his left hand so he could cover Jacqueline's closest hand. He didn't know which it was, because it totally disappeared in his large paw.

His heart beat enormous blows in his chest and he asked, "Who's there?" But he realized his mistake, and Jacqueline didn't move her hand away.

Then, all the flowers bloomed in a single stroke and a marvelous melody filled the countryside. It was the Major humming the choral movement of the Ninth Symphony. He'd come back to inform them the car had been repaired.

III

Outside of Clermont the car rolled between two power lines in full flower and they perfumed the air with a delicious ozone odor. Leaving Clermont, Oliver carefully sighted Aurillac and continued on his trajectory. He didn't need to steer, and once more with his right hand, he imprisoned Jacqueline's.

With delight the Major sucked in the fragrant electric air, his nose in the wind, and the dog on his lap. He sang the blues while mentally trying to calculate how many days one could spend in Carcassonne on 22 francs. He ended his calculation with the division of 22 by 460. He got a migraine and grew disinterested, deciding simply to remain a month in the best hotel.

The same wind that struck the Major's nostrils scattered Jacqueline's curls and refreshed the reddening temples of a distracted Oliver. Shifting his gaze from the rear-view mirror, adjacent his right foot he could see Jacqueline's charming shoes of live lizard closed with gold clasps so you couldn't hear their cries. The delicious curve of her amber calves settled on the cream leather of the front seat. He'd have to replace the leather. It already was in shreds because she changed position so often. But Oliver hardly bothered about it, and it would be a precious souvenir for him.

Now the road had quite a time straightening out under the car tires. The glance Oliver had aimed at Aurillac while leaving Clermont was so precise that the least turn was imperceptible. The slightest error, and the steering wheel pivoted a few degrees, returning to position at the expense of extenuating contortions. It didn't regain its initial balance until late at night, thus causing considerable drawn-out collisions.

Aurillac, Rodez, and then the borderland of tropical Auvergne appeared before the three travelers. On maps they call it *Languedoc,* but geologists know better.

After Aurillac, Oliver occupied the back seat with Jacqueline. Major and the dog were charged with driving. With a skillful turn of the monkey wrench, the Major reestablished the exact position of the rear-view mirror, and could consecrate himself to the exclusive examination of the road they'd just followed.

The borderland of tropical Auvergne disappeared as night fell, but soon reappeared because the dog had turned on the headlights.

An hour from Carcassonne, and it wasn't yet midnight. They entered Carcassonne at one o'clock. Jacqueline's room and that of Oliver had been reserved for a long time. The Major, along with the dog, found it convenient to get in bed with one of the hotel maids. Then he got into the maid herself, stopped there, and slept snugly. He'd change rooms in the morning, wishing to choose it carefully.

IV

The following morning they reunited around a round breakfast table. The dog, seated underneath the table at an equal distance from each, neglected except in stature, easily was confused with the center pole. One movement from the Major made him a dog again. This consisted in leaving the hotel garden. The dog followed, wagging his tail and barking out of politeness. The Major whistled a stomp and polished his monocle.

Left alone, Jacqueline and Oliver, intimidated by the brown ceiling girders, looked the other way. The sun back-lighted Jacqueline's profile on one of the windows with small panes. It designed her silhouette several times before arriving at a perfect resemblance, but at that moment she truly was ravishing.

The smooth skin of her cheeks accentuated her extremely youthful appearance and the rose tea-colored complexion near her bronze hair took on an allure hitherto unknown to Oliver. Jacqueline's bright eyes – and that's all. At his very center Oliver tasted an apricot that he'd just swallowed to sample its return, as unicorns do. He felt happier and happier, and how could he explain this happiness if he omitted

74

Jacqueline? With a limber movement she got up, pushed back her chair and held out her hand.

"Come," she said, "We're going for a walk before lunch."

At the tobacco shop opposite the station, the Major bought some postcards. He took some for twenty-one francs and gave the remaining twenty sous to the dog to pay for a kit and caboodle with all the kits inside, of course. With one leaden eye and the other of glass, the Major watched the couple depart.

Arms entwined, they took the country road. She had on a dress of transparent material, and wore light sandals with high heels – and her hair always imprisoning the sun.

The Major substituted a slow tune for the stomp, and comfortably seated himself on the café terrace of the Albigensian and United Station.

The country road was like other country roads, beautiful as always. It consisted of the road and an intermediate zone divided into grassy banks, a shallow ditch, a bank planted with trees, and finally, the fields with all the expected ingredients – mustard, summer rape, wheat, different and indifferent animals.

There was Jacqueline with her long legs and rounded breasts underlined by the white leather belt, and her arms – bare except for the small balloon sleeves ready to fly away with Oliver's heart suspended by a fragment of aorta just long enough to make a knot.

Upon their return, when Jacqueline withdrew her hand from Oliver's forearm, it left a transparent imprint on a brown background. But it didn't leave a single impression on her own body. Maybe Oliver was too shy. They reached the station terrace as the Major was getting up to mail eleven cards scribbled in nothing flat. Knowing they cost nineteen sous each, you can calculate yourself how much he had left.

At the hotel, lunch was ready.

V

The dog was scratching fleas in front of the Major's room, so Oliver stepped on his tail as he left his room for the lunch bell.

The night before had been marvelous with a car ride down to the river. The dog had protested because, only now having killed the fleas, had he the time to pay attention to Oliver. Jacqueline had stretched out near the water in a white bathing suit with water pearls on her hair, water like brilliant cellophane on her legs, her arms – water simply wetting the sand where she'd lain. Then, he'd bent down and patted the dog's back and the dog condescendingly had given his hand a huge lick.

But he hadn't dared ask her the words that are so embarrassing when you're shy. He came back late with her, but simply – "good-night" as on other nights.

This morning he wanted to tell her the words. Then the Major's door opened and Oliver was standing behind it in the hall. Jacqueline left the Major's room wearing white silk pajamas open at her breasts. She crossed the hall to her own room to re-do her hair and dress.

VI

They tried to close the Major's door, but salt-water tears had rusted the hinges fast.

FOG

I

The director of the asylum watched André leave. He walked
with his elbows glued to his body and his head bent backward
at a right angle. He's completely cured, the director thought.
When they'd brought him in three months ago, this calm
inmate could only flail his spread arms while staring at his
navel and imitating the sound of a bumblebee.

A remarkable case, the director told himself. He took out
a pack of cigarettes, stuffed one in his ear, and chewed the
match while hopping from foot to foot – reaching his office
on all fours.

André walked two hundred meters, then, feeling tired, he
spread his arms, bent his head forward, filled his cheeks with
air and let go with a "Bzzzzzzzzzzz." The earth wriggled underfoot as the trees on the road wagged the tail. Small graceful
houses covered with deflowered vines closely examined André's bearded physiognomy as he passed, but couldn't draw
one single salient conclusion.

Seeing the streetcar arrive, André sprinted, and the howl
from pain to his parietals muffled the concomitant noise
produced by the trolley. While it was waiting, he was taken to
the pharmacy for an alcohol solution (though it was Tues-
day). He left a small tip and took the road back.

II

From his window on the fifth floor, he could see the lower roof of the house opposite. The shutters had been pulled back for so long that they marked the wall with horizontal stripes, which were invisible because the shutters always were open. On the third floor, a young girl undressed in front of a mirrored dresser and he could make out the bedstead of chilled Brazilian rosewood attached to two impatient feet and draped with a cheerful yellow American comforter.

On second thought, perhaps she wasn't a young girl and the sign on the door – "Sports Hotel – Rooms by the Hour, the Half Hour, and Passing Through" – proved it. But the hotel was pretty with a mosaic on the façade at street level, drapes on all the windows, and only one slightly disorderly tile in the middle of the roof. After the last bombing, red tiles had replaced the brown ones. They designed the pregnant profile of Mary Stuart and were signed by the artist: Gustave Laurent, roofer, Red Shark Street. The house next to it hadn't been repaired. A tarp still covered the gaping hole on the right end. Plaster rubble and scrap iron were piled at the base of a wall populated with wood lice and venomous snakes that rattled their voodoo Black Mass late into the night.

The last bombing had other repercussions; in particular, it sent André to the asylum. It was the second bombing he'd sustained, and his brain, used to being sated on the evangelists according to Saint Zano, took an accentuated vertical gyration, thus dividing him in two nearly identical parts.

For those who saw him in clockwise profile, his skull projected forward, necessitating the spread of his arms to balance himself. He completed this highly original state of mind with a slightly rhythmic "Bzzzzzz." Due to these circumstances, people tended to give him plenty of elbowroom. Slowly the condition abated, thanks to the good services of the director of the asylum. Donning his old comportment as soon as he was out of this affable man's sight corresponded to his comprehensible need for freedom, as well as his need for capricious invention.

On the floor below, the lawyer's clock struck five. The hammer on the bronze resounded in André's heart as though it had struck simultaneously in the four corners of the room. Not a church around. Only the lawyer's clock bound André to the exterior world.

It was made of varnished oak with a round smooth face in dull metal and numerals in copper. Lower down through the glass you could see the short cylindrical balance wheel terminated by a bobbin sliding on another shapely shaft that formed the stopwork at the transverse bar rounded by the pendulum weight. A good electric clock never stopped, and the weight was invisible.

The evening of the bombing, André had seen the clock through the lawyer's open door. It said six o'clock, half an eternity, and at that moment the bomb surprised him – showing him a menacing door, and blowing death into his face. He fled. His fall down the stairs stripped eleven steps of corrugated brass, and he didn't stop until he was in the basement.

She'd halted, but as soon as she was his, the clock would let André throw her weight back into time.

III

The heat continued to mount and collide with the low ceiling, slowly compressing the breathable atmosphere into a narrow band flush with the doorsill onto the landing. Stretched out on the floor in front of his bed, with deep inhalations André breathed the slightly fresher air. This imperceptible movement produced clouds of dust from the grooves of the worn floorboards. The faucet over his sink wearily released a stream of cold water on a second bottle of alcohol so it wouldn't combust. The contents of the first bottle were boiling in André's intestines, spreading through his pores in small geysers of gray steam.

Gluing his head to the floor, he distinctly heard the regular tick of the clock. He positioned himself so he could find its zenith. With the strongest blade of his pocketknife, he tried to gouge a hole in the overly scrubbed pine boards so that he could see the clock. The strong yellow grain of the wood resisted the steel blade, but the scrub brush-worn valleys succumbed. First cutting crosswise, he sectioned the fibers, then pressing down along the grain, he made match-size splinters fly.

Through the blinding frame of the open window a high plane buzzed like a brilliant point that flickers before the half-closed eyes of someone on the verge of a migraine. Not a bombing. The anti-aircraft unit guns on the far end of the nearby bridge were silent.

He continued to cut with his knife.

If there were another bombing, maybe the lawyer would leave his door open again.

IV

The lawyer pushed up his sleeves. Through an opening of his robe, he vigorously scratched his chest. It sounded like someone currying a horse. He placed his magistral cap on the head of a shiny banister beside him and started his counsel's speech.

"Gentlemen of the jury," he said, "we will disregard the motive of the murder, the circumstances in which it was committed, and the murder itself. Under these conditions, with what do you accuse my client?"

The jury, struck by a side of the case they hadn't considered, was silent and rather uneasy. The judge slept, and the public prosecutor was sold to the Germans.

"Let's present the problem differently," the lawyer said, happy with his initial success. "If you discount the regrettable suffering of the victim's parents before which I bow down, if you set aside my client's necessity to plead self-defence – permit me to add that my client also killed the two police-men charged with his arrest – finally, if you take nothing into account, what is left?"

"Nothing," a jury member who was a teacher was forced to concede.

"This established, if we consider that from his youth my client only knew robbers and assassins, that all his life he had before him an example of debauchery and decadence, that he gave himself to this life-style and adopted it as normal to the extent that he became a debauchee, robber, and assassin himself, what can we conclude?"

The jury was confounded by such eloquence, and an old bearded man on the extreme right with wise diligence watched for an involuntary splutter from the floor. But once more the teacher thought obliged to answer: "Nothing," and blushed.

"Eh! Yes, sir!" retorted the lawyer with such strength that some fragments of glass he'd eaten that morning fell on the public. "We will conclude that submersed in an honorable milieu, my client only would have contracted honorable traits. *Asinus asinum fricat,* as the proverb goes." He didn't point out that the contrary also could be true.

For a while, the teacher searched in his mind for the contrary of an ass. The effort so taxed him that he grew weak and died on the spot.

"But," concluded the lawyer, "what I told you just now wasn't true. My client is of a perfectly reputable family, has received an excellent education, and killed the victim volun-tarily and in full conscience so that he could steal his ciga-rettes."

"You're right!" the jury shouted unanimously. After deliberation, the murderer was condemned to death. The lawyer left City Hall and headed home on his bicycle, taking care to place his derrière directly on the seat so that the wind sweeping under his Piguet robe would disclose his hairy thighs, as was the fashion. Underneath, he wore red bloomers with elastic at the ankles.

Some distance from his place, he stopped before the window front of an antique shop. To his amazement, a Dutch clock offered its complex multiple frame depicting the phases of the moon in successive crescents, illuminating the black and gold splendors of the new and full moons. On the engraved face he could read the days, months, days of the month, and the age of the clockmaker.

As a retainer fee, the client had willed the lawyer his entire fortune. Aware that he was about to become an inheritor because they'd just condemned him to death, the lawyer judiciously decided to celebrate by purchasing the clock. He already had a watch so he didn't take it with him, but said he'd have it picked up.

V

A light filtered through the small square hole in the floor and crushed itself lazily beside the spider on André's ceiling. The spider nibbled at the edges of the spot, slowly forming it into a clockface, then started working on the numbers. André realized that they were talking about *Her* on the floor below. He placed his ear at the opening and the light filtered into his ear. So, of course, he heard the words resonate in clear letters before his eyes.

The lawyer had a guest for dinner. "I'm going to sell this clock," he said, showing the guest its pendulum casing. The weight of the pendulum jumped and then continued on its course.

"Doesn't it work?" his friend asked.

"Oh, quite well, but just awhile ago I saw a prettier one." The lawyer emptied half a glass of wine. "Drink!" As an example, he refilled his glass.

"What's the other clock like?" the friend asked.

"It has the phases of the moon on it."

Then André heard no more because the two men had stopped talking about the clock. He got up. So as not to be discovered, he'd turned out the lights, and the chink of light shined through the hole and settled on the sloped ceiling of the mansard roof. To meet all expectations, a full round bomber's moon completed the lighting, and trembled slightly because it was getting hotter and hotter.

In the sink the faucet water still ran over the bottle of alcohol. André rested on his bed and the clock chimed incessantly in his head. Time passed all about him, but he hadn't the weight to stop it.

There was no wind or rain and despite André's attempts to beat the heat, it rose as on most evenings and pressed so hard against the windows that he could see them bulge toward him, distend, shatter one by one, and reform like soap bubbles in a cracked bowl.

When one of the windows shattered, for an instant he could faintly hear the exterior noises: the patrol marching down on the street, the yowl of cats on a neighboring roof, the din of the wireless behind the drapes drawn on large open windows. When he leaned over, beneath him he could see bright spots on the shirt of the man and dress of the woman concierge who were seated on two old chairs in front of his apartment. But he had to hurry, because the windows were reforming. The stream from the water faucet subsided, signaling that it had been turned on below him.

The metal mattress spring accompanied André's rhythmic breathing with a small noise. The bed clawed at the ground like a cat, curling up its feet, raising them slightly one after another, and balancing itself with a regular movement. The floor would be ruined tomorrow and the feet buried into it. To reduce the damage, André got up and, after having slipped an old shoe under each of the bed feet, he stretched out on the floor. With shoes on, it was amusing and easy to walk, and the bed took advantage of André's absence by making a turn of the room and raising its foot against the wall.

The lawyer's friend had just left, and the lawyer must have left the dining room because the light on the ceiling had gone out. Faintly, he heard the radios, and from somewhere he heard the jammed BBC station-call, modulated on five notes. Suddenly in the sky there was a distant murmur and a plane passed over at such high altitude that he couldn't identify its direction.

The minutes continued to dissipate because André still didn't have the weight. When he remembered that the clock soon would be leaving, perspiration soaked his neck and thighs. Then far off he heard the screech of sirens in the neighboring community, and a few seconds later, the Town Hall joined in.

The anti-aircraft unit hadn't sounded their alert, but searchlights projected uncertain spots in the sky, gigantic beams focusing their nebulous excited wavelengths. A few rays of light delineated the window frames with drapes scrupulously pulled, and the apartments filled up with muffled murmurs. There were cries from a child awoken with a start, then footsteps going downstairs, and the concierge stumbling in the basement – he recognized her vocabulary.

The lawyer hadn't opened his door. No doubt he was laid low by the wine he'd drunk in great quantity at dinner, and was still sleeping. Suddenly, there was a total blackout. On the floor, André crawled to the window and fearfully awaited the arrival of the planes and the crash of the bomb that would wake up the lawyer.

He got up and tried to get the tap water to run, but only elicited a raucous gurgle. The concierge had just locked the cellar. Even so, he drank the alcohol in the bottle. It tailspun in his esophogus with a strange whirring and, at the last, sounded like the plug pulled from a bathtub.

His human sense demanded that he warn the lawyer. Warily in the dark, he took the two shoes from the bed and painfully extracted its feet. He had to fight with the bed to retrieve them, and the iron castors tore ten centimeters from his wrists. Cunningly, he loosened two screws from underneath, and the bed caved in, defeated in a crash of dead metal.

The ruckus hadn't awakened the lawyer. André would have to go down. He went onto the landing, mechanically closing the door behind him, and realized that his keys must be in his vest on the chair. To check, mechanically he dug into his pants pockets where he found only a handkerchief and his knife.

Cautiously, so as not to make the second step squeak, he descended, glued against the wall. The black shaft of the stairwell, an abyss from which some unknown horror could escape at any moment, exuded the noxious stale odors of cabbage cooked that afternoon, and the sewer.

The lawyer's doorbell was to the left and a meter twenty centimeters from the ground. After knocking first, without rushing he leaned to the side, and let his hand ramble over the casing. Finally, he encountered the brass doorbell cap and pressed the center. The contact with the plastic nipple gave him a shock. The electricity had been cut, but a small current still ran through the wires. Maybe it would waken the lawyer. To make doubly sure, André kicked at the door. It hadn't been carefully closed by the inebriated lawyer, and gave way with his kicking. He entered in darkness, stumbled, bumped into the wall, and came upon the dining room. The wide-open window let in fifty high-caliber moon rays and the impeded pendulum weight gleamed slightly under its crystal casing.

Time finally stopped. André didn't hear the lawyer leave his room because he already lived in a world older by a minute. But he saw him far off, and must have thrown his knife to clear the distance. He watched the lawyer flee, carried by time, his throat bleeding in his flaccid lawyer's body.

The end of the alert imposed its dissonant pitch on the night. All at once the light came back on, and the clock pendulum ceased to exist.

VI

The darkness of the stairwell already grew lighter near the small stained glass-leaded windows. André's feet, heavy and sad, pushed him into the street. Two white cats filed before him, flying from the garbage pail like bubbles from champagne.

The bridge wasn't far, and the smooth surface of the railing was easier to walk on than the asphalt side walkway. Suddenly, the silhouette of the Major, furious at being left out of the story, rose behind him and seized André by the collar. His shoulders hitched up, arms askew, and head forward, André gesticulated from a few meters above the railing, crying, "Let me go!" But because the Major was invisible, André was the only one who knew the Major had lifted him. As for everyone else, they thought he'd jumped into the river.

86

GOOD STUDENTS

I

Moon and Paton came down the stairs of the Police School. They'd left the Tax Payers Anatomy Class and were about to lunch before resuming probation in front of the Conformist Party building where ranting troublemakers just had broken windows with their clubs.

Gayly, they swung their blue capes while whistling a policeman's march, stressing every third beat with a hearty whack of their billy clubs at a neighbor's thigh – an assault ideally suited to an even number of policemen. At the bottom of the stairs they turned and took the vaulted corridor to the dining hall. The march resonated beneath the old stones, because the air vibrated on A flat of the fourth octave, a note composed of no less than 336 vibrations. To the left, in a long narrow street lined with scorched trees, prospective policemen limbered up – playing leapfrog, and studying the quadrille to a violin, their green exercise clubs hammering the calabashes they were ordered to split in one blow. Moon and Paton paid no attention to the spectacle since they participated in it daily, except on Thursdays when the policemen rested.

Moon pushed open the large door to the dining hall and went in first. Paton waited a minute to finish the march because he was a slow whistler. The students arrived in twos and threes, chattering excitedly because they'd just taken exams that morning and the previous day.

Moon and Paton made their way toward table seven where they found Arrelent and Poland, a pair that compensated for being the most backward policemen in the school with an overabundance of impudence. With a shuffle of broken chairs, they all sat down.

"How did it go?" Moon asked Arrelent.

"A real bummer!" Arrelent answered. "They gave me a drudge who was at least seventy years old and tough as a horse, the bitch."

"I broke nine teeth in a single blow," boasted Poland. "The examiner congratulated me."

"I was unfortunate," Arrelent said. "She made me so mad that I blew the livid pilgrim."

"I know why. They no longer can find enough of them in the poor district so they give us the ones that are better fed," Paton remarked. "They hold up better. Mind you, it still works with the women. But this morning I had a rough time driving my club into this guy's eye – "

"I anticipated that problem, and fixed up my club a bit," Arrelent said, showing them the sharpened tip. "It went in like butter. I really tried, and I recouped the two points I'd lost yesterday."

"Children are tough this year, too," observed Moon. "The one yesterday morning I had to break a wrist at a time, and I was forced to kick at his ankles with my boots. It's disgusting."

"Same here. We can't have them on Welfare anymore," Arrelent commented. "They're children from the pound, so you never know. You get a good one or a bad. It's luck. The well-fed are hard to work over fast. They've got tough skin."

"The weights in my cape have come unstitched. Only seven

of the sixteen are left," Poland said. "I had to hit twice as fast, so I was dead tired, believe me – The sergeant swore up and down when he saw that. He told me simply to sock it to them harder next time. I was penalized.

When the soup came they stopped talking. Moon seized the ladle and plunged it into the pot. It was goat soup with grease swimming on top. They took large servings.

II

Moon waited on duty in front of the Conformist Party building. He looked at the books in the bookstore, and the titles gave him a headache. He never read anything but his police manual with the four thousand examples of quadrilles to memorize – from pissing in the street to talking too much with a policeman. The reading of the manual always sent him into conniptions as soon as he came to page fifty and an illustration of a man crossing a main street outside the white lines. Each time he saw it, he spit on the ground and turned the page so that he could regain his composure, looking at the portrait of the "good policeman" with shiny buttons. By strange coincidence, the good policeman resembled his friend Paton, who at that moment tiptoed silent as a rat on the other side of the building.

A large flatbed loaded with steel girders approached from down the street. A small apprentice was perched on the end of the longest girder sticking out behind. He waved a big red scarf to warn pedestrians, but some frogs attracted to the scarf leapt on him from everywhere, and the unfortunate child fended himself from their slimy skins. The truck constantly lurched on four hard black tires and the child danced as if he were on a shuttlecock. The truck passed by the building. The simultaneous jolt of the truck and the landing of a large spinach-green tree frog in the child's armpit caused him to let go. Screaming, he described the arc of a shooting star and landed right in the bookstore window. Feeling courageous, Moon whistled with all his might and rushed on the child. He pulled him by the feet to the opening, and began to bash the child's head against the nearest lamppost. A large splinter of glass in the child's back reflected sunlight, and the luminous spot danced on the dusty sidewalk.

"Another Fascist!" exclaimed Paton, who arrived on the scene.

The bookstore employee approached them. "Perhaps it's an accident," he offered. "He looks too young to be a Fascist."

"You think so?" asked Moon. "I saw him. He did it on purpose!"

"Hmmm," said the bookseller.

Furious, Moon let go of the child. "Are you taking over my job? I'll take care of you if you persist!"

"Ok," said the employee. He picked up the child and went into the bookstore.

"What a bastard," said Paton. "You'll see what that will cost him!"

"You tell them!" Moon said with satisfaction. "It's progress in perspective. Maybe we'll be able to retrieve that Fascist for the school – "

III

"What a boring day," Paton said.

"Sure is. Remember last week? We should do something special once a week. That would be great," Moon said.

"Yeah. Hey look!"

Two very pretty girls were in the bistro next door.

"What time is it?" asked Moon.

"Another ten minutes and we're off," Paton answered.

"Great!" Moon looked at the girls. "Are we going for a drink?"

"Sure," Paton said.

IV

"Are you seeing her again, today?" Paton asked Moon.

"Nope. She couldn't make it. What a day." They were on guard at the door of the Ministry of Profits and Losses. "Nobody's coming by here. It's – " He stopped himself because an old woman addressed him.

"Pardon me, sir, where's School Street?"

"Go on," said Moon, and Paton struck the woman's head with his billy club. They propped her against the wall. "Old slut! Can't she speak from my left like everyone else? Well, at last a distraction."

Paton wiped off his club with a checkered handkerchief. "What does she do, your girl friend?"

"I don't know. But, you know, she's nice."

"Does she – well?" Paton asked.

Moon blushed. "You're disgusting. Don't you know anything about feelings?"

"Then you aren't seeing her tonight?"

"No. What can we do tonight?"

"We could go to the General Stores," suggested Paton. "There always are people there scrounging around for stuff to eat."

"We aren't on duty."

"We can go hang out. It'll be fun. Maybe we'll find someone to arrest. But if you want, we could go to – "

"Paton, I knew you were an ass, but really, you don't understand. I can't do that now."

"I've got your number. Ok, I won't be a bore. We'll go to the General Stores. But bring your equalizer. We might make a hit."

"Now you're talking! We'll get a few dozen at least."

"You look to me like you're in love for real," Paton told him.

V

Paton went first. Moon followed closely. They skirted the brick wall and reached the opening carefully guarded by the carekeeper to prohibit thieves from scaling and damaging the wall. They went in. The opening overlooked a straight path adorned here and there with barbed wire that allowed thieves the only possibility of escape. Every so often, holes were dug in the ground so the policemen could squat and sight carefully. Moon and Paton each chose one. They comfortably installed themselves and scarcely two minutes had passed when they heard the motor of a bus bringing the thieves on site. They listened to the ringing of the bell and the first thieves appeared at the opening. Moon and Paton covered their eyes so they couldn't see them. It was more fun to kill them on their way back. The thieves were all barefoot because shoes were noisy and expensive.

"Swear that you'd rather be with her," Paton said.

"Yes," Moon admitted. "I don't know what's wrong with me. I must be in love."

"I told you. Did you give her any presents?"

"Yes. I gave her a bracelet of blue fir. She was very pleased with it."

"Then she's pleased with very little. Nobody wears those anymore."

"Who told you that?"

"It's none of your business. Do you cuddle up when you're with her?"

"Shut up. You shouldn't kid about that."

"You always had a weakness for blondes. But you'll forget her like the others. She's skinny."

"Talk about something else. I don't like you saying that, either."

"You annoy me. You'll lose your place at the school if you only think of her."

"I won't," Moon said, and then, "Look sharp. They're returning."

First, they let a man go by with a sack of candy mice. And then Paton fired. A tall thin one fell, making a *couic* sound, his packages rolling onto the ground. Paton showed him what he was capable of, and Moon fired a round. He brought down two, but they scrambled up and reached the opening. Moon cursed and Paton's pistol jammed. Three others escaped under their noses. A woman came last and Moon angrily emptied his cartridge on her while Paton left his hole to finish her off. A pretty blond. Her toenails were polished red by the blood and on her left wrist she wore a brand-new bracelet of blue fir. She was thin. She'd died young. It's better for your health.

ONE-WAY STREET

I

A young man was to be married. He was finishing up his studies in all types of tombstone engraving. He came from a good family. His father managed section *K* of Tubular Boilers, his mother weighed sixty-seven kilos, and they lived at 15 Two Brothers Street. Unfortunately, the ugly dining room wallpaper hadn't been changed since 1926. On it were orange oranges on a Prussian blue background. Now, it would be papered with nothing on perhaps a lighter-colored background. He was called Faithful, and his father, Just. His mother also had a name.

As on most evenings, he rode the metro to get to his course, a gravestone under his arm, and his tools in a small case. Because of the stone, he paid for a berth to avoid the often vitriolic remarks that one can encounter in ordinary passenger cars when traveling with such a cargo.

At the Denfert-Rocherau stop a student from the advanced course got in the same compartment. He was carrying a larger gravestone and in his tool box, moreover, he had a beautiful violet pearl cross. Faithful greeted him. The course discipline was strict. They had to wear black suits and change their underwear twice a week. They also had to abstain from ill-bred manifestations such as going out without a hat, or smoking in the street. Faithful envied the violet cross, but the year was moving forward, and in two months he would graduate into the advanced course. Then he would have access to large tombstones with two crosses, one of pearl and the other of granite. They weren't permitted to work on them at home because of their value. The materials were stamped with the course director's name. But the students were authorized homework on certain esthetic arrangements in order to fully benefit from their instruction.

The school had a placement bureau and generally coupled students that passed the examination into pairs – a planner and a realizer – chosen according to their respective talents after a series of tests modeled on the Parisian Transport Society. The planner also studied the commercial side of the trade and public relations with the clientele. This required perfect manners and dress.

The two students got off together at Station Saint-Michel and walked back down the boulevard. The recreation headquarters were in the ruins of the Thermal Baths of Julien the Apostolate by special permission from the Cluny Fathers. And a part of the instruction took place at night in open air amidst the ruins. The idea was to place the students in a state of receptivity appropriate to the flowering of modern and refined funeral esthetics.

As they neared the ruins, the bell tolled and they quickened their pace because it was time to start.

II

An hour break interrupted the courses at midnight. The students spent the time breathing the fresh air in the ruins and amusing themselves deciphering Hebrew inscriptions on the tombstones, which the Julien Baths had in imposing number.

During this hour, they also could have a drink at the

nearby museum bar of the Cluny Brothers – Lazare Weill and Joseph Simonovitch. The conversation of these two men, rich in instruction on the art of marble engraving, plus their original insights of every nature, greatly charmed the studious Faithful. His thoughts were distracted from the stones only to linger awhile on the contours of a graceful vision – his fiancée Naomi.

Naomi, whose father was an inspector and whose mother was still well-preserved, lived simply in a second-floor twelve-room apartment on Boulevard Saint-Germain. She had two sisters her age, and three brothers, one of which was one year older, and thus was called the eldest.

Sometimes Naomi spent time with her fiancé at the museum bar under the paternal eye of Joseph Simonovitch, and the two young people exchanged sweet vows while drinking Joseph's masterpiece, the Gravestone Ghost. Normally, the students were permitted only black coffee with a drop of cream, but there were exceptions to the rule without serious consequences to their morality. They always maintained perfect decorum.

That evening, Naomi wasn't meeting Faithful. He had a rendezvous with Laurent, an old high school buddy and an intern at General Hospital. Laurent often had night duty and he escaped the ward when the duties weren't all-consuming.

Laurent arrived at about twenty minutes to one. He was late. They'd brought in a drunk and as usual, six or seven policemen accompanied him. At first they didn't know he was drunk. But they had to take the word of the policeman who'd knocked him senseless. As the drunk was in a coma, they listened to a policeman's testimony.

"He cried, '*Vive la liberté!*'" said the policeman. "Then he crossed the street outside the white lines."

"Then we locked him up," the other policeman said. "You

have to admit that a drunkard is a bad influence for the young people in the students' quarter."

Feeling guilty, the guy died under the chloroform before they could operate. So Laurent was late. Luckily, his colleague Peter Gna took over night duty, and the drunk.

"So when are you getting married?" Laurent asked.

"Next week."

"And when will you bury your childhood? You've got to be prepared for that sport."

"My God!" Faithful was amused. "I suppose I'll do that next week too."

"You know," Laurent said, "you should start thinking of it seriously."

"I will."

"Who will you invite?"

"You, Pierre, and the Major."

"Who's the Major?"

"A friend of Pierre's. Pierre absolutely has to introduce us."

"What's so special about him?"

"It seems that he's visited a lot of cemeteries and he could be useful in my career. Besides, he's very funny."

"Good, the Major. And the girls?"

"Oh, no girls!" Faithful exclaimed, shocked. "I'll be married three days later."

"So? Why do you think we bury our childhood?"

"A burial's a serious thing," Faithful said, "and I want to give my fiancée what she'd expect from me."

"Perfect virginity?" Laurent asked.

"At least recent virginity," Faithful said shyly.

"All right. Then it will be a stag party."

"Right. Wednesday evening at seven o'clock at my place."

When the bell chimed one, Laurent shook his friend's hand and said good-bye to Joseph as he left. Faithful joined his buddies in the south crypt where the course was being held. It also served as an exposition room at the end of the year. The course dealt with painting gravel black at the base of miniature boxwoods. The boxwoods were vegetal decoration for model #28 – a granite stone with a cross in demi-relief.

Faithful took out his notebook and sat on a block of whimsical red marble.

III

At four o'clock Faithful left with a buddy for half-an-hour break in the ruins. He saw some stars, practically all of them except Betelgeuse, which was temporarily extinguished because of too consummate a glow the previous month. Faithful wrapped his scarf around his neck. A slight breeze wafted from the boulevard through the iron gate, and he managed to stay in the quiet air behind the rails.

He neared the corner where the Hebrew tombstones were piled so they could examine the details, and he sat on one.

Before him lay the fragment of an arch, a piece from a half-buried column. Strangely, it resembled an oyster, perfectly cylindrical with one side flat and the other hemispheric. Faithful tried to turn it over and did so with difficulty. Underneath, two intertwined earwigs slept beside a millipede and three perfectly preserved mint lollipops from Cambrai.

He tasted them one by one, then let the stone fall back into place. Next, aware of its striking resemblance to an oyster, kneeling before it, he took a chisel from his pocket and tried to open it.

After fruitless attempts, he succeeded in forcing the extremity of the chisel into a lateral opening half plugged with earth and moss. He exerted strong force. The chisel broke.

He took another. Discouraged, the stone gave up. Carefully, he set aside the cover and looked. Reposing on a bed of fine sand was a photograph of Naomi under rose-tinted glass with a carved wood frame. He placed the rose in his buttonhole, seized the portrait, then put it back on the sand.

Naomi's lips moved and he broke the glass to hear her. He also told her how much he loved her. The day was starting. This would be his last course. A bird left its nest and one by one shook out the twigs, took a dust bath, stretched, flew away, and returned with their dinner. But Faithful had gone. The bird ate both portions and was sick the entire morning.

IV

Naomi was reading in her room. Breakfast just had been brought to her – a nut tart and Norway lobster in mayonnaise. Her liver was very delicate and she was paying special attention.

The book was a biography of Saint Elisabeth of Hungary by the Viscount of Montalembert. And Naomi had cried copiously because she was at the death of the young valiant Signor from Bourg, Elisabeth's courageous husband. But she felt light-hearted now so she closed the book and instead took up *Three Men in a Boat*. Suddenly, she thought of serious things and stopped reading because she had to get up and look for a book corresponding to her mood. Nothing was left on her bedside table but the telephone directory.

To rest mind and spirit, she did a few Finlandish exercises. They're practiced without budging from a horizontal position and consist in tensing followed by the relaxation of judiciously chosen muscles.

She got up, put on a colorful linen dress, walked up three steps, and fell from fifty centimeters into the next room on level with her own. With a slight sprain, she hobbled into the bathroom to bandage her ankle. Then she sat before the mirror, smoothed her dark red hair, and smiled at her image. But the pain from her ankle stopped it from smiling back. Moved, Naomi began to cry. Her reflection forced a courageous smile to reestablish calm, and everything, although already quite replete, fell into place.

V

Faithful began to prepare for the party. There wouldn't be any parents. Sometimes their proximity's compatible with freedom, but it's just such parents who decide to go to the movies so their children can have a good time. Faithful didn't envisage an orgy. Nevertheless, shy reserve poses certain restrictions of verbal expression in front of adults, and Faithful at least wanted to depict his happiness with phrenological revelry. It made him shiver just to think of it.

The long high dining room lent itself comfortably to a meal. Photographs of deluxe tombs and Faithful's project models enlivened the walls with their gray note of old stones. Not much furniture. A long low buffet of sorry birch supported two silver candlesticks decorated with red candles. A table of the same wood. Some Moroccan leather-covered chairs of dark, nearly black African birch – which, literally translated, is ebony. Faithful would sit with his back to the windows.

The only flaw was the orange oranges on the Prussian blue background. Faithful telephoned to have the wallpaper changed. He wanted blue Prussian oranges on an orange background. On second thought, he decided that a plain granitelike beige wouldn't be bad.

The painter interposed bands of ivory and cream with a bright red border to match the Moroccan leather chairs. And he replaced the tomb photographs with a portrait of Naomi. He took it from his portfolio with a smile of complicity.

VI

Naomi luxuriated in bed until late morning. But she wasn't totally inactive. She took up her knitting. In the varnished wicker basket were three large balls of white angora, and a skein of ordinary red wool. She finished the top of the front. Fourteen rows to go. The front was in white angora with two horizontal rows of red stripes, then two rows of white – which left ten rows. She was going to Jacquard-knit her fiancé's first name in red at the bottom. The white angora fur would half hide it and would keep him very warm. So it would be easier for her, she would do it in runic letters. So for ten rows she had to count eight stitches backward in white and two in red. It would be a handsome sweater.

In the afternoon she went with a friend to see Manfred Carote's latest movie, and a girl in the film was wearing a pullover just like the one she was knitting. So that she wouldn't miss the beginning, but arrive after the shorts which she'd seen nineteen times already, she had made her appointment at the Green Bird for 4:30.

VII

The same morning, Pierre, one of Faithful's guests, shaved carefully and put on a clean shirt for work. He was an engineer in a venturesome enterprise. Pierre was waiting for the Major to call and give him Faithful's address, and meet him so they could drive together to the dinner.

But the Major had landed in his special plane at 2:20, left his empty suitcase in the baggage room, and to compensate, carried the suitcase of a fellow-passenger, loudly hailed a taxi, advised the driver he had a spot on his nose, gotten out to take the metro (took it, not leaving any for the others), and arrived at the station he wanted at 3:00 o'clock. On foot he reached the Ball of Gold, and the entrance to his private hotel in Lion-Hearted Street.

He left again half an hour later, allocating the task of the disgusting mess he'd made in record time to the maid. He'd changed his suit, twirled an elegant striated blond cane, and his glass eye shone like a beacon, once and for all blinding the rare people he honored with a glance.

The Major entered a café, decapitated an inoffensive customer with a backlash of his cane, threw a large tip into the mouth of a protesting waiter, double-locked himself into a telephone booth, dialed defectively, and the floor gave way under his weight.

The Major found himself in the café wine cellar and took advantage to distribute a few choice bottles among his various pockets. He went up the stairs, left the café with great dignity, and looked for a more solid establishment. He found it, situated himself, put a token in the slot, and called Pierre, who was waiting.

VIII

Assisted by Peter Gna, Laurent operated on his fourth hipparion of the ovary since daybreak. He was going to proceed with the fixation. The patient rested on a support of nickle tubing — a kind of trestle in the form of an *A*. Her spine balanced on the bridge of the letter, her head and feet hung from both sides of the *A*, and her stomach was hanging like a perch. The pain of this position made her forget the cruel twinges caused by the hipparion. A large white reflector flashed on the operating table with strident light, and the hipparion vaguely moved under the skin. The light bothered Laurent.

"Hexobarbital!" he ordered.

Peter Gna prepared the syringe, wiped blood from the patient with a wad of cotton soaked in alcohol, and shot the needle into the blue corded vein. It exploded with a small humid noise. He looked for another entrance, and not finding it, with a quick gesture he planted the bent point under the hairy armpit. Slowly, the silver liquid was released under pressure. Consequently, a small conical protuberance formed under the patient's right eye.

"Count to ten," Laurent told the patient.

The patient counted to six.

"Strange! Ordinarily they don't go to sleep for twenty seconds." Peter Gna commented.

"I'm not sleeping," the patient bawled. "I don't know how to count any further." And all of a sudden she went to sleep on the support. Her spine, unfettered by the nervous tension of sitting up, suddenly collapsed and followed the exact sharp profile of the tubular assemblage.

"Do you see it?" Laurent whispered.

"Yes!" breathed Peter Gna.

The hipparion, seriously endangered, tried to escape the reflector light.

"Needle!" Laurent ordered.

Peter passed it to him. It was a large blue steel needle with a nickle fist. Laurent aimed carefully and planted the sharp needle in the dark mass which ceased to move under the skin. He held it with all his might. After a minute, he relaxed his grip.

"It's fixed," he said. "Now we can operate. Let's hurry, I have an appointment at a friend's tonight at 7:00."

IX

Faithful welcomed Pierre and the Major at the entrance where the maid just had opened the door.

"Isn't Laurent with you?" he asked, shaking hands.

"He's coming alone," Pierre said. "Let me introduce the Major."

"My pleasure," Faithful said. "Anyhow, you aren't late. I told Laurent 7:00 and it's only 6:15. We'll talk."

"You're so kind to reassure us," the Major said. "We could wait on the landing – " Faithful took this as a joke and burst into laughter. The two others joined in chorus, ending up on an augmented fifth.

"Let's go into my studio," Faithful suggested. They went into the dining room with wallpaper depicting green oranges on a violet-mauve background. There was a small bar, a compact bookcase, a table, some leather armchairs. "Grape juice?" Faithful asked.

"Fermented and distilled for me," the Major requested. "Sometimes they call it cognac, sometimes armagnac, depending on the region."

"You've traveled a great deal," Faithful commented admiringly.

"I have – " the Major said. (The other two sat on the couch, glasses in hand, and the Major took the place of honor in a deep down-lined armchair.) He continued, " – seen oceans and seas, the old and new worlds – the new world first as a matter of taste, and the old world in time, as one should. I've visited the pockets of a good number of my fellow countrymen. I've burned the pavements of towns considered fireproof. I've carelessly littered the asphalt pavement of world capitals with gold-tipped cigarette butts while wearing my Roubai overcoat – always conscious of the miracles I'd discover the next day."

"Have you seen cemeteries?" Faithful asked.

"I've filled them!" the Major answered coldly. "I could describe the red ditches of the Windward Island, where at moonrise the natives bury their dead in winding sheets of naked pandas. The Tahitian women with their breasts in the wind sing the melodious words of the *Song of Ancestors:*

> *Oari ména*
> *Oara méni*
> *Tatapi oya Tatapi*
> *Arhûu Arhûu Oari*
> *Ména Tatapou*

And there are other words I won't tell you, because you're Christian – I suppose. And the witch doctor of the island burns a short candle while leaning toward the heavenly body of night."

"Do they put stones on their graves?"

"Tons of stones," the Major assured Faithful.

"Engraved?" Faithful asked.

"All engraved," the Major answered.

"How?"

"In the form of stones," concluded the Major, adding, "Are we dining soon?"

"Huh, perhaps we should wait for Laurent."

"Then go phone him and tell him to hurry!" the Major ordered.

"Huh, yes, I'm going," Faithful complied. He got up and went into his father's study. The Major took advantage of his absence to try various drinks at the bar, and sat back down when Faithful returned.

"So?" he asked.

"He can't make it right away," Faithful explained. "A woman just arrived with black eyes and a broken skull. Her husband did it."

"Can't she do it back?" the Major proposed.

"Do you know what she told Laurent? She told him – 'I couldn't do it in front of the child. It would be a bad example.' "

"Common women often are so virtuous," the Major sighed. He hiccuped, and with indecent aplomb, blamed it on his eye.

"Ah yes, well, because of this woman Laurent thinks he'll finish up in a quarter of an hour," Faithful said.

"Good, so much the better," the Major said. "So as I was saying, in Greenland – "

X

On her friend's arm, Naomi left the Imperial-Cujas Cinema where Manfred Carote just had succumbed to the pitiless blows of a cruel band of torturers much older than he. Her eyes were full of tears and her sprained ankle hurt. The evening fell fast, and the rain-filled air formed halos around the electric lamps. There was a lot of traffic and heavy traction vehicles for mass transport.

XI

" – and, far from preserving the dead in a perfect state," the Major said, "it's convenient to note that the polar ice freezes them so totally that they're like meat taken from the freezer in which there's not one particle of ice. I leave it to you to explain this anomaly."

"Do Eskimos sculpt the ice blocks they place on their tombs?" Faithful asked.

"No," the Major answered, "for the simple reason that the tombs are hollow. They take out a chunk of ice, put the client in, and pour water over him, but not to the edge."

"Wait! Why?"

"It's explained by physics. The water they pour comes from the piece of ice removed, and everyone knows that ice loses volume when it melts."

"But if it freezes again – " Faithful protested.

"Yes, but you're forgetting the penguins," the Major said.

"Ah!" Faithful exclaimed, not really understanding what was meant.

"They're always thirsty!" the Major explained. "And they aren't alone," he added with discretion, looking into his glass.

Faithful refilled the Major's glass. "Now Pierre, old buddy, go telephone Laurent," the Major commanded. "He must have finished."

Pierre went into the office and they heard the echo of his insistent voice. He returned and announced, "He can't come."

"Still the wife?" complained the Major.

"No, it's the husband. He has two broken ribs, a smashed nose, and a fractured collarbone."

"Luckily, she was worried about the child," the Major sighed. "But tell me," he continued, turning toward Faithful, "I hear you're getting married tomorrow?"

"Yes, at the town hall."

"And how is your fiancée?"

"She's pretty," Faithful said. "She has cheeks smooth as polished porphyry. She has eyes like huge black pearls, dark red hair set in a crown, breasts of marble, and the air of being isolated from the rest of the world by a small wrought-iron grill."

"Suggestive!" the Major appraised with a shiver up his spine.

XII

Naomi truly was pretty, even after the truck hurled her against the sidewalk. Her head rang and her teeth clashed violently. Her friend began to cry. The ambulance didn't come right away and the General Hospital was closest.

So they carried her on a stretcher. In the corridors the nurses passed, emptying buckets full of tonsils and appendices that the surgeon's assistants just had deposited outside the operating rooms. Two of the nurses were playing with a large oxygen ball with red and yellow edges. On the stretcher Naomi still had beautiful red well-defined lips, dark red hair, and a straight nose. But her eyes were closed.

XIII

"Anyway, this time tell him to hurry, or I'm going," the Major said.

"Yes, I'm going to insist. His patients aren't our business," Faithful agreed.

"But I can't," Laurent told Faithful over the phone. "They've just brought in a girl hit by a truck."

"Come anyway. Let someone else take care of her," Faithful urged.

"Listen, it bothers me. She's pretty and besides – "

"You're disgusting. This time you're blackballed for sure. I'm begging you. Try!" Faithful said.

"All right, but if this ass Duval fails, it'll be your fault." Laurent said.

"Let's eat. Let's eat!" bellowed the Major.

XIV

Naturally, the operation was a success, but not the one on Naomi, who died. And as there was nowhere to put her body, her parents were called immediately to take her home. When they arrived she already was covered with a sheet because you can't imagine the work necessary for a fractured skull. But they gave them her hair because it was very long, and they were forced to cut it.

BY BORIS VIAN

Vian's work has had a ripple effect very much in keeping with Pataphysical design, spiraling into larger and grander editions, reprints, and collections of newly discovered, unedited material. Some of the books overlap, but this is inevitable in a mop-up operation of such magnitude. The following bibliography is arranged chronologically from the earliest date of publication. Titles are given in English only for those books that have been translated and published in English.

NOVELS

Vercoquin et le Plancton. Paris: Gallimard, 1946, 1968, 1973; Le Terrain Vague, 1965; Christian Bourgois, 1982; Folio Éditions, 1989.

L'Écume des jours. Paris: Gallimard, 1947, 1981. Pauvert, 1963, 1981. Plon Éditions 10/18, 1963. Super-bibliothèque, 1979; Christian Bourgois, 1982; Le Livre de Poche, 1984. Translated as *Froth on the Daydream* by Stanley Chapman, London: Rapp & Carroll, 1967. Translated as *Mood Indigo* by John Sturrock, New York: Grove Press, 1968.

L'Automne à Pékin. Paris: Éditions du Scorpion, 1947. Éditions de Minuit, 1956, 1980. Plon Éditions 10/18, 1964. Christian Bourgois, 1983.

L'Herbe rouge. Paris: Éditions Toutain, 1950. *L'Herbe rouge* followed by three short stories, *Les Lurettes fourées,* Le Livre de Poche, 1962, 1972, 1981. *L'Herbe rouge* (only) Christian Bourgois, 1975.

L'Arrache-coeur. Paris: Vrille, 1953; Paris: Le Livre de Poche (Pauvert), 1962, 1975, 1981. Translated as *Heartsnatcher* by Stanley Chapman, London: Rapp & Whiting, 1968. Paris: Christian Bourgois, 1975.

Trouble dans les Andains. Paris: La Jeune Parque, 1966. Christian Bourgois, 1976. Union Générale d'Éditions (UGE), 1984.

NOVELS BY VERNON SULLIVAN

J'irai cracher sur vos tombes, Paris: Éditions du Scorpion, 1946. Translated as *I Shall Spit on Your Graves* by Boris Vian and Milton Rosenthal, Paris: Vendôme Press, 1948. Adapted for theater and performed in Paris, 1948. Adapted for film by Vian and Jacques Dopagne and directed by Michel Gast in 1958. *Le Dossier sur l'affair "J'irai cracher sur vos tombes"* (notebooks on the trial), edited by Noël Arnaud, Paris: Christian Bourgois, 1974, 1982. UGE, 1986.

Les Morts ont tous la même peau. Paris: Éditions du Scorpion, 1948. UGE, 1970. Christian Bourgois, 1975.

Et on tuera tous les affreux. Paris: Éditions du Scorpion, 1948. Christian Bourgois, 1975.

Elles se rendent pas compte. Paris: Éditions du Scorpion, 1950. Le Terrain Vague, 1962. UGE, Paris, 1974. Christian Bourgois, 1982.

SHORT STORIES

Les Fourmis. Paris: Éditions du Scorpion, 1949. Le Terrain Vague, 1966. UGE, 1970. Paris: Christian Bourgois, 1982.

Les Lurettes fourées. Paris: Pauvert, 1962, 1982. (*See L'Herbe rouge* – three stories follow the novel.)

Le Loup-garou (thirteen unedited stories), Paris: Christian Bourgois, 1982. Paris: UGE, 1984.

Le Ratichon baigneur (fifteen unedited stories). Noël Arnaud, ed., Paris: Christian Bourgois, 1981. UGE, 1983.

PLAYS

L'Équarrissage pour tous with *Le Dernier des métiers.* Éditions Toutain, Paris, 1950. Translated as *The Knacker's ABC* by Watson Taylor. Grove Press, New York, 1968. Translated as *Knackery for All* by Marc Estrin, New Directions, New York, 1966.

Les Bâtisseurs d'empire ou le schmürz. L'Arche, Paris, 1959. Translated as *The Empire Builders* by Watson Taylor, Grove Press, New York, 1967; also Methuen, London, 1971. Reprinted in Arrabal and Vian, *Panorama du théâtre nouveau,* Appleton, New York, 1967.

Le Goûter des généraux. Collège de 'Pataphysique, Paris, 1962. Pauvert, Paris, 1965. Translated as *The Generals' Tea Party* by Watson Taylor, Grove Press, New York, 1967.

Théâtre (three plays listed above). Paris: Pauvert, 1965, 1972. Paris: UGE (10/18), 1971.

Théâtre (unedited), includes *Tête de Méduse, Série blême tête, Le Chasseur français,* Paris: UGE, 1972.

OPERA LIBRETTI, SONGS, JAZZ ESSAYS

Le Chevalier de neige (unedited opera libretto) to music by George Delerue, 1953 and 1957 performances, Paris: Christian Bourgois, 1974. Paris: UGE, 1978.

Fiesta (opera libretto) to music by Darius Milhaud. Paris: Éditions Heugel, 1958.

Opéras (above opera libretti plus *Le Marquis de Léjanes, Arne Sakussem, Lily Strada, Le Mercenaire*), edited by Noël Arnaud. Paris: Christian Bourgois, 1982.

En avant la zizique. Paris: Le Livre Contemporain, 1958; *En avant la zizique . . . ici les gros sous,* Paris: La Jeune, 1966. Paris: UGE, 1971. *Derrière la zizique:* Textes de Pochettes de Disques de Jazz et de Variétés, UGE, 1981.

Textes et chansons. Paris: UGE, 1966, 1970. Edited by Noël Arnaud, Christian Bourgois, 1975.

By Boris Vian 113

Chroniques de jazz, edited by Lucien Malson, Paris: La Jeune Parque, 1967. UGE, 1971.

Manuel de Saint-Germain-des-Prés. Paris: UGE, 1951 (unedited). UGE: 1974.

Petits Spectacles: Receuils et sketches. Paris: Christian Bourgois, 1977. UGE, 1980.

Jazz Hot. Claude Rameil, ed. (two volumes), Paris: Christian Bourgois, 1981, 1982.

Chansons. Paris: Christian Bourgois, 1984.

RECORDS

Vian, *Chansons possibles et impossibles,* Philips 76.042, 1955.

Vian, Magali Noël, Philippe Clay, *Boris Vian,* Philips 77.922, 1965.

Vian, Serge Reggiani, Pierre Brasseur, Magali Noël, Marie-José Cassanova, *Boris Vian, Intégrales,* vol. I, Jacques Canetti Records, 1965.

Béatrice Moulin, Yves Robert, *Pas avec le dos de la o.i.r.,* Adès 33 vs 587, 1965.

Marie-José Cassanova et Jacques Higelin, *Marie-José Cassanova et Jacques Higelin chantent Boris Vian,* Canetti Records 48.813.

POETRY

Barnum's Digest. Ten monsters illustrated by Jean Boullet and translated (borrowed) from the American by Boris Vian (chapbook edition of 250 copies), Paris: Aux Deux Menteurs, 1948.

Cantilènes en gelée. Five illustrations by Christiane Alanore (signed letterpress edition of 200), Limoges: Éditions Rougerie, 1950.

Je voudrais pas crever. Paris: Pauvert, 1962.

Cantilènes en gelée (above collections – without illustrations – plus Vian's letters to the Collège de 'Pataphysique and unedited work), Noël Arnaud, ed., 10/18 Paris: UGE, 1970. Christian Bourgois, 1976.

Cent Sonnets (unedited). Paris: Christian Bourgois, 1984.

114

MISCELLANEOUS COLLECTIONS

Chroniques du menteur (essays). Paris: Christian Bourgois, 1974. Edited by Noël Arnaud, UGE, 1980.

Romans, poèmes, nouvelles (668 pages of Vian). Paris: Pauvert, 1978.

Mémoire concernant le calcul numerique de dieu par des methodes simples et fausses (monograph). Cahiers, Collège de 'Pataphysique. Commemorative edition (350 numbered copies), 1978.

Cinéma, science-fiction. Paris: Christian Bourgois, 1978. UGE, 1980.

Écrits pornographiques. Edited by Noël Arnaud, Paris: Christian Bourgois, 1980. UGE, 1981.

La Belle Epoque: Variétés. Paris: Christian Bourgois, 1982; UGE, 1987.

Traité de civism (Vian and Laforet). Paris: UGE, 1987.

Rue des ravissantes: et autres scènes. Paris: Christian Bourgois, 1989.

TRANSLATIONS

Kenneth Fearing, *The Big Clock (Le Grand Horloger),* Les Nourritures Terrestres, Paris: Gallimard, 1947.

Raymond Chandler, *The Lady in the Lake (La Dame du lac),* translated with Michelle Vian, Série Noire, Paris: Gallimard, 1948. *The Big Sleep (Le Grand Sommeil),* Série Noire, Paris: Gallimard, 1948.

Peter Cheyney, *Ladies Won't Wait (Les Femmes s'en balancent),* Série Noire, Paris: Gallimard, 1949.

Dorothy Baker, *Young Man with a Horn (Le Jeune Homme à la trompette),* La Méridienne, Paris: Gallimard, 1951.

James M. Cain, *Love's Lovely Counterfeit (Le Bluffeur),* La Méridienne, Paris: Gallimard, 1951.

Omar Bradley, *History of a Soldier (Histoire d'un Soldat),* Paris: Gallimard, 1952.

A. E. van Vogt, *The World of Null-A (Le Monde des A),* and *The Adventures of A (Les Aventures des A),* Le Rayon Fantastique, Paris: Gallimard, 1956.

Nelson Algren, *The Man with the Golden Arm (L'Homme au bras d'or),* Du Monde Entier, Paris: Gallimard, 1956.

Corbett H. Thigpen and Hervey M. Checkley, *The Three Faces of*

Corbett H. Thigpen and Hervey M. Checkley, *The Three Faces of Eve* (*Les Trois Visages d'Éve*), L'Air du Temps, Paris: Gallimard, 1958.

August Strindberg, *Miss Julie (Mademoiselle Julie)*, and *Erik XIV (Erik XIV)*, Paris: L'Arche, 1958.

Brendan Behan, *The Quare Fellow (Le Client du matin)*, Le Manteau d'Arlequin, Paris: Gallimard, 1959.

STRIKE

STRIKE

D.J. MacHale

razOr
bill

An Imprint of Penguin Group (USA)

razOr
bill

A division of Penguin Young Readers Group
Published by the Penguin Group
Penguin Group (USA) LLC
345 Hudson Street
New York, New York 10014

USA / Canada / UK / Ireland / Australia / New Zealand / India / South Africa /
China
Penguin.com
A Penguin Random House Company

ISBN: 978-1-59514-669-4

Printed in the United States of America

1 3 5 7 9 10 8 6 4 2

For Bobby "Jake" Russell.
I hope you got the silk shirts.

FOREWORD

We are rapidly approaching the end.

No, I'm not talking about the "imminent destruction of the world as we know it" kind of end. I mean "the end" of another adventure. (Though I'm not making any promises about the possibility of world-destruction.)

I'm particularly excited about wrapping up the SYLO Chronicles because, well, I've been getting grief from a lot of readers. Seems as though the endings of SYLO and STORM were, shall we say, a big tease. Guilty. I admit it. As much as each of those books had a definite conclusion, both times I added one of those pesky last chapters that throw you over that proverbial cliff and give you a maddeningly slender thread to hang on to. I know, I know, the more I revealed about the plight of Tucker and friends, the deeper the mystery became. Again, guilty. What can I say? I love that stuff.

So that's why I am very happy to submit for your approval, the conclusion of the SYLO Chronicles. There are no more cliff-hangers. No more unanswered questions. No more "To be continued..." And yes, it WAS freakin' Uncle Press who gave Bobby

Pendragon his journals in that last chapter of The Soldiers of Halla. There! I said it. How could you not have gotten that? It was so obvious! (If you have no idea what I'm talking about, it's okay. We won't hold it against you. Much.)

Okay, I feel better now. Moving on.

We're here to talk about SYLO and learn the fate of our brave refugees from Pemberwick Island. But before heading back into the sky, as tradition dictates, I'd like to offer some acknowledgements. I sound a bit like a broken record with these but, as you might imagine, it takes a number of people to bring a book to publication and ultimately into your hands. An author is the beneficiary of a lot of hard work and support from many people. That doesn't change from book to book and I want them all to know how much they are appreciated each and every time.

Thank you to all of my friends at Razorbill, especially Ben Schrank and Caroline Donofrio. Caroline took up the SYLO reins and did a wonderful job editing STRIKE with Ben's wise guidance. Thanks to both of you for making this a grand conclusion.

Richard Curtis, Peter Nelson, and Mark Wetzstein have been in my corner looking out for my best interests for many years now. Thank you guys.

I've had the pleasure of meeting and working with many school and public librarians from all over the country. You all hold the keys to an incredible kingdom and I thank you for encouraging us all to enter.

One of the great joys in travelling the country to talk about my books is getting the chance to meet booksellers. Whether they are from tiny "mom and pop" shops or giant mega-stores, they all have one thing in common: they love books, and they encourage readers. Getting the right book into the hands of the right reader is an art, and these guys are the best. We all thank you for that.

I have to give a big thanks to the guys who have been helping me with my DJMACHALEBOOKS.COM website . . . especially Jason and Geoff. You have no idea how much easier you make my life by keeping a watchful eye on things for me.

My two girls are the most important people in the world to me. I'm often asked where I draw inspiration from, and that's never an easy answer because inspiration comes from everywhere. But if I were to narrow it down, I would have to say that most everything I write about comes from real life, and my girls are my real life. I love you guys.

Of course I can't name each and every one of the hundreds of other people who had a hand in bringing this book to you, though I'd like to. Please know that I am grateful to all of them for their talent, support, and dedication.

The final "thank you" has to go to you, the person holding this book. Yes, you. Don't look over your shoulder, I'm talking to you. Whether you've read every last one of my novels (and seen all of my TV shows) or if you just so happened to have picked this book up because you thought the cover looked cool, thank you. (BTW . . . if you DID randomly pick this book up, close it, put it down, and pick up SYLO first. Seriously. Go. Hurry.)

Okay, is that it? I think so.

Time to launch.

Where were we? Oh yeah, the cliffhanger.

We left Tucker and his friends hovering in a SYLO helicopter over the mysterious dome in the middle of the Mojave Desert. Below them were the wrecks of hundreds of SYLO planes that had been shot out of the sky while trying to destroy that structure. Tucker and Tori believed they had finally defeated the Air Force by blowing away their entire fleet of marauding drones, but while flying over the dome they discovered plenty more of those nasty little planes were still around . . . and they were taking off to attack.

Oops.

Turned out "the end" of that story was really just the beginning of this one.

At least their cliffhanger is about to be resolved.

And so is yours.

Turn the page and brace for the boom.

Hobey ho,

D.J. MacHale

ONE

"**S**trap in, this is going to get bumpy."

Not words you wanted to hear from a pilot who has your life in his hands.

Six of us were trapped in a military helicopter that was under attack, spinning out of control and headed for the ground. Fast.

I sat shoulder to shoulder with Tori Sleeper on one side of the craft. On the other side sat Kent Berringer and my mother, Stacy Pierce. None of us wanted to be there. Reaching to my right I grabbed hold of Tori's leg. Her good leg. The other one had a bullet in it. She clutched my arm for whatever comfort it might give.

It was too dark outside to see what our altitude was, or when the impact might come. All we could do was huddle together and brace for the inevitable.

"It can't end like this," Tori said with surprising calm.

Well, yeah it could.

I suddenly felt pressure on my chest. It was as if a heavy weight had been dropped into my lap and was pushing me back into the seat. We were gaining altitude. The wild spinning stopped a moment later. The pilot was back in control.

"Get us outta here!" Captain Granger screamed at him through our headphones.

"Gee, you think?" Kent Berringer said sarcastically.

"Hold the chatter!" Granger scolded.

The helicopter's rotors whined as we lifted back into the sky. I looked across the cabin to my mother. I didn't think for a second that she wasn't as terrified as the rest of us, but her expression seemed to be one of, I don't know, resignation? It was almost as though she had accepted the fact that the Retro forces on the ground would shoot us out of the sky and there was no use stressing about it.

Kent, on the other hand, looked wide-eyed and frantic. He clutched the straps of his safety harness as if that would do any good if we slammed into the ground. He twisted left and right, struggling to look out of the window and get a glimpse of . . . what? The ground? The Retro forces down below that were shooting at us? A miracle swooping in from the heavens?

All four of us wore headphones that connected us with the cockpit where Captain Granger, the SYLO commander, sat strapped into the copilot's seat. At the controls was the marine commando named Cutter, who was doing his best to keep us flying.

"Help is incoming," Cutter announced casually as if he had just said, "Looks like rain."

Was a miracle about to arrive after all?

The helicopter was buffeted by another shot fired from the ground. And another.

Tori yelped. Kent did too.

"Why aren't we shooting back?" Mom said calmly into her microphone.

"Skyhawks aren't attack birds," Granger replied sharply. "No weapons on board. We leave that up to the Cobras."

The chopper shuddered and we were thrown violently against our harnesses as the craft pitched to our right, but we stayed airborne and under control. At least, I think we were under control. The Retro forces weren't shooting conventional missiles. Their weapons fired invisible yet powerful bursts of energy that worked silently but with no less destructive force than a rocket-propelled explosive. The blasts were only one example of the impossible technology the Air Force possessed . . . and that the Navy, SYLO, didn't. Though they were both branches of the United States military, the Air Force had a serious technological advantage. The civil war that had these two forces going at each other was definitely an unfair fight.

"Evade," Granger commanded.

"Trying, sir," Cutter replied. The guy remained cool, but not that cool. The tension in his voice proved that he was flying his ass off to try to keep us alive.

Cutter banked hard to the right and nosedived, intentionally. The last thing he wanted to do was travel in a straight line, allowing the ground cannons to anticipate our course. The move pulled me out of my seat, straining the harness. My head spun and my stomach twisted, but I wasn't complaining.

Kent was.

"Losing it," he announced. His head was pressed against

the fuselage in a desperate attempt to maintain his equilibrium. "Fighting the puke."

Mom leaned back with her head pressed into her seat to try to keep herself stable. When she saw that I was looking her way, she lifted her right hand and held out her index finger. It was a gesture we had done with my dad for as long as I could remember. We would touch index fingers as a way to say "I love you." It was very *E.T.*, but it meant a lot to me when I was a kid. I don't remember the last time we had done it, or at least the last time I acknowledged my mother when she did it. A fourteen-year-old doesn't do that kind of stuff . . . especially one who has been through as many battles as I had.

Then again, maybe facing the imminent end of the world made me the exact kind of fourteen-year-old who *should* be doing that kind of stuff.

I raised my hand and pointed my finger toward her. Though our fingers were several feet apart, the contact was made. I hadn't yet forgiven my mother and father for the lies they told me about why we had moved to Pemberwick Island, but I was open to try to understand. Besides, no matter what had happened, she was still my mom.

She gave me a little smile and dropped her hand.

"Now we're talking!" Granger exclaimed with his slight southern accent.

"What do you mean?" Kent asked.

The answer came in the form of double streaks of white light that flew past us, headed for the ground. A second later we heard two explosions. Our miracle had arrived. Two SYLO gunship choppers flashed past, one on either side of us, headed for the Retro base. The clatter of machine gun fire was a welcome addition to the tortured whine of our engine.

"Those would be the Cobras," Granger announced.

Cutter banked hard to the right, which gave me a perfect view of the two SYLO attack helicopters as they streaked toward the Retro base, unleashing rockets one after the other. The spray of missiles they shot toward the ground left thin trails of smoke that eventually led to multiple eruptions on the surface. I hoped they were finding targets.

"They're going to save us," Tori said in a small but confident voice.

For the record, I thought they were going to save us too.

I was wrong.

A second later, one of the Cobras exploded. It was a spectacularly horrifying sight as the flying gunship burst into a brilliant fireball that lit up the ground, revealing dozens of the antiaircraft cannons that were all pointed to the sky. Toward us. The burning mass that just moments ago was a chopper with pilots on board fell like a molten brick and crashed to the sandy surface of the Mojave desert.

"We're not out of this yet," Granger cautioned.

Our chopper made another sudden lurch. I thought it was Cutter making an evasive maneuver until . . .

"I've lost lateral stability," he announced. "Our tail rotor must have taken a hit."

"What?" Kent shouted with panic. "We've been hit?"

The chopper started spinning, much more violently this time.

I heard Cutter's heavy breathing through the headphones. He was struggling to fight gravity and control a hurtling machine. "I'll put us down as softly as I can but I can't control where—"

The front windshield shattered.

"Look out!" Granger screamed . . . too late.

Glass sprayed everywhere. Cutter was hit with a wave of razor-sharp shards and instantly went limp in his seat. I couldn't tell if he was unconscious or dead. Either way he wasn't flying the helicopter anymore. Granger went for the stick but Cutter had fallen onto the controls, making it impossible for Granger to take over.

The spinning picked up and we started dropping again.

I quickly unlatched my straps.

"Tucker, stop!" Mom called, no longer calm.

I ignored her. If we slammed into the ground it wouldn't matter if I was held in by safety straps or not.

I threw off my headphones and climbed forward to where Cutter was slumped forward in his seat.

"Pull him back," Granger yelled. "Keep him off of the instruments."

Cutter's straps hadn't been snugged tight and he was a big, muscular guy. It took all of my strength to pull him back into his seat.

"Can you fly this thing?" I yelled at Granger.

My headphones and mic were gone so he couldn't hear me. Didn't matter. I would find out soon enough.

Granger struggled with the copilot's stick but it didn't stop the spinning. The SYLO commander had always come across as supremely confidant. Not anymore. He looked as terrified as I

STRIKE

was, but that didn't stop him from doing all he could to try to save us.

"Prepare to crash!" Granger called. He gestured with his head for me to go back to my seat.

There was nothing more we could do.

I turned to scramble for the rear of the chopper when . . .

Boom!

The side door blew in with a force so violent it was torn off its track. The metal door bounced around the interior like a whirling buzz saw. If I had moved to the back a second sooner it probably would have killed me. As it was, I was launched off of my feet and sent careening to the far side of the chopper, where I hit hard and fell to the deck. I looked up in a daze to catch a brief glimpse of the terrified expressions of my mother, Tori, and Kent as debris swirled everywhere. The engine whined, desperate to provide enough power to keep us airborne. I heard someone scream but the roar of the engine and the explosions outside were enough to drown it out before I could tell who had lost it.

Boom!

The chopper was hit again. The entire craft lurched forward, throwing me to the deck.

I hit my head.

The sound stopped.

The spinning ended.

The chaos was over.

Everything went black.

———

I found myself lying flat on my back as a cool breeze blew over me. It was a welcome relief from the violent mayhem of a few moments before.

I moved my hand to feel the ground beneath me. I wasn't in the helicopter anymore. I was lying on sand. Cautiously, I opened my eyes to see a bright, blazing sun overhead. How long had I been here? What had happened? Without moving, I strained to hear anything that would give me a clue. What I heard was the unmistakable far-off cry of a lonesome seagull.

What? In the desert? It was followed by another sound that made even less sense.

It was the crashing of a wave.

I got my wits together and sat up to see . . . the ocean. I was lying on a sandy beach not twenty yards from the waterline. That explained the cool breeze, but it didn't begin to tell me how I had gotten here . . . wherever *here* was.

Sailboats cut through the sea out beyond the break, running with the wind as they were pulled along by colorful jibs. The waves weren't big enough to surf, but plenty good for boogie-boarding and bodysurfing. The water was full of kids splashing and playing inside the break. The beach to either side of me was dotted with brightly colored sun umbrellas. Families were staked out everywhere, lying on their blankets to sunbathe, read, and snack. A couple of guys tossed a football around. There was a high-pitched squeal as one of the kids picked up a girl and tossed her into the surf. She was kicking her legs while shrieking in protest, but she wasn't kidding anybody. She loved it. Young kids used neon-colored shovels and pails to build sand castles. A guy jogged by with a golden retriever trotting at his heels. Radios played a mix of hit songs. A single-engine plane flew by over the water, parallel to the shoreline and dragging a banner that advertised two for one lobster dinner at the Lighthouse Inn.

It was all so impossible . . . yet familiar.

"Pemberwick Island," I whispered to myself.

I was home.

It was the beach where I had been hanging out for the last five years, first with my parents and then with my friends. It was on the eastern shore of my island home . . . the same home that had been overrun by SYLO soldiers and quarantined against a virus that didn't exist. SYLO had set up a base on Pemberwick Island to make a stand against the Air Force, which was being controlled by people called Retros. SYLO came to protect the island from the gruesome fate that the Retros brought to the rest of the world. Calling it genocide would be an understatement. The Retro Air Force went on a fierce killing spree, wiping out three quarters of the world's population.

Their justification was that they were protecting the world from an even worse fate, though it was hard to believe that there could be anything worse than a cataclysmic, systematic mass execution.

I never expected to see my island home again, yet there I was with my feet in the sand, lying on a scratchy striped towel, catching some rays. I was even wearing board shorts and a T-shirt. What had happened? Was I knocked unconscious and shipped home with amnesia? It was the only logical explanation I could come up with.

That logic went right out the window at the very next moment.

"Tucker!" a familiar voice called out. "'Bout time you got here!"

I was almost too stunned to turn around. Almost. I looked over my shoulder to the stretch of sea grass that bordered the beach to see my best friend trudging over the sand berm, headed my way.

Quinn Carr was alive.

He carried a beach chair and had a bright orange towel draped around his neck. His mop of curly blond hair and thick glasses were unmistakable. My best friend, the guy who was disintegrated when he was hit by a killer beam of light fired from three Air Force fighters, was somehow headed my way.

"Jeez," he said. "Could you have picked a spot a little further away? My feet are on fire."

Quinn dropped his towel and stood on it directly over me, blocking the sun so that I didn't have to squint. I saw him in silhouette, a dark, impossible ghost.

All I could do was stare in wonder and ask the only question that made sense. "Are we in heaven?"

"Yeah right," he said with a scoff. "I know you think Pemberwick is, like, nirvana but . . . heaven? That's over the top, even for you."

My mind was reeling, desperate to understand what was happening.

"You okay, Tuck?" Quinn asked with concern.

"Okay? I'm about as far from okay as you can get. What the hell is going on?"

"You tell me," he said. "Your leg looks gnarly."

"My leg?"

I looked down to see that my right leg was covered in

blood. The instant I saw it, I registered the pain. It was vaguely numb at first, but the sensation quickly grew into a vicious, angry ache.

"My folks can fix you up," Quinn said. "But I don't know how you're going to ride your bike to the hospital."

"I rode my bike here?" I asked, bouncing between confusion and panic.

"I was hoping we could take a midnight ride later," he said. "I miss those rides, Tuck. Hell, I miss *you*. I wish things could go back to the way they were."

I tried to stand up but the pain in my leg forced me to stay down.

"What is happening, Quinn?" I cried. "Why am I here?"

Quinn laughed in that casual way he had of letting you know he knew so much more than anybody else in the world and said, "Because this is where you want to be. Hopefully you'll get back here someday. For real."

"But I'm here now!"

Quinn took a step back and the sun blasted my eyes.

"I'm proud of you, buddy. You're officially my hero."

"Quinn?" I shouted.

The only reply I got was a sudden rush of sound. At first I feared that a rogue wave had hit the beach and I was about to be washed away. But the sound was too steady for that. I looked for Quinn, but he was gone. The whole beach was gone.

I was still lying in the sand, but it was Mojave sand. It was night. The blinding light revealed its true nature: It wasn't the sun at all, but a searchlight on a helicopter that was shining down on me. The rogue-wave sound was the steady whine of its engine.

I had only visited Pemberwick Island in the dazed stupor of a teasing dream. My pounding head was proof of that. The only thing real about any of it was my bloody leg. I was hurt. Badly. The pain was excruciating. I didn't dare touch it for fear I would feel a bone sticking out.

I waved to the chopper, hoping it was coming to get me. It answered by killing the searchlight and flying off. It was hard to see any detail, as I'd just had a bright light shining directly into my eyes, but I could still make out the rising-sun SYLO logo on its belly.

Whoever was in that chopper, they didn't care about me.

As the sound of the helicopter's engine faded I looked around to try to figure out my next move. I was definitely in the middle of nowhere. I did a slow three-sixty until I spotted something that rocked me fully back to reality: the wreck of our helicopter.

A dozen thoughts flashed through my brain. None of them were good. My mother, Tori, and Kent were on board. So were Granger and Cutter. It looked as though I had been thrown clear of the wreck. That might have happened because I was near the door that was blown open. Whatever had happened, I was lucky to be alive, even though my leg was useless.

I tried to get up but there was no way my leg could handle any weight. Still, I had to get to the wreck. People could be trapped inside. The only way I could move was to crawl on one knee, dragging my dead leg behind me. The pain was unbearable. It felt as though my limb was being wrenched off, and on fire, but I didn't stop.

The chopper was dead. The engine was silent. It wasn't burning so I didn't think there was any chance of an explosion. How long had it been since the crash? I could have been lying there for hours. Why didn't the SYLO helicopter land? I didn't hear any sounds of battle. The action seemed over.

As I crawled nearer to the wreck, I realized that my leg wasn't my only problem. My head was spinning. I must have had a concussion, not that I knew what that was like. I'd had my bell rung a few times playing football, when I'd see colors and hear a sharp ringing for a few minutes. This felt like that, except it wouldn't go away. The world was spinning and so was my stomach. I heaved, losing whatever I had eaten earlier that day in Las Vegas.

Las Vegas. That seemed like centuries before.

I wiped my mouth with my dirty sleeve and kept going. I had to know who was inside that wreck, even if there was nothing I could do to help them. When I finally reached the downed chopper, the first person I saw was the pilot through the shattered windshield. Cutter. He was dead. The marine commando who helped lead the rebels in Las Vegas but was secretly part of SYLO was gone. He came across as an arrogant jock, but the guy had compassion. He actually told us that he was honored to know us. In the end, I was honored to have known him.

I dragged my way to the side of the chopper and the huge gash that had once been a door. The spinning got worse. So did the nausea. I wasn't going to last much longer, let alone help anybody who was inside. But I had to know. These were the only people I had left in the world. My mother. My friends. Granger, too. It's weird to say that I hoped Granger survived after all he had done, but nothing was turning out the way I expected it to.

I pulled myself toward the opening and hesitated. What would I find inside? It could be gruesome. I wasn't sure what was hurting more: my leg, my head, or my heart.

The chopper was a twisted wreck. It didn't seem likely that anybody could have survived such a violent crash. It took every bit of physical and mental strength I had left to poke my head inside the downed craft.

What I saw inside was . . . nothing. No bodies. No survivors. No sign that anybody had lived or died. Even the copilot's seat was empty. Granger was gone, along with my mother and my friends. The shock of seeing the empty craft and realizing that I was totally on my own was the last straw.

I gave in to the spinning.

The world turned upside down and I dropped into oblivion.

TWO

I should have been hurting a lot more than I was.

That was the first conscious thought I had. My right leg had been pretty much hanging by a thread; my head had been battered so hard that my skull must have cracked like Humpty-Dumpty; and after being tossed from a crashing helicopter I probably had any number of other injuries that I hadn't noticed only because the other two were so vicious.

I had the brief fear that I might be dead, but I didn't think a trip to the afterlife involved having an IV stuck into your arm. The only real physical discomfort I felt was a stiff left wrist from the needle that pumped liquid into me from a plastic bag hanging overhead. I was definitely alive, so why wasn't I in pain? I didn't even feel numbed by drugs. I forced myself to focus on my surroundings. Part of me wanted to be back on that beach on Pemberwick Island, but since that was only a dream, it was just as well that I wasn't. Instead I was lying on my back in what looked like a hospital ward. There were two long lines of beds that faced each other. Most were occupied by a patient. Rather than some antiseptic institution, though, the building looked more like a long wooden hut. This place was brand new, with the smell of freshly cut wood overriding any typical hospital smells.

I lifted my head slightly and saw that all of the patients, including me, were wearing the same thing: bright orange one-piece coveralls. My bloody jeans and dark hoodie were gone, replaced by an outfit that made me look like I was ready to work on a road crew . . . that handled plutonium. On my feet was a pair of clean gleaming-white sneakers.

I reached down to my injured leg to discover it was no longer injured. How long had I been unconscious? Was I in a coma long enough for my leg to have healed completely?

The answer came quickly and it wasn't a good one. I suddenly registered that the medical staff all wore black-and-gray military fatigues.

The uniform of the Air Force. The Retros.

I instantly realized why I wasn't in any pain. They had given me the same miracle medicine that had healed Tori's gunshot wound and brought Mr. Feit back from the brink of death. It was probably being pumped into me through the IV. I may have been healed but it came at a steep price.

I was in the hands of the Retros.

The realization gave me a shot of adrenaline that brought me into full focus. I wanted to jump up and run, but I had no idea where I was and wouldn't know which way to go. I had to force myself to calm down and understand the situation before doing something stupid. I didn't want to let anybody know that I was awake so I did my best to scope out the situation without sitting bolt upright.

It was daytime. Bright sunlight shone in through windows set near the ceiling. As I focused I realized that they weren't windows at all, but openings for ventilation . . . and they weren't doing a very good job, because it was hot. The only relief came from ceiling fans that were spaced every ten feet or so, gently moving around the warm, dry air. This was no high-tech medical center. It was more like how I imagined a hastily erected battlefield hospital must feel.

Every last one of the patients seemed to be in the same situation as me. They were on their backs, hooked up to an IV. There were both men and women, and all appeared to be adults. I watched through squinted eyes as a Retro approached the guy in the bed next to me. He held a small device that could have been an iPod and scanned something at the foot of the bed. He checked the screen, dropped it into his pocket, and lifted the guy's leg to examine his foot. He rotated it a few times as if to see that it was working properly. His casual manner made it seem more like he was checking out a piece of machinery than a human being. Satisfied, he dropped the foot, went right to the guy's IV, and pulled it out.

"Go," the soldier said. That was it. "Go."

The patient stood up obediently, and after spending a few seconds to test his foot, he walked off down the line of beds headed for . . . somewhere. Spread across his back were four large black numbers: 4242.

The soldier made an entry into his device and moved on.

I cautiously looked around to the rest of the ward to see similar scenes playing out. Retro doctors, or whatever they were, checked on patients while entering information into their electronic devices. A few of the patients were unplugged and given the same "Go" command as the guy next to me. The rest were left to continue whatever healing process was going on.

A few minutes later another patient in an orange jumpsuit was wheeled in on a gurney and transferred to the bed next to me. It was a woman and she was a mess. She was unconscious, and that was a good thing, because her right leg was twisted into such a grotesque angle that it made me want to gag. A small blossom of blood grew in the orange material below her right knee. It seemed as though her leg was in just as bad a shape as mine had been. The medical guy hooked her up to the IV, entered some notes, and moved on.

The scene was disturbing for all sorts of reasons. These patients were being treated no better than animals. Or robots. Very few words were exchanged. Nobody asked any questions or spoke about how they were feeling. The doctors didn't even pretend to care. Who knows? They might not even have been medically trained. That miracle medicine healed the body at an impossible speed; it wasn't like the doctors had to do anything more than stick the IV in.

Also disturbing were the numbers printed on the patients' backs. Nobody was called by name. It was all so . . . inhuman. It followed what Jon Purcell, the Retro infiltrator we met in Portland, told us. He called us primates and said we were all dead already. The Retros thought the only value we had was to rebuild the world for them. I saw that plan in action at Fenway Park. Tori and I watched with horror as survivors of the attack were treated like slaves, fed the Ruby (which gave them impossible strength and speed), and forced to work on the project that Granger called the gate to hell.

Is that what these orange-wearing people were being used for?

Is that what I was being healed for?

Most upsetting of all, I had no idea what had happened to my mother. Tori, Kent, and Granger were missing too. Part of me hoped that they had died in the crash so they wouldn't be forced into becoming robot slaves like the people surrounding me.

And me.

The reality of the situation hit me with a wave of despair. Whatever hope we had of putting an end to the Retros' plans of resetting society ended when our chopper crashed into the desert floor. I may have survived, but the Retros did too. Destroying their fleet of planes hadn't put them out of business. Our moment of victory was short-lived. We had failed.

"You are Zero Three One One," a woman said.

Without thinking I turned quickly to see that she was standing at the foot of my bed. I wished I hadn't looked to her so quickly. It proved that I was awake.

"I'm not a number," I said defiantly.

I saw a few of the other patients shoot a quick look toward me as if I had broken the cardinal rule by opening my mouth.

"Do not speak," the woman said harshly.

"Why not?" I asked.

She raised her electronic device, aimed it at me, and a second later I felt a painful jolt of energy shoot through my body. It only lasted a few seconds, but it was brutal enough to convince me to keep my mouth shut. That was some device: iPod and torture-shooter all in one handy package.

"You're new," she said with no emotion, as if she'd given this same speech a hundred times. "You're allowed one mistake. You won't be allowed another."

I didn't dare say, "Oh yeah? And then what?" That might have been suicide. The Retros had no hesitation about wiping out three-quarters of the world's population. They wouldn't think twice about destroying a wiseass kid with too many questions . . . especially one who had a hand in blowing up the entire Retro fleet of attack planes at Area 51.

I truly hoped they didn't know I had anything to do with that.

The woman grabbed my leg and worked my knee around like she was kneading bread dough. She didn't ask how I felt or if she was hurting me. (For the record, I felt fine, and she wasn't.) She learned all she needed to know from her incredibly thorough five-second exam. I think all she was doing was checking to see if my lower leg was still attached. Once that was established, I was good to go.

She yanked out my IV (without swabbing my arm with alcohol to stop any bleeding, I might add) and simply said, "Go."

I almost said, "Where?" but didn't want to get zapped again.

I wanted to question her. I wanted to ask where we were. I wanted to know how long I had been out. Hell, I wanted to punch her in the head.

But I also wanted to find out about my mom and the others. For that I needed to be alive.

I slowly stood up. The last time I had moved I was broken

in a dozen places and so dizzy I couldn't see straight. I expected my head to go light and pain to shoot up my leg. Instead, I felt surprisingly strong. There was no pain. No dizziness. No nausea . . . and no fatigue whatsoever. I felt great. At least physically.

"Follow me, Zero Three One One," came a man's command.

Standing between the rows of beds was another Retro soldier. This guy wasn't part of the medical staff. The black baton weapon he held proved that. I'd seen that weapon in action and knew that the charge it shot out could knock somebody into next week . . . or kill them, depending on its setting. I'd used one myself to threaten Mr. Feit—Colonel Feit of the United States Freakin' Killer Air Force. The fear of getting zapped convinced him to turn a giant attack craft back from its mission of wiping out the rest of the population of Los Angeles.

The Retro soldier motioned for me to walk ahead of him between the two rows of beds. I obeyed and walked slowly past him toward a door that was thirty yards away. The whole way, I stole quick glances at the poor victims who were being healed, hoping to catch a glimpse of my mom or the others. Many were awake, staring blankly at the ceiling. None made eye contact with me. It was like being trapped in zombie-land.

I pushed through the door at the far end of the building and entered another structure that looked nearly as long as the hospital ward, but it was twice as wide. Rather than hospital beds, there were dozens of white domes that looked like igloos lined up neatly in two rows.

The Retro soldier pushed past me and hurried up to one of them. He used his weapon to rap on what looked like a door. A second later a panel slid open with a quick, sharp *hiss*.

"Inside," the guy commanded. "Sit down. Wait."

"Why?" I asked.

At the sound of my voice, the guy stiffened as if I had just slapped him in the face. He started to bring the weapon around to shoot me for daring to open my mouth, but he took a deep breath and got hold of his emotions.

"If you keep asking questions," he said, "you won't be alive long enough to get any answers. Inside. Sit down. Wait."

Message received. I ducked down and entered the dark dome.

Inside was a black wire chair with a wide back that faced a flat, blank white wall. That was it. The entire inside of the dome was white, except for the chair. I sat down, as instructed, like a good little primate prisoner.

With a hissing sound, the door closed, plunging the dome into total darkness. I felt panic rising. What were they going to do with me? If they knew I planted the bomb that destroyed every last Retro plane at Area 51 and killed one of their leaders, I could be in for a rough time. Was this my prison? Was I sentenced to live the rest of my life in dark solitude? Or would it be my execution chamber?

I sat there in pitch darkness for what felt like an hour, though it might have been only a few seconds. I was a breath away from screaming out, "Why am I in here?" when words appeared in front of me. They were white letters that looked to be floating in space.

YOU ARE ZERO THREE ONE ONE. ACKNOWLEDGE. I heard it spoken as I saw the words written in front of me. It was said aloud by a woman who spoke with no emotion and not much inflection.

It felt like a computer-generated voice, but it sounded way more natural than that.

The words disappeared, only to be replaced by the single word: acknowledge.

"ACKNOWLEDGE," the voice repeated.

"That's what they tell me," I replied.

I figured that was a good answer. I wasn't accepting the fact that they considered me a number rather than a human being, but I didn't want to pick a fight with a machine that was probably way smarter than me.

Each time the computer spoke, the words appeared in front of me. I guess it was in case I was deaf or something.

"YOU ARE FORTUNATE, ZERO THREE ONE ONE," the voice said. "YOU HAVE BEEN SELECTED TO HELP REDIRECT THE COURSE OF THE WORLD."

"You mean I'm lucky because I wasn't killed when you guys wiped out most of the population," I said.

I couldn't help myself.

The machine didn't acknowledge that.

"THE WORK WILL BE DIFFICULT," the computer voice and the floating words continued. "BUT YOU WILL BE REWARDED WITH THE KNOWLEDGE THAT YOU ARE PERFORMING AN IMPORTANT SERVICE TO MANKIND."

"And if I get hurt you'll just plug me into the magic medicine machine and fix me right up so I can get right back to work, right?"

"YOU WILL BE FED WELL AND GIVEN MEDICAL TREATMENT WHEN NECESSARY," was the reply. "AS LONG AS YOU COOPERATE AND WORK HARD, YOU WILL BE TREATED FAIRLY."

The conversation had turned ominous.

"And what if I don't cooperate and work hard?" I asked.

"YOU WILL BE ELIMINATED," was the horrifyingly matter-of-fact answer.

"My name is Tucker," I said, belligerently.

"IRRELEVANT," the machine replied. "WHAT USEFUL SKILLS DO YOU POSSESS?"

"Useful skills? What do you mean?"

"DO YOU HAVE A PARTICULAR TALENT? ARE YOU ACCOMPLISHED AT SOMETHING PRACTICAL?"

"Like what?" I really didn't know where these questions were going.

"ARE YOU A PLUMBER? AN ELECTRICIAN? A WELDER? DO YOU WORK WITH WOOD? CAN YOU COOK? WE ARE ALWAYS LOOKING FOR THOSE WITH USEFUL SKILLS. WHAT ARE YOURS?"

I really had to think about that. What could I do? If I had some kind of skill it might get me out of doing hard labor. Or *dangerous* labor. The trouble was, I had nothing. I was a fourteen-year-old second-string running back on my high school football team. What was that going to get me? Suddenly all those hours studying math and writing essays in school felt pretty wasted.

"Wait," I said. "I have a skill. I'm a landscaper. I design gardens and know how to care for pretty much anything that grows. They say I've got a green thumb."

That was totally overselling my abilities. The truth was I mowed and raked grass for my dad's gardening business. I knew a little bit about fertilizer and how to trim plants to keep them looking good, but that was about it.

"IRRELEVANT," the machine said.

Gee, thanks.

"What happened to my mother and my friends?"

As soon as I said that, I regretted it. This machine didn't know who I was. If it connected me with the others there was a better chance we'd all be found out. But I couldn't help myself. Without my friends I wasn't sure how I'd have enough strength to go on.

"YOU NO LONGER HAVE A MOTHER AND FRIENDS," the machine said. "YOU ARE ZERO THREE ONE ONE. THAT IS YOUR HISTORY AND YOUR FUTURE."

I wanted to jump out of my chair and throttle this person, or whatever it was. But there was nothing to grab on to but glowing white letters that came and went as if blown by the wind.

"DO NOT SPEAK WITH AIR FORCE PERSONNEL UNLESS YOU ARE REQUESTED TO SPEAK. DO NOT COMMUNICATE WITH THE OTHER WORKERS UNLESS IT REGARDS THE TASK AT HAND. THERE ARE SEVERE CONSEQUENCES FOR DISOBEDIENCE."

I didn't have to question that. I believed it.

"YOU WILL SLEEP IN A COMMUNITY BARRACKS AND EAT IN A COMMUNITY HALL. YOU WILL NOT SLEEP IN THE SAME BUNK TWICE SO DO NOT HOARD PERSONAL ITEMS."

This was going to be even more horrible than prison. They were taking away everything that made a person unique, starting with their name. "WHAT YOU WERE BEFORE ARRIVING HERE DOES NOT MATTER; THEREFORE NAMES ARE IRRELEVANT. WORK HARD, OBEY THE RULES, AND THE REST OF YOUR LIFE WILL BE WORRY-FREE."

"Yeah, except it probably won't last very much longer."

"GOODBYE, ZERO THREE ONE ONE."

The door to the igloo slid open. I shielded my eyes from the bright light and saw the Retro guard waiting outside for me. I stood and shuffled out.

"So I guess I'm registered," I said. "Now what?"

The guy zapped me with the baton.

I screamed, but it was more out of surprise than pain. His weapon was dialed to shoot a very light charge . . . just enough to keep the rowdy in line.

"Do not speak," the guard warned. "I'll bring you to your unit."

There wasn't anything else I could do but follow the guy. If there was any hope of finding out what happened to my mom and my friends, I was going to have to play along . . . at least until I saw a chance to escape. As I followed the Retro guard through this frightening new world, there was only one thing I knew for sure: I was not going to live out the rest of my life as a slave to these murderers. That would have to become my focus because all hope of bringing down the Retros was gone.

The guard led me through several more buildings that were connected by wooden walkways. Each time we left one building we stepped out into the blazing-hot desert. After a few steps we'd enter the next long building in line. It wasn't much cooler inside the structures than out in the open. Each building had ceiling fans that didn't do any more than push the hot air around, but it was still better than being under the sun.

The buildings we passed through were nearly identical. They were barracks similar to the wooden hospital ward but with one big difference: The beds here were empty. The buildings themselves looked and smelled brand-new. The wooden beams were fresh and there was none of the grime that came from use. It looked to me as if the Retros were preparing for an influx of more people. Many more people.

When we were given the briefing back in Las Vegas before setting out to sabotage the Retro fleet of planes, the leaders of the survivors said how the Retros were heavy on equipment but light on manpower. They were absolutely correct. Area 51 was home to well over a thousand attack drones, but we saw almost no people. Wherever this camp was, it looked to be just as under-manned. But from the number of empty beds I was seeing, that would change. People were coming. But who?

After passing through a dozen identical empty barracks, I began to hear the sounds of work. There was hammering and sawing and the general cacophony one would expect from a large work force. We exited the final building and arrived at a busy construction site. Three more barracks in various stages of completion were being worked on by several dozen workers. Prisoners. It looked as though I was going to be put to work along with all the other orange-wearing, number-given slaves. This was my future. At least my immediate future.

The guard led me through the work zone when a new sound entered my consciousness. It was music. Eerily familiar music. I froze. It was a sound I'd heard far too many times. Slowly, I turned around to see what I knew would be there and was greeted by an even more disturbing sight.

Looming high above the new structures, no more than a few hundred yards away, was the giant steel igloo-like dome.

The gate to hell.

I had to fight from falling to my knees.

A black Retro attack plane rose up next to it. It lifted vertically into the air until it cleared the top of the dome, then its musical engine kicked in and the killer craft shot off like a rocket. In seconds it was out of sight.

I knew exactly where I was . . . the Mojave Desert, not far from where our SYLO helicopter was attacked and downed. Captain Granger had made a foolish mistake by flying us by here to see this structure. He should have known they'd be watching. Before we were attacked, we saw a Retro fighter plane float out from inside the dome. It proved that in spite of the fact that we had obliterated their entire fleet at Area 51, the Retro Air Force had not been defeated. More of these deadly craft were arriving from whatever factory was churning them out. How long would it be before the entire fleet was replaced so they could continue their ghastly purge of the planet's population?

From the sky we had seen the wrecks of hundreds of SYLO fighter jets strewn across the desert floor that had tried to destroy this monstrous structure . . . and that were blasted out of the sky by drones and antiaircraft guns.

The dome was untouchable, the Retros were still very much in business, and I was their prisoner. The war, or at least my part in it, was over.

I found myself wishing I hadn't been thrown free of the crashing helicopter. I wanted to be together with my mother and my friends, however dire their fates were.

THREE

The guard pushed me toward a long half-completed wooden building that would eventually look like all the others. Next to it was a deep trench that looked to be the beginnings of the foundation for yet another building. This pit was being dug by hand, painstakingly. A large group of tortured-looking men and women in orange coveralls used simple shovels to move the dry desert sand. They methodically filled wheelbarrows that were carted off by other equally exhausted-looking prisoners.

The Retros were at it again, forcing the survivors of their attack into slave labor. Seeing the vacant stares of the beaten and abused prisoners as they worked under the hot desert sun made my heart race with anger. How could a group of people who said they were trying to right the course of civilization treat their fellow men so badly?

A Retro wearing camouflage, but unarmed, stood next to the growing pit, monitoring what looked like an oversized iPad in her hand. She was a severe-looking woman with short, steely hair and broad shoulders. The guard I had been following approached her and said a few words I couldn't hear. The woman gave me a quick look and turned away, shaking her head. I guess she didn't need any more workers, which was fine by me.

The guard came back to me and said, "This is your unit. Unit Blue. Do whatever your supervisor orders you to do. The more productive you are, the easier it will be for you. More food. *Better* food. Shorter shifts. Better bunks. If you don't produce, then . . ." He let his voice trail off and he shrugged.

I wanted to hit him, and might have, if he hadn't made eye contact with me.

Up until that moment he had been totally cold, as if I were an annoying dog that needed training. But in that brief moment I thought I saw something in his eyes that looked strangely like sympathy.

Or maybe I just imagined it.

He gave me a slight nod and headed off, leaving me alone with the silver-haired supervisor who didn't look any happier about being there than I was.

The guard hadn't told me the supervisor's name and I didn't dare ask. Maybe her name was as irrelevant as mine supposedly was.

"Grab a shovel," the woman barked without looking at me. "We need to move two tons of earth before nightfall. Get to work."

Nightfall. Was that how it was going to be? Were the prisoners forced to work until it was too dark to see? I picked up a shovel from a pile near the edge of the pit and gazed over the side to see at least twenty people laboring in the furnace that was to be the foundation of yet another bunkhouse. The hole was roughly six feet deep. Grave depth. But it was only half the size of one of the long buildings. There was a lot of work to be done.

I didn't want to go down there. I feared that I might never come out. In that one moment, all the horror I'd been through since the night of Marty Wiggins's death on Pemberwick Island came flooding back in a rush of violent images that sprang from my memory. I couldn't catch my breath. My heart raced. What was going on? Was I suddenly overcome by sorrow? Or was it fear?

No, it was anger. Who were these Retros and how were they able to use the United States Air Force to take over the world and enslave the survivors? They had turned the world upside down. For what? Nothing could justify the deaths, the destruction, the loss. To make it worse, they were treating the survivors like animals in a slaughterhouse. We were given numbers. Numbers had no personality. No history. No humanity. What was next? Would they brand us with a burning hot iron?

I gripped the shovel tighter as my rage grew. I glanced at the silver-haired Retro supervisor who still didn't think enough of me to make sure I was climbing down into that pit. She was busily scanning her tablet. In that one second I felt as though she alone represented the heartless force that had destroyed our world. I wanted her to suffer for what they had done. I raised the blade of the shovel and strode toward her. I'm not crazy, or a killer, but in that moment I didn't feel like myself. I was a number. Zero Three One One. If they could treat me like I was nothing, then I could do the same to them. I raised the shovel, poised to bash it over her head and exorcise the demons that had taken control of my emotions.

I lifted the shovel higher, ready to strike . . .

. . . as a military jeep came screaming out from behind the last of the completed barracks. The sound jolted me back to my senses. I assumed it was carrying Retro guards who were coming to stop me from beaning the unwary supervisor.

I was a heartbeat away from dropping the shovel and running when the jeep turned hard and an orange-clad body was thrown out. He hit the ground with a sickening thud and tumbled in the sand like a broken doll before coming to rest.

Three Retro soldiers sat in the jeep. One behind the wheel, the second in the passenger seat. The third Retro was in back. That was the guy who had tossed the prisoner to the dirt. The jeep slid to a stop near the edge of the foundation pit, kicking up sand and dust that hung in the air and giving a coughing fit to a few of the workers.

The unit supervisor stood there staring. Apparently she didn't understand what was going on any more than I did.

The guy in the passenger seat twisted and pulled himself out. He wore black-and-gray Retro fatigues but carried himself more casually than the other soldiers. He rolled more than walked, as if every joint in his body was loose—the exact opposite of the ramrod-straight Captain Granger. His shirt was unbuttoned to the middle of his chest, showing off deeply tanned skin. Though he looked to be about my dad's age, he had longish, bleached-blond hair that had to be constantly swept out of his eyes. Other than the uniform there was nothing military-like about this guy. He looked more like somebody who played tennis at the uppity Arbortown Racquet Club with Kent Berringer than a soldier at a military prison camp.

The other three soldiers were on high alert. They kept their eyes locked on this guy as he strolled toward the pit. He may not have looked like a respected military leader, but from the body language of his own soldiers, he was somebody you didn't dare mess with.

He stood on the edge of the pit and leaned forward slightly to get a full view of the workers toiling below.

"Hello!" he called down in an overly friendly tone. "Come up here for a moment, would you please? Take a break. All of you!"

The workers in the pit looked to one another, confused. But they weren't about to pass up a chance to take a breather, so they quickly dropped their shovels and climbed out to stand in a loose group on the edge of the hole.

I stood apart from them, closer to the woman supervisor who still hadn't moved since the jeep arrived.

"Thank you," the blond guy said with a slight bow. "Forgive me for taking you from your work."

Right. Like they were upset.

"We don't use names here," he announced. "But I want you to know mine. It's Bova. Simon Bova. Major Bova, if you'd prefer to be formal. I share that information only because I believe you should know who your host is."

He smiled at the prisoners as if he wanted them to like him. The guy came across like a gracious host, rather than the commander of a work camp. His eyes had the silver sparkle of someone who was either seriously smart, or dangerously insane.

"Now!" he announced. "A bit of business. I trust you all know . . ." he slid over to the guy lying in the dirt and leaned over to take a look at his back ". . . Eight Six Seven Five."

Nobody reacted.

"Of course you do," Bova said with a wink. "You've worked next to him for days. I'm sorry to have to tell you that he has been a very naughty boy."

Bova motioned to the soldier in the back of the jeep. Instantly, the soldier jumped down, ran to the prisoner, and pulled him up to his knees.

Bova took a quick step back as if he didn't want to risk coming in contact with the filthy sand that swirled around the poor guy.

The prisoner was a mess, but he was conscious. His hair was tangled and blood dripped from the corner of his mouth. Caked sand clung to his face, surrounding a pair of swollen eyes.

He'd been beaten. Badly.

Bova bent down so his face was close to the prisoner's, but not close enough to risk contact. "You know you've been very bad, don't you?"

The prisoner didn't react.

"Go ahead, you can admit it," Bova said, cajoling. "We have no secrets here."

Bova was talking to him in a singsong voice, as if he were a little kid.

The prisoner looked to the ground. I couldn't imagine what he might have done that deserved getting beaten like that.

"Tell you what," Bova exclaimed with excitement. "We'll play a game." He gave a broad smile to the group and added, "One of my favorites. I used to play it with my parents. It's simply called *Please*."

The prisoner started to collapse back down to the ground but the soldier grabbed him and pulled him to his knees again.

"Now, my friend," Bova said to the prisoner, who was anything but his friend. "The rules of my game are quite simple. You must answer my questions and do as I say . . . but only if I say *please*. That's all. A simple courtesy. I believe that even under the most difficult circumstances we should always do our best to maintain civility. This game helps us remember that. Agreed?"

The prisoner wet his parched lips. He needed water, badly.

"Agreed!" Bova announced for him.

He strode to the jeep and grabbed a canteen from the passenger seat and walked back to the prisoner. He held the canteen out close to his face and said, "Take a drink."

The prisoner reached out for the canteen . . . and Bova kicked his hand away. Violently. So violently that it made most of the other prisoners jump with surprise. It threw the guy off balance and he fell down onto his elbows.

Bova shook his head and chuckled. "You've forgotten already? I didn't say *please*."

He motioned to one of his soldiers, who ran over quickly. I thought he was going to help the prisoner back up to his knees, but instead he wiped Bova's boots with his sleeve, taking away any offending grime that may have come off of the prisoner.

"Very good, let's try this again," Bova said, holding out the canteen. "Won't you have a drink of water?"

The prisoner pushed himself off the ground until he was back on his knees. One side of his sweat and blood-covered face was encrusted with dirt. It was gut-wrenching to see.

He glared at Bova but didn't move.

"Very good!" Bova exclaimed with joy. "Now we're on the same page. This is going to be fun."

There were a lot of words to describe what was going on. "Fun" wasn't one of them.

"Now. *Please* lift your right arm."

After a painfully long few seconds, the prisoner raised his right hand. Barely.

"Wonderful!" Bova declared.

He really was having fun.

For the record, he was the only one, including the other Retro soldiers, who watched with no expression. "Now," Bova continued. "Tell us all what you did that was so naughty."

I willed the guy not to answer.

The prisoner didn't say a word. His eyes seemed unfocused, as if he were about to pass out.

"Very good!" Bova declared. "Tell us what you did that was so naughty . . . *please*."

All eyes were focused on the poor, tortured guy.

His eyes flashed around, looking for some clue as to what he should do.

"You have to tell me," Bova said, wagging his finger. "I said *please*. Those are the rules of etiquette."

"I . . ." the man said, sounding as though his throat was on fire. "I tried to bring water to my unit."

"Precisely!" Bova exclaimed giddily. "You tried to bring water to your unit. *Extra* water. Now, *please* tell me, is this your unit?"

Bova gestured to the group at the edge of the hole.

Reluctantly, the prisoner nodded.

"Of course it is. *Please* tell me, did anyone in this unit drink the water?"

I felt the people in the group stiffen. What had been a sadistic torturing of a single prisoner now had the potential to include them.

The prisoner shook his head.

"No," he whispered. "I never made it back."

Bova walked up to the unit supervisor, who looked ready to faint. He got right in her face and said, "Is this true? There were no extra water rations distributed to your unit?"

The woman blinked a few times. She was terrified of this man.

"No sir," she said with a shaky voice. "No extra water was given to this unit today."

Bova stared directly into her eyes. Into her brain.

I was standing ten feet away, but I saw a bead of sweat grow on her temple that slowly trickled down her cheek.

He kept his eyes locked on hers for a solid ten seconds, then grinned.

"I know it wasn't," he said with happy lilt. "We discovered his treachery long before he had the chance to come back here."

Bova stepped away from her.

The woman visibly relaxed.

"Eight Six Seven Five?" Bova said as he backed toward the kneeling prisoner. "*Please* tell me, did you know it was wrong to steal water and bring it to your unit?"

For the first time, the prisoner showed life. He straightened up, though he was still kneeling, and said, "It was a mistake. I didn't steal it. I thought I was bringing the normal ration."

"It was a mistake all right," Bova said to the whole group with a smile, as if he expected everyone to laugh at the joke.

For the record, nobody did.

"*Please* tell me, were you wrong?"

The prisoner hung his head. "Yes, I was wrong."

"*Please* tell me, will you ever make that same mistake again?"

The prisoner lifted his head, showing signs of hope. "No, never."

"Of course you won't," Bova said.

He turned away from the prisoner and faced the bulk of the group.

"The rules of my camp are clear and simple," he announced. "We expect you to follow them, and to work hard. Do that and you will be rewarded."

Bova gestured to the driver, who pulled out a large green Jerry Jug from the jeep and lugged it toward the group of prisoners.

"You have been working hard in the sun," Bova announced. "You deserve extra water."

The guard placed the jug in the sand and backed away.

The prisoners didn't move.

"Well go on!" Bova said. "It's yours."

Still, nobody moved.

"*Please!*"

That was the magic word. Like a group of hungry puppies, everyone went for the Jerry Jug. One guy lifted it and took a deep drink of water. The others clamored to be next as the first guy passed it on. They each took a deep, refreshing drink while careful not to spill a precious drop before passing it along. It was a surprisingly civilized process for people who were so desperately thirsty.

Bova stood back, watching the scene with a satisfied smile like he was some generous benefactor. The whole event was meant to be a warning. He was making an example out of the prisoner to show how much power he had. He could give extra water, or command a brutal beating.

"*Please*, everyone, don't forget your friend," Bova said.

The last guy with the jug brought it to the kneeling prisoner and placed it gently on the ground in front of him.

"Very good," Bova said. "You see? When you follow the rules, you will be rewarded."

Allowing these poor people to get a few extra swigs of warm water didn't exactly seem like a huge reward, but I wasn't going to point that out. I didn't even get a drink, which I guess was fair. I hadn't been working.

Bova went back to the kneeling prisoner, leaned over, and said, "There. It was all just a silly misunderstanding. I trust that there will be no more. Have a drink and rejoin your unit."

Bova turned and walked toward his jeep. The show was over.

The prisoner lunged for the Jerry Jug and greedily took a deep drink.

Bova was about to board the jeep, when he stopped suddenly. He turned and quickly strode back toward the kneeling prisoner.

The entire group of prisoners froze in place.

Bova walked quickly, heading directly for the prisoner. As he moved past one of the guards he grabbed the black baton-weapon from the soldier's belt without breaking stride. He marched right up to the kneeling prisoner who still held the Jerry Jug up high, trying to get the last few drops of precious water. When he saw Bova standing over him, he froze.

"Sorry," Bova said with what seemed like genuine sympathy. "I didn't say *please*."

Bova brought the weapon up and aimed it at the prisoner's chest.

Nobody made a move to stop him.

Bova fired.

The weapon made no sound.

The prisoner did.

With a pained yelp he was thrown backward. The Jerry Jug clattered to the sand and came to rest near the head of the poor guy.

He didn't move. He wouldn't move again.

The unit supervisor dropped her head in what seemed like genuine anguish.

The rest of the prisoners remained frozen. I thought I heard a small whimper, but it was quickly squelched.

Bova spun back to the others and calmly announced, "Like I said, the rules are simple. Follow them and you'll all live a long and fulfilling life. Choose not to and, well . . ." he gestured to the dead prisoner. "Let's get back to work now, shall we?"

Nobody moved.

I saw a flash of anger cross Bova's face, but it was quickly replaced by a smile of realization.

"Oh, forgive me," he said playfully. "*Please!*"

The prisoners instantly scrambled toward the hole. They couldn't get away from him fast enough.

I wasn't sure what I should do. I stood frozen in shock.

Bova spotted me and took a few steps in my direction.

"Is this where you should be?" he asked.

I looked away, not wanting to make contact with those crazed, sparkling eyes.

"*Please,*" he said. "Time to get back to work."

I glanced to the unit supervisor. She gave me a small nod and motioned to the shovel I had dropped in the dirt. The shovel I had almost beaned her with. She might not have wanted me there before, but now I was a replacement for the murdered prisoner.

I reached down and picked up the tool.

"Very good," Bova exclaimed. "Enjoy the rest of the day."

He turned and strode back toward his jeep. The other Retros boarded and they took off, leaving a choking cloud of dust in their wake.

The body of the murdered prisoner remained.

I had been awake in the Retro camp for less than half an hour, and already I had gotten my first taste of what life was going to be like if the Retros won this war.

FOUR

I spent the next few hours shoveling dirt and sand into wheelbarrows. It was hot. It was mind numbing. It was torture. Painful blisters formed on my hands that burst and made it a challenge to grip the wooden handle of the shovel. I was in good shape, but nothing could have prepared me for that kind of manual labor. And that kind of pain.

None of the other prisoners said a word to me or even made eye contact. They had become drones. After a few hours, I understood why. It was easier to put your mind in neutral than to stress and constantly wonder when the day would end.

Every so often a prisoner came through to give us each a small cup of water. It wasn't anywhere near enough to replace the fluids lost through sweat, but it was better than nothing. Every drop was priceless.

Throughout the torturous day I often heard the musical sound of an Air Force plane powering up and lifting into the sky before rocketing off. In just a few hours at least a dozen new planes appeared above the tops of the wooden buildings. They were obviously coming from the steel dome. I figured it must have been the final assembly point for these death machines, which definitely made it a gate to hell.

Each time a new plane lifted off, my feelings of hopelessness and desolation grew deeper. Not only was the Air Force still in business, but there was every reason to believe that my mother and friends were dead. My one hope was that my father was still safe on Pemberwick Island.

I was probably kidding myself. For all I knew, Pemberwick had been laid to waste like the rest of the country. Though I was among hundreds of people trapped in the same desperate situation, I felt totally alone. The harsh reality had finally set in that there was no chance of a return to my old life, only the promise of a grim future.

"That's it!" the unit supervisor finally shouted. "Climb out and drop your shovels."

It took a second for me to register what was happening. Looking around the pit I could easily believe that we had moved the ton of dirt that the supervisor said she wanted. We had dug a huge rectangular hole, six feet deep and roughly the size of one of the barracks. I wish I could say I had a feeling of accomplishment, but all I felt was tired and sore. And miserable.

We climbed out of the pit to see two Retro guards, armed with batons, waiting for us.

"This way," one guard commanded. "Single file."

We shuffled into a ragged line and followed the guard away from the worksite. The second guard picked up the rear. We were led in the opposite direction of the giant steel structure. Just as well—I didn't want to be anywhere near the gate to hell. We shuffled by several more newly built but empty barracks until we finally arrived at one that showed signs of life. There were no windows, but I heard what sounded like running water inside.

The guard stopped and turned back to us.

"Showers," he said. "Drop everything in the bins and pass through. Give your number on the far side for a clean set. Move it."

The others obeyed without question and began stripping. It didn't matter that there were both men and women together. Nobody cared. Except for me, that is. I guess I hadn't been there long enough to be completely numb to the degrading treatment.

I got undressed, peeling off my sweat- and dirt-crusted overalls. There were three large plastic bins outside of the large door that led into the shower building. One was for the coveralls, the second for socks and underwear, the third for sneakers. I kept my eyes on the ground, trying not to look at any of the women. Or any of the men, for that matter. It was humiliating. I kept my head down and shuffled in line toward the shower doors. The smell of sweat was so overpowering I nearly gagged. Showers would be a good thing, no matter how degrading the experience was.

"Keep moving!" a guard commanded.

Overhead were six parallel bars that ran the length of the building and sprayed powerful jets of water down on us. The showering would last for as long as it took to shuffle in line from one end of the building to the other. The water was cold, but I didn't mind. It felt good to wash away the thick grime that was caked on every inch of skin that had been exposed during the day. I furiously rubbed at my scalp to get rid of the imbedded sand but it was a losing battle.

There was definitely some kind of soap in the water because my blistered hands stung. So did my eyes. I cupped my hands to capture as much as I could and gently rubbed them together to clean and soften the dead skin. As much as it hurt, I had to do it or risk infection. We shuffled along on the slick cement floor in two parallel lines. Halfway through the ordeal the burning sensation stopped, which meant we were being doused by pure water. When we finally reached the far side we stepped out into the harsh glare of the late-day sun to air-dry. There were no towels waiting for us. A few yards beyond the exit were tables set up with stacks of clean coveralls, underwear, and shoes.

"Number?" a guard asked me.

It took a second for me to understand what he meant.

"Number?" he barked, more insistent.

I hated having to give my number, but I also didn't want to be naked for any longer than I had to.

"Zero Three One One," I muttered, begrudgingly.

A pair of white socks were shoved into my hands along with tighty-whitey underpants. On top of that was a pair of size-ten white sneakers. Finally, I was given clean orange coveralls . . . with the number 0311 in bold letters on the back.

It was a dehumanizing experience, made all the more so by the cool efficiency of how it was run. Throughout the process, and all during the torturous day, I kept trying to understand how this could possibly be considered a positive reset of civilization. After all, that's what Feit said the Retros were after: a reset of civilization to save us from destruction.

I wasn't seeing that.

I wandered a few yards away from the group and started getting dressed. It felt good to be clean and wearing fresh clothes. I had to appreciate the positives when they came. Once I was dressed I took a second to size up my own condition and realized, with surprise, that I felt pretty good. I was tired, yes, but I didn't feel all that sore. Most surprising, my destroyed hands were no longer blistered. I rubbed them together, thinking it might be an illusion because they had been softened by the water, but they truly felt and looked fine.

My brain jumped to the only explanation: The water in that shower contained the miracle medicine that healed wounds. I'd seen it work too many times to doubt it. Now I understood that the Retros could use it to keep their work force in top shape.

At least they weren't forcing us to take the Ruby. None of the people I saw were operating with super-human capabilities. Maybe the Retros had learned their lesson. The short-term benefits of using that stuff was outweighed by the fact that it killed people. The Retros were a lot of things, but they weren't stupid.

"Blue Unit," a Retro guard called. "This way for chow."

I wound my way through the crowd of people still getting dressed to find the line of workers I had been with all day. Other units were also being herded together by Retro guards.

"Red Unit!"

"All Black Unit workers over here!"

"Green unit! This way!"

Workers scrambled to find their group. With the promise of food, it wasn't the time to slow down and take it easy. I was starving and had no doubt that everyone else was too.

There were hundreds of orange-clad workers and only a few guards. It crossed my mind that the guards could easily be overpowered by the prisoners. If we took a few hostages we might be able to bargain our way out.

It was only a fleeting hope because reality told me otherwise. The Retros had little concern for human life. After wiping out a few billion people, what would a few more deaths matter? Any uprising would be met with ruthless consequences, even if it meant wiping out some of their own soldiers. I had no doubt about that. The rest of the prisoners must have understood as well, which is why they obeyed like mindless sheep.

The Blue Unit regrouped and in no time we were trudging along in line, all cleaned up and smelling fresh, headed for dinner. We passed several more barracks. Unlike the ones we had been digging near, these looked to be occupied, for I saw movement through the narrow windows. We were led into yet another long building that was clearly the mess hall. We each grabbed partitioned plastic trays and made our way through the food lines. Prisoners in orange coveralls and aprons worked in the kitchen. I wondered how they got those jobs. It looked a heck of a lot easier than digging ditches. The meal itself wasn't horrible. We were given slices of ham, seasoned rice, broccoli spears, loads of bread with butter, and a fruity drink that reminded me of Gatorade. I want to say that the Retros were being benevolent by giving us decent food, but the truth was they needed us to be well fed in order to keep up our strength to work. At the end of the food line were plastic utensils, but no napkins. We shuffled silently toward long rows of tables with bench seats. I kept walking until the guy in front of me sat down. When the time came, I dutifully stopped and sat beside him.

We ate in silence. The only sound was the din made from the food being eaten and trays being moved on the tables. We were given five minutes. Unlike the SYLO camp on Pemberwick Island, no second portions were offered. My cue to get up was when the guy next to me got up. It didn't matter if you were finished or not; it was time to go. The silence was eerie. We all moved in line away from the mess hall and continued our journey past the many barracks buildings until at last we were directed to one. This would be my home. At least for that night. Inside were two rows of beds against the long wooden walls. Unlike the hospital that had rows of single beds, this barracks had bunk beds stacked three high. The place already smelled of sweat. We may have been freshly showered, but this was still the desert.

I had no choice as to where I would sleep. When the guy in front of me turned and crawled into the lower bunk to our left, I took the bunk above him. There was a three-inch thick mattress but no sheets, only a thin cotton blanket that was folded at the foot and a pillow that looked more like a ravioli than a comfortable cushion to lay my head on.

Even so, lying down was a relief. It could have been on a bed of nails—resting still would have felt great. I lay there on my back, closed my eyes, and listened as the rest of the barracks filled up.

A few minutes later, I heard a strange sound. I couldn't make it out at first because it was so out of place. It took a few seconds to recognize it for what it was.

Whispering.

People—prisoners—were actually communicating.

I looked to my right and saw a woman in a bunk who reminded me of my homeroom teacher back at Arbortown High. She was small, probably no taller than five feet, with long red hair that I imagined would go to her waist.

"Hello," I whispered.

She turned to me and smiled.

"Hello," she whispered back.

It was such a simple thing, but hearing another voice made me feel like a person again. Especially since it wasn't barking orders at me.

"Are we allowed to talk?" I asked.

She nodded. "It's the only time they let us," she whispered. "But only for a short while."

"What's your name?" I asked.

"I'm Scottie. I've been here about a week. They brought me here from Los Angeles."

"I'm Tucker," I said. "I'm from Maine."

"You're a long way from home, Tucker."

"Yeah."

I didn't mention that I was from Pemberwick Island. I was afraid that would lead to a huge conversation that I didn't feel like getting in to. All I wanted was to communicate with another living person for a few moments to pretend as though life was still normal.

All around us, people were doing the same thing. Voices were low, but there were many of them. It sounded as though everyone was letting out a day's worth of pent up thoughts.

"Do you know why we're building these barracks?" I asked.

"All I know is that more people are coming," she answered.

"More prisoners?"

"No, more of *them*, I think. I overheard the guards talking about it. They're preparing for a lot of people to show up. It's kind of scary. If the rest of them are anything like these guards . . ."

She didn't have to finish the sentence. I knew how she felt.

This war didn't make sense. The Retros were set on wiping out as much of the population as possible, while SYLO was trying to stop them. It seemed pretty clear that the Retros were winning, but winning what exactly? They hadn't taken over any territory or started a new government. There seemed to be no point to the deaths except . . . death.

Mr. Feit told Tori and me that SYLO was leading the world to calamity and the only thing that would save it was a reset of civilization. He said the Retros' drastic tactics were necessary so that they could save the world. But what had they done other than wipe out millions of people and force the survivors to build more of those giant steel gates to hell?

The Retros controlled the United States Air Force and had used some incredibly sophisticated technology to further their plan. But what exactly was their plan, and who was calling the shots?

Knowing that the prisoners here were building what amounted to a facility to house thousands of Retros made me believe that whatever the plan was, this was going to be the staging area. Other Retros could be headed this way from all over the world.

Once again, I found myself in the middle of the action.

Only this time I was alone.

"I've got a dumb question," I whispered to Scottie.

"What?"

"This is kind of embarrassing, but where do we go to the bathroom?"

Scottie smiled and I no longer felt embarrassed. But I still had to go.

"There are portable bathrooms outside each of the barracks," she said. "You're allowed to go any time."

"Thanks. That time is now."

I slid out of my bunk and walked down the center of the room to the door on the far end of the building. When I stepped outside I saw that even though night had fallen, massive floodlights perched on towers lit the camp, making it look as bright as an evening football game.

A Retro guard stood outside of the door. When he saw me he gestured to a row of Porta-potties. He knew exactly why I had come out, because many other prisoners were doing the same thing. I passed several who were either coming or going from the facilities.

I found an empty stall, went inside to do my business, and got out before the putrid smell made me gag. After walking a few steps back toward the barracks, I stopped to take in the surroundings.

It seemed like we were in a prisoner-of-war camp right out of the history books, complete with wooden huts, armed guards, and high light-towers. The one thing I didn't see was any kind of fence surrounding the place. Perhaps the miles of dry, empty desert that surrounded us were fence enough.

Out of nowhere, the sound of a car horn tore through the quiet night. Moments later two jeeps came screaming into a large clearing between the barracks. Both drivers were laying on their horns.

Two Retro guards standing near the potties looked to each other and smiled knowingly.

This wasn't a normal occurrence. Something was definitely up.

The prisoners who were already outside made their way toward the clearing. Others wandered out from the various barracks to see what the commotion was.

The two jeeps rattled into the clearing and started chasing each other in a circle while kicking up dust into the cool, desert night. After multiple laps they stopped and faced each other about twenty yards apart. Each had their headlights shining on the other.

By now a circle of prisoners had gathered, forming a ring around the two vehicles. The guards lay back, keeping a watchful eye on them, poised and ready for trouble.

I pushed my way forward through the crowd until I had a good view of the dueling jeeps.

A soldier got out of one, strode forward, and stood in the beams from the two sets of headlights.

It was Major Bova.

I hoped he wasn't there to play another warped game of Please.

He stood with his hands on his hips and slowly turned to survey the crowd that circled him.

The jeeps killed their engines.

The prisoners were dead silent.

"I hate this," a guy next to me whispered.

"What's going on?" I whispered back.

The guy didn't answer, he just stared at Bova.

"Good evening!" Bova exclaimed. "I trust you all had a productive day."

Silence.

"Yes, I'm sure you did. Before you retire to a well-earned rest, I'd like to provide you with some light entertainment. You know how much emphasis I put on the importance of running a safe, orderly camp. We don't have many rules here and you are expected to obey them without question."

Yeah, right. The Retros didn't have many rules, but the rules they *did* have meant we lived like dogs . . . while working like silent slaves.

"Unfortunately," he continued. "There are those who choose not to accept our system. That is why we are gathered here for tonight's entertainment."

It looked as though another example was about to be made. Bova was like a sadistic ringmaster in a circus of horrors. He strode around the inside of the circle with his arms raised, loving the attention. Besides the hundred or so prisoners who stood circling the jeeps, there were thousands of others who watched from inside their barracks, peering out through the small windows.

"Earlier today, two young men foolishly tried to leave us. To escape. The desert is a cruel and punishing place where they would surely have died from exposure. The way I see it, by preventing their departure we actually saved their lives. They will be allowed to thank me afterward."

He smiled, brushed his hair from his eyes, and added, "At least one of them will."

A pair of guards emerged from each jeep. Each pair held a prisoner between them. The prisoners struggled to get away but the guards were too strong. They dragged the orange-clad victims into the beams of the headlights.

"I am a forgiving man," Bova continued. "I will let this lapse of judgment go unpunished . . . for one of them."

The guy next to me sighed and turned to walk away.

"Wait, what's going to happen?" I whispered.

"I've seen this sick game before, I don't need to see it again," he said and trudged back to his barracks.

"One will be forgiven!" Bova declared. "The other will die. We'll leave it up to them to decide who deserves to live."

The guards shoved the two prisoners down into the dirt.

The overhead floodlights went out. The only light on the field came from the headlights of the two jeeps. I realized with horror that this had been staged for full dramatic effect. Bova stood between the two prisoners who lay in the dirt.

"One will sleep well tonight," he declared. "One will die . . . at the hand of the other."

"No," I whispered to nobody in particular. "They're going to fight to the death?"

Bova raised his arms and said, "The rules of this game are simple. Whichever of you deserves to live . . . will. Good luck!"

Bova backed out of the light.

The circle of prisoners watching this horrible spectacle was deathly silent. All I could hear was the steady, labored breathing of the two fighters.

They looked to each other and slowly, cautiously, got to their feet.

I finally got a good look at their faces.

It felt like a punch to the gut.

One of the fighters . . . was Kent Berringer.

FIVE

Kent stood a few inches taller than his opponent. His beach-blond hair had started to darken and grow longer since we'd left Pemberwick Island, a reminder of how long it had been since we left home. Seeing him was a relief, not only because he had lived through the crash, but because it meant there was a chance that my mother and Tori had survived as well.

I actually felt a surge of hope for the first time since I had woken up in this nightmare of a camp.

Kent Beringer was alive.

At least for the moment.

He was a strong athlete. I knew that from playing football with him at Arbortown High. He was a few years older than me, a senior, though thinking of life in terms of high school years felt so strange to me now. He was a rich kid—there's no other way to put it. But as privileged as he was, he was also tough. And fast. If he wasn't too terrified to move, he'd have a chance.

The other guy was short but stocky, as if he'd spent a little too much time lifting weights. Or countless shovelfulls of dirt. He looked as though he had the advantage in strength, but Kent knew how to move.

The question was, did Kent also know how to kill?

The two faced each other, tentatively.

Kent looked scared and I didn't blame him.

His foe seemed more focused as he stared back, sizing up the guy he would have to kill in order to survive.

"The short guy's done this before," a guy next to me whispered. "The blond kid doesn't stand a chance."

The two stood there for a solid thirty seconds, like two gunslingers waiting for the other to twitch.

I wanted to jump in and help Kent but that would probably mean suicide for both of us. I doubted that Bova's rules covered fan interference.

The crowd of prisoners watched with silent anticipation.

Major Bova stepped up onto the hood of the jeep to my left.

"Was I wrong?" he bellowed. "Perhaps neither of you deserves to live."

That was all the encouragement the dark-haired guy needed. He let out a low growl that came from somewhere deep and primal . . . and charged for Kent.

Kent put up his fists as if getting ready to box. It was probably the only way he knew how to fight.

He was in way over his head.

The guy was nearly on him when Kent took a swing. He actually caught the guy in the side of the head, but he might as well have hit him with a pillow for all the good it did. The guy blasted right into him, stuck his head into Kent's chest and knocked him back off of his feet. Kent hit the ground hard, flat on his back, grunting from the impact.

The guy went right for his throat. He wrapped his hands around Kent's neck and started to squeeze.

Kent's adrenaline must have finally kicked in because he grabbed the guy's hands, but rather than pry them off, he kicked his legs up and back, flipping the guy over his head. The dark-haired prisoner hadn't expected that and landed on his back.

"Bravo!" Bova shouted, clapping his hands with delight.

The Retro guards cheered and whistled like it was some MMA event, not a battle to the death. I wouldn't have been surprised if they had put bets down on who they thought would walk away alive.

None of the prisoner spectators reacted. They seemed as horrified at the scene as I was . . . or maybe they were also imagining what it would be like if they were the ones who had to fight for their lives.

Kent was now fully into the fight. He flipped over and jumped to his feet faster than his opponent, who was still struggling to catch his breath. I'd seen Kent hit ball carriers on the football field. He was fearless and fast. I willed him to drive into this guy and take him down like he did so many running backs. He charged at the squat guy and hit him just as he was standing up and turning around. The guy didn't have time to brace himself. Kent got low and drove his shoulder into his chest. I heard the man grunt at the moment of impact.

Kent kept driving his legs, pushing the guy backward until he hit the grill of the jeep to my right. There was a sickening thud and another sharp groan of pain when his body made contact.

The guards in the jeep didn't so much as flinch. They'd seen fights like this before.

Kent leaned back, pulled his opponent up by the front of his coveralls with one hand, and nailed him with a punch that snapped the guy's head to the side.

That woke his opponent up. He threw a punch at Kent, but held back before connecting. It was a fake.

Kent threw up an unnecessary block. That gave the guy the opening he needed to deliver the real blow. He used his foot to sweep out Kent's legs and sent my friend crashing to the sand. The guy looked as though he had some martial arts training. Before Kent hit the ground, he was already throwing controlled kicks to his head and chest.

Kent landed flat on his stomach and threw his arms up to try to ward off the vicious blows. It was no use; he was losing. In desperation, he crawled for the jeep he was lying next to and scrambled underneath, while being continually kicked.

"Please! No hiding!" Bova called out, taunting.

Kent wasn't hiding. He didn't stop under the jeep but kept crawling until he came out the other side.

His opponent rounded the jeep to try to get there before Kent could stand up.

Too late. Kent leapt up, grabbed the hood of the jeep and launched himself feet first at the attacker. His timing was perfect. He caught the guy in the gut with both heels, sending him tumbling backward while pinwheeling his arms in a desperate attempt to stay on his feet. He failed and hit the ground, again.

I expected and hoped that Kent would take advantage and jump on the guy, but he was exhausted. After getting kicked multiple times, he couldn't catch his breath. He had to hold onto the side of the jeep to keep from falling over as he gasped for air.

His opponent wasn't in any better shape. He lay flat on his back with his chest heaving.

Both of them were exhausted and probably badly injured.

"Good show!" Bova exclaimed. "I think we're all ready for round two!"

It was as if he expected the crowd to roar back their approval.

For the record, they didn't.

"We don't have to do this," Kent's opponent called to him, sucking wind.

I was surprised to hear him say anything to Kent, let alone something that showed defiance to Bova.

"They're just using us to threaten everybody else," he added.

I looked to Bova.

The commander stood on top of the other jeep with his arms folded across his chest. He seemed intrigued by this new development.

The guards hadn't moved, though they kept stealing glances at Bova, expecting him to do something.

The circle of prisoners pulled in a bit tighter, as if drawn to the drama that was playing out.

"Yeah, so?" Kent called out between pained breaths.

"We're all going to die here," the guy called back. "I don't want to do it for their entertainment. I'd rather make a stand."

Kent glanced up to the guards who stood over him in the jeep. They didn't budge.

He looked over to Bova.

Bova gave him a shrug as if to say, "Don't look at me. This is your fight."

I didn't know what to think. I didn't want either of these guys to kill the other. But if they refused to fight, would Bova kill them both? After what I'd seen him do to the prisoner who tried to steal water, I didn't doubt it.

Though there were hundreds of people watching the drama, it was so deathly quiet in that clearing that I could hear the heavy breathing from both fighters.

Kent did a slow scan of the circle of prisoners who were all staring at him. He was looking for help. Or at least some sign that he wasn't in this alone.

He didn't get any.

The dark-haired guy slowly pulled himself to his feet.

"What do you say?" he called out. "Are we going to die with dignity? Or for their entertainment?"

Kent took a deep breath, let go of the jeep, and stood up tall.

"Alright," he called out. "I'm done." He backed away from the jeep while looking up at the guards who loomed above him. "This is bull. If we're going to die, you've got to kill us. We're not going to put on a show for you."

A concerned murmur went through the crowd. Nobody called out or cheered. It was more a muted sigh of relief, but it was the first sign of life I'd seen from the prisoners. It proved that they hadn't given up yet, and it gave me a small hint of hope.

I couldn't have been any more proud of my friend. I dreaded to think of what might happen to him because of his stand, but he had shown something I'd never seen from him before.

Courage.

Kent turned his back on the guards and walked slowly toward the crowd, limping. He was hurt but didn't let that stop his show of defiance.

The dark-haired guy walked toward the jeep.

I expected Bova to shout out a warning to them, but none came. He watched them both with a cautious yet amused eye.

The short prisoner made it to the jeep. He stopped there and then, with one quick and surprising move, he reached inside and pulled out a dark piece of metal that looked like a heavy crowbar or a piece of pipe.

Before the guards could react, the guy took off running . . . after Kent.

Kent was still turned away from him. He had no idea.

The people in the crowd barely had time to react. A few people called out, "Look out!" and "No!"

Too late.

The guy jumped Kent and swung the bar around his neck. The two fell to the ground as the guy jammed his knee into Kent's back for leverage while pulling the bar back against his throat.

I reacted without thinking.

I jumped from the crowd and ran for them.

Kent grabbed at the bar, desperate to relieve the lethal pressure. It was futile. The guy was about to crush his windpipe. He had seconds to live . . . unless I could get to him first.

The guy's back was to me, which gave me an extra few seconds. When I got to within a few yards I threw myself at him, nailing his back with my shoulder. If it hurt me, I didn't feel it. I was too charged up to care. The guy grunted and went limp for a brief moment, just long enough for him to drop the metal pipe and release Kent.

He tensed back up quickly and the fight was now between the two of us. We rolled in a jumble of arms and legs, each thrashing to get away from the other.

I saw the pipe on the ground and stretched for it.

The other guy went for it too.

I got it first. I swept it off the ground and swung it in his direction with everything I had. I caught him square on the side of the head and he dropped instantly. Either I had knocked him out cold, or he didn't want to fight any more, because he lay there in the sand without moving. I waited a few seconds to make sure he wasn't pulling another cowardly fake, but he didn't budge. He was truly done.

Looking around I saw Kent lying on his back a few feet away. I crawled over to him, but kept hold of the pipe . . . just in case.

Kent was on his stomach. I grabbed his shoulder, ready to roll him over, but hesitated out of fear for what I might see. Was he dead? How long did it take to crush somebody's windpipe?

I steeled myself and pulled him over to see that his eyes were open . . . and searching. He was dazed, but alive.

"It's me," I said. "Fight's over."

It took a few seconds for Kent to focus on me. There was a

moment of confusion in his eyes as if he thought he was seeing a ghost. A moment later, he smiled.

"Rook!" he said with a raspy whisper. "Who won?"

"I'd call it a draw," Bova said.

I spun quickly to see the commander strolling toward us, followed by two of his guards. He was in no hurry. We weren't going anywhere. He now carried a black baton gun.

"This didn't play out anything like I expected," Bova said, half to us and half to the crowd. "Though I can't say I'm disappointed. Such drama! An even fight. A bold show of defiance that turned out to be a cowardly betrayal, and of course, a selfless act to save a life. Bravo!"

The idea that he had enjoyed this horror as if it were a show put on for his amusement turned my stomach. I thought about taking a swing at him with the pipe but realized he would shoot me before I got close enough to do any damage.

"What is your number?" he asked me. "You can speak. Please."

"You tell me," I said and turned my back to him.

Bova stopped walking suddenly, as if I had slapped him. He stared at me with those sparkling eyes. I tensed up, expecting him to raise his weapon and blast me into oblivion.

Instead, he laughed.

"I remember you, Zero Three One One," he said, almost jovially. "You were there to enjoy my little game earlier. Quite the busy day for such a young lad. I trust you will remember it for a good long time."

Bova stepped away and addressed the circle of anxious prisoners.

"I trust you will *all* remember this for a good long time," he announced. "In spite of the dramatic turn of events, punishment must still be given."

Kent's opponent sat up slowly, shaking himself back to clarity.

"We gathered here to determine which of these escapees deserved to live," Bova continued. "That has not changed. If not for the interference of this young man, the tall one would most certainly be dead."

Bova strolled toward the dark-haired prisoner and held out his hand.

"Please," Bova said with a smile.

The guy tentatively took Bova's hand and was helped to his feet.

Bova stepped away and addressed the crowd.

"This prisoner saw that the fight was very much in doubt and made a tactical decision, hoping it would turn the tide in his favor."

Bova strolled up to Kent and me. I felt Kent tense up, preparing for the worst.

"He deceived the tall one into making a grand, rebellious gesture that would demonstrate the disdain he felt toward his captors . . . and lower his defenses. It was a clever ploy, for his treachery almost won him the fight."

The dark-haired prisoner actually smiled as he soaked up the praise.

Bova walked back to him and stood staring him square in the eye.

"Almost," Bova repeated. "I'm not against treachery, if it's effective. Your stunt proved to be futile. Therefore, you are not deserving."

The smile dropped from the dark-haired guy's face. "But—"

Bova jammed his weapon into the guy's gut and pulled the trigger.

The guy let out an anguished cry and fell to the ground. Dead.

Shocked gasps rumbled through the crowd.

Bova was coldly oblivious. He did an about-face and strode back to us.

Kent and I sat in the dirt, staring up at him.

I tensed up, ready for the shot.

Bova stood over us.

"Thank you," he said. "That was quite surprising, and entertaining. The best bout we've had in weeks. Perhaps tomorrow evening the two of you will do us the honor of fighting each other. Two friends. A duel to the death. That will be quite the show!"

"Forget it," I said.

Bova laughed. "Don't count on that, Zero Three One One. Don't count on that."

He walked past us toward his jeep, still laughing as the guards dragged the dead prisoner to the other vehicle. Moments later both jeeps roared to life and drove away, forcing the spectators to scatter or be run down. No sooner were the jeeps gone than the floodlights came back to life, bathing the clearing in harsh white light, making the assembled squint and cower.

Kent and I sat in the dirt. Nobody came to help us or to see if Kent was okay. We watched in silence as the crowd dispersed and shuffled back to their barracks. Eventually, we were left alone in the center of the dirty field.

"I'm not going to fight you, Rook," Kent said through gasping breaths.

"Don't worry about it. We'll take it one day at a time. Are you okay?"

"Better than the other guy."

"What happened to my mother? And Tori? Did they make it?"

Kent massaged his throat and shook his head. "I don't know. I remember you getting blown out of the door just before we hit. I saw stars, man. Literally. I was hurt so bad I had streaks of light flashing past my face. Must have been a concussion. It was all just a jumble. I couldn't focus on anything, so I don't know what happened to them. Next thing I knew I was in the hospital plugged into an IV."

"Yeah, same with me."

"I'm sorry, Tuck. Maybe they made it, but I just don't know."

Kent had nothing to be sorry about because he had done something for me that only a few minutes before I wouldn't have thought possible.

He had given me hope.

"You know we're square in the middle of Retro-central," he said, his voice finally clearing.

"I do," I said. "I know something else too."

"What's that?"

I looked up at the giant steel dome that loomed over the camp to see a black plane rising up, lifted by its musical engine.

"They're going to wish they never brought us here."

SIX

"I can't move, Tucker," Kent said.

Now that the adrenaline had left his system, the pain from the beating had taken hold.

"It's hard to breathe. I think I have a couple broken ribs. My knee is totally out of whack too."

"We gotta get you to the medical building. That miracle juice will fix you up."

I stood up and tried to help Kent to his feet, but he howled in pain.

"I can't," he cried. "Jeez, that scum really did a number on me."

"I'll get help," I said.

"From who? The guards don't care. Neither do the other prisoners. Everybody stays in their own little orbit so they don't draw any attention."

"Well we can't stay here."

Kent tried to get up again, and again he sat back down, wincing with pain.

What had been a fiercely hot day had quickly become a cold desert night. The barracks were dark. No guards were around.

We were alone . . . until a set of headlights appeared, moving our way.

"Great," Kent said sarcastically. "What are they going to do now? Kill us for being out past curfew or something? That Bova guy is a real piece of work."

There was nothing we could do but wait and see who—or what—was coming our way. The vehicle was quiet, which made sense as it got closer. It was an electric golf-cart looking thing. At the wheel was a Retro guard. He glided up next to us and came to an abrupt stop.

"Get him in back," the guard commanded brusquely. "I'll take you to the infirmary."

It was a rare show of humanity from the otherwise heartless guards.

"Let's go," I said to Kent. "Take it slow."

"No problem there," Kent replied.

I wrapped his right arm around my neck and gently stood up.

Kent strained not to yell out but said, "Jeez, I can't breathe!"

I didn't know what to do other than to ease him down again. Before I realized what was happening, the guard was kneeling at Kent's other side.

"We'll both lift him," he said, all business. "Hold him behind his back and under his butt."

We both slipped our arms under Kent from opposite sides.

"Now, lift together. One . . . two . . . three."

We both stood up as Kent grit his teeth and did his best to keep from howling. The two of us quickly shuffled to the back of the golf cart, where there was a flatbed for cargo.

"Easy now," the guard cautioned.

We eased Kent over the deck and gently lowered him to the surface.

"I'm good. . . . I'm good. . . . I'm good. . . ." Kent said, straining. He wasn't even close to good.

"Ride in back with him," the guard said. "Don't want him falling out."

"Thank you," I said.

The guard didn't acknowledge me. He went right to the driver's side, hopped in, and slowly accelerated. He was careful not to bounce the cart too much, which wasn't easy as we traveled over the rough dirt roads of the camp.

"That juice works every time, right?" Kent asked through gritted teeth.

"You'll be better by morning," I said with confidence.

"Maybe I don't want to be better," he said. "Things just keep getting worse, Tucker."

It was hard to argue with that.

"You're not a quitter," was all I could think to say. "Stop talking like one. We're not alone anymore. That's something."

I almost asked the helpful soldier about my mother and Tori but decided not to. I still feared that the Retros would put together that we were the team that destroyed the fleet of planes at Area 51. The less information we gave them about us, the better.

But I so desperately wanted to know what happened to my mother.

The trip wasn't far, but it seemed to take forever because

Kent let out a soft squeal of pain each time we hit a bump in the road.

"You guys took a big chance," the guard finally said. "Both of you. How old are you? Sixteen?"

"Fourteen," I said. "He's sixteen."

"Seventeen," Kent said.

The guard sighed and shook his head. "Damn. I don't believe it. You're just kids."

What *I* couldn't believe was that this Retro was actually talking to us like we were humans, let alone showing sympathy.

"I was an idiot," Kent said through clenched teeth. "I trusted that weasel."

"He probably saved your life," the guard said.

"Really? By setting me up and then crushing my windpipe?"

"If he hadn't, Bova would probably have killed you both."

"Why?" I asked. "To make an example?"

"That," the guard said, "and because he hates you. All of you. It's why he volunteered to run this camp. He enjoys making you all suffer."

"That's sick," I said.

"That's Bova," he replied. "If you want to stay alive, avoid that guy."

"Gee, you think?" Kent said with sarcasm.

"Why are you telling us this?" I asked.

The guard didn't answer right away. He must have been thinking hard about what to say.

"Do you know why you're forbidden to use your names here?" he asked.

"To degrade us," I said.

"No. They don't care about you enough to want to degrade you. It's about us. They don't want us to see you as real people with personalities and a past. It makes it easier to . . ."

His voice trailed off.

"To what? Kill us?" Kent asked.

The guard didn't answer. He didn't have to.

"Why are you helping us?" I asked.

"Not everybody believes in this war," he replied. "We weren't given a whole lot of choice. What I saw you guys do back there, you know, standing up to Bova and then running out to help your friend? It gives me hope."

"Hope?" I said. "Hope for what?"

The soldier thought for a moment and then said, "Humanity."

"What is it you Retros are trying to do? Reset civilization by wiping out most of it? It's crazy, you know."

"Crazier than you can imagine," he said.

I looked to Kent, who gave me a wide-eyed shrug.

"Who's calling the shots?" I asked. "The Air Force is just a weapon. Who is leading them?"

"You don't want to know," the guard said.

"Well, yeah we do."

"We're here," the guard announced and stopped the golf cart in front of the infirmary building where I first woke up.

I jumped from the back of the cart and ran to face the guard as he got out of the vehicle.

"Tell me the truth," I said. "Who is running this show?"

The guard shook his head.

"I can't tell you that," he said. "It would only make things tougher for you. Besides, you wouldn't believe me."

"Then tell me why we have to build all of these barracks? What's going to happen here?"

The guard looked around wistfully.

"The answer you're looking for is coming. Soon these buildings are going to be packed with more of us. Many more. That's what this is all about, after all. It's the whole point."

"So it's like . . . an invasion?" I asked.

The guard chuckled ironically. "Yeah. That's exactly what it is."

"A few days ago I asked one of your officers who you were. His answer was, 'We're you.' Those were his exact words. 'We're you.' What did he mean?"

"Exactly what he said," the guard replied.

The door to the infirmary flew open and two more medical types came out wheeling a gurney.

"Look for the Sounders," the guard said quickly so that the others couldn't hear. "Stay alive and find them. They're the only chance you have."

The guard stepped back and made an odd gesture. He put his right hand over his heart, but then dropped it quickly.

"What?" I asked, confused.

"Quiet!" one of the medical guys barked.

Our conversation was done.

The two medical personnel pulled the gurney up to the golf cart and quickly lifted Kent's body to load him on.

"Ahh," he screamed in pain. "Easy. I think I've got a couple of busted ribs."

The medical guys didn't care. To them, Kent was just a slab of breathing meat.

"I'm staying with him," I said.

"Go back to your unit," one of the technicians barked curtly.

"No, let him stay," the guard who brought us commanded. "They've earned it."

"Earned it?" the technician said with disdain. "What's that supposed to mean?"

The guard strode up to the two medical guys and stared them down. It was clear who the alpha dog was. It looked as though the guards who dealt with the prisoners were more badass than the soldiers who worked in the hospital.

"It means I ordered you to let them stay together," the guard said coldly. "Am I going to have a problem with you?"

The soldier backed down and shrugged.

"Whatever. They'll be out of here by morning anyway."

The two soldiers wheeled Kent inside and I followed right behind. Before going through the door I looked back at the guard. He was already in the golf cart, driving away. Still, I was glad he added one more piece to this strange puzzle.

Sounders.

What were Sounders and how could they give us hope? Instead of getting real answers from the guard, he had only deepened the mystery. At least our few minutes with him proved that not all of the Retros were cold-blooded killers. Just most of them.

The soldiers wheeled Kent past the double row of patients until we came to an empty bed. A minute later Kent was lying down with an IV in his arm.

Before leaving, one of the soldiers pointed a threatening finger at me. "Keep quiet or you'll end up in one of these beds yourself."

I nodded and the two of them left.

The bed next to Kent's was empty so I pulled it closer to my friend and sat.

"You okay?" I asked softly, so as not to disturb any of the other patients, or draw attention from the guards.

"I feel like hell."

"That won't last. Soon you'll be back up to speed like nothing ever happened."

"I know," Kent said. "This is cake compared to the broken back I had."

"What?" I exclaimed, a bit too loud.

"The crash. When I first woke up here I couldn't move. The pain was incredible. I wanted them to put me out of my misery just to make it stop. They knocked me out right away and when I woke up again, I was fine. Sort of. This stuff may heal your body, but it doesn't make you forget the pain."

"And you have no idea if my mother and Tori are alive?"

"I don't, Tucker. It was all so crazy. After we hit I couldn't even lift my head to see what was going on. I know a lot of people came into the helicopter but I couldn't understand what they were saying. I was really out of my mind. It was so confusing. I don't know if they made it or—"

"They made it," I said with more hope than confidence.

Kent nodded but didn't seem as confident about it as I was.

"When you were sucked out of the chopper," Kent said. "I thought you were done."

"I thought so too, but after a dose of the magic medicine it's like nothing ever happened."

"Crazy, right?"

The two of us sat there silently for a good long time. I watched with fascination as the liquid dripped into the tube leading to Kent's arm. What kind of chemical could this be that would instantly heal wounds and stitch together bones? And why had we never heard of it before?

"You saved my life, Tucker," Kent finally said. "Thank you."

I didn't know which was stranger: Kent sincerely thanking me for something, or hearing him call me Tucker. I'd grown used to his sarcastic nicknames. I guess bumping up against death a few times is enough to mellow anybody.

"I wasn't thinking," I said with a shrug. "I saw the guy sneaking up on you and I just went for it."

"It was a totally stupid thing to do."

"Yeah, well, nobody ever accused me of being bright."

Kent shrugged. "I'm not surprised that you did it. I'm not so sure I would have done the same."

There was a huge elephant in the room that had to be talked about. It felt like as good a time as any to deal with it, especially since Kent couldn't yet move.

"I'm sorry about Olivia," I said.

Kent stared up at the ceiling fan. His eyes started to glisten. I knew he was thinking back to the moment when a Retro soldier fired his weapon at me and Olivia jumped out to protect me. She took the full charge and it killed her. It was one moment among many that had been forever seared into my memory.

"I wanted to kill you for that," Kent said.

"I know."

"Losing her was like giving up on whatever decent future we might have. Things are never going to be the same. I get that now. It hit me when we were maybe halfway across the country. We hadn't seen anybody for days and I realized there was no way we'd ever go back to anything even close to normal. Not even if these Retro a-holes gave up and went away. Too much had happened. So I started looking ahead, wondering how this new life might play out. The only thing that made it bearable was knowing Olivia would be with me. I wasn't just some stupid kid with a crush on the hot girl. I really loved her. I thought we would be together until . . . well . . . turned out I was right. We were together until one of us died. I just didn't think it would be so soon."

There was nothing I could think of to say that would make him feel any better. Olivia's death took something out of me too. She wasn't only a friend, she sacrificed her life to save mine.

"I don't blame you for what happened," Kent added. "You don't have any more control over what's going on than anybody else. She wanted to save you and that's what she did. Just like you saved me today."

"We've all been helping each other from the get-go," I said.

"I know," he said, his voice clutching. "I just . . . wish she was here."

I wanted to say that I did too, but I thought he should be allowed to grieve on his own.

"I don't want to die in this hell hole," Kent said.

"I don't see how anybody can die here," I said. "Not with this miracle medicine."

"You can die here all right," Kent said. "If you cross Bova. That guy's a psycho."

"We've got to be good little prisoners," I said. "Don't break the rules, don't call attention to ourselves. At least not until we find my mother and Tori."

"And then what?"

"Something is about to happen, Kent. It's why we're building the barracks. I think the next phase of this war is going to take place right here."

"Yeah, so?"

"So when it does, we're in the exact right spot to cause some trouble."

Kent smiled. "I like causing trouble. Why the hell not? It's not like we've got anything to lose."

"For now let's just do what we're told and keep our eyes open."

"What do you think that guard meant by Sounders?" he asked.

"I have no idea, but it makes me think that we aren't the only ones who want to stop the Retros."

"What about SYLO?"

"Yeah, SYLO. They'll be back. This isn't over. I think we should do all we can to stay alive until things start hitting the fan. That's when we'll move."

"I'm with you, Tucker. But right now I've got to sleep. This medicine is knocking me out."

"I'll stay right here," I said, but Kent didn't hear. He was already asleep.

I pushed the bed back into position and lay down. It wasn't until that moment that I realized how weary I was. Whatever rejuvenating effect the shower had on me had long since worn off. I put my head down on the flat pillow, hoping that sleep would come quickly.

It didn't. I couldn't stop thinking about my mother. And Tori. And for that matter, Granger. Had the SYLO leader died in the crash? As much as being with Kent gave me the confidence to start talking big about causing trouble for the Retros, I had trouble looking beyond that into the future. Even if we got out of this camp, what kind of life would we be looking at if everyone I cared for was gone? With the kind of firepower the Retros had, I couldn't imagine SYLO being able to protect Pemberwick Island for long. For all I knew it was already overrun by the Retros, and if my father was working with SYLO, what were the chances of his having survived the attack?

I was looking at the very real possibility that I was now alone in this new world. Alone with Kent Berringer. How ironic was that?

I had to force myself to stop looking beyond the next day. The next hour. The next minute. As I had done since deciding to escape from Pemberwick, the best I could do was exist in the moment . . . and hope that I was going to fight for a future that I might actually want to be part of.

Eventually I fell into a desperately needed deep, dreamless sleep . . . that didn't last anywhere near long enough. I was soon jolted awake by the sound of an explosion. It was still dark out. There was no way to know what time it was. Another explosion erupted soon after, this one even closer than the first. Next came the sounds of people running and yelling. What was happening? Was SYLO attacking? Had their missiles gotten through? Was the gate to hell about to be pulverized like the one under construction back in Fenway Park?

All around me the recuperating prisoners were waking and sitting up in their beds, looking as dazed as I felt.

"Nobody move!" a Retro soldier yelled as he ran past the beds, wielding his black baton threateningly.

Kent sat up, rubbing his eyes.

"Is this a dream?" he asked.

Another explosion hit, followed by screams.

A second soldier ran through and was stopped by one of the medical staff.

"Is it another air raid?" the nurse asked.

"No," the soldier replied. "It's a breakout."

SEVEN

"How do you feel?" I asked Kent.

"Like ass. But better."

"Stay here, keep healing," I said. "I'll go see what's happening."

I jumped out of bed and ran for the door on the far end of the infirmary. Some of the patients were sitting up, groggy and confused. Most didn't move. They couldn't be roused from their deep, healing sleep . . . even by the sounds and excitement of a massive prison break.

I jumped outside of the door in time to see another explosion erupt on the far side of the compound. It didn't seem big enough to cause any real damage. The base wasn't being attacked by SYLO, at least not as far as I could tell.

Retro soldiers ran from every direction with their baton weapons raised, headed for the latest explosion.

Boom!

There was another explosion that seemed to be a few hundred yards from the first. I turned back to the infirmary and scanned for a way to get up onto the roof where I'd be able to survey much of the camp. Using the skills I learned from climbing up and down the drainpipe on our house on Pemberwick Island, I put my foot up on the window frame, then grabbed on to a light fixture, which allowed me to crawl onto a small awning over the door. With a few kicks and a little struggling I hoisted myself up and over the top.

The roof was long and flat, and from that high angle I had a view of the entire camp. Or base. Or whatever it was. There looked to be dozens of similar buildings either completed or in various stages of construction. They were clustered in groups of four or five with large empty areas between them, like the one where Kent and that weasel prisoner fought.

At the center of it all was the giant steel igloo. It was like the hub of a wheel, with camp roads and buildings stretching out from it like spokes. There looked to be a runway leading out from the massive door. This was where they launched the black fighter aircraft. Since the planes took off and landed vertically, the runway didn't need to be very long. The dome was surrounded by a concrete tarmac where a few idle fighters sat.

My perch on top of the infirmary allowed me to view the extent of the Retro city. The entire camp was surrounded by black. The desert. What I couldn't see were the hundreds of antiaircraft cannons that had protected the dome from SYLO attacks, nor the wrecks of fighter planes that had crashed into the desert while trying to blow it off the face of the earth.

I registered all of this with only a quick look because what was happening far off to my right was way more interesting. I'd never seen a prison riot before, but this sure looked how I imagined one to be. Individual clouds of black smoke rose in several areas, probably from the explosions. There were several fires burning, but they were each contained, as if the bombs had gone off in between the buildings. None of the buildings looked to be damaged. It made me think that the explosions were more about making noise than causing destruction.

At the edge of one clearing, beyond three burning fires, a crowd of prisoners was gathered. There looked to be a few hundred of them and they were growing in number. Their arms were locked as they chanted something that took me a while to decipher.

"Water! Water! Water!"

This might not have been a prison break after all, but more of a demonstration. During the day we were forced to do backbreaking labor under the hot desert sun and weren't given anywhere near enough water to keep us hydrated. This nighttime riot seemed more like a massive show of anger over how we were being treated than a breakout attempt.

I didn't think for a second that it would do any good.

Facing the chanting crowd was a row of Retro soldiers. Though the prisoners outnumbered them ten to one, the Retros had weapons they weren't shy about using. I hoped the demonstrators knew what they were doing because they would certainly pay a heavy price for this insurrection.

The Retro soldiers didn't move. They held their baton weapons with both hands but had yet to aim them at the protesters.

The crowd was getting more animated. Their shouts of "Water!" grew louder and more insistent. Tension was high. If either side made a move against the other, it would certainly trigger violence. Part of me wanted the prisoners to rush and attack the Retro guards. There were enough of them to be able to grab a few weapons and do some real damage. But that meant many prisoners would be shot, and from the look of things nobody was willing to risk that.

I relaxed, thinking there wasn't going to be a mass execution that night. It was at that moment that I caught a glimpse of movement on the other side of the camp. It was a bus, not much different than a school bus, but painted in dark colors. It moved without headlights along a narrow section of barracks and finally came to a stop at the building one over from where I stood.

I hurried along the roof to get a closer look at this new arrival. My fear was that the bus was bringing Retro reinforcements with heavier artillery to put an end to the midnight protest. I ran right up to the edge of the roof, peered down, and saw that I couldn't have been more wrong. The bus was empty. What was it doing there?

The answer came soon after.

Several orange-clad prisoners hurried out from the barracks next to the bus and quickly boarded. They moved without a word as they quietly filled the vehicle.

The true purpose of the demonstration now became clear. It wasn't a protest. It was a diversion. The bombs, the chanting, the standoff . . . it was all to draw the attention of the Retro guards to the other side of the camp so that these people could load onto the bus.

It was a prison break after all, and the Retros didn't have a clue.

The people in the courtyard were sacrificing themselves in order to help a handful of prisoners get away.

Up until that moment I thought that the prisoners in this Retro camp had been turned into mindless workers who had given up and accepted their fate. It now appeared that Major Bova's rules did nothing to stop them from communicating and working together to fight back against their tormentors. It gave me a rush of pride and excitement like I hadn't felt in a very long time.

This was definitely a well-rehearsed plan. The prisoners moved quickly out of the building and entered the back door of the bus. Part of me wanted to jump off the roof to join them, but this wasn't my show. All I could do was watch and root.

I looked back at the action in the clearing. Even more Retro soldiers had arrived. They now stood two deep. It was an intimidating show of force, which meant there were fewer of them back in the camp who might happen upon the real event. The plan seemed to be working perfectly.

I looked back to the bus as the last few prisoners scampered out of the dark barracks . . . and nearly fell off of the roof when I saw a girl among them.

A girl I knew.

There was no mistake. The long waves of curly black hair were a dead giveaway.

It was Tori Sleeper.

Alive and well.

"Tori!" I called out and immediately regretted it.

I was so surprised to see her that it came out before I could think.

Tori froze and looked back to see who had called her name.

Several prisoners stopped abruptly and turned to look up at me.

They seemed horrified that somebody would have called out like that, inviting attention.

I wasn't so happy about it myself. I could have blown the whole plan.

At least my dumb move confirmed one thing: It really was Tori. I was so excited that I wanted to scream out again and say, "It's me! Tucker! I'm alive too!" But I'm not that much of a fool. All I did was give a small, embarrassed wave.

The other prisoners snapped back to their senses and pushed her onto the bus. They moved with urgency, thanks to the screaming fool on top of the infirmary. I scanned the area quickly but didn't see any Retro soldiers running their way. No sooner did the last escaping prisoner board than the back door closed tight and the bus began to roll.

It seemed as though every Retro guard in the camp was facing off against the protesters. None of them had any idea that they were in the wrong place looking the wrong way. I actually punched the air in triumph and would have shouted "Yeah!" but I'd learned my lesson.

The next day there would be hell to pay. I didn't even want to think about what punishment Major Bova would condemn the rest of the prisoners to for helping the others escape. I had to believe that they had all considered this and chose to go through with it anyway. These were incredibly brave and selfless people. Once again it gave me hope that the Retros hadn't completely triumphed.

Best of all, Tori was on her way to freedom. It was a very good night . . .

. . . until I heard a sound over the distant protest chants of the prisoners. It was music. The kind of music I didn't want to hear.

Near the steel dome, three black fighter planes on the ground had come to life. The ground beneath them lit up. The planes were about to take off.

What were they going to do? Was this why the Retro guards hadn't moved on the protesters? Were they going to bring in the heavy guns and attack the mass of prisoners? I thought about running to the far end of the building to scream out a warning, but it wouldn't have done any good. The protesters were chanting too loudly. They wouldn't hear one lone voice. . . . They couldn't even hear the music of the planes.

I was totally helpless.

The three planes lifted slowly into the air and hovered near the dome.

Three planes.

The situation was even more dire than I thought. It was dark. The laser weapon the Air Force used to wipe out so much of the earth's population only worked in the dark. It took the combined power of three planes to make it work. I couldn't breathe for fear these three planes would hover over the protesters and fire their deadly light on them. Every last one of them would be obliterated in seconds.

I couldn't take it anymore. I had to do something. I ran to the far end of the roof screaming, "Run! Get out of there! They're coming!"

It was futile. I was a lone voice lost in the wind. These brave people were all about to die. I wanted to think they were prepared for the worst, but how could anyone prepare for something like that?

I looked back to the dome where the three aircraft continued to hover. It wouldn't be long before they drifted over the crowd and each shot a ray of light that would combine with the others to sweep the ground and wipe away everyone there. I'd seen it happen before.

It was how Quinn died.

"Run!" I yelled one last time.

I needn't have bothered because they couldn't hear me . . .

. . . and the planes were on the move.

In the opposite direction.

My brain didn't comprehend at first. The planes weren't going for the protestors. For one fleeting moment my hope soared that they were headed somewhere else. Planes had been coming out of that dome and leaving for parts unknown all day. This might be just another scheduled departure. The protestors, at least for the moment, were safe. I had a brief moment of total relief.

Very brief.

The planes banked and moved off in unison. They weren't headed toward the protestors. . . .

They were going for the bus.

"No!" I shouted and ran back in the other direction.

I sprinted along the length of the building, getting no closer to the planes as they moved away from me. In the distance I could still see the bus. It was a dark spot moving between buildings with Tori Sleeper on board . . .

. . . being stalked by three flying marauders.

The dark planes were in no hurry. They didn't chase so much as drift ever closer to their quarry.

"Tori!" I shouted in absolute futility.

I couldn't bear to watch, but I had to. The three dark shapes moved closer to their prey. In seconds they would be over the slow-moving bus. I hoped the people on board that bus had no idea of what was about to happen and that their end would be quick and painless. They had all suffered enough already.

Especially Tori.

I stood with my legs locked and my feet planted firmly. I wanted to witness it. I wanted to remember it.

The three planes stopped advancing and floated in place directly above the bus. I knew what would come next. I saw it over the ocean when Quinn fell victim to this kind of ruthless attack. Now I would have two memories to haunt me . . .

. . . and add fuel my rage.

A narrow, intensely bright beam of light shot from each of the three stingray-shaped planes. The lights joined together and continued on as a single more-powerful beam that hit the bus. The vehicle was instantly enveloped in light and began to glow brightly, lighting up that section of the camp as if it were daytime.

Though my knees went weak, I managed to stay upright and focused. I had to see what happened next.

The glowing bus continued to move for another second. That was all. A moment later, it was gone. Vaporized. The light dissipated to reveal there was nothing left. There was no wreck, no scorched ground. No bodies. It was as if the bus and its passengers never existed.

But it did exist. So did the people on board.

People who were now dead and gone.

Including Tori.

The beams of light retracted and the planes flew off. Their job was done. They had deadly business elsewhere.

My legs couldn't hold me anymore. I fell to my knees, too stunned to know how to think. Or feel. I stayed that way for longer than I can say. I was in shock. In a single few minutes I had gone from feeling the joy and relief of learning that Tori was alive to witnessing her execution. Was it my fault? Had I called the attention of the Retros to the bus? I hoped not. It had happened too quickly. They were all dead. Tori was dead. With all that I had seen and been through since the invasion of Pemberwick Island, I had never cried. This time, I had no choice.

I sat there, alone, and let the tears flow.

Tori had survived the helicopter crash after all. Freedom was within her reach. Now, no amount of healing miracle-medicine would bring her back. I had lost another best friend. My hope was that she died with the confidence she was about to escape and had no idea of what had been hovering in the air above her.

"Tucker?" came a girl's voice.

I thought it was a dream. Or another hallucination caused by my grief.

"Are you okay?" she asked.

I spun around to see her standing on the roof, not five feet from me.

Tori.

Or Tori's ghost.

"I . . . I . . ." Finding words was impossible because I couldn't even find my brain.

I dumbly pointed back in the direction of where the bus had been obliterated.

"You saved me," she said.

"I saved . . . ? What?"

"Once I saw you there was no way I was going to leave. I got on the bus and ran straight for the door in front."

She looked off beyond me and I could see that she was crying too. "All those people. They took me in because I was in their work unit today. Now they're . . . gone."

The reality of the situation was gradually sinking in. She wasn't an illusion created from my paralyzing grief. She was really there.

Alive.

I got to my feet and threw my arms around her.

"I thought you were gone," I said.

"I would have been if you hadn't called to me."

"It was a stupid thing to do."

"I know," she said. "But it saved my life."

We stood there for a good long time, hugging and crying. The different emotions that were bouncing around my brain, and my heart, made my head hurt. I was devastated by the murder of so many prisoners and fearful for whatever punishment Bova would dole out to the others, but I was also back together with my friends. With Tori and Kent. We weren't alone anymore.

"The crash?" I asked. "What about my mother? And Granger?"

"And Kent," Tori added.

"He's down below getting healed. He's fine."

Tori wiped her eyes and let out a small, happy laugh.

"Thank God," she said, sniffling.

"What happened to you?" I asked.

She shook her head. "I don't know. I saw you get sucked out of the chopper and then we went down and everything went black. The next thing I knew I was lying in the infirmary hooked up to an IV. I was fine. Even the gunshot wound I got on the Retro plane was healed. But I don't know what happened to your mother. I'm sorry."

"Cutter is dead," I said flatly. "I think he died before the chopper even crashed."

Tori nodded. She wasn't surprised.

"This just keeps on getting worse," she said.

"Not entirely. I found you and Kent. At least we're together. That makes things a whole lot better."

"Do they know we were the ones who destroyed the fleet?"

"No," I said. "But I'll promise you one thing, before we're done here, they will. They're going to know exactly who we are."

EIGHT

"**W**hat the hell are you doing?"

It was a rude awakening from what had been, up until that moment, a very restful sleep. I opened my eyes to see a Retro soldier standing over me with an angry scowl and an electronic device in his hand ready to zap me. It was the same guy who didn't want me staying in the hospital with Kent in the first place. When he saw that Tori had now joined me on the bed, his head must have exploded.

I didn't move but braced myself for the shock.

"It's all right," another soldier said as she rushed up to the bed. "We'll send them back to their unit."

The new arrival was a woman who wore Retro fatigues but had no weapons. She was probably on the medical staff.

"Damn right," the first soldier said as he slipped the device back into his pocket. "I want them out of here, now."

He stormed off, leaving the woman soldier standing over us.

"It's time you all went back to your units," she said kindly, which was totally odd because from what I'd seen, none of the medical staff had any conversations with the patients other than to bark single-word commands.

She went to Kent and carefully removed the IV from his wrist.

I felt Tori's weight behind me on the bed. We had come back down from the roof to be with Kent and had fallen asleep while lying together. It probably wasn't the brightest thing to have done, but now that we were all back together, I didn't want to risk losing them again by splitting up.

Kent sat up, groggily, wiping the sleep from his eyes.

I raised both my hands in a "So? How are you doing?" gesture.

He shrugged and gave me a thumbs-up. The juice had done its job. Kent was healed. When he caught sight of Tori, his eyes lit up. But he didn't say anything. He knew the drill.

The soldier leaned down to me and said softly, "You are a very brave young man. I wish you all well."

She put her hand over her heart in the same gesture used by the soldier who brought Kent and me to the hospital.

Sounders.

Was she a Sounder? Who were Sounders anyway?

I nudged Tori to get up. The three of us got on our feet and left the hospital without a word. I took one last quick look at the woman soldier who stood at the foot of the bed. Her hand was still on her heart. When she saw me, she lowered it and walked away quickly.

Once outside, Kent grabbed Tori in a big bear hug.

"Jeez, Sleeper, I thought I'd never see you again," he said with genuine joy. "You okay?"

"I'm good," she replied. "Hate the Retros. Love their medicine."

"Do me a favor and stop getting shot, okay?" he said.

That made Tori hug him even closer.

It was still dark but the sky to the east was beginning to lighten, which meant sunrise wasn't far off.

"Let's go back to the barracks with my unit," I said.

The three of us walked through the quiet, dark camp shoulder to shoulder. The simple presence of friends was more than comforting. Knowing we were all safe and back together gave me a shot of confidence that made me believe we might actually stand a chance of surviving this latest ordeal.

"What's the plan, Rook?" Kent asked. "I know you've got one."

I was so happy to be together with these guys that I didn't even mind that he called me Rook. I actually kind of liked it, though I'd never admit that to him. It was our own private connection to another life.

"I've got to find my mother," I said. "If we all survived the crash, there's a good chance she did too."

"And Granger," Kent added.

"Yeah, Granger," I said with no enthusiasm.

"Hard to believe that guy's on our side," Tori muttered.

"But he is," Kent said. "He's SYLO and SYLO is all about stopping the Retros."

Tori stared at the ground. Her jaw muscles were working. It was Granger who ordered the attack on the camp of rebels that killed her father. Though it turned out that the attack was about rooting out Retro infiltrators, knowing that Granger was responsible for the death of her father was hard for her to deal with.

We rounded the corner of one of the long barracks and stopped to face the huge steel dome looming in the distance. The early morning sun was beginning to creep up over the mountains. It threw a warm light on its silver shell.

"What is that thing? Really?" Kent asked.

"I think it's the key to everything," I replied. "SYLO has tried to destroy it more than once. It's important enough that they blasted the one in Boston to dust. Who knows how many others are under construction, but this one—this one here—this is the one that counts. This is where they're launching their attacks from. This is where they're putting up buildings to house an invasion force. If we solve the mystery of that thing, we'll know exactly what this war is all about."

"So how do we do that?" Kent asked.

"We stay alive," I said quickly. "We do whatever they ask. And we wait."

"For what?" Kent asked.

"I don't know. A chance. A weakness. An opportunity. We won't know it until we see it. Maybe finding these Sounders is the answer."

"Sounders?" Tori said. "What are Sounders?"

"A Retro soldier helped us," Kent said. "He told us to look out for Sounders because they were our only hope."

"So then what are they?" Tori asked with growing enthusiasm. "Where are they?"

"I think they're right here," I said. "All around us."

Kent and Tori exchanged looks.

"Seriously," I went on. "Remember that Native American guy

who helped us before the raid on Area 51?"

"Yeah."

"Something he said really stuck with me. He couldn't believe that anyone was capable of committing such wicked crimes against their own kind."

"I thought you didn't buy my alien invasion theory," Kent said.

"I don't, but I also have trouble believing so many people could be convinced to wreak this kind of destruction on humanity. There had to be some push back. I don't care how badly the Retros believe things are going, wiping out billions of people isn't something you just go along with. Most of the guards are treating the prisoners worse than cattle, but a couple have gone out of their way to show a little kindness. What if some of the Retros are having second thoughts?"

"You mean like a revolution inside the revolution?" Tori asked.

"Maybe. I might be reading too much into this, but if enough of these Retros don't want the killing to continue, the Air Force may not be as invincible as it seems."

The giant steel monstrosity was growing brighter as light from the morning sun spread across its surface. The beast was coming to life before our eyes.

"The gate to hell," Kent said in a soft whisper.

"Everything that's happened, everything we've done, it's all led here," I said. "This is what's it's all about. The key to stopping this nightmare has got to be inside that thing."

"Yeah," Kent said. "I'd like to get a look inside that bad boy."

I looked to Kent, then to Tori. Glancing around the compound

I didn't see a single Retro soldier.

"Me too," I said. "Let's do it."

"What do you mean?" Kent asked, suddenly sounding uncertain. "Do what?"

"Let's go knock on the door," I said and started walking toward the dome.

"Whoa, wait," Kent said, hurrying after me. "Now?"

"Why not?"

"Because they're not going to let us just walk inside, that's why not," Kent argued. "Not if it's as important as we think."

"Only one way to find out," I replied.

I glanced to Tori, who gave me a wink and a smile.

"Let's do it," she said with confidence.

The three of us strode through the empty compound, headed for the monolithic dome. I had no idea of what we might find inside but was totally confident that whatever it was, it would give us a clue as to what we should do next.

We passed several quiet barracks, moving ever closer. The sheer size of the steel structure took my breath away.

When we were roughly fifty yards away, we rounded a building and came face-to-face with a team of Retro guards. Armed guards. They strolled casually across the dusty road, seemingly bored. That is, until three prisoners walked up to them.

When they spotted us, there was a moment of surprise and confusion as if they couldn't believe three prisoners would dare approach them, let alone three kid prisoners.

"Stop right there," one of the guards commanded, raising his black baton.

Instantly, five of them formed a line, standing shoulder to shoulder.

"We're looking for the bathrooms," I said, trying to sound innocent. And dumb.

"This is a restricted area," the guard said sharply. "You know that."

"We just arrived," Tori said sweetly. "Why is it restricted?"

The guard answered by firing his weapon at our feet. The charge of energy tore into the ground, kicking up a cloud of sand that washed over us and hit us in the eyes.

"All right, all right," Kent said, backing off. "We get it. We're going."

The three of us turned and hurried away.

I grit my teeth, expecting to get shot from behind. We took a quick turn to put a building between us and the guards but kept moving until we felt we were a safe distance away.

"That settles one thing," Kent said, breathless. "They don't want anybody near that thing."

"Which is exactly why we have to get inside," I said.

"I don't see how," Tori said. "Not if they've got guards ringing it."

"Neither do I," I said. "Not yet, anyway."

I saw movement through the windows of one of the barracks. The prisoners were waking up. Two Retro soldiers appeared and strolled toward the building, probably to start the prisoners on the new workday.

"We just have to be ready when the opportunity comes up," I added.

"We'll be ready," Kent said with confidence.

"You know we will," Tori added.

I loved those guys. Even Kent. He had become my brother.

The Retro guards started blowing whistles to wake up the prisoners. The three of us hurried back to the barracks where I had been the night before for a grand total of five minutes. My hope was that we could all blend into Blue Unit.

We reached the barracks as some familiar faces started piling out. It was an easy trick to mix into the group and move along with them as if we had been inside sleeping all night. The fact that the Retros didn't keep names or seem to care about who any of us really were gave me confidence that we wouldn't be questioned. We were numbers, not people.

The group filed into the mess hall where we were fed a decent breakfast of scrambled eggs, greasy sausage, and orange juice. I made a point of downing as much juice and water as I could get my hands on. It was already getting hot outside, which meant the day was going to be a scorcher.

As we silently followed our leader out of the mess hall and toward our workplace, I thought of the failed escape attempt the night before and the decoy demonstration. Would there be some punishment doled out? There were hundreds of prisoners who staged that mini-riot. If Bova didn't think twice about murdering a prisoner for trying to sneak a drink of water, I hated to think of what he might do to the group who tried to help others escape.

When our unit marched past the field where the demonstration had taken place, I had my answer. There was going to be punishment, but not the physical kind.

At first I thought there was a line of orange-clad prisoners standing shoulder to shoulder across the clearing, but as we got closer I realized that the coveralls were empty. They were strung up by a long line that was threaded through the sleeves, giving the illusion that people were standing side-by-side. It was a creepy sight that I didn't understand at first.

But Tori did.

"It's them," she whispered so the guards couldn't hear.

"Them who?" Kent asked.

"The ones who tried to escape on the bus. Their numbers are on those coveralls."

We were being marched around the clearing to view the grisly display. These orange suits were symbolic of the fifty or so people who were incinerated on the bus. I didn't know any of them but it still hit me hard. I could only imagine what the other prisoners who were part of the doomed plan felt like.

Many prisoners kept their eyes on the ground while others seemed to be steeling themselves to look at the macabre memorial. Several were crying.

Bova knew exactly what he was doing. He didn't need to physically punish these people. Hell, they were already driven to the edge of insanity by the hard work under the desert sun. What he was doing was much worse. This was a psychological beat down. He was taking away any hope they had for escape and shoving it down their throats. No words were needed. No speeches or warnings. No games. The sight of those empty coveralls was torture enough.

We were forced to march around the large field three times. By that time the sun was up and the temperature was climbing. Our workday hadn't even begun and we were already burned out.

Our unit finally broke away from the main group and we were led to our workplace for the day. The steel-haired woman Retro guard met us at a new structure that already had a cement slab poured. At first I was happy we wouldn't be digging dirt anymore. That relief was short-lived when we learned what our job was going to be.

"There are thirty trucks loaded with lumber for the construction of this building," the woman announced. "They're sitting over there, about a hundred yards away. Our first job today is to unload those trucks and stack the lumber right here where I'm standing. I want every truck unloaded by noon. Get that done and there will be extra water distributed. That's it. Get to it."

That was our morning: the brutal, physical labor of unloading endless heavy lengths of lumber, carrying them a hundred yards and stacking them near the work site. It made me wish I had some better skill to offer than gardening.

There was nothing to do or say. We all just got to work. Fortunately the supervisor didn't question why Kent and Tori were there. She probably didn't even realize she had inherited a few extra workers. We were indistinguishable to her.

It was brutal, backbreaking work. We weren't given gloves, which meant we ended up being jabbed with splinters on most every trip. The healing waters of the shower that night would take care of the wounds, but that didn't help with the pain we suffered while doing the work. After only a few trips, the front of my coveralls had massive bloodstains from where I'd wiped my bleeding hands.

Kent and Tori worked together while I teamed with the woman named Scottie who had given me the heads-up on the bathrooms the night before. Fortunately she was strong, so I didn't have to carry more than my half of the weight.

After about an hour we were given a much-needed water break. I sat next to Kent and Tori as the three of us leaned against a stack of wood. We didn't say a word to one another. What was there to say? We made eye contact, shared quick smiles, and tried to find a sliver of shade to wait for the water carriers to come by with our meager ration.

"Attention!" the woman supervisor announced.

There were a few groans because we had only been resting for a few seconds and most people hadn't gotten water yet.

"Inspection!" she announced.

Inspection? What the heck were they inspecting for? The three of us exchanged puzzled looks.

A jeep screamed up and stopped twenty yards from us.

"Uh-oh," Kent muttered under his breath.

Out of the passenger side stepped Major Bova. As far as I could tell, nothing good ever happened when that guy showed up. He gave a half-hearted salute to our supervisor, who saluted back crisply.

"Forgive the intrusion," Bova said to her. "We'd like to take a quick look at your workers."

"Is there a problem, sir?" she asked nervously.

"No, no. You are all doing a fine job. We are looking for three individuals that arrived yesterday."

"Prisoners come and go all the time, sir," the woman said subserviently. "It's hard to keep track."

"Understood," Bova said. "If they're here, we'll find them."

He punctuated his sentence with a grin that showed no humor. Something was up and it couldn't be good.

"This is it," Kent whispered nervously. "He's coming for us now. He's gonna force the two of us to fight. I'm not going to fight you, Tucker."

"I don't think you'll have to," I whispered back. "He said he's looking for three people, not two."

Another soldier stepped out of the jeep. An officer. He had short blond hair and wore freshly cleaned fatigues. He stood up straight and set his gaze upon our ragged group of prisoners.

"Oh my God," Tori whispered.

In that instant I knew exactly who these soldiers were looking for, and why. They were hunting down the three saboteurs who were responsible for destroying the entire Retro fleet of planes at Area 51.

They were looking for us.

Seeing this soldier answered a question that had been bothering me for days. When the final explosive charge erupted, destroying the massive attack craft that had wiped out Las Vegas, I had seen a mysterious dark shape blasting away from the doomed craft. It wasn't until that moment, when the officer stepped out of that jeep, that I understood what it was.

It was an escape pod.

I thought Mr. Feit was killed in the explosion.

He wasn't.

He was very much alive. . . . And he was here at Camp Retro looking for us.

NINE

"If he sees us we're dead," Tori whispered.

We were asked to line up, shoulder to shoulder, to be inspected. We stood at the end of a line of thirty people, watching Bova and Feit move closer. They strolled slowly, almost casually, past the tired, sweaty workers who wouldn't dare look their tormentors in the eye.

Bova was more focused on Feit than on the prisoners. He had no idea of what we looked like. Feit, on the other hand, knew us all too well. Bova kept watching him for a reaction, waiting for him to identify his prey.

Us.

Feit was in no hurry. He must have known we'd either be in the camp, or dead. There was no way we could have survived the helicopter crash and made our way out of the desert alone. He looked at each person in turn, sometimes using his black baton weapon to lift their chins so he could look them square in the eye. It was like he didn't want to actually touch any of us dirty primates with his fingers for fear we might contaminate him.

When I first met Feit on Pemberwick Island he seemed like a typical older surfer dude with long hair, a hoodie, and an earring. He was all sorts of casual . . . while dispensing a killer performance-enhancing drug to see how far he could push the human body before it crashed. His true identity wasn't revealed until we met him again in Fenway Park, where the Retros were building another steel dome. It turned out Mr. Feit was actually Colonel Feit of the United States Air Force and a major player in the Retros' campaign to change the course of civilization. Later on, when we confronted him aboard the flying death machine that had obliterated Las Vegas and was headed to wipe out the remaining survivors of Los Angeles, he was amazingly cool, as if he never doubted that he was in total control.

That had changed. It was subtle, but Feit's entire attitude was different. His laid-back surfer manner was gone. He stood military straight and moved with precision. His eyes had gone cold. It even seemed as though the sadistic Bova was wary of him. Feit's nose looked no worse for wear, considering I had broken it when I smashed his face into the hatch of the plane we were aboard. I shouldn't have been surprised. All it took was a dose of the magical medicine.

Feit moved from prisoner to prisoner, appraising them like pieces of meat at the grocery store.

"He's pissed," Kent said under his breath. "What do we do, Rook?"

I had no idea. We couldn't just cut and run. That would be futile. We couldn't attack him, or bargain, or turn invisible. I stood there between Tori and Kent in total brain lock.

Feit and Bova moved closer. There were halfway down the line. In seconds they'd be standing in front of us.

"It's you, isn't it!" a woman prisoner shouted.

Everyone looked to see that one of the prisoners had stepped out of line to call out the guy Feit was about to inspect.

The screamer was Scottie, the woman from the barracks.

"Don't go pointing at me," the guy she was accusing yelled back at her. "This is your fault!"

The guy gave her a shove. Scottie took a step back and then leapt at him angrily, wrapping her arms around him and pushing him back.

The entire line of prisoners swung around to see what was going on.

Feit and Bova did too.

We had our chance.

I grabbed Kent and Tori by the hand and pulled them away from the group. They didn't need convincing. We sprinted toward the pile of lumber we had been stacking all morning and skirted around to the back side. It was the only place that was close enough for us to hide quickly. It was a weak escape at best, but better than standing there until Feit walked right up to us.

The three of us fell to the sand and pressed our backs against the wood. We were all breathing hard as our hearts raced with fear. Nobody said a word. We just listened.

The sounds of the fight between the prisoners continued.

"They're looking for you!" Scottie yelled. "Admit it!"

"I think it's *you* they're after!" the man shouted back.

"Enough! Stop it!" Bova shouted, sounding surprisingly frayed.

None of us dared peek around to see what was happening. We could only guess from what we heard. There was a lot of scuffling and heavy breathing.

"Grab them!" the woman supervisor yelled, which meant Retro soldiers had entered the dispute.

"What is wrong with you animals?" Bova yelled, sounding flustered. He must have been trying to impress Feit with his total control of the camp, and having two prisoners punching it out definitely didn't look good.

"He's not doing his share of the work," Scottie cried. "He's the one you're looking for."

"Me? I've been doing my own work and yours too! If you want to take someone, take her!"

The three of us exchanged looks.

"They're doing this for us," Tori whispered.

She was exactly right. We were the new arrivals, and just kids to boot. The rest of our unit knew that, even if our supervisor didn't care enough to register us. Scottie had created a distraction so we would have a chance to do exactly what we did. Hide.

I hoped those two wouldn't suffer because of it.

"You aren't the ones we're looking for," Bova announced. "Control yourselves."

"Back in line!" the supervisor shouted. "Now!"

The ruckus died down and I had to assume that everyone had dropped back into line.

"My apologies for that, Colonel," Bova said, his voice shaken. "Shall we continue? Please?"

This was the moment. Would they realize the unit was suddenly three people short? The only sound we heard was the faint scuff of boots on the sand as Bova and Feit continued their inspection. I did all that I could to control my breathing so as not to give us away.

I squeezed Tori's hand. Kent pressed his head against my back with his eyes closed.

A minute passed. I looked up, expecting to see Feit's head looming over the top of the stack of boards. Another minute passed. Sweat dripped from my forehead into my eyes. It burned but I didn't dare move to wipe them.

Another few agonizing seconds went by and then we heard the sound of the jeep's engine powering up and the vehicle driving away.

We exchanged quick, hopeful looks.

Tori cautiously peered around the end of the stack of boards and gave us thumbs up.

"That's it," the supervisor bellowed. "Break's over. We've still got two trucks to unload before noon."

The group walked past our hiding place, headed for the trucks.

The three of us scrambled to our feet and melted into the moving crowd.

I was relieved to see that Scottie and the guy she had shoved were still there. There had been no punishment for their fight.

I took her hand and squeezed it, mouthing the words "thank you."

Scottie smiled and gave me a wink.

I took a chance and put my hand over my heart. It was the

gesture used by the mysterious Sounders. I thought maybe the prisoners might be part of the group.

Scottie nodded and smiled, but didn't put her hand over her heart. If she was a Sounder, she didn't admit it. She was just a nice brave lady trying to help out a fellow prisoner.

The three of us got back to work with the knowledge that we might have dodged a bullet, but we weren't out of trouble. Not with Feit prowling around. He wouldn't give up that easily. Sooner or later he would find us, and who knew what he would do once that happened? There was nothing I could think to do at that moment except continue unloading the trucks. We would have to come up with a new plan, fast. With Feit looking for us we couldn't lay low and wait for an opportunity to make trouble.

There was only one option: escape.

For the next two hours we slaved in the hot sun. The whole time I kept glancing around, expecting Feit to return. Some workers passed out from heat exhaustion and were carried away, only to be replaced by other nameless workers. At midmorning we were given a short break and fed some kind of oatmeal-like gruel. It was disgusting but nourishing. Whatever was in it quickly filled my belly and restored some of my strength. I wondered if they had mixed in a little bit of ground-up Ruby.

The reprieve didn't last long. In no time we were back at it, lugging huge lengths of lumber and stacking them near the construction site. We emptied the trucks by noon, just as our supervisor wanted. When the last length of lumber was off-loaded, the trucks pulled away . . . only to be replaced by twelve more trucks that were packed solid with more wood.

"And there's our afternoon," the supervisor announced. "Get to it."

Complaining wouldn't have helped. All I could think of was the evening shower and the rejuvenating water. The day couldn't end fast enough.

I thought for sure that we'd be working until the sun dropped below the surrounding mountains, so I was surprised when the supervisor blew her whistle early.

"Whatever you've got, drop it right there," she announced. "Fall in line."

I didn't think for a second that we were being given a break. Something was up.

We all dragged ourselves into a raggedy line. When the supervisor was satisfied, she blew her whistle again and we trudged on, following her.

"We gotta get outta here," Kent whispered.

"I hear you," I said. "Tonight. After dark."

"I'd rather take my chances in the desert than with Feit," Tori said.

With that quick exchange, it was settled. We were all thinking the same thing. After nightfall we'd make a break. It wasn't what I had wanted. Running away wasn't going to get us any closer to the truth about the Retros, or finding my mother, but Feit's arrival changed that. The first thing we needed to do was survive. Staying in that camp while Feit was hunting for us would make that impossible. It was time to go.

The supervisor led us back to the clearing between buildings where Kent had fought the night before. A huge crowd of prisoners was gathered under the hot sun. They were encircled by dozens of Retro soldiers. Something was up. Something different. I couldn't help but feel like a cow being led to the slaughter.

Our unit was pushed into joining the crowd of prisoners. It was lucky that we had arrived late. The first people who got there were in the center of this mess, pressed together by hundreds more bodies that kept arriving.

On the far side of the crowd was a military flatbed truck. Two Retro soldiers stood on the ground to either side of it. Though it was a huge crowd, it was eerily quiet. These people had been tortured into submission. They didn't dare resist. At least not in any obvious way. The escape attempt the night before proved that there was a lot more communication and planning going on between them than the Retros knew about, or understood.

"Here we go," Kent whispered.

I looked forward over the sea of prisoners to see Major Bova climb up onto the flatbed. He stood with his legs apart and his fists on his hips like some twisted version of Superman. He surveyed the tortured sea of humanity before him with an oily smile.

"May I please have your attention," Bova called out, like we had any other choice. His voice was amplified and sprang from unseen speakers.

"An urgent matter has come to my attention that I must now bring to you," he announced. "Please pay close attention. Your future will depend on it."

Bova stepped to the side as Mr. Feit, *Colonel* Feit, climbed up onto the truck.

"This can't be good," Kent whispered.

Feit surveyed the silent crowd. Not that there was any chance of him seeing us from as far back as we were, but I crouched down just the same.

All eyes were on him, silently waiting for a speech that nobody wanted to hear.

"My name is Colonel Feit," he began boldly. "I am one of the architects of your new future. *Our* new future."

I held back the urge to boo. I'd guess every last prisoner felt the same way.

"You are all experiencing hardships. I understand that. It is the price that must be paid to build a better, safer tomorrow."

Tori whispered, "Right. They're rebuilding what the Retros destroyed, just like every other war in history. It's all about destruction until it's about rebuilding. So pointless."

"I can assure you," Feit continued. "The sacrifices you make today will help create a new and better world order for you and your children. Your children's children. Hard choices have been made. Difficult choices. We are making them today in order to assure that mankind will not only survive, but thrive in the future."

Feit was a different version of himself than any I'd seen before. He was deadly serious and used his words sparingly. The easygoing beach dude was long gone.

"Your cooperation and hard work are essential to guaranteeing your own safe future. You will not always be working in this camp. Soon you will be transferred to other parts of the country. Perhaps to your own hometown. From there you will begin your new, intelligently guided lives and take part in the transformation that will help ensure that we will pass on a better world to those who follow."

He was speaking as if he expected to get a round of applause after each statement.

For the record, he didn't.

"However, there are those among you who want to end this important progress. They don't have the foresight to understand that until we stepped in, the world was on a collision course with disaster. To those people I say that it's entirely your choice. You do not have to be part of the new order. But be warned. If you are not with us, you are against us, and you will be treated accordingly."

Crickets. The crowd was deadly silent.

"I must now make a plea," Feit went on. "There are three criminals in your midst. They have committed crimes against the new order and must face judgment."

"Here it comes," Kent said. "He is really pissed at us."

"I ask that you reveal these traitors to your supervisors. Once they are in our custody, you will be rewarded with a full day off from labor."

That finally got the crowd buzzing. A day off from work was a luxury that seemed impossible . . . until just then.

We were in trouble.

"Help me to purge the rot from this camp," Feit bellowed. "Bring them to me."

There were murmurs as people looked around at each other, probably looking for us.

We didn't move. Where would we go? If we ran we'd have every guard come down on us and probably a few prisoners as well.

Our only hope was that nobody knew who we were.

I glanced to my right to see Scottie staring at me. Would she turn us in to get a work-free day?

She smiled and subtly shook her head. She wasn't about to give us up.

"Very well," Feit bellowed, the ragged edge of frustration creeping into his voice. "You are fools for not cooperating."

Bova stepped forward and announced, "Do you understand the opportunity? The reward for compliance is a day free of work. The penalty for not cooperating will be harsh."

"No," Feit interrupted. "That won't be necessary. I understand why they might not be willing to help us. They believe that by standing up to us, they are helping their own cause. They couldn't be more wrong. We are here to help you! To save you! In time you will come to understand that."

Nobody was buying what he was selling.

"Very well," he continued. "If no one is willing to step forward, we will use another means to root out the traitors."

Feit gestured to someone. A second later another Retro guard climbed up onto the truck, along with an orange-clad prisoner. A woman. She struggled against the guard but was no match for him. He pulled her up onto the flatbed of the vehicle with ease, as if she were nothing more than an annoying little child.

Tori gasped.

My knees went weak.

"You gotta be kiddin' me," Kent said.

Standing next to Feit, holding her head up defiantly, was Stacy Pierce. My mother.

TEN

My mom looked more exhausted than I'd ever seen her. She squinted and held her hand up to block the bright sun as if she had been held in a dark cave up until that moment. Her long blonde hair was pulled back in a ponytail, making her look younger than her forty some odd years.

But she stood there courageously, with her eyes fixed on Feit.

Mom was alive. That was my first thought. The relief was so dramatic that for a moment I actually felt light-headed. The moment I saw her it was as if the thousands of other people in the clearing had suddenly disappeared. It was just me, my mother . . . and Feit.

That was my second thought.

Feit had her.

I took a step forward but Tori grabbed me.

"Don't," she whispered with urgency. "That's exactly what he wants you to do."

I had some vague understanding that by my revealing myself I'd also be putting Tori and Kent in danger. I wish I could say that it mattered to me but in that moment, it didn't. All I could see was my mother being manhandled by my enemy, and that wasn't going to fly.

"Feit!" I screamed.

It was like a gunshot in an empty auditorium. Every last person spun to look at me.

"And . . . we're done," Kent said with a sigh.

Tori let go of my arm.

For the first time since he had reappeared, Feit smiled. Even from that distance away I could see it and it made my blood boil.

My mother's reaction was much different. She deflated and dropped her head. She must have been hoping that Feit was wrong and that I had somehow escaped from the grasp of the Retros.

"Let her go!" I screamed.

It was a lame demand. It wasn't like I could do anything about it if he refused.

Bova leaned down to one of his soldiers and whispered something. Immediately after, several Retro soldiers started making their way around the perimeter of the mass of prisoners to close in on me. On us.

"Hello Tucker," Feit called out with his familiar, casual voice. "Good to see you again."

The guy must have been under some serious pressure from his superiors for having been outsmarted by a bunch of kids. It cost the Retros a thousand fighter planes. Having found me seemed to have instantly taken some of that pressure off.

"If you want me, leave her alone," I shouted.

"How exactly do you figure that?" he called back. "I already have you! I trust my other good friends are close by."

That's when it fully hit me that by revealing myself, I had also doomed Kent and Tori.

"I'm sorry," I said to them sheepishly.

Kent shrugged.

"This isn't over," Tori said with conviction. "We've gotten through worse."

It may not have been over, but in that moment it sure felt like it.

There must have been over a thousand prisoners there, as well as dozens of armed Retro guards. They all stood silently, listening to our exchange. All but the handful of guards who were headed our way, that is.

"Get out of here," I whispered to Kent and Tori, without taking my eyes off of Feit. "Blend into the crowd. He doesn't know for sure that you're here."

Kent nodded quickly and started to move deeper into the crowd, but Tori stood still.

"Go," I insisted.

She stood her ground.

Kent glanced back and saw that Tori wasn't moving. He deflated, rolled his eyes, and pushed his way back to us.

"I don't like being noble," he grumbled.

"But you're still here," Tori said with a smile.

"Reluctantly," he added.

The Retro soldiers moved toward us, pushing through the crowd from both sides. Most of the prisoners didn't budge, making it tough going for them.

"Please," Bova called out to the crowd. "Clear a path for my men. We don't want to see anyone get hurt unnecessarily."

"What do you think they'll do to us?" Kent asked nervously.

I wished I had an answer to that.

The soldiers finally reached us. There were six of them who stood facing us as the nearby prisoners finally backed away.

One soldier raised his black baton weapon, ready to aim it at us.

"Is there going to be trouble?" he asked.

I wanted to say I planned on giving them as much trouble as humanly possible, but that wouldn't have been wise.

"No," I said flatly.

"Then walk," he commanded.

I didn't hesitate and walked straight at the six soldiers, who had to get out of our way to let us pass. The prisoners pushed back and gave us a wide opening so we could move out of the crowd. Once we left the mass of humanity and walked through the ring of guards that held the crowd together, we turned forward and began the long walk to Feit.

Kent and Tori stayed right behind me.

The Retro soldiers were close behind them.

There was no escaping this fate. Once again, we would have to face Feit. We had beaten this guy before. More than once. I had to hold on to the belief that we could do it again. It seemed impossible under the circumstances, but it was all I had.

As we walked, we passed several Retro soldiers, who glared at us, stone faced, as if we were lower than all the other primates they had so much disdain for. Each look made me stand a little straighter, as if to show them I wasn't afraid or intimidated, though I was both.

We were in a situation that seemed totally hopeless . . . until I made eye contact with a soldier who was still a few steps away.

He lifted his hand and put it over his heart.

I was so surprised I stopped walking.

The soldier quickly dropped his hand, as if not wanting anyone else to see the gesture.

Kent and Tori bumped into me from behind.

"What?" Kent said, annoyed.

"Keep moving," The guard commanded from the rear.

I started walking again but kept my eye on the soldier.

Without warning he lunged for me, grabbed me by the front of my coveralls, threw me on the ground, and put his face right in mine.

"Vermin!" he screamed with rage. "You animals don't deserve our pity."

I was too surprised to fight back.

Kent and Tori tried to pull the guy off of me but he was too strong.

He leaned down close to my ear and whispered, "Slow down. Help is on the way."

"What?" I said, stunned.

The soldier pushed off of me and got back to his feet. He spit on the ground with disgust and walked away.

Tori and Kent quickly helped me to my feet.

"You all right?" Tori asked.

I wasn't. My mind was spinning. What had just happened? Was that soldier a Sounder? I had to get my act together and come up with a way to deal with what he just told me. Was help really on the way? What kind of help? Was there actually hope?

I turned to the leader of the guards who were escorting us and walked boldly up to him.

"Can't you control your people?" I asked, indignantly. "You call us animals? What was that all about?"

"Keep moving," the guard growled without a hint of sympathy.

"Not until you guarantee to protect us."

"Wha . . . ?" the soldier replied, stunned. "Protect you? You can all disappear for all I care."

"What's the delay?" Bova called from the truck, still fifty yards ahead.

I didn't know if I could believe the soldier who attacked me or not, but if help was really on the way and I needed to slow down, I was going to slow down.

"We're coming!" I shouted. "But you have to promise me you won't hurt my mother."

A murmur rippled through the crowd when they heard that the prisoner who stood next to Feit was my mother. There was a growing swell of sound that I could imagine turning into anger, and a thousand angry people would make a pretty powerful force.

"Quiet!" Bova ordered. "Discipline!"

He wasn't talking to the crowd. The Retro soldiers that formed a ring around the crowd all turned inward, raised their batons, and fired.

Instantly, dozens of prisoners screamed and fell to their knees. They weren't injured or even knocked unconscious, but a direct and violent message had been delivered. The crowd instantly went silent.

"You're in no position to make demands, Tucker," Feit called. "I have no issues with your mother, unless you continue to give me grief."

"I think we better keep moving, Rook," Kent said, his voice shaking.

He was right, but I wanted to take as much time as possible for . . . what? I walked right to the lead soldier with the baton, stared him square in the eye, and said, "Why don't you have a couple of your robots walk in front of us so nothing stupid like that happens again."

The idea of doing something that a lowly primate suggested probably made him nauseated. It definitely made him mad. I saw his jaw muscles tensing as he attempted to control his rage.

"Just a thought," I added, snarky. "Your call."

The guy swallowed hard, grabbed one of his men by the arm, and pushed him forward.

"Walk in front of these . . ."

He didn't finish the sentence.

"Animals," I said. "I think the word you're looking for is animals."

The soldier moved past us and waited.

"Now," the lead soldier said. "Move."

I smiled at him and politely said, "You got it. Thank you."

I turned away and walked back to Kent and Tori.

"What was all that about?" Tori asked.

"I don't know yet," was my reply.

The three of us started walking again, this time with Retro escorts in front and back. I set the pace, deliberately walking slowly. As we drew closer to Feit and my mother, the reality began sinking in that help was not on the way. Whoever that soldier was, he didn't know what he was talking about. Or maybe he did and it was just another form of torture by offering a faint glimmer of hope before crushing it. . . .

A shrill whistling sound tore through the sky and . . . *boom!*

An explosion erupted on the surface of the steel dome.

Every last person spun to look as . . . *boom!*

Another explosion followed, only this one hit the ground beyond the dome.

My first instinct was to look for my mother.

She was already gone. So were Feit and Bova.

Every last Retro soldier took off running, including our escorts. They ran with purpose, as if this was a drill they had practiced many times.

"What the hell?" Kent shouted.

His words were cut off by the shrieking sound of two gray fighter planes screaming by overhead.

"SYLO," Tori called.

Help had arrived after all.

With the soldiers gone and an aerial attack underway, there was widespread panic among the prisoners. Unlike the soldiers who had run off to whatever post or shelter they were assigned to, the prisoners had no clue of what to do or where to go. The base may have been under attack, but that meant the prisoners were square in the line of fire. Many ran toward the barracks buildings and piled inside for whatever protection the flimsy wooden structures would provide.

Retro fighter planes soon appeared in the sky as they lifted off vertically from around the dome. They hovered around the steel structure, forming a protective perimeter. Others shot off to meet the intruders head on.

Four more Navy jets appeared over the mountains, headed for the dome. Within seconds they each unleashed two missiles that streaked for the towering structure. SYLO hadn't come to help the prisoners. They were going after the gate to hell . . . and a Retro soldier knew the attack was coming.

A Sounder.

There really was hope.

Several black Retro fighter drones swooped in like angry wasps. The impulses of power they fired from their impossible weapons were invisible, but effective. Most every one of the SYLO missiles exploded in midair before getting close to their target.

The three of us hadn't moved. We stood on the edge of the clearing, staring up in wide-eyed wonder as the aerial bombardment intensified.

Multiple SYLO fighters appeared, crossing paths with the screaming jets that had just fired their own missiles ineffectively. Unlike Fenway Park, where there was no Retro defense to protect the half-built dome, this monster in the desert was well defended. Not only were there ground-based antiaircraft weapons outside the desert base, but the Air Force drones weren't solely in defense mode. While the ring of hovering craft stayed near the dome to protect it, dozens of other Retro fighters went on the attack.

"My God, look," Tori said pointing to the horizon.

The air battle taking place beyond the borders of the camp was monstrous. It sounded like distant thunder as dozens of SYLO fighters streaked along the perimeter, looking for an opening to make an attack run on the dome. For every SYLO jet there were three or four Retro drones battling to keep them at bay. It was a depressing sight, especially since it had only been a few days since we had destroyed a thousand of those black monsters. This proved what Granger had said. The Retros weren't even close to being finished. We may have set them back at Area 51, but their resources were deep. The Air Force must have been building these high-tech weapons for a very long time in order to have manufactured so many.

But how was that possible? Where had these new fighter drones come from? How could they have gotten to the desert so quickly?

"Move!" Kent shouted and pushed Tori and me away from the field.

"Look out!" Tori screamed, pointing skyward.

I heard it before I saw it. A Navy jet tumbled out of the sky in flames, and it was headed our way.

We ran for the nearest building, scrambling for whatever protection it might offer. We hit the side of the wall and crouched down just as the jet slammed into the open field at full throttle. There was a massive eruption that spewed flames, debris, and burning jet fuel.

There were no survivors.

I pulled Kent and Tori away from the building and made a desperate run to get around to the far side. The heat at our backs was so intense I feared our coveralls would ignite. The moment we rounded the corner of the building, the structure was hit with burning debris. The wooden barracks were peppered by pieces of flaming wreckage, large and small. The terrified screams of the people hiding inside could barely be heard above the roar of the fire that engulfed the downed jet.

Seconds later the building erupted in flames, sending people flooding out, desperate to escape the burning deathtrap.

I should have helped them out. I should have run to the windows, broken them, and pulled as many victims out as possible. But I didn't. Who knows if I could have made a difference anyway? In that moment, another opportunity had presented itself. One that was more important. I had to take it.

"This is it," Kent said, breathing hard. "This is our chance. Look."

Terrified prisoners were not only running for cover, they were sprinting for the camp borders.

"The Retros are hiding in bunkers," Tori said, breathless. "They don't care if any prisoners are killed."

Kent added, "Yeah and as soon as this attack is over they'll come back and they'll have us. This is it. This is our chance to get out of here."

I watched hundreds of people fleeing from the camp, sprinting toward freedom.

"What about Tucker's mother?" Tori exclaimed.

"She's with Feit!" Kent yelled with frustration. "I'm sorry Tucker, we can't help her. But we can help ourselves. This is the chance you were talking about. We can get out of here."

My brain locked. Could I leave my mother? I couldn't imagine doing that, but to save her I would have to fight my way through Feit and Bova and whatever Retro guards were protecting them. Not to mention survive this bombing. That seemed impossible. Suicidal.

Boom!

Another missile got through the defense and exploded on the skin of the dome, its thunderous echo rolling through the camp.

"Listed to me Rook," Kent said. "The only way to help your mother is to get out of here and maybe get picked up by SYLO."

I looked to Tori, hoping she would help me make the right decision.

"He's right," she said, wincing. "Feit wants you. He wants us. As long as we're free, he'll keep her around because he knows you'll come for her. We have a better chance of helping her if we escape."

My mind raced, calculating the possibilities. The opportunities. I glanced around the corner of the burning building and saw the target of the attack.

The dome.

There were two scorch marks on its skin from the missiles that hit it. Other than that it looked untouched. SYLO's attack was doomed to fail. Again.

In that split second I made my decision. This really was the chance we were looking for.

"I'm not leaving," I said.

"Tucker!" Tori exclaimed. "Staying here is suicide."

"Running into the desert is no better," I said quickly. "We're in the middle of nowhere. We have nothing. As soon as the attack ends Bova's going to send out soldiers to round everyone up. There's nowhere to hide out there. Every last one of those people who bolted is going to be right back here before nightfall."

"So what do you want to do?" Kent asked. "Going after your mother is as good as giving ourselves up."

"There's a third choice," I said.

A shrill whistle warned of the arrival of another shot. A second later an explosion erupted on the skin of the dome. Though the ground shook on impact, it was another useless effort that did nothing to damage the structure.

"The Retro guards are gone," I said. "This is our chance."

"Yeah, to get out of here," Kent said.

"No. To go for the dome."

Kent and Tori exchanged quick, stunned looks.

Kent said, "The target? You want to run straight for ground zero?"

Two more SYLO fighters flew by. They were coming less frequently. The antiaircraft weapons were doing their job. The attack wouldn't last much longer.

"If I'm going to die here," I said. "I want to know why. I want the truth."

"This is crazy," Kent whined.

"Look, I won't blame you guys if you don't come with me. But I don't think you're going to have a better chance out in that desert. You told me we were better together, Kent. You're right. We are. We need each other. I have no idea what we'll find in that dome or if it will make any difference in this fight, but the best chance of finding that out is if we do it together."

Tori looked away from the dome, where many more prisoners were flooding out of the barracks and running for the border of the camp.

"Or we could get out of here, find SYLO, and bring them back," she said.

It was clear what Tori wanted to do. There wasn't time to argue.

"You're right," I said. "Get out of here. Disappear into the desert and try to get to SYLO. But I can't. I gotta stay here. I love you guys."

With that I took off running for the dome before I could change my mind.

Once again, I was alone. I hated leaving them but there was no other choice. I forced myself not to look back, instead staying focused on what was ahead. The dome. The truth.

I sprinted along the sandy road, hugging close to the buildings for whatever protection they might offer. I came upon a prisoner who was lying on the ground. He had been hit by shrapnel. His pants were soaked with blood and he was in excruciating pain.

"Help me!" he called, with his hand raised. "I can't move!"

I didn't think twice. I blew right by him. I'm not proud to admit that, but I had been given an opportunity, the opportunity I had been waiting for. I wasn't going to waste it.

A missile tore by overhead and slammed into the dome. The explosion was so powerful it rocked the ground, knocking me off my feet. When the smoke cleared I looked up to see that the missile may have found its mark, but it had still done no damage to the dome. The only sign that it had blasted into the steel surface was another scorched scar.

Two more SYLO jets blasted through the antiaircraft fire and made a run at the dome. Several black drones broke off from their protective ring around the structure and flew to meet them. It was a game of chicken with both sides firing as they streaked toward one another like an aerial joust. One of the Navy jets launched its missile . . . a second before the jet was hit by an impulse from the Air Force fighter that obliterated it in midair. A storm of burning shrapnel rained down on the far side of the camp.

The missile shot past the dome and screamed by overhead. It lost altitude quickly and made a direct hit on the barracks building that was already on fire. Thank God it had been evacuated. The second Navy jet broke off without firing.

That was the moment. While insanity continued to escalate around me, I had severe doubts. What was I doing? Was finding the truth worth abandoning my only friends in the world? Would knowing whatever was inside the dome make any difference anyway? Would it help save my mother? I thought about running back to join Kent and Tori but feared it was too late. I had committed. There was no turning back.

I ran to a large building right next to the dome that seemed more permanent than the others. It was made of cement and looked to be more of a command center than a barracks. I hugged the building and made my way along the outside wall, careful to avoid windows where I might be seen from inside. When I reached the end of the long building, I took a cautious look around the corner to see I was only fifty yards away from my destination. It was the exact spot where the Retro guards had stopped us that morning.

But now the guards were gone. They were probably huddled safely in underground bunkers, riding out the attack. It was the exact situation I had been hoping for. The dome was unprotected.

"This is crazy!" Tori exclaimed.

I spun around to see Kent and Tori running up to join me.

"No!" I screamed. "What are you doing?"

"Sticking with the plan," Tori shouted, struggling to be heard over the constant sounds of the not-so-distant air battle. "We're not splitting up. Not anymore."

"Even if that means running toward a target that everybody else is running away from," Kent added. "Just sayin'."

"We're going together," Tori said adamantly.

I opened my mouth to argue but thought better of it. I'd seen that look in Tori's eyes before. More times than I could remember. When her mind was made up, there was no changing it.

I looked to Kent.

"This is crazy," he said, deadly serious. "But we came here together and that's how we're going to leave. You're not flying solo on this, Rook."

I looked between both of them. My friends. My family.

"You sure?"

"No," Kent said.

"You know we are," Tori added.

It was what I wanted to hear. I was tired of being alone.

"All right," I said and turned back to our objective.

"This is it," I said. "Ready?"

Tori nodded. Kent nodded.

There wasn't a living soul between us and the dome, only small piles of burning plane wreckage.

"I am too," I said. "It's time to find out what the hell this is about."

I got to my feet and ran.

Kent and Tori were right behind me.

It was the last leg of a journey that began on Pemberwick Island and would end at the gate to hell.

ELEVEN

We sprinted directly for the dome and the massive door that was a quarter of the way around the structure from us. A missile shot by overhead, streaked past the huge steel igloo, and slammed into the ground causing a minor earthquake-like rumble that nearly knocked us off our feet but didn't stop us from moving. We had committed and there was nothing that would keep us from reaching our goal.

"Damn, this thing is big," Kent exclaimed.

He was looking up at the structure that towered over us. From this close we couldn't see the top since the shape of the building curved in to a center point. The sheer enormity of it took my breath away.

Tori put her hand on the surface.

"I thought it would be hot," she said. "I don't know why."

"Because it's a doorway into hell, that's why," Kent said.

I started moving again, quickly making my way counter-clockwise around the circular base of the building, headed for the giant door.

"You realize we're running square into a bull's-eye," Kent said.

I picked up the pace and sprinted. There was no reason to be cautious. We would either be hit or we wouldn't.

We ran for a solid thirty seconds without reaching the door. That's how massive this thing was. I finally caught sight of what looked like a vertical beam running up the side of the building in front of us.

"It's the edge of the door frame," I announced. "We're almost there."

I slowed down, more to catch my breath than out of caution. We were only a few yards from the opening when a black shape appeared, moving out from within. I put on the brakes and got down on one knee as the others joined me to watch a Retro fighter drone float out from within. It moved slowly, only a few feet off of the ground. The three of us crouched close to the outer wall of the dome in the hopes that whoever was controlling this killer drone wouldn't spot us. The musical sound of its engine grew louder as the entire length of its stingray-shaped fuselage was revealed. The craft drifted forward slowly until it completely cleared the door frame. Once it was in the open, the fighter instantly picked up speed and launched skyward to enter the dogfight.

"This place is like a freaking clown-car," Kent said, stunned.

"They must be assembling the drones inside," I said.

"How is that possible?" Tori asked skeptically. "We've watched planes come out of there for days but I haven't seen a single shipment of parts going in."

"So you think they're just magically appearing in there?"

"I don't know what to think," Tori said with frustration. "But I'm dying to find out."

I could have kissed her. She wanted to see what was in there as much as I did.

"You okay, Kent?" I asked.

He hesitated a second, giving the question some real thought. He then nodded and said, "Yeah. Yeah I am. I'm tired of wondering who these guys are."

That was all I needed to hear. I jumped up and took off running the last few yards to the doorway. I stopped when I reached the outer edge of the frame and looked back at Tori and Kent.

"Keep going, we're with you," Tori said with confidence.

I felt my gut twist. This was it. From the moment SYLO had invaded Pemberwick Island, we had wondered what the forces were that had turned our lives inside out. We were finally going to find out. The idea suddenly terrified me, though not enough to stop me from pushing on.

I took a cautious peek around the corner in case there were any Retro soldiers, or Retro drones, on their way out. I didn't see a single soul, so with a quick nod to the others I rounded the corner and entered the dome.

I had no real expectations as to what we would find in there. Part of me thought it would be like the giant hangar at Area 51 with several Retro drones waiting to be activated. Or maybe there would be some kind of high-tech assembly line that was spitting out the fighter planes. I wouldn't have been surprised to see teams of Retro soldiers hunkering down in the seemingly indestructible dome, waiting for the attack to pass, or harried Air Force officers in front of a massive map, plotting the eradication of the rest of the world's population.

Seeing any of those things would have made sense.

What we actually saw made no sense at all.

The cavernous space was empty. No soldiers, no parts, no planes, no clue at all as to why SYLO would want to throw its might into destroying it. The floor was so clean you could eat off it. The internal framework of the super structure, with its heavy-duty steel girders, rose high into the air, meeting at the peak, which had to be at least forty stories overhead.

Halfway around the dome, one on either side, were two rounded, egg-shaped structures that looked to be built into the outer walls. They were iron pods of some sort with open hatches that showed their walls to be well over a foot thick. The interior of each pod looked to be the size of a small room. The word EMERGENCY was stenciled in bold red letters on each door.

Other than these two odd, heavily reinforced little emergency rooms, there was nothing in the colossal space but air. The dome was no more than an enclosed void . . .

. . . with one notable feature, and it was a big one.

"You're kidding, right?" Kent said.

It was a movie screen.

At least it looked like a movie screen. It was gigantic, like the kind you'd see in an old-time drive-in movie. It reached from side-to-side of the cavernous dome and rose at least thirty feet into the air. The entire "screen" was encased in a massive, solid frame that looked like it could have been manufactured a century ago. It was three feet wide all the way around and looked to be made out of cast iron and painted light green. I guess you could call it old-school industrial looking. There was nothing about it that looked even close to something that was built by the same people who had the advanced technology to create the predator drones that fired incinerating lasers.

"It doesn't look like a gate to hell," Tori said, stunned. "Or to anywhere else."

The only sign that this monstrosity was anything other than a simple screen was the surface itself. It was arctic white, but it gave off a soft glow that made me think it was somehow energized.

"It's like, I can't focus on it," I said.

"Maybe it's a giant computer monitor," Tori said. "I mean, these guys are pretty high-tech, right?"

I walked slowly to the left, with the idea of looking behind the screen to see if it might be hiding something on the opposite side of the dome. Our footsteps echoed through the silent cavern. The only other sound came from the ongoing battle that raged outside. Every so often another explosion would rock the dome, but its foundation was solid enough that there was barely any shaking.

"Are we crazy for being in here?" Kent asked. "SYLO is trying to blast this thing into oblivion."

I ignored him. I was too curious about the screen.

We reached the far left side, where we could see that the frame was about four feet thick. It was definitely a massive piece of industrial hardware. Rounding the structure we could see the back surface of the screen. It was a plain jet-black wall with no glow.

"Whatever this thing does, it's all about the front side," Tori said. "Maybe they control the fighter planes from in here and—"

"Wait," I said. "There's a plane coming. I hear music."

We hid behind the screen, while peering around the edge to

the open door of the dome. I expected to see a black drone floating in from outside at any second.

Four more Navy jets screamed past in the distant sky, being chased by a half dozen Retro fighters.

"This battle's not going to last much longer," I said. "There are too many Retro planes."

"Yeah," Tori said, numb. "And here comes another one."

The nose of a Retro drone appeared . . . not at the door of the dome, but out of the screen right next to us.

"Whoa," Kent exclaimed. He backed quickly away until he hit the far wall of the dome.

We crowded together and watched in awe as a Retro fighter, complete with its musical engine humming, floated out of the glowing screen.

"That's . . . that's not possible," Kent muttered, numbly.

From where we stood we could see both sides of the screen. The plane was definitely not coming through from the back side. It was appearing out of the screen itself.

"It's being created," Tori said with a gasp. "That's how they're making so many planes. They don't need parts. Or workers. This screen, or whatever it is, is creating them."

"You mean like a design program that actually spits out something real?" Kent asked.

"I don't know *what* I mean," Tori shot back. "Except whatever this thing is, it's giving birth."

The plane was nearly out, but the screen wasn't finished.

Something else came out of the screen that made Tori's theory fall apart.

It was a Retro soldier.

"No!" Kent exclaimed, too loud.

The soldier stopped abruptly and shot a look our way. As soon as he registered three prisoners dressed in orange, he tensed up and raised his black baton.

"Scatter!" I screamed.

The others moved instantly. The only way we could avoid getting shot by his baton-weapon was if we became three different moving targets.

Kent ducked behind the screen; I ran toward the floating plane to use it as a shield and Tori went straight for the door.

The soldier fired wildly, missing all of us. The burst of energy from his weapon hit the inner wall of the dome with a sharp crackle of power and dissipated quickly.

Both Tori and I dodged and weaved, trying to be difficult targets. My idea was to stay near the plane, thinking the soldier wouldn't risk damaging it. I hoped that Tori would make it out of the dome entirely. Kent, on the other hand, had disappeared behind the screen. He may have been protected from being shot right away, but if Tori and I went down he'd be trapped back there.

"Come on!" I shouted to the soldier. "You know you want to blow me away."

I was trying to taunt him into coming after me and forgetting about Tori.

The guy looked indecisive. He waved the wand back and forth between the two of us, unsure of which he should target. That's exactly what I wanted in order to buy Tori enough time to get out.

"Can't get me, can you?" I shouted. "You look scared. Why

don't you put that down and come after me? I'm a lousy primate. You're a trained soldier. But you're scared because you know you can't take me."

I was throwing out everything I could think of to keep his attention on me.

The guy fired and I dove to the ground, rolled, and bounced back up. A quick glance showed that Tori was nearly at the door. She would get out and I hoped she wouldn't stop until she had left the camp.

I found myself directly between the floating aircraft and the soldier.

"What's the matter?" I taunted. "Afraid you might get busted for missing me and hitting one of your drones? Drop the weapon and fight fair."

The guy fired. He didn't care about the drone, or fighting fair.

I hit the deck again. The charge missed me and pinged off the wing of the aircraft. The jolt was like a wake-up call to whoever was controlling it. The musical engine powered up and before I could get back to my feet, the craft blasted out of the dome at full speed.

I was left on the floor, twenty feet away from the soldier, with nothing to hide behind and nothing to stop him from spraying his weapon in my direction until he hit me.

The soldier knew it too. He was in no hurry. With a confident laugh he slowly raised the baton in my direction. All I could do was wait until he was about to fire and then dodge to try and make an impossible target. But that wouldn't save me for long. He would eventually connect and I'd be done.

"What is this thing?" I called to him. I wanted to buy as much time as possible. "How did the plane come out of there?"

The soldier wasn't about to start a conversation. He raised the baton and took aim.

I waited until the last possible second and then . . .

Kent tackled the guy from the side.

The soldier never saw him coming. The force knocked the weapon out of his hand but rather than go for it, he fought back against Kent. Kent was bigger but the soldier was, well, a soldier. He was a trained fighter. Once the surprise was gone, Kent wouldn't have much hope of beating him.

Unless I got to the weapon.

The two of them were locked in a vicious wrestling match. Kent tried desperately to pin the guy down but the soldier was too strong. He got to his feet, lifting Kent up on his back like a pro-wrestler, and threw him to the deck. Violently. Kent hit with a sickening thud.

The soldier turned back to retrieve his weapon and saw me going for it. He broke into a run, but didn't get far because Kent wasn't done. He grabbed the guy's legs, trying to tackle him. The guy kicked to get away but Kent was tenacious. He got his own feet back under himself and yanked the soldier back to keep him away from the baton.

That gave me time to sweep the baton up off of the floor.

"Let him go!" I screamed to Kent but I don't think either of them heard.

The soldier turned on Kent and threw a punch. Kent let go of him and ducked. It was a good thing because the roundhouse was powerful. If it had connected, Kent would have been knocked cold. He dodged the punch and charged the solder again, nailing him with his shoulder and wrapping his arms around him.

"Shoot!" Kent yelled.

I couldn't. I would stand just as much chance of hitting Kent as the soldier.

"Back off!" I screamed at Kent. "Let him go!"

Kent must have thought I was yelling at the soldier but all I wanted was for Kent to get away from the guy so I could get a clear shot.

With an adrenaline-fueled cry, the soldier shot both of his arms upward, breaking Kent's grip. He then charged at him like a bull going for a red cape. Kent ducked to get out of the way, but wasn't fast enough. The soldier nailed him hard in the chest and wrapped him up like a charging linebacker. He kept his legs pumping, driving Kent backward . . .

. . . directly for the glowing screen.

Kent was off balance and couldn't get his feet under him. I braced myself, ready for the collision when Kent hit the flat surface.

The soldier kept driving.

I winced.

The two hit the screen . . .

. . . and disappeared.

There was no crash. No collision. No broken bones.

One moment the two of them were there, and the next second they had been swallowed up by the glowing screen.

"What was that?" Tori cried as she ran up to me.

"I . . . I don't know," I said, stunned. I then focused on her and said, "You were supposed to get out of here."

She didn't reply. All she could do was stare at the blank screen, dumbfounded.

"They're dead," she said, stunned.

I looked to the screen, my mind racing.

"I don't think so. The soldier came out of there. So did the plane and probably all the other planes we've ever seen. That's not a computer screen—or an incubator or a magic box that makes planes and people."

"Then what is it?" Tori asked.

"I think it's a doorway."

"But there's nothing behind it," she argued.

"Not here there isn't," I said. "I think that doorway leads to someplace else."

"You mean like . . . hell?"

"Maybe. But those drones didn't just appear out of thin air. They came from somewhere. And that soldier stepped out like there was nothing to it. I think there's something through there and that's what this dome is all about. SYLO doesn't care about blowing up this metal can, they're trying to get to that thing."

We stood there, breathing hard, staring at the glowing, white wall.

"It's over," Tori said.

"What is?"

"The attack. Listen. No more explosions. No more screaming fighters. SYLO's given up."

"That means the Retro soldiers will start crawling out of their holes," I said.

Tori gave a quick look to the door of the dome, then back to the glowing white screen.

"This is it, Tucker. The answers are in there. Kent's already made it."

"He saved my life, again," I said.

"He did. You owe him. You want the truth? We'll find it through there."

I could already hear the sounds of activity outside of the dome. The soldiers were on their way back.

"Are you sure?" I asked.

"It's the most sure I've been about anything since we left home," she replied.

My heart was racing. Was Tori right? Were we about to find the answers we had been so desperately searching for? Or would we be vaporized?

I handed Tori the black baton.

"Take this," I said.

"Don't get all macho-protective. I can handle myself."

"I know. That's why I want you to have it. You're a way better shot than me."

Tori gave me a small smile and took the baton.

"I meant what I said before, Tucker," she said.

"What did you say?"

"I love you."

I couldn't help but chuckle. "I love you too."

"Good," she said with finality. "We agree. Let's stop being victims and start fighting back."

I took her hand.

Tori squeezed mine and gave me a wink.

We turned to face the screen.

Together we ran to the blank wall . . . and jumped into the light.

TWELVE

When we stepped through the frame the first thing that hit me was the smell. It was a nasty, chemical odor that burned my nose and made my eyes water.

The second thing that hit me was another Retro drone.

Actually, I did the hitting because it was floating directly in front of us when we jumped through the frame and I ran into its nose, stomach first. The impact knocked the wind out of me and forced me to let go of Tori's hand. I hit the ground, gasping for breath while looking around to try to understand what had just happened.

The Retro fighter drifted forward, the underside of its fuselage not two feet over my head. If the drone knew that it had been hit by someone coming through the portal, it didn't show it. The craft continued moving ahead and into the large frame, disappearing into the white light that now shone from the backside. Behind us.

I was left on my stomach, my heart racing and my lungs desperate for air. I caught movement to my right and saw the Retro soldier kneeling over Kent. Kent was flat on his back and the soldier had his hands wrapped around his throat. These were the last moments of a battle that Kent had lost. I rolled over and struggled to get to my feet, fighting for breath, to try and help my friend.

I made it as far as getting to my hands and knees when the soldier suddenly went stiff. His back arched and he fell away from Kent.

Turned out I had made the right choice by giving the baton weapon to Tori. She was only a few feet from me on one knee with the black weapon balanced against her forearm for stability. One shot and the Retro was done.

I managed to crawl to Kent, fearing it was too late. When I saw that his eyes were open but staring at nothing, my heart sank.

"Kent?" I said, still gasping for breath. "Talk to me."

I leaned into him, desperately searching for a sign that he was still alive. When I got right over his face and looked into his eyes, he blinked.

He was breathing and suddenly I could too.

His eyes darted around, confused, searching for something to focus on. He finally looked right into my eyes, recognized me, and relaxed.

"You still with us?" I asked.

"Barely," he said with a raspy voice. "Did you have to cut it that close?"

Tori ran over and knelt down next to us.

"We gotta move," she announced with urgency. "Now."

We helped Kent sit up.

"Are we in hell?" he asked.

Tori gestured to the fallen soldier and said, "Get him. Bring him over there."

While she helped Kent to his feet, I went to the soldier, who was either out cold or dead. Either way he wasn't going to be a problem . . . until somebody spotted him. Or us. I grabbed his legs and dragged him to one side of the frame where a bunch of crates were stacked up. I pulled him between the pile of boxes and the wall, hoping he would be hidden from curious eyes. Kent and Tori soon joined me.

"He's alive," I announced as I checked the Retro's pulse. "How did you know the shot would only stun him?"

"I didn't," Tori said absently.

Her mind was already past the soldier. She was too busy taking in our new surroundings. Kent was too. I turned my attention from our enemy and got my first real look at where we had landed.

"Whoa wait, we're still in the dome," Kent said with amazement. "I think."

It looked as though we had stepped through one side of the frame and out the other, with one major difference: The dome was no longer empty. The place had suddenly come alive, like a massive, busy beehive. A long line of hovering Retro drones started just inside the enormous open doorway and stretched outside to who knew where. The killing machines floated a few feet off the ground, one behind the other, patiently waiting their turn to move into the dome and drift through the portal. The music from their engines joined together to create a strangely hypnotic soundtrack, which only added to the surreal scene we were witnessing.

"No we're not," Tori said with confidence. "This isn't the same dome."

"It's like a mirror image of what we left," I added.

Stacked against the walls were thousands of containers of every shape and size. Some were about the size of a basketball, others looked big enough to hold a car. They were all made of a plastic-like light green material. Each had a unique raised black bar code on one side that must have been used to identify the contents. There were no recognizable words, English or otherwise. Just the bar codes.

"Look," Kent said, pointing up.

Above us were several round platforms stacked with more crates. Nothing supported them or tethered them in place. They were floating freely. The platforms must have been using the same technology that allowed the Retro planes to fly. They hung at all levels, taking up much of the empty air above the screen like decorative lanterns at a tea party.

One loaded pallet floated up and over from the far side of the frame then dropped down slowly until it settled in ahead of the next Retro drone in line. It never stopped moving as it drifted forward and disappeared into the white screen.

"Jeez," Kent said, stunned.

"Supplies," Tori said. "This is where the Retro's gear is coming from."

"And weapons," I added. "That frame is some kind of transporter."

"Transporter?" Kent said, incredulous. "There's no such thing."

"There's no such thing as a lot of things we've been seeing," I said. "Add this to the list."

"I'm telling you," Kent said. "They're aliens. Nothing like this exists on Earth." His eyes got wide as he glanced around nervously. "We might not even be on Earth. What if that frame is like a 'Beam me up, Scotty' thing? We could be anywhere in the universe."

"It's an automated shipping depot," Tori said thoughtfully. "Everything the Retros have been using in this war must have come through here. It's why we never saw anything delivered to the prison camp. It all comes through here and gets spit out in that dome in the desert. It must be why they're building more domes. They want other places around the world to receive their equipment from here."

"But where is here?" I asked.

"Wherever we are," Kent said, "it stinks. Literally."

"It smells like some kind of factory," I said. "There's definitely chemicals in the air."

Tori's eyes went wide. "Maybe that's why nobody is here. This place could be toxic."

I glanced to the giant door that was the entrance for the Retro aircraft.

"Answers are out there," I said. "We gotta go see."

"Not dressed like this we don't," Kent said. "We're bound to run into more soldiers."

"As soon as we find other clothes we'll change," I said. "Until then we've gotta try to be invisible."

"Yeah, like we're going to blend in wearing orange clown suits with big numbers on the back," Kent said with a scoff.

"The only other choice we have is to go back through to the camp," Tori said. "And we'd be right where we started."

Kent frowned. His mind was racing, desperately trying to come up with a third option. He eventually sighed and shrugged.

"Fine," he said with resignation. "Just keep that shooter handy."

I started walking around the perimeter of the dome, headed for the door. Unlike the nearly empty structure in the desert, this dome was so full of stacked crates, floating pallets, and fighter planes that we were able to creep along while taking cover. At least that's what I told myself. With the kind of technology the Retros had, we could easily have been under electronic surveillance from the moment we stepped through the frame.

"They're getting ready," Tori said.

"For what?" Kent asked.

"The occupation. An army needs supplies."

It made all sorts of sense. Feit had told us that the Retros were working to reset society and change the course of mankind. Killing off billions of people just for the sake of wiping out the population like Noah's flood couldn't have been their entire plan. At some point the Retros would have to take charge or the world would collapse. The barracks being built in the desert was the first evidence of what their plans were for the next phase of this war. This shipping depot was the second. Once organized society was reduced to rubble, they would step in and rebuild.

But who were they? Did they come from all over the world to gather here in preparation for the invasion? Did that mean the western United States would be the seat of a new civilization? And where was here, exactly? These guys had advanced technology that the world at large had no idea existed. How was it possible that they could have created advanced weapons and transportation devices without major governments knowing about it? Without *anybody* knowing about it?

As we approached the large doors that led outside I had to believe that some of those answers would be on the other side. I stopped a few feet from the door. It made my knees weak to be so close to one of the Retros' killer planes. At any second it could sense us, turn, and fire.

"Is there a plan?" Kent whispered, as if the black plane might hear him.

"No," I answered honestly.

"So then what are we doing?" he asked impatiently.

"We're here to learn the truth," Tori answered. "If we can find out what's behind this whole thing, we'll bring the information back to the camp. To the survivors. From there we might be able to spread the word. Like the Las Vegas survivors did on the radio."

"And then what?" Kent said. "It's not like it'll change anything."

"It might. The prisoners outnumber the guards at that camp. Maybe the truth will give them the will to fight back."

"You mean commit suicide," Kent said with disdain.

"Whatever," Tori shot back. "But we deserve to know who's doing this and why. We're not primates. We aren't inferior beings."

Kent shook his head. "I hear you, but I'd rather be clueless and alive than smart and dead."

"So go back," I said coldly.

He glared at me, and for a second I saw the old, arrogant Kent who bristled when challenged.

"Keep moving," he said.

I continued walking until I reached the edge of the colossal doorway. There was no doubt in my mind that we were on the verge of learning the secrets of the Retros. I glanced back to Tori and gave her a smile.

She nodded.

"Just go," Kent commanded impatiently.

I rounded the corner . . .

. . . and stepped into a nightmare.

The dome was on the edge of a vast gray city full of cube-shaped buildings of all sizes that stretched out for as far as I could see. A single avenue led straight up to the dome and it was clogged with traffic. Not car traffic, black fighter-drone traffic. There had to be a hundred planes in line, waiting for their turn to glide through the portal and wreak havoc on the other side.

"We're okay," Tori announced.

"Okay?" Kent exclaimed. "How is this okay?"

She pointed to a group of orange-clad workers who were sweeping sidewalks and washing street-level windows.

"They brought prisoners through to work here too," she added. "We won't stick out."

The prisoners were being watched over by a Retro soldier who leaned against a building, bored.

"Hide the weapon," I commanded Tori.

She quickly slid the dark baton up her sleeve. It was only around eighteen inches long and fit easily, with one end resting in the palm of her hand.

I walked toward the group of workers. The others followed without question.

A platform stacked with tools hovered several yards away from the prisoners. Before the soldier could turn around, I grabbed a push broom and a shovel then hurried away and ducked down a side street. Once out of earshot I handed the broom to Kent.

"If we get stopped we'll just say we were ordered to clean up," I said.

We walked along the narrow street until we came to another wide avenue that didn't look much different from the last. The buildings had no character. They ranged from three to ten stories high, all with identical rectangular windows. The streets and sidewalks were paved with a light sand-colored material, probably to hide the fact that actual sand collected in the gutters.

The streets were busy with people, all hurrying along as if they had somewhere important to be. There were Retro soldiers wearing the black-and-gray camouflage uniforms, which actually gave the illusion that they blended into the surroundings. There were also more groups of orange-clad prisoners who were constantly sweeping up the sand. It seemed like a never-ending task.

Most of the hurrying people were dressed in civilian clothes. Both men and women wore black pants but with different brightly colored shirts. There were no patches or markings of any kind, but the clothing definitely looked similar enough to seem like uniforms. It could be that the color you wore indicated a group you were in.

Or a job you performed. Or a rank that you held. Or none of the above.

Though it wasn't raining, many people held open silver umbrellas.

"These people sure are neat," Kent said. "They've all got the same haircut."

The men all had their hair cut short while the women all wore their hair the exact same length, which was barely over their ears. It was in marked contrast to all the prisoners, who looked shaggy and unkempt. Most of the prisoner men had beard stubble. Compared to the clean-cut locals, the prisoners really did look primitive.

"They must all go to the same barber," Kent said.

"It's military," I said. "They may not all be in uniform, but they're all part of the same operation."

"Are those street signs?" Tori asked.

The corners of each building, just above eye-level, had a raised black symbol that looked like the bar codes we had seen on the crates in the dome.

"This isn't a normal city," Kent declared. "I swear we're not on Earth."

"The chemical smell is getting to me," Tori said. "It's worse than inside. Look at the sky."

We all gazed upward to see a gray sky full of brightly colored clouds that moved across in rainbow-like waves. There were multiple layers of brilliant reds, greens, and yellows that lazily drifted by, blotting out a hazy-brown sun. It was almost pretty. Almost. This wasn't some gorgeous, natural phenomenon. It was thick, chemical pollution.

"Ahh!" Kent screamed and grabbed his hand. "I just got burned."

"By what?" Tori asked. "Oww!"

She grabbed at her neck.

"It's raining," Kent complained. "Acid."

We ran for the protection of a building to get away from the microburst that had opened over our heads. The mini-squall moved down the street, dropping a light mist that sizzled and spit where it hit the ground.

"Now we know what the umbrellas are for," Kent said. "That hurt."

Another mini-squall sprinkled tainted rain on a group of people on the far side of the street. They instantly raised their silver umbrellas to protect themselves.

"You guys okay?" I asked them both.

"Yeah, it didn't break the skin," Tori replied. "What a nightmare."

We rounded a corner and were faced with a building that looked unlike any of the others. It was shaped like a half-dome and took up an entire block. It stood only a few stories high and there was one large door that looked to be made of iron that was shut tight. In front were two armed Retro guards.

"Guess that's where they keep the good stuff," Kent said.

Directly across the street from the low dome was a huge building that towered over everything else. It was set back from the street with a large cement-paved courtyard in front. The front doors blew open and a crowd of people flooded out. Like the people on the street, they wore the dark-pants-and-bright-shirt combo. In this case, their shirts were all electric blue. Some raised silver umbrellas, others glanced to the sky for fear of getting dripped on and burned. The one thing that nobody did was talk. At least not to each other. Many had their eyes glued on handheld devices that were probably smart phones. It was a miracle there wasn't a major pileup of these human drones bumping into one another.

"Looks like a meeting of the blue-club just got out," Kent said.

"It's eerie," Tori said.

"What is?" Kent asked. "Besides everything."

"All those people and nobody is talking to anyone else. It's like they're all operating in their own little world even though they're part of a crowd."

"I want to see what they've got going on in there," I said and headed across the street.

Kent and Tori followed, both glancing to the sky for fear of getting burned again.

There was a small group of blue-shirt civilians standing in the courtyard, all staring at handheld devices. One guy spotted us, nudged his friend, and dropped a plastic cup onto the ground.

I ignored him and moved past.

"Hey!" the guy yelled.

"I guess they speak after all," Kent whispered.

I knew he was talking to me so I stopped. The last thing we needed was to cause a scene and draw attention.

"Pick that up," the guy ordered.

I wanted to swing the shovel at him, but I grit my teeth, took a few steps back and picked up the cup.

"That's a good boy," the guy said, taunting. "Get used to it. It's your turn to clean up after us."

I looked the guy in the eye and saw something I didn't expect. At first I thought he was a typical bully who was showing off for his friends. That's what bullies did for laughs and to prove their superiority. That's not what I got from this guy. He wasn't laughing. His buddies weren't either. They all glared at me with contempt. Though I was the one being abused and had every right to be angry, it felt as though these guys truly hated me. This wasn't some dumb prank, it was punishment.

"Say thank you," the guy said through gritted teeth.

I didn't get it. Why was I supposed to thank him after I picked up his cup?

"Thank you," I muttered. It wasn't worth getting into a fight over and drawing the attention of Retro soldiers.

The guy held up a threatening finger and said, "You're lucky to still be here. Remember that."

With that, the group moved on.

I wanted to run after them and ask what he meant, but Tori grabbed my arm and pulled me toward the building.

"Let it go," she ordered.

"What was that about?" I asked, more confused than angry.

"Yeah," Kent said. "I'm not feeling all that lucky to be here."

"Did you see him?" I asked. "He wanted to take my head off."

"I saw it," Tori said. "I don't get it either."

We continued on toward the building and came face-to-face with a single Retro soldier who stood blocking our way. It was a woman who looked to be my mom's age, wearing fatigues and a black beret.

"Hold it right there," she commanded.

We stopped and immediately looked to the ground to show subservience. After all, we were lowly primates.

"What's your number?" she asked.

For a second I didn't know what she was talking about.

"He's Zero Three One One," Tori said for me.

I saw the outline of the baton weapon up Tori's sleeve. She was ready to bring it out the second things went south.

The Retro soldier frowned. Something was wrong. It seemed as though she knew we weren't supposed to be there, but how could she? She raised her handheld device and quickly input something.

Tori grabbed my arm and pulled me away from the curious woman.

"Sorry, ma'am," Tori said. "We've got orders to report inside and we're very late."

"No, wait!" she called out.

We didn't.

I expected the soldier to pull out a baton and start firing at us. Or sound an alarm. I stole a quick look back to see she was watching us, but more with curiosity and confusion than with disdain. For some reason she was having trouble processing our existence.

"Are you crazy?" Kent whispered urgently to Tori.

"Crazier to stay there," Tori said back. "I'm not gonna just sit still and let them grab us."

Kent glanced back and said, "She's not coming after us."

"Just keep moving," Tori commanded.

We picked up the pace, and seconds later we entered through the swinging doors of the large building. Once safely inside, we stopped in what was a huge atrium-like lobby.

"Did you know her?" Tori asked me.

"No. How would I know her?"

"She sure seemed to know you," Kent said. "I'll bet she's texting Bova right now. Or Feit."

"All the more reason to keep moving," I said and walked on, moving deeper into the building.

"Pretend like you're sweeping," I said to Kent.

He dropped the broom to the floor and gave it a few half-hearted pushes.

The place was bustling with people moving quickly as if late for appointments. There were a few soldiers in uniform scattered through the crowd, but mostly everyone wore the dark-pants-colorful-shirt combo. There were both men and women, and all sorts of ethnic groups represented as well. What I didn't see were any kids or elderly folks. It was an evenly mixed, racially diverse group. The only thing they had in common, besides their outfits, was their total disdain for us. People blew by us like we were air. A few threw angry glares at us, but there was no more contact than that.

As with the group of people outside, none of them spoke to one another. There was no socializing. No chatter. No laughter. These people were all business.

A long, wide corridor stretched out from the far end of the lobby. A group of people all wearing red shirts hurried through as if they had just been released from a meeting. Nobody spoke.

Nobody laughed. Nobody communicated in any way other than to look at their handheld devices.

They all seemed as emotionless and drone-like as their black fighter planes.

"I want to see what's going on back there," I said and made my way through the busy lobby.

To either side of the corridor were large rooms that appeared to be lecture halls. Each room was filled with people, all wearing the same colored shirt, all facing someone behind a lectern giving a speech. The rooms were open so it was easy to hear what each speaker was saying.

The speaker in the first room was a gray-haired guy who could have been a college professor. He wore the black-and-gray camouflage fatigues of the Retros. Floating in space behind him was a 3-D hologram of some sort of device with pipes and gauges.

". . . continuing the supply of safe, clean drinking water is crucial. You will each be assigned to a critical filtration plant where your principal duty will be to keep the water flowing. If there are native survivors you can press into service to take advantage of their expertise, all the better, but our goal here will be to educate you on how to maintain and repair these systems without the need for native support."

As he turned to refer to his floating diagram I motioned for the others to follow me to the next speech. We passed a wall that separated the two groups to find another lecture hall packed with people who all wore the same forest-green-colored shirts. On the stage was a woman in fatigues who was backed by the 3-D image of what looked like a massive herd of cows.

". . . this feedlot in Greely, Colorado, was left intact. We have sent in operatives to ensure the continued health of the herd, but the effort to feed the colonies will be a great one that will require massive manpower. There are feedlots similar to this one all over the globe. They will be the principal source of our meat. Our protein. Refer to your tablets to learn of your assignments and the farms where you will be assigned."

We moved on to the next lecture to find the audience was filled with uniformed Retro soldiers. My heart started to beat faster. Tori clutched my hand.

Giving this lecture was a heavyset guy with a buzz cut and golden eagles on his shoulders.

". . . these are not your friends. They are not your brothers. When you look at the natives, there is only one thing that you should be thinking: You reap what you sow. Feel no pity for them. They have brought this on themselves. They are culpable and now they have paid the price. Do not form emotional bonds or friendships in any way, shape, or form. Do not deviate from the mission. Treating the natives like humans is a treasonable offense. Let me repeat that: a treasonable offense. Are there any questions?"

Nobody raised a hand.

"I'm guessing we're the natives they're talking about," Kent whispered.

"They're being brainwashed to hate us," Tori added softly.

We continued down the long corridor of lecture halls hearing talks on topics like waste removal, housing, future dome construction, electrical power, and the proper use and administration of the Ruby to the natives. Us.

The three of us made it to the far end of the corridor after hearing an earful. A door led out of the hallway and into a stairwell where we could talk freely. We stood there for a long while, trying to get our minds around what we had just witnessed.

"It's an invasion all right," Kent finally said. "They're training people to run the world. *Our* world. I'm telling you, they're aliens."

"I just can't believe that," I said.

"Really?" Kent shot back, exasperated. "Then what makes sense to you? That thousands of crazies from all over the world left their normal lives, got together to build this crappy city, and convinced the United States Air Force to wipe out most of the rest of the world's population so that they could step in and run things their way? Oh yeah, and along the way they invented freaking mad technology and figured out how to manufacture it all without anybody knowing they were up to no good until it was too late? Is that what works for you?"

I wanted to argue and offer a reasonable counter-theory, but I had nothing.

"I think maybe Kent's right," Tori said meekly.

"Damn right I am!" Kent shouted, pacing anxiously. "We were invaded by aliens. They could be robots for all we know. They sure act like it. They studied us, they know how everything works, they think we're no better than bugs, and they are about to overrun the planet. It's over, Tucker. We lost. Get used to that orange suit because you'll be spending the rest of your life in it. Or what's left of it."

"Suppose it is aliens," Tori said. "That still doesn't explain how they were able to construct this city and take over the United States Air Force."

"I don't think we're on Earth, that's how," Kent said. "That transport thing shot us to the other side of the universe and this is planet Torchyourbutt."

"No," I said bluntly. "That isn't it."

"Why not?" Kent said. "Because it's too hard to believe? I'll believe just about anything right now."

"Because there's something odd about this place," I said. "I can't put my finger on it but there's something wrong here."

"Gee, you think?" Kent said sarcastically.

"I want a better look at this city," I said and went for a flight of stairs that led up.

I took the stairs two at a time, climbing higher through multiple floors until I reached a dead end and a door that I didn't hesitate to push open. We were hit with a rush of stinking hot air as we stepped out onto the vast, flat roof of the huge building.

We were higher than any of the surrounding buildings and now we could see for miles. The city before us was an extensive, clogged mass of similarly ugly structures. The hideous sprawl went on for mile after mile. There were no parks, no ball fields, and no green spaces whatsoever. None of the buildings had any character. It was one squat, sand-colored cube after another.

Again, the chemical smell hit hard.

"That's where it's coming from," I said, pointing to my right.

Far in the distance, one end of the city was taken up by what looked to be factories. Soaring stacks belched dark, colorful smoke that joined to form massive clouds of industrial particles that hung over the city like a filthy rainbow.

"That's what we're smelling," I said. "It must be where they're building the planes."

The only other structure that stood out was the giant steel dome that loomed high, not far from us. The rest of the city was a crowded, filthy dump.

"We really did come through the gate to hell," Kent said, soberly.

"This is . . . this is wrong," Tori said, stunned. "I've never heard of any city that looks like this and rains acid."

"I don't think anybody has," I said. "This place must have been built secretly to prepare for the invasion. This is where the Retros have come to live and prepare to take over the world."

"How is that possible?" Tori asked with growing frustration. "You can't just build a secret city. Forget the government; anybody could see it on Google Earth."

"But we're not on Earth," Kent said, adamantly. "You'd have more luck checking Google Pluto! That's the only explanation. Whatever crappy planet this is they've found a way to transport themselves across the universe. And why not? Compared to this dump, Earth is a pretty sweet place to move in on."

"I don't know," Tori said, bewildered. "Maybe you're right."

"Of course I'm right!" Kent shot back.

There was still something bothering me. It wasn't just because it was hard to wrap my head around the idea that we had been transported to a strange, filthy planet in a galaxy far, far away. It was just the opposite. As alien as this place was, it also felt somehow . . . familiar.

"I still don't buy it," I said and strolled across the vast rooftop.

"There's a single yellow sun in a blue sky. It's hot, but bearable. It may be polluted but we can breathe in this atmosphere. The people not only don't look alien, they represent every ethnic group that exists and they speak English. How is it possible that another planet could be so much like Earth?"

"I told you," Kent said. "They've studied us. They probably shape-shifted themselves to look and act like us. They did their homework."

"No," I said. "We're missing something."

I gazed out at the city. It truly was a wasteland. It didn't add up that the people who built it had the knowledge to use such advanced technology, yet lived in obscene squalor.

My eyes wandered further out, beyond the edges of the city. We sat on pancake-flat land that was surrounded by arid, rocky mountains. I did a slow turn, taking in the full panorama.

That's when it clicked.

Maybe it was the heat, or the small rocky ridge that rose up close to the city. It might have been the image of the giant steel dome backed by the distant range. Or maybe it was just the constant swirl of sand that collected in every corner and parched my throat. It was probably the combination of everything.

The reality of what I suddenly understood made my head go light.

"We're not on another planet," I declared.

"Rookie!" Kent shouted in exasperation. "You're killing me. What other explanation is there?"

"I don't know," I said. "I can't explain why, or how, or what it all means, but I know exactly where we are."

"Where?" Tori asked. "Where did that portal take us?"

"It didn't take us anywhere," I said. "We're still in the Mojave Desert in the Retro camp."

My words stunned the others into momentary silence.

Kent was ready to argue but took a look around and said nothing.

Tori walked in a daze to the edge of the roof as she scanned the horizon.

A small blood-red cloud passed over, dropping a second's worth of rain that crackled when it hit the surface of the roof. Nobody paid any attention.

The three of us stood together, looking out over this filthy city and the exact same Nevada landscape that had become all too familiar.

"This is impossible," Tori finally said.

"Or maybe not," Kent said numbly.

"Seriously?" I shot back at him. "You backing off your alien theory?"

"I don't know. Maybe," he said with a nervous hitch in his voice. "I've read about stuff like this."

"Where?" I asked, incredulous. "Graphic novels?"

"Well, yeah."

"That's science fiction, Kent," I said, scoffing. "Fiction. That means not real."

"I know, but a lot of that stuff is based on real theories. Even Einstein thought this might be possible."

"What are you talking about?" I demanded.

"We could be in another dimension," he said flatly.

We stood staring at him, too numb to respond. I wanted to laugh, but there was nothing funny about it.

"You can't be serious," Tori finally said.

"I'm dead serious," Kent said, his excitement growing. "There are these theories that different realities can exist in the same physical space. I'm not talking about stories, this is from real scientists. Maybe that portal thing sent us from one dimension into another. Who knows? There could be others too. Hopefully one of 'em is good because this place is total crap and ours is sinking fast."

I wanted to tell Kent that he was being idiotic, but I held back because I couldn't come up with a better explanation. Inter-dimensional travel was as good a theory as any.

Tori said, "So you think there's a whole different reality that exists right alongside ours in some alternate spooky dimension and the people somehow figured out how to break through the barrier so they could invade us? Is that it?"

Kent kicked at the roof nervously. "Well when you put it like that it sounds stupid."

"Then put it some way that *isn't* stupid," Tori said, scolding.

"Zero Three One One?"

We all spun quickly to see the female Retro soldier who had stopped us on the street outside of the building. This time she wasn't alone. With her was another Retro soldier . . . who had a weapon.

"What exactly are you doing up here?" she asked.

I did my best to act as if nothing was wrong. I raised the shovel and said, "Cleaning up. Our unit leader sent us here."

"Your unit leader is building a barracks in the forward base camp, Tucker," she said.

So much for acting as if nothing was wrong.

"Wait, what? You know my name?"

She held up her communication device. On the screen was my picture.

"This is you, isn't it?" She asked. "And you're Tori Sleeper and Kent Berringer?"

"I thought you didn't keep records of prisoners?" Tori asked.

"Just the ones we're watching out for," she replied. "You need to come with me."

I acted without thinking and threw the shovel at the armed soldier. He was so stunned that his first reaction was to catch it . . . and drop his weapon. I lunged at the guy and tackled him before he could get his wits back.

Tori didn't hesitate either. I let go of the soldier and rolled away from him because I knew exactly what she would do.

She dropped the baton out of her sleeve and shot him.

The soldier let out a gasp, went stiff, and lay still—out cold.

The woman didn't move. She stood there, coolly appraising us.

"You're making a mistake," she said casually, as if fights like this happened to her every day.

"Give me that thing," I said, holding my hand out.

She shrugged and handed me her electronic device.

After giving it a quick look, I dropped it onto the roof and raised my foot to smash it.

"No don't!" she cried, finally showing some emotion.

I brought my foot down and slammed my heel into the device, cracking the screen.

"There's nowhere to hide, Tucker," she said with a sigh.

"We'll see," I replied and took off running.

Kent and Tori were right behind me.

We sprinted back to the door we had come up through. I had no plan in mind except to climb down and somehow disappear into this twisted city. We were twenty yards away from the door . . .

. . . when it blew open and a Retro soldier stepped out.

The three of us put on the brakes and skidded to a stop. We all looked around, desperate for another escape route.

"Door!" Kent announced and took off running across the roof toward the far side.

I was breathing hard and coughing as I sucked in polluted air that burned my lungs.

"Damn!" Tori screamed and wiped at her hair as she was hit with a spit of burning rain.

Whatever this place—this dimension—was, it was a nightmare.

Two more Retro soldiers appeared through the door we were running toward. The roof had suddenly become a very crowded place. We changed direction again, only to see three more soldiers had appeared. They were spread out across the roof, surrounding us and closing in like a tightening noose.

Running was useless. We were trapped. We stopped in the dead center of the roof and stood with our backs to each other, helpless as the circle of Retro soldiers grew closer.

Tori lifted her weapon but I put my hand on hers to stop her.

"Don't," I said. "You won't hit enough of them before they start shooting back."

She fought me and kept holding the weapon up, ready to fire.

Each of the Retro soldiers had a baton trained on us. It was seven to one. Six actually. The soldier that Tori shot was unconscious. One of the larger soldiers had him slung over his shoulder.

Tori realized the futility and reluctantly lowered the weapon.

Kent held his broom threateningly, as if that would do any good.

"Back off," he warned. "I'm serious."

He said it as though he didn't realize how stupid he looked. At least the Retros didn't laugh at him.

The woman soldier who had first confronted me raised her hand as a signal and the others stopped advancing.

"Throw down the weapon, Tori," the woman said calmly.

Tori didn't budge.

"Do what she says, Tori," I said.

"No!" Kent yelled. "I am not going back to that camp."

"We're not sending you back," the woman said.

"So then what are you going to do?" I asked.

The woman stood staring at us as though trying to decide the best way to answer. After an uncomfortable few seconds, she slowly raised her right hand . . . and put it over her heart.

Tori gasped.

One by one, the other Retros followed her lead and put their hands over their hearts.

"We've been trying to find a way to get you here for a few

days," the woman said. "I should have known you would have found your way here on your own."

Tori lowered the black baton as if the weight was suddenly too much for her to bear.

"I don't understand," Tori said, numbly. "You're Sounders?"

"We are," the woman replied. "I'm glad you already know about us, but I guess I shouldn't be surprised at that, either. You three have quite the reputation for being resourceful. It's an honor to meet the team that took out half of the Air Force's attack fleet."

My head was spinning.

Kent dropped the broom, letting it clatter onto the rooftop.

"How do you know who we are?" he asked.

"I told them," one of the Retro soldiers said. It was another woman. "I don't think they believed most of the stories until you showed up here," she said. "You just validated everything I've been telling them about you."

My heart started racing faster than it had when we were running. I was seeing it and I was hearing it, but I wasn't believing it. It was easier to accept that we were on another planet or that we had somehow stepped through a magical portal into a parallel universe than it was to believe the sight in front of us.

The soldier stepped forward and pulled off her beret to reveal the short blonde hair of the beautiful girl who had sacrificed her life to save mine.

Or had she?

"Oh my God," Tori said with a gasp.

"Surprise," she said with a flirty smile. "Miss me?"

Olivia Kinsey was alive and back in the game.

THIRTEEN

"**H**ow?" was all I managed to say.

Kent couldn't even get that much out. He stood there with his mouth open staring at Olivia with a stunned expression that I couldn't read. I didn't know if he was overjoyed or if his head was about to explode.

"Obviously that shot didn't kill me," Olivia said. "But don't let that take away from the fact that I took it for you, Tucker Pierce. You still owe me."

I stammered out a lame, "But—"

"Attention," an amplified voice boomed.

Everyone spun and looked up to see a dark, ominous mechanical device floating closer to us from above. It was a miniature version of a Retro attack drone with a wingspan that was maybe four feet across. The faint musical tone it emitted proved that it was powered by the same advanced engine as their larger counterparts.

"This is an unauthorized operation," the voice from the plane commanded. "Drop your weapons and step forward to be scanned and identified."

There was a frozen moment. This drone wasn't after us, it was after the Retro soldiers. The Sounders. We all stood in the middle of a wide-open rooftop, totally exposed, with nowhere to run for protection. There was only one possible choice.

Olivia lifted her baton and fired at the plane.

Yes, Olivia.

The impulse of power blasted the hovering craft and spun it away from us.

"Let's go," the woman commander ordered and ran for the door we had first come through. The Sounder carrying the unconscious soldier hurried after her while the others dropped to their knees, lifted their weapons, and shot a steady stream of impulses at the craft.

Olivia was one of them.

Tori, Kent, and I stood there, stunned. For all sorts of reasons.

"Olivia?" I said, numbly.

"Go!" she barked in a commanding voice that was both familiar and impossible. "We'll catch up."

Tori snapped out of it and pulled us both to get us going.

"We gotta move," she declared.

Kent pulled away from her and knelt down next to Olivia, who continued to fire on the hovering craft.

"You were dead," he said in a voice that was loaded with confusion and fear.

"You really want to chat about it now?" Olivia shouted.

I grabbed Kent at the exact instant another hovering craft appeared over the edge of the roof, rising up from the street below. It fired.

One of the Retro soldiers screamed as he was blasted off of his feet. The guy wasn't just stunned, he was killed instantly. These drones weren't there to take prisoners.

"Drop back," another Retro soldier commanded. "There's bound to be more."

The small squad might have been able to battle one craft, but not multiple predators. Retreat was the only smart move. That made it easier for me to get Kent moving and we all sprinted for the door. Olivia and the Retro soldiers moved backward, spraying the air with charges from their weapons as . . .

Boom! the first drone exploded into a spectacular fireball that sprayed molten bits of flaming material over the surface of the roof.

"That'll draw more attention," the second Retro soldier said.

On cue, a third craft swooped in, focused on our position, and fired.

The surface to my right exploded so violently that I felt the roof give way beneath my feet. Tori grabbed me and pulled me forward, keeping me from falling through.

"Move!" the woman commander shouted from inside the door.

The three of us ducked inside, followed right behind by Olivia and the rest of the soldiers.

We all scrambled down the stairs as the door we had just come through was blown off of its hinges. It crashed around inside of the service hallway, slamming into the fleeing soldiers.

"We can't go down there," Kent shouted above the echo of footsteps as we all charged down the stairs. "The place is full of Retros."

The Sounders were way ahead of him. When we reached the next floor, rather than continuing down the stairs, the commander led us through a door that opened onto a long, brightly lit corridor.

Every last Sounder suddenly slowed to a calm walk as if they were casually passing through. It was almost comical how quickly they went from fleeing in terror to taking full control of their emotions. Or at least of their appearance.

The corridor was lined with sealed windows behind which people sat wearing white shirts and dark pants. They were at high-tech workstations with flat panels on the desks that their fingers slid across expertly to manipulate 3-D images that hovered over each screen. Some were working on complex calculations. Others seemed to be manipulating detailed designs of machinery. I had no idea what any of it was but I was no longer amazed or surprised by the advanced technology the Retros possessed.

"Bring him directly to the medical unit," the commander ordered authoritatively.

The soldier who was carrying his unconscious pal moved ahead of us quickly. The other Retro soldiers were behind us, including Olivia. They held their baton weapons across their chests and walked shoulder to shoulder, as if escorting their prisoners.

Us.

"Bring these natives to Security Six," she commanded. "Wait for me there."

She was putting on a show for the benefit of the eggheads who were working behind the glass. She needn't have bothered. They were all so focused on whatever they were working on that they didn't notice the group of soldiers and prisoners passing by outside.

We all walked quickly—but without panic—to the far end of the long corridor, out the door on the far side, and then through another service stairwell, where the soldier carrying the injured soldier was waiting for us. Once through, the boss-woman immediately shed the casual act and started pulling off her clothes.

"Wake him up, now," she ordered. "Secure the door."

One of the soldiers pulled out a small hand-tool and jammed it into the lock. I had to believe he had just destroyed the mechanism, making it impossible for anybody to follow us. Another soldier dug into his pocket and took out a small glass vial, cracked it open, and jabbed one end into the arm of the unconscious soldier like an injection, right through his sleeve.

Everyone else pulled off the small backpacks they had been wearing and began tearing off their camouflage uniforms.

"That's why I'm still here," Olivia said, pointing to the vial of medicine.

"That brings people back from the dead?" I asked.

"No, but it can bring them back from the brink." She slammed her backpack into my stomach. "Here. We brought you clothes."

I took the bag numbly and flipped it open to find a pair of black pants and a green shirt.

"You too," another soldier said to Tori and gave her a pack.

A third soldier did the same for Kent.

The three of us were too stunned and confused to move.

"Or you could keep wearing those snappy orange outfits," Olivia said.

That was all we needed to hear. The three of us instantly joined in and stripped off our clothes. There was no time for modesty as each of the soldiers peeled off their camouflage uniform and put on black pants and a green shirt.

"Hurry please," the commander said.

"I hope I guessed right on the sizes," Olivia said.

"You arranged all of this?" Tori asked, incredulous.

"I knew you guys would end up here sooner or later."

"Olivia, what the hell—" I said.

"Shhh," she replied. "Not until we're somewhere safe."

I dressed quickly. There were even black leather shoes and dark socks for all of us.

Kent moved as if in a daze. He couldn't take his eyes off of Olivia, as if not believing she was actually there.

For the record, I was having trouble believing it too.

There was absolutely nothing that made sense about her presence. We watched her die after she jumped in front of me to take the charge that was fired by a Retro soldier. Though I can't say which was more surprising: the fact that she was still alive or that she was a Retro soldier.

At least one mystery was finally solved: Captain Granger had been right. One of my friends who escaped with us from Pemberwick Island was indeed a Retro infiltrator.

I had befriended her months before and spent an incredibly fun summer showing her around the island. When SYLO invaded, we had been thrown together by circumstance and eventually made our escape. We then traveled across the United States, seeking survivors who wanted to fight back against the Retros.

The idea that she had been playing us the whole time was mind-blowing.

I heard a groan. The soldier Tori had shot was coming around. Whatever was in that glass vial really did bring him back from the brink. The other soldiers didn't waste time offering him sympathy. They were too busy tearing off his uniform and redressing him in the civilian clothes.

"Walk out casually," the commander said. "We were all here to attend a lecture on herd management. Leave the gear but slip the pulsers up your sleeves."

Pulsers.

I finally knew what those baton weapons were called.

"I don't have to remind you that we're going to have a very small window of time to get out of this building before the place is locked down," she continued. "Once outside, separate and make your way to Safe House Tango."

"Uh, what?' Tori asked.

"Stay with me," Olivia said as she finished tucking in her shirt. "It'll be just like old times."

"You were killed during those old times," Tori said.

"Yet here I am," Olivia said brightly.

The three of us could only stare at her in disbelief.

"Are you with us?" the commander asked the soldier who was being treated.

The guy stood up, took a deep breath, and said, "I'm good."

"All right then, everybody ready?" she asked.

I raised my hand to ask a question. I actually raised my hand. For a moment I felt like I was back in kindergarten, being swept along in a flurry of activity that I had no control over or understanding of.

"Yes?" the commander said patiently.

"What exactly is happening here?" I asked. "Are we your prisoners?"

The commander started to answer quickly. I'm sure she was ready to say something bold, like "Shut up and keep moving!" Instead, she caught herself and took a step back.

"You are not our prisoners," she said thoughtfully. "We may be in the Air Force but we're doing everything we can to prevent the invasion."

"Good enough for me," Kent said.

"And you're going to help us do it," the commander added.

She stood staring directly at me.

"Oh," Kent said, sober. "Didn't see that coming."

I didn't break eye contact with the woman. I wanted her to know that we wouldn't be manipulated. By anybody.

"If you want us to help you," I said. "You're going to have to trust us with a whole lot more information than we have now."

"That's a deal," she said without hesitation. "Can it wait until we're someplace safe?"

I looked to Kent and Tori.

Kent shrugged. He was too stunned to have any other comeback.

Tori gave me a reassuring nod and said, "Let's get the hell out of here."

"We'll follow you," I said to the commander.

"All right then," she said. "Stay calm. Don't hurry but keep moving."

The woman started down the stairs, followed by the soldier who had been unconscious only minutes before. We went next, closely trailed by Olivia and the rest of the Retros.

The commander moved quickly but with control down three flights of stairs until we hit the bottom floor. She stopped at the door and looked back to us.

"Remember, act like you belong and nobody will stop us."

She yanked the door open and a flood of sound rushed in. The lobby was loaded with people moving about like high school students during a class change. It was the perfect situation to blend in unnoticed, though I felt like a fat fly buzzing through a pack of hungry spiders.

Olivia stepped up behind me and put her hand on my shoulder.

"Breathe," she whispered.

Easy for her to say. She knew how to come back from the dead.

The commander walked boldly into the mass of people.

Olivia had to give me a shove to get me going. Once we were in the crowd, Olivia pushed her way to get in front of us and announced, "C'mon, we'll head out on the north side."

The tension could not have been higher, yet Olivia gave such a casual performance that I truly believed she would be able to get us through. It also made me realize how fully capable she was of coolly infiltrating Pemberwick Island, becoming our friend, and traveling across the country pretending to be someone she most definitely wasn't.

The question was, who was she really?

We moved in a loose group, following Olivia. It was a constant traffic-ballet as we moved through the crush of people . . . and soldiers. I kept telling myself to act normally, but didn't know how to do that in a place that was so completely different from anything I was used to. The harder I tried to be casual, the more awkward I felt.

Everyone else seemed to be headed somewhere important. There were no conversations and definitely no laughter. It was the same as with the people we saw outside. There was no interaction. Every so often we'd cross paths with a Retro soldier and my back would stiffen. Though we had only been to the prison camp in Nevada for a short time, I was already conditioned to fear our captors. Back there, one wrong look meant severe punishment. Or worse. I had to keep telling myself that these people didn't know I was a prisoner. A native, as they called us. They weren't going to zap me . . . unless I gave them reason to.

A few times I made eye contact with a soldier and had to force myself not to look away too quickly. I could only hope that they wouldn't recognize me. I made a point of not smiling because, well, nobody else was smiling.

We made our way across the vast lobby to a set of doors beside the main entrance. Just twenty more feet and we'd be out.

"Olivia Kinsey!" a guy called.

Olivia stopped short. Her whole body stiffened. If you didn't know her as well as I did, you might not have noticed.

The rest of us slowed down and drifted apart to find a spot to stand and wait for her. I stood beside a massive column that looked as though it helped support the roof.

Olivia turned back as a Retro soldier hurried up to her.

She instantly put on a big, dazzling smile as if running into him was the highlight of her day. Olivia was good at that.

"Hello, Alec," she said sweetly. "So good to see you."

Olivia was strangely formal with the soldier, though they were obviously friends.

I threw a quick look to Tori and Kent. They both had their eyes focused on her. If they were like me, they were also holding their breaths.

"When did you return?" the soldier asked. He too sounded formal, like Mr. Spock or something.

Alec didn't look any older than Kent. He had short dark hair and was built like a defensive end. He was handsome too, a fact I'm pretty sure wasn't lost on Kent.

"Just a few weeks ago," Olivia said brightly. "How is your training proceeding?"

The guy shrugged. "Adequately. It's nothing I haven't heard a thousand times before. I've been assigned to the first group that will land on Catalina Island."

"Congratulations," Olivia said. "That's a dangerous assignment."

I knew she was trying to act as though nothing was wrong, but her manner was strangely stiff. Was that how Retro friends acted with each other?

"Not really," Alec replied. "They won't know what hit them."

My stomach twisted. There was a SYLO ark on Catalina Island off of Los Angeles. This guy was talking about an invasion.

"What about you?" he asked. "I thought you were on Pemberwick?"

She shrugged and said, "I was. I got homesick."

Alec gave her a surprised look. It was the first time he showed any emotion. "You were homesick for this dump?"

Olivia reached up, touched his chest, and with a flirty smile said, "No. I was homesick for you!"

That was the Olivia I knew. She was a master when it came to manipulating guys.

I think the soldier blushed, which is exactly the response she was going for.

He said, "Maybe we can get together tonight and—"

Olivia backed away from him, heading toward the door. "Ooh, not possible. I haven't finished my report about Pemberwick and it's overdue. Another time?"

"Any time," he said. "But, uh, it should be soon because, well, you know."

That was ominous.

"I promise! Bye!"

Olivia spun around and practically skipped toward the door. It was yet another technique she used to attract attention, and drive guys wild.

The enchanted soldier named Alec watched with his mouth open until she reached the door. He may have been robotic, but it was hard to resist Olivia Kinsey. Compared to the other emotionless types who were moving through the building, Olivia stood out like, well, like Olivia. Playing her part to the end, she turned to give him a flirty smile and a wave. With a giggle, she headed out.

Alec waited a second more, probably hoping she might change her mind and come back.

Grateful the diversion was over, I walked straight for the door and marched outside.

Olivia was there waiting. The flirty smile was long gone.

"Keep moving," she commanded. It was back to business.

Tori and Kent were right behind me, as were the remaining soldiers. Or Sounders. As we made our way through the busy courtyard headed for the street, my hope grew that we were not only going to find out what the Sounders were all about, but we would also learn about the Retros and what was going on here. Olivia had known exactly who they were all along, but of course she didn't share it with us. How could she? She was an infiltrator. An enemy. I was torn between feeling angry at her, bewildered as to what her true intentions were, and afraid of the truth.

She led us quickly through the silent crowds until we reached the sidewalk. Without hesitation she moved across the street and turned down a narrow side street where two white vans were waiting.

In the driver's seat of the front van was the woman commander. She was the first and only one to have arrived.

"Jump in back," Olivia said to us.

We obediently piled in.

Olivia sidled into the shotgun seat next to the woman commander, who sat with both hands gripping the wheel.

"We'll move as soon as the others arrive," the commander said, matter-of-fact.

Olivia looked at her as if wanting to say something to her superior but not sure if she should. It took her a few seconds to finally make a decision.

"I'm sorry about Conner," she said with compassion. "I know what a good friend he was."

"He was with us from the beginning," the commander said. "He'll be missed."

It sounded as though she was trying to keep her emotions in check. I had to believe they were talking about the Retro soldier who was killed on the roof.

"There's nothing they can use to trace us through him," the commander added.

"I wasn't even thinking that way," Olivia said.

It was odd hearing Olivia speaking with such sincerity and respect. I was more used to her complaining. Then again, it was odd seeing her shooting down an enemy drone too.

"Here they come," the commander said.

I was hoping she meant the other Sounders, but instead there were several more small drones that swooped by overhead on their way to the building we had just escaped from. They were soon followed by dozens of armed Retro soldiers who sprinted for the building and set up in the courtyard, their eyes trained on the entrance. The drones hovered overhead, keeping a watchful eye out . . . for us.

"We got out of there just in time," Olivia said.

"Maybe," the commander said, ominously.

Thankfully, the rest of the Sounders arrived and hurried to the rear van. The commander fired up our engine, but rather than the throaty roar of a gasoline engine coming to life, the cabin was filled with the familiar musical tones that came from the Retro jet fighters.

The commander stepped on the gas, or whatever it was that they called the accelerator here, and the car rolled forward. We were under way and nearly home free when a squad of Retro soldiers appeared from around the building in front of us. Their leader, a tall dark-skinned guy with probing eyes, raised his hand for us to stop.

The other soldiers with him took up positions in front of the car, blocking our way.

Olivia calmly pulled her pulser out from her sleeve and held it close to her thigh, out of sight but ready.

The commander lowered her window as the squad leader strode up to her.

"Identification," the leader said curtly.

The commander handed him a plastic ID card that the squad leader took and passed it over his own handheld device.

"Make this quick," the commander said with authority. "My team is deploying in ten minutes."

The leader looked at his device with a scowl, then to the commander.

"Colonel Pike?" the leader said.

"Yes?" the commander, Colonel Pike, replied.

"You aren't in uniform," the leader said, suspiciously.

"As I said, my team is about to deploy," she said curtly. "And you're wasting my time."

The leader didn't flinch. "There has been Sounder activity in the Academy. They destroyed one of our security craft and tried to escape with three native prisoners. I need to see everyone's credentials."

That wasn't going to happen.

Olivia gripped her pulser tighter, though it wouldn't help us much seeing as four other armed Retro soldiers were standing directly in front of us.

"*Tried* to escape?" the Colonel said. "That means they're still inside?"

"We believe so," the leader said. "We've sealed the building."

"Then why exactly are you wasting my time by checking my team's credentials out here?" the Colonel said with disdain. "If we miss our deployment window you will need to explain that to your commander. Is that how you want to spend your evening?"

The squad leader looked shaken. His eyes shifted to us, then back to the Colonel.

"Your choice," the Colonel added.

The squad leader handed back the Colonel's ID card and waved for his men to move aside.

"They're clear!" the squad leader said.

The Colonel stepped on the accelerator and we lurched forward, barely missing one of the Retro soldiers who hadn't moved away fast enough. We quickly picked up speed and drove away from the building called the Academy, which was now under total lockdown . . . a few minutes too late.

"Idiot," the Colonel said with disdain. "I should report him."

Olivia laughed, but quickly held it back since her Commander wasn't really the joking type.

We sped along the narrow streets of the filthy city, passing hundreds of soldiers and civilians that clogged the sidewalks. There were very few vehicles. Most everyone traveled on foot.

Kent continued to stare at Olivia. Or at least, at the back of her head. I had to think he was still in shock over her resurrection. I knew the feeling.

Tori reached over and grabbed my arm. She needed the support. I did too. I wanted to trust these people but everything was happening way too fast.

"Olivia?" Kent finally said in a small voice.

She turned to look at us.

"Why aren't you dead?"

"I couldn't feel your pulse," I said. "You were past the brink."

"Apparently you don't know how to take a pulse," she said. "I was hanging from a thread, but I wasn't gone."

"I gave your body to some of the other survivors from Las Vegas," Kent said.

"And they were ambushed by a squad of Air Force personnel from the base," she explained. "Lucky for me they actually knew how to read a pulse, and shot me with the field meds."

It all seemed plausible. If Feit could come back from the dead, twice, why not Olivia?

"I was back here before morning," she added. "Good as new."

"And where exactly is here?" Tori asked.

It was the simplest, most straightforward question possible.

It meant everything.

Olivia gave a questioning look to the Colonel.

The Colonel waited several long seconds before saying, "Your call."

Olivia nodded. I felt as though she was bracing herself to deliver some very bad news. The pained look in her eyes only made it seem worse. She looked to me, then to Tori and to Kent.

"I know this will be hard to believe," she said. "But I love you guys. I truly do. I hope I'll be able to prove that to you."

"Answer the question, Olivia," Kent said, his voice cracking with emotion. "No more lies. What is this place?"

Olivia took a nervous breath and said, "That's the wrong question. I think you already know what this place is. What you really need to know is . . . *when* it is."

I felt Tori stiffen.

Kent shot me a confused look.

"What does that mean?" I asked, though I wasn't sure I wanted the answer.

"We're not aliens," Olivia said. "We're not from another place. We're you. We're from The United States of America . . . in the year two thousand three hundred and twenty-four. This is the twenty-fourth century."

FOURTEEN

Silence.

That's what Olivia's revelation was met with.

Total silence.

I can't speak for the others, but I had to believe they were having the same stunned reaction as me. I want to say that it was disbelief, but I was long past trying to find logical explanations for our new lives. It wasn't so much that I couldn't believe it; it was more about trying to wrap my mind around the possibility that what Olivia had said was true.

On the one hand it quickly answered the question as to why the Retros had such incredible technology. Three hundred years was a long time. But it didn't explain what we were seeing outside the windows of the speeding SUV. This was the future? Where were the moving sidewalks? The flying suits? The modern buildings that proved we had found a way to live in harmony with our environment? What I saw instead was filth. This was not some utopian city that proudly displayed the wondrous advances of mankind. It was a crowded slum of bleak buildings that could have been built in a faraway nation before I was born, not three hundred years into the future.

And it rained acid.

"Not exactly what you expected?" Olivia asked, reading my mind.

"On any level," Tori replied, while staring out the window with a look that was a mix between wonder and disgust.

"Does the rest of the world look like this?" I asked.

"No," Olivia replied. "This city is here because of the Bridge. The doorway between this time and the past. The rest of the world is nothing like this."

"Thank God," Tori said.

"It's way worse," Olivia added.

That brought the silence back.

We travelled for several minutes along the crowded, grimy streets. The nondescript buildings made it impossible to tell one block from the next. There was a constant swirl of dust in the air that forced the people to cover their mouths with stained bits of cloth. Some wore surgical masks to block the choking clouds of chemical dust as they hid beneath their silver umbrellas.

I couldn't imagine what "worse" might look like.

"Where are we going?" Tori asked.

"Olivia's quarters," Colonel Pike answered. "You'll be safe there until you're needed."

"Needed for what?" I asked. "You've got to give us a lot more to go on before we do anything to help you—"

The Colonel hit the brakes and the vehicle slammed to a stop. She quickly spun around to face us and said, "Olivia tells me you came all the way across the country to join a group of people who were willing to fight back against the Retros, as you call us. Is that true?"

Nobody replied.

"Answer me," she said, insistently.

"Olivia's a liar," Kent said. "Everything she said to us from the moment we met her was a lie."

Olivia slumped in her seat.

"She was doing her job," the Colonel said tersely. "Under incredible stress and impossible circumstances. You were swept up in this. She volunteered. I'd trust her with my life and I suggest you three do the same. Now I'll ask you again, do you truly want to fight back?"

"We destroyed about a thousand of your planes," I said. "Does that answer your question?"

The Colonel gave me a small smile.

"But we have to know the truth," Tori said. "All of it."

"You'll get it," she said, then nodded toward Kent. "What about you, All-American?"

Kent looked away.

"He wants to stop the Retros as much as any of us," I said. "Give him some time to process what's going on."

"Fair enough," the Colonel said.

She hit the accelerator. The vehicle lurched forward and we were back under way.

Olivia stayed focused on the street ahead.

A small tear ran down her cheek.

I was too stunned to know what to say. Or think.

2324.

The future.

Was it possible? All we could do was go along for the ride and put our trust in the one person who turned out to be the most untrustworthy of us all.

After careening through the crowded streets for fifteen minutes, Colonel Pike stopped the car in front of a tall gray building that looked exactly like every other tall gray building.

"Are you all right?" Pike asked.

"No," Kent replied.

"I was talking to Olivia," she said curtly. "Can you do this?"

Olivia nodded.

"The timetable is going to accelerate," the woman said. "Keep them here until you hear from me."

Olivia sat up straight as if bracing herself to take on a new challenge.

"Got it," she said with confidence that seemed genuine.

The Colonel looked back to us. "Are we good?"

"Not even close," Tori said coldly.

"Stay with Olivia," Pike added. "She'll tell you everything you need to know and probably more than you'll want to hear. If you don't want any part of us after you hear what she has to say, we'll get you back to your time safely."

"And into the hands of Feit and Bova," I said.

The woman shrugged. "Or you could stay here, but you'd be on your own."

"I really hope there's a third choice," Kent said.

"There is," the woman replied. "That's what you're here to talk about."

Olivia sighed and quickly got out of the car. She was done with conversation.

"Go with her," Colonel Pike said to us. "Try to keep an open mind."

I was done with conversation too. I got out of the car and went right up to Olivia.

"Give me one reason to trust you," I demanded.

"Sure," she said without thinking for even a second. "I didn't stop you from sabotaging the drone fleet at Area 51 and nearly died saving your life. How's that?"

Tori and Kent joined us as the Colonel sped away.

"It gets our attention," I said. "No promises after that."

"Fair enough," Olivia said curtly.

She walked toward the building and disappeared through the grimy double glass doors.

"What do we do?" Kent asked.

"We have to hear her out," I said. "If she can tell us what this is all about, it'll be worth it."

"Is it possible?" Tori asked. "Did we really come through a doorway into the future?"

"If it's true," Kent said. "The future sucks."

We followed Olivia into the building, where she waited for us at an open elevator. We all boarded and rose to the top floor. The fifth floor. At the end of a long corridor was a doorway marked with a similar bar code as the signs we saw on the street. Olivia pulled a black communication device from her pocket and waved it in front of the door. A short hum followed and the door swung open.

If we truly were in the future, rather than having evolved into something amazing, the world had become a sad, tired version of itself.

"This is my home," Olivia said. "My real home."

"So you were lying about living in New York City too," Kent said with disdain.

"No, I lived there with my mother until I joined the Air Force. She's still there. In this time, that is. I lied about living there in your time."

"This is making my head hurt," Kent said.

Olivia led us into a dark, simple apartment that had no personality whatsoever. There were no pictures on the walls or books on shelves. The furniture was functional but plain. There was one main room, a kitchen, and a bedroom. There was nothing about this place that seemed like Olivia at all. Then again, we didn't know who Olivia really was.

"Depressing, isn't it?" she said, as if reading my mind. "This is standard quarters for lower-level personnel. I'm an Airman. First Class, for the record, as you'd say Tucker. I just got a promotion for making it back from your time alive. It's not great but I don't spend much time here anyway. Who's hungry?"

She headed into the kitchen.

"Are you serious?" Tori said, incredulous. "We're not here for afternoon tea."

"Good," Olivia said as she reentered with a cardboard box. "I don't have tea. Or anything else delicious. These are nutrition bars. They taste like dirt but they're loaded with nutrients."

She dropped the box on a low table, took one for herself, and gnawed on it.

"Yum," she said with fake delight. "Not like an Arbortown lobster roll but better than going hungry. Eat."

Kent took a bar, shrugged, and ate. Tori and I passed.

Olivia plopped down on her dusty couch and propped her feet up on the plain table in front of it. All of the furniture was bland and functional. There was nothing made from wood. It all looked to be molded out of some sort of synthetic material.

"I'm guessing the future isn't exactly what you thought it would be," she said. "I can't complain though. I've got this place to myself. Most people have to bunk four or five to an apartment. It's one of the sweet perks I got when I risked my life by going undercover."

"How is this possible?" Tori asked. "That thing in the dome is a time machine?"

"Not exactly," Olivia replied. "It's a time bridge. A gateway between different ages."

"Uh. . . ." Kent muttered. "What?"

Olivia sat forward and slid back a panel on the table to reveal what looked like a keyboard, but with symbols I didn't recognize.

"Quick history lesson," she said. "January 27, 1951."

Her fingers danced over the touchpads and an animated three-dimensional holographic image appeared in the air over the table. This future world made no sense. Most everything looked like a tired, dirty version of the past. But every once in a while some amazing piece of technology appeared that would never have existed in our time. It was like all the efforts of mankind had gone into advancing technology and the weapons of warfare while everything else was left to decay.

The hologram grew from the tabletop and slowly rose until it became a recognizable form. It was a three-foot-tall mushroom cloud . . . the result of a nuclear detonation.

"The first atomic test explosion at the Nevada Test Site. That's where we are, by the way, in case you hadn't figured it out."

"We hadn't," Kent said.

I watched in awe as the perfectly rendered image grew with incredible detail. The image was so realistic I took a nervous step back, afraid the growing cloud of smoke might actually be radioactive.

"Hundreds of nuclear devices were tested right here. At first they were set off above ground. That was until they realized the radioactive fallout was spreading cancer. Duh. After that all the detonations were done underground. What doesn't get mentioned in the history books is that there was an interim step. Project Alcatraz. Named after the prison I guess. Not sure I get the connection."

Olivia touched a few more pads. The mushroom cloud disappeared and was replaced by a two-foot-high hologram of the familiar dome. The gateway to hell.

"The idea was to create a structure that could contain the force of the blast and the radioactive material. They only made one test. January 24, 1952. The bomb went off inside. The dome didn't blow apart. No radioactivity escaped. Everything went as planned except for one tiny little detail. When they went into the dome, they discovered that by containing and concentrating the blast they had accelerated matter to such an incredible degree, it produced an event even Einstein couldn't have predicted. I can't explain the science but what they had done, by dumb luck if you ask me, was to blow a hole through time. A kind of black hole right here on earth. When somebody finally got the guts to go through it, they found themselves still here in the desert, but three hundred years later."

She touched a few more pads. The dome disappeared to reveal a miniature version of the glowing frame we had stepped through.

"It was as simple as that," Olivia explained. "The Bridge was permanent and safe. They built a big old frame around it but that was just for looks. Travelling back and forth between these two eras was as easy as stepping through a doorway. A doorway between times."

I knelt down to take a closer look at the image of what they called the Bridge. It seemed impossible, yet explained so much.

"It's incredible," I said with awe. "Can it be controlled? I mean, can you pick what time you want to go to?"

"No. I told you, it isn't a time machine. We were briefed on the physics once. It has to do with nuclear fission accelerating particles past the speed of light and countering gravity and the actual shape of the dome and I don't know what else. They don't even know why it ended up opening the door to this particular time. But it did, and that's why we're sitting on the edge of disaster."

"Why didn't anybody know this happened?" Tori asked, incredulous. "You can't keep something like this a secret."

"Well, yeah you can. And they did," Olivia said. "Think about it. If people found out they could step into the future, it would have destroyed every known concept of science and God. People's basic beliefs would be blown out of the water. And who wouldn't want to see their own future? You could find out how you died and avoid the circumstances that got you there. Heck, you could find out who won the next thirty Super Bowls. Or invent the iPad before Apple. Knowledge of the future was the most powerful weapon ever imagined. You gotta give credit to the U.S. government. They kept it quiet for over seventy years and only shared it with a few select people."

"Did the people of this time know about it?" I asked.

"Not at first. The U.S. government on this side stepped in and sealed the area. It had been a secure military base since the 1940s so keeping the Bridge a secret was fairly simple. Knowing what to do with it wasn't."

She worked the controls again. The frame disappeared and was replaced by a detailed globe of planet Earth that slowly rotated before our eyes.

"The years haven't been kind to our little planet."

"Seriously," Kent said. "There's lots of modern stuff but mostly it looks like everything just got old and crappy. Was there a nuclear war or something? What happened?"

"Nothing," Olivia replied. "That was the problem. Nothing happened. Things just kept on going the way they were. I'll throw some highlights at you."

She stood and pointed out specific areas on the globe. It was definitely planet Earth, but the landmasses had changed.

"Climate change melted the polar ice caps, flooding low-lying regions all over the world. Lower Manhattan is underwater. So is much of Los Angeles. New Orleans is gone along with a dozen other major cities. Pemberwick Island no longer exists. Sorry. The population continued to grow while livable space shrank along with farmland."

I stared at the image of the globe and the reality of what Earth had become. It was a devastating reality that, unlike everything else we'd seen, seemed possible.

"Living in a city is like being jammed into a crowded ant colony. There are no private homes, only government-controlled housing. Don't even ask about crime. These buildings we're in? These beautiful buildings? They're all made from recycled plastic and other waste. They're trash. Literally. Tori ran her hand along the arm of the chair she was sitting in, trying to grasp the concept of a world that was made from recycled junk.

"If that weren't bad enough, the inevitable happened. Fossil fuels dried up. Natural gas, oil, coal . . . all spent. That threw the world into chaos. The Middle East spiraled into anarchy because the money dried up along with the oil. The stock market didn't just crash, it crumbled and disappeared because the rules of normal commerce didn't apply anymore. Fortunes were lost, big and small. The world came dangerously close to going dark. Everyone saw it coming, the same as with climate change, but no practical alternative energy had been developed. Private industry didn't bother trying to develop anything because it was too expensive. The only realistic alternative was nuclear power. Now it's the prime source of energy. Everything you've seen, like the planes and the cars and the weapons and even this computer right here, is nuclear powered. It's convenient and practical and there's an endless supply. That's the good news. Bad news is that it needed to be developed so quickly that precautions weren't taken. After all, the lights had to be kept on. But there was a cost. The radiation from billions of nuclear powered devices increased the cases of cancer a thousand fold."

"What about the miracle medicine?" Tori asked. "Doesn't that help?"

"No. It regenerates tissue, but it doesn't cure disease. People are physiologically better off than ever. They're more athletic. They're stronger. They never have to worry about injury. It's great, except that the average lifespan for a man living in the United States is now only forty-two years old. Women live slightly longer. Forty-three. Haven't seen many elderly people around, have you? With the lack of farmland, growing enough food to feed the population is next to impossible. What we get is mostly beans and rice. Yum."

"It's a nightmare," Tori said.

"And those are just the highlights."

"No wonder everyone's walking around like robots," Tori said. "It's like mass depression."

"That's exactly what it is," Olivia said. "The number-one concern on everyone's mind is survival. There's no value put on art, music, or literature. We all just live day to day, waiting for the next disaster to strike."

"With no joy," Tori said.

"It's everyone's worst fears come true," I said.

"Not everyone's," Olivia said. "That's where things got really ugly. By stepping into the future, the government and military leaders of your time got a glimpse of what was to come. But they didn't do anything about it. I can't say they didn't try, but they failed. They didn't push for the development of safe alternative fuels, because the business community didn't see the potential for profit. They didn't press the issues on climate change because they couldn't convince enough people that it was real. People still drove their big cars and kept burning coal to create the electricity that kept the factories pumping out goods. The population kept increasing while the food supply dwindled. They saw what was coming, but it didn't make any difference."

"That seems . . . impossible," Tori said.

"But it isn't. The fact that nothing changed is at the very heart of the war we're fighting. The people of my time live in hell, and they hold the people of your time responsible. There were nearly seventy years of diplomacy when the United States Governments from two different eras worked together to try and avert this nightmare. They failed. Miserably. The people of the past were given a gift, a chance to reverse the fate of the world. That stupid bomb test offered a chance to get it right . . . but they didn't. It was out of desperation that my government, and the military, quietly devised a plan to try and save our people. To save our planet."

"They invaded the past," I said, hardly believing the words.

"They went public a few years ago," Olivia said. "They revealed the existence of the Bridge. They told us about the years of futile negotiations to try to get the people of the past to change course and how they were met with nothing but resistance. It was all part of the plan. They were building up hatred for those who were responsible for the horror. It was the only way to get the people to accept . . ."

"Genocide," Tori said.

"Yeah. Genocide."

"Whoa, wait," Kent said. "What if the people in the past listened? If they made any changes, even small ones, it would have completely altered the future. What's it called? The Butterfly Effect? Everything would have changed. Different people would have been born. People from here might suddenly disappear because every little change would create an entirely different future. If the people of the past made big changes it might have actually destroyed the people trying to save their own future."

"Except it didn't work that way," Olivia said. "They did simple experiments to see how changing the past would alter the future. What they found was it didn't. Nothing changed. They planted time capsules in the past and when they went to dig them up in my time they weren't there. They planted newspaper articles in major publications back in the fifties and sixties but when they searched for them in the archives of the present, they no longer existed. They finally concluded that if an event happens, it can't be altered. The two eras exist completely separate from one another. The past is yours. This future is ours. The two can't be mixed. It's like they're two different worlds."

"Or two different dimensions," Kent said softly, trying to allow the reality to take hold in his own brain.

"So then what was the point?" I asked. "If this future couldn't be avoided, why did they even try to get people from the past to change?"

"Good question," Olivia said. "They said they were doing it for the good of mankind. It was the right and noble thing to do, even though we wouldn't benefit. That's what they said, but they were lying. It was all part of the plan."

Olivia changed the hologram from the globe to a bird's-eye view of an airfield that was filled with ominous black attack planes.

"Nobody in power admits it, but invasion became an option the moment they realized changing the past wouldn't help the billions of diseased and starving people of our time. It's a story as old as history. If a tribe can no longer sustain itself on its own land, it must expand. Since we never created colonies on other planets, there was nowhere for us to expand to."

"Except the past," I said gravely.

"Exactly. Once that decision was made, my people continued trying to convince the people of the past to see reason and change their ways, but it wasn't to try to fix our world, it was to make sure that once we conquered and colonized the past, the new future would be a better one for us to live in."

"Why didn't they just tell them the truth?" Kent asked. "People from the future could just filter back and live in the past, right?"

Olivia gave Kent a sideways look and said, "Seriously? Filter back? Overpopulation is already a problem in your time. The world's population has quadrupled since then. Where exactly would they go? You have some extra room at the Blackbird Inn?"

"Not funny," Kent said with a frown.

"So they decided to just wipe out the population of the past to make room," I said soberly.

"That's about it."

"And our government had no idea it was coming," Tori said, dazed.

"Oh they knew," Olivia said. "Or at least they suspected. That's why they created SYLO. SYLO was supposed to be the force that held us back. But they had no idea of the firepower the Air Force was building. It took years, but the Air Force created a massive, lethal attack force. The people of the past didn't stand a chance."

"These guardians protect us from the gates of hell," I said. "Or not."

"Yeah, or not," Olivia echoed.

Olivia turned off the hologram and sat back into the couch with a sigh.

"I joined the Air Force to help feed my family," she said. "The military figured out pretty quick that I wasn't one to carry a pulser and fight, so they made me a spy. An infiltrator. There were thousands of us who leaked through time over the years to blend in and learn about SYLO and the bases they were creating to stage their defense. That's why I was on Pemberwick Island. There were dozens of us there. Granger knew that, he just wasn't sure of who was who. Those people who were shot or arrested weren't innocent islanders trying to escape, they were Retro spies."

"Not all of them," Tori said, bristling.

"No, not all of them," Olivia said with sympathy. "Your father got caught in the crossfire. I'm so sorry for that."

"We all got caught in the crossfire," Kent said. "I lost my dad too."

Olivia said, "Those SYLO bases were meant to preserve your old way of life and rebuild once the Retros were turned back. SYLO had no idea that so many of us were already inside those bases, waiting for the command to rise up and finish the job."

"And SYLO had no idea how powerful the Retros really were," I said.

There was a painfully long silence as we let the incredible information sink in. Everything Olivia said rang true. It all fit. It answered every question and made total sense . . . even the concept of stepping through time. That may have been the most outlandish concept of all, yet strangely it was the least disturbing.

"Can I ask you something?" Kent said in a meek voice.

"Sure," Olivia replied.

"You talk about your government like they're villains who fooled the people of the past into believing they were trying to help them while secretly planning their destruction. I get that, but what makes you any different? You're just as cold-blooded as they are. Did we mean anything to you? Or were you just sticking with us to help root out survivors?"

Olivia didn't answer right away. Tears welled in her eyes. She tried to speak but her voice cracked.

We all just stared at her, waiting for an answer.

"The more I learned about what they were planning, the more disgusted I became," she said. "I tried to hide my real feelings because they don't have much patience for traitors. I guess I didn't do such a great job of keeping it to myself, because I was approached by the Sounders. They saw I had doubts. I learned that I wasn't alone in thinking that the invasion would be a monstrous act against humanity. I planned on working with them from the inside to try to put an end to the madness, but that's when I got shipped out to Pemberwick Island."

"So you went along with the Air Force program after all," Tori said.

"I didn't have a choice," she said, trying to keep her emotions in check. "I was being watched constantly. Even after the attack began and we escaped from Pemberwick, I had to report in daily. Just like Jon Purcell."

"Did you know Jon was a Retro?" I asked.

"Eventually. It made it that much more difficult to tell you the truth, but I did what I could to protect you. I didn't want to go to Fort Knox because I feared we'd uncover another SYLO base. I didn't want to go to Nevada and find survivors because I knew I would be leading the wolves to their door. That's why I wanted to bail and go to Florida. I thought maybe we could just get out of the crossfire until everything settled. I was fully prepared to desert."

"But you didn't," Kent said.

"I didn't because I cared about you guys," she said boldly. "And because I'm a Sounder. There are hundreds of us. None of us wanted the invasion but we didn't have the power to stop it. I'm not even sure we had the *will* to stop it. That is, until it was too late and the horrible theory became a reality."

"Why do you call yourself Sounders?" Tori asked.

"They had to come up with something that we could use to refer to each other without raising suspicion. Sound thinking doesn't lead to genocide. There's no justification for mass murder. I'm not sure I fully understood that until I saw what happened for myself. In Portland. And Boston. And every other place we visited from there to Las Vegas. The idea that so many lives, so many stories, had just ended was . . . it was mind numbing. All I wanted to do was get back here and reconnect with the Sounders. They needed to hear about what I saw. What *we* saw. They had to know the reality. It was the only way to convince them that we had to take action and do something before the rest of the people from the past were executed."

"That all sounds very noble, but are there enough Sounders to derail the Air Force?" I asked.

The mischievous sparkle returned to Olivia's eyes. I hadn't seen that in a good long time.

"In pure numbers, not even close," she said. "We can't battle them outright. But there is a plan. We couldn't set it in motion until we found a critical piece of the puzzle. Now we think we've got that piece."

"What is it?" Tori asked.

Olivia smiled slyly and said, "You."

FIFTEEN

I had heard enough.

"Why?" I asked, staring straight at Olivia.

"Why what?" she asked in her most innocent voice.

"Why should we believe anything you say? You've been playing us. Every single thing you've said about yourself for the last five months has been a lie. Give us one good reason why we should trust you now."

Olivia took a moment to collect her thoughts, then stood up slowly and faced me.

"Because you want your life back, or at least you want to live the rest of your life as close to normal as you can. If that's what you want, Tucker, I'm your only hope. The Sounders are your only hope. Is there anything you've seen since stepping through the Bridge that makes you think I'm lying now? Is there anything you've seen since it hit the fan on Pemberwick Island that makes you think I'm not telling the truth about all this? Tell you what, I can show you something that'll freak you out even more than the story I just told you."

"Oh please don't," Kent said.

Olivia reached down to the control panel and let her fingers hover over the keyboard.

"I can show you history. My history. When that bomb opened the Bridge in 1952 it started the clock on an entirely new existence. But the old existence didn't go away. It's still there. You're in it right now. Like I said, you can't change events that already happened."

She waved her fingers over the controls, teasing us.

"You want to see the history of my time, Tucker? *This* time? I can show you what became of you as an adult. What do you think of that? Do you want to know the day you died? What about you, Tori? Your dad lived to a ripe old age. You know what else? Marty Wiggins went on to play for USC. Your father didn't die from an overdose of the Ruby, Kent. And Quinn wasn't killed out on that boat. I looked it all up. That's my history . . . the history that led to the world you're in right now. When we go back through the Bridge, we're not just going back in time, we're going back to a different existence. A new existence that was created when that bomb went off. The future of that reality hasn't been written yet."

"I think I like our old existence better," Kent said.

"Really?" Olivia shot back. "You like this? You like how the world turned out?"

"No, but I like that the Retros didn't wipe out billions of people. And oh yeah, my father."

"There's the trade-off," Olivia said. She walked toward the large window and stared out at the filthy desert city. "Which is the bigger crime? Wiping out most of humanity in a single invasion, or slowly destroying an entire planet for multiple generations to come?"

"It sounds like you're agreeing with the invasion," I said.

Olivia spun away from the window to face us. Her eyes were wild and her breathing was heavy. She was way more upset than I had realized.

"Nobody is innocent here," she said. "But we have to live with what we do and I can't live with being an executioner. That's why I'm a Sounder and that's why I want to stop the invasion. But don't think for a second that going back to your old life would make everything all better because it wouldn't."

Through the window behind her, a large dark shape floated down from above and hovered outside.

"What the . . . ?" Kent said.

"Get down!" I screamed.

Olivia's eyes went wide and she spun around to face the black attack drone that loomed outside.

I reacted without thinking, jumped at her, and tackled her to the floor. An instant later the window exploded from the impact of the energy cannon that had been fired at us.

The Retros had tracked us down.

Bits of glass and recycled garbage rained down on us as the plane continued to fire, pulverizing the outside wall and the contents of the small apartment.

"Crawl back to the door!" Tori screamed over the sounds of destruction.

We were all flat on our bellies. Safe, but for how long? Once the outside wall was destroyed there would be no more protection.

Olivia went first, crawling for the front door of the apartment. The rest of us followed, pushing our way through the growing rubble as the black marauder pounded away unmercifully. Kent shot past her and got to the door first. He bravely reached up and opened the door so we could all scramble into the corridor.

"The elevator," Tori yelled and started running for it.

"No!" Olivia shouted. "They'll take control of that. The stairs."

She led us in the opposite direction, sprinting for the stairwell on the far end of the corridor. As she ran, Olivia held her communicator up to her ear.

"They tracked us to my quarters," she screamed over the sounds of her apartment being blasted apart. "We need to come in. Now!"

She pushed open the fire door that led to the stairs and ran down faster than was safe.

"Four of us," Olivia shouted into the device without breaking stride. "Give me a location."

"Location for what?" Kent asked, breathless.

"We'll get picked up and taken somewhere safe," Olivia called back to him.

"Safe like this place?"

Olivia didn't have a comeback to that.

"Understood," she said into the device. "Five minutes." She jammed the communicator into her pocket and called back to us, "We'll get picked up five blocks from here."

"Or they'll pick up our pieces downstairs," Kent said. "What the hell is going on?"

"They must have identified me from the roof of the Academy," Olivia said. "Like I said, they don't appreciate traitors."

We hit the ground floor and blasted out of a back door to find ourselves in a narrow alley between buildings. All four of us instantly looked to the sky for fear of seeing the black plane hovering above.

"Gee, just like old times," Kent said.

"Does the Air Force know about the Sounders?" I asked.

"They know there's an underground but I don't know how much they actually know about us, or who any of us are."

She took off running down the alley and we followed closely. When we reached the corner we all cautiously peered out to see two Retro attack planes hovering high above the building, pulverizing the spot that used to be Olivia's apartment.

"I guess they know about *you*," Tori said.

Olivia shrugged and said, "Yeah, guess I've been dishonorably discharged from the Air Force."

She then led us on a race through the narrow streets of the filthy city. Olivia seemed to know exactly where she was going, dodging down multiple narrow alleyways while keeping off the wider streets. We passed hundreds of people who were either dressed in camouflage fatigues or the dark-pants-colorful-shirt uniforms. None of what we were seeing seemed real, least of all Olivia, who led us with such confidence.

She had played the role of the spoiled rich girl well. The only hints she had given up that there was more to her were the few times she did something totally uncharacteristic, like when she cared for Tori's wound after being shot by the SYLO sniper or when she saved Kent from being crushed in the Las Vegas casino. I saw her perform heroically those few times but thought it was a fluke. I had no idea just how much she was hiding.

"Walk," she commanded. "There's less chance of us being spotted."

Gratefully, we slowed to a walk. I was totally winded. It was torture sprinting through a jammed, polluted city in the burning desert.

"This city only exists because of the Bridge?" I asked.

"It's the training and staging area for the invasion and colonization," she answered. "Every last person here is preparing to move into the past. They all have specific jobs and have already been assigned a new home."

"What's your assignment?" Tori asked. "Pemberwick Island?"

"Hardly," she said with an eye roll, flashing a hint of the Olivia we used to know. "Because of my advance work I was given my choice of where to settle."

"And where's that?" Kent asked.

"Paris. I always wanted to see the City of Lights."

"You've never been there in your time?" Tori asked.

"It doesn't exist in this time. Paris is a polluted salt marsh."

There was no escaping the reality of what the world had become. It almost made me feel sorry for the people of 2324. Almost. They may have been backed into a desperate corner by the ignorance of those who lived before them, but they were still a cold-blooded society who believed mass murder was the solution. At least most of them did.

Then there were the Sounders—proof that some people still had a conscience. Whatever their plan was for derailing the invasion, it was looking more like the best (and only) hope for salvaging whatever remained of the world we knew. Our world.

As we moved through those dusty desert streets I knew in my heart that I would do whatever it was they asked of me. I was going to have to become as cold-blooded as the people we were trying to defeat. I would become as ruthless as Feit. As callous as Bova. I would do whatever it took and I welcomed the chance. I owed it to my friends, and to my family. My mother was back in that Retro camp. As far as I knew, my father was still on Pemberwick Island. I had to fight for them. For us.

Olivia threw up her hand and we stopped at the edge of an intersection that was crowded with people. I listened for the telltale musical sound of the attack planes, but only heard the white noise of a few hundred people shuffling on their way to wherever.

"There it is," she said and took off quickly, leading us through the intersection until we came upon a black military-looking vehicle.

"Get in," she commanded and went for the shotgun seat.

Kent grabbed her arm to stop her.

"Tell us where we're going," he said.

"To a safe house," she said.

"I'm not going," Kent said adamantly. "Being with you guys is too risky."

"Seriously?" Olivia shot back. "Taking you in is a far bigger risk for us. Feit wants your heads."

"So then why protect us?" Tori asked.

"Because the invasion is about to happen. People are going to start moving through the Bridge to repopulate the past. Before that happens they plan on wiping out millions more from your time. Either we stop them now, right now, or blood will start flowing again. We have a plan but we need you three to pull it off. I'm trusting you. Can you trust me?"

"I . . . I don't know," Kent said.

He wanted to grab some control over the situation, but he was floundering.

Tori shot past him and got in the car.

"Wait, no," Kent whined.

We were starting to draw the attention of people in the street.

"Get in, Kent," I commanded. "Now."

Kent snapped a surprised look at me. He'd never heard me talk to him like that before because I hadn't. But this was no time to worry about hurt feelings. The Retros were coming after us. They were coming after the Sounders. People were going to die. It was now or never.

"C'mon, Kent," Tori said, coaxing him sternly. "We don't have a lot of choice here."

Kent was mad and still hurting over Olivia's deceitfulness. I wanted to feel sorry for him but I couldn't. Not just then.

"Please, Kent," Olivia said gently, sounding like her old self.

Kent may not have trusted Olivia. But he still cared about her. With a huff, he climbed into the backseat.

I jumped in right after.

At the wheel of the vehicle was a bald guy with dead eyes wearing Air Force fatigues. Under any other circumstances I'd be afraid of that guy, but I was glad he was in charge of getting us out of there and away from a predator drone. You want that job to go to a steely eyed professional.

"Name?" Olivia asked.

"Statham," he replied with no emotion.

"Situation?"

"Bad boys are circling. I'm to get you and three packages safely to Mayberry. Priority One."

"Good. Go."

Statham hit the accelerator, the music grew, and the vehicle launched forward.

"Packages?" Tori said skeptically. "Mayberry? Isn't that a little cloak and dagger?'

"It's a lot cloak and dagger," Olivia said. "It's what's kept us alive."

Statham knew how to drive and it had nothing to do with being safe and obeying traffic laws. We screamed down the narrow street, forcing people to jump out of our way.

Olivia pulled back a panel in the ceiling to reveal a sunroof. She wasn't trying to get light. She was looking for the drones.

"How far?" I asked.

"The edge of the city," Olivia answered. "In the industrial sector. Ten minutes away."

I realized she must have been talking about the area of the city I saw from the rooftop that was belching colorful smoke from tall stacks.

Statham took a couple of quick turns, I assume to make it more difficult for us to be followed. I don't know how he knew where he was going since every building looked exactly the same.

"We've lost them," Olivia finally said.

"How did they find you in the first place?" I asked. "Just because they saw you on the roof?"

"That must be how," Olivia said. "I've never been under suspicion before."

We drove past the last of the tall buildings to find ourselves in a section of town that was cluttered with low industrial-looking structures, enormous tanks, and old-fashioned soot-belching smokestacks. I watched as they poured colorful, deadly clouds into the sky that fell back to earth as burning rain.

"We're going just beyond the sluice," Olivia explained.

"Sluice?" Tori said.

"It's a huge gutter for industrial waste. Every last one of the factories dumps its runoff into it. It's disgusting. I don't even know where it goes. Somewhere out in the desert. When we drive over it, don't breathe."

"Over?" Kent said, nervously.

We were headed directly toward a two-lane bridge that spanned the "sluice." There were similar bridges spaced fifty yards apart, all crossing the wide river of filth. It looked to be a few hundred yards to the far side. We hit the bridge, which ramped up until we were speeding high over the foul-smelling sludge. Looking over the edge we saw it was a long way down to the dreck, which was just as well. It smelled bad enough from where we were. If we were any closer it would have been impossible to breathe.

"Once we're over, Mayberry is only another minute—"

"Communicator," Statham said, holding out his hand to Olivia.

"What?" Olivia asked, thrown.

"Give me your communicator."

Olivia wasn't sure of how to react. Reluctantly, she handed it to the driver.

He took the black device . . . and smashed it against the dashboard, destroying it.

"Are you crazy?" Olivia screamed.

"That's how they're tracking you," Statham said, and pointed up through the sunroof.

We all looked up to see a black Air Force drone hovering above us.

"We're trapped on this bridge," Kent said.

The drone started firing, blasting out chunks of the roadbed around us.

Statham swerved, doing his best to become a difficult target. It seemed futile, considering it was only a two-lane bridge.

"Faster!" Olivia screamed.

No sooner did she get the word out than the vehicle was rocked by a shot from the craft that hit the bridge directly in front of us. It was too close for Statham to avoid. He spun the wheel and we slipped into a dangerous skid, hitting the damaged section. The vehicle flipped, doing a complete rollover before skidding closer to the edge.

The squeal of metal scraping across cement was deafening. Or maybe it was the sound of Kent screaming. We skidded nearer to the edge until we finally came to rest back upright, but with our front wheels dangling over the edge of the bridge.

It all happened so fast that I didn't have time to be scared.

"Get out!" Olivia screamed.

She didn't wait to find out if anybody was hurt or knocked out or even dazed. She knew what was at stake. We were totally exposed with an attack plane on the prowl . . . and we were inside a car powered by a nuclear engine that had just been tumbled. The sound of the engine powering up was unmistakable. Those engines were fragile. We saw what happened in Portland when a drone was rammed by a car. You didn't want to be anywhere near one if it exploded, and this engine sounded as though it was headed in that direction.

Luckily, Tori and Kent were conscious and still with it. We all yanked off our seatbelts and dove out of the car. Without our weight, the vehicle shuddered and slid further over the edge of the bridge. It was either going to explode, or fall into the polluted abyss. Or both. We all sprinted back to the ramp that led onto the bridge.

All of us but Statham.

"Wait, the driver," Kent screamed and slowed down.

Statham was still in the doomed vehicle.

We stopped to look back to see that the man was strapped in the front seat, his head tilted to the side, unconscious . . . as the vehicle slipped closer to the edge.

Far in the distance, hovering above the bridge was the Retro drone. It remained there as if watching and waiting to see what would happen with the vehicle.

"We can't leave him there," Tori yelled with desperation.

"Yes we can," I shouted. "He may be dead already. C'mon."

I tried to pull Tori away, but she wouldn't go.

I was out of my mind. In those few seconds all I could think about was the Sounders and the one chance we would have to save our world. Millions of people had died. Millions more would follow. I didn't want to leave Statham there either, but he was just one man. We couldn't jeopardize the entire future for the fate of one person.

"We have to get out of here!" I screamed.

I tried to pull Tori away but she wouldn't budge.

"We can't leave him," she argued.

Kent didn't argue with me.

He sprinted back to the vehicle.

"Whoa no!" I shouted.

Kent had his head down and his legs pumping. He went right to the driver's door and tried to yank it open. The damage from the rollover must have jammed the lock. Kent pulled like a mad man but it wouldn't budge.

Behind him, the attack plane started to make its move. It dipped down low and picked up speed, headed our way.

"Kent, get out of there!" I yelled.

Kent hammered on the glass with his fists but it wouldn't break. He threw his shoulder into it but only bounced back.

Tori pulled away from me and started back toward him but I grabbed her and stopped her.

"They'll be killed," she screamed.

"And so will you." I shouted, "Kent! It's coming!"

The attack plane was picking up speed.

"Kent, run!" Olivia yelled.

That got through to him. Kent glanced to the sky, saw the plane, and stumbled away from the vehicle. He was breathing hard and crying and could barely keep his balance but he ran back our way.

"Get down!" Olivia shouted.

Kent half fell/half dropped to the ground.

A second later the drone fired. The invisible pulses of energy shot toward the doomed car. When they hit they knocked it onto its side and triggered a fiery explosion that created a wave of intense heat that hit us like a fast-moving truck. The force instantly knocked us all to the ground.

The burning vehicle teetered on the edge of the bridge for an agonizing second, then with the shriek of tearing metal it dropped over the side, fell quickly, and then crashed into the chemical river far below. The instant it hit it ignited the sludge, creating an inferno beneath us.

The drone continued on, gained altitude, and streaked off.

"Why is it leaving?" I asked nobody. "Does it think we're dead?"

Olivia got to her feet and ran for Kent.

"I hope to God he's okay," I said to Tori.

Tori was staring at me with such cold eyes it made me gasp to catch my breath.

"You all right?" I asked.

I stood, gingerly, and held out my hand to help her up.

Tori didn't take it. She stood up on her own and staggered toward Olivia and Kent.

"What's the matter?" I asked.

"You didn't want to help him," she said coldly.

I pulled myself to my feet and followed.

"He was as good as dead already," I argued.

"And what's one more death, right?" she said angrily.

She was wrong. Kent was wrong. Statham's death was tragic,

but it was nothing compared to the larger challenge. We were trying to save millions of people. It would have been wrong to risk our lives—and our entire future—to save one individual. I truly believed that.

When we reached the others, Olivia was on her knees holding Kent's head. I was relieved to see Kent's eyes open and focused on her.

"He was still alive," he cried, fighting back tears. "He looked at me but he couldn't move. I tried to open the door but—"

"I know," Olivia said, soothingly. "There was nothing you could do."

"I'm proud of you, Kent," Tori said.

"I'm proud of you *all*," came a voice from behind us. "Together again. This is so absolutely awesome."

I suddenly knew why the drone had flown off. It didn't think we were dead. It left because it was no longer needed.

Standing on the bridge, flanked by two armed Retro soldiers, was Mr. Feit.

SIXTEEN

We were done.

While Feit's soldiers kept their weapons aimed at our heads, several Retro vehicles showed up behind them. Feit wasn't taking any chances. Now that he had us, he wasn't going to risk losing us again. We were each taken by a different armed soldier, loaded into separate vehicles, and driven away from the burning river. It was like being imprisoned in a rolling steel cage. I wanted to scream. Or punch the roof.

Or better yet, put my fist through Feit's smug smile.

We had come so close to learning about the Sounders' plan to stop the invasion. Olivia said they needed us for it to work. Since Feit had us, did that mean the plan was finished? Was the last hope of stopping the invasion gone? That seemed likely because now that the Sounders had revealed themselves, the Retros were actively hunting them down.

Everything was unraveling.

Though it was impossible to tell one city street from the next, I could see where we were headed. They were taking us back toward the dome. When we neared the giant structure, the line of vehicles turned into the open garage door of a tall, plain building. We stopped inside the large, empty garage, where I was pulled out of the car and manhandled into the building. With two Retro soldiers flanking me and holding my arms, I was hurried down a long corridor and pushed into a tiny room that looked like a prison cell. There were two cots with thin mattresses, a steel sink, and a toilet.

A second later, Tori was shoved in behind me and the heavy steel door was closed and locked with gut-wrenching finality. Nobody had said a word to us since we were on the bridge. We had no idea if we were going to be there for a few minutes, a few hours, or the rest of our lives.

The two of us stood there awkwardly and more than a little dazed. After a few moments Tori dropped onto one of the cots and curled up with her arms hugging her legs. She wasn't crying. Tori never cried. She sat there silently, staring at the wall.

"We don't know anything about the Sounders' plan," I said. "They can ask us whatever they want but there's nothing we can tell them. Then again, Olivia knows everything. If they make her talk the plan might be—"

"Stop, all right?" Tori snapped at me. "It's over. Stop pretending like it isn't."

"We can't give up hope."

"Hope for what? Humanity? Hope that we can change the way these people think? This is a society of animals who will do whatever it takes to survive, even if it means murdering billions of people. There's no coming back from that. This really is hell, and it has nothing to do with the living conditions."

"What about the Sounders?" I asked.

"What about *you*?" she shot back.

"Me?"

"You didn't care that the driver was about to die."

"He was beyond help, Tori," I argued. "Kent almost died for nothing."

"At least he tried," she said flatly.

"Are you serious? You're angry at me for not risking everything to try to help a guy who was as good as dead already?"

"I'm not angry," she said. "I'm confused. We're condemning the Retros for invading the past to save themselves. We're amazed that they have such little regard for human life, but we're just as willing to let people die to get what we want."

"It was one guy!" I argued.

"It wasn't just one guy," she said, her voice growing more urgent. "How many died when we sabotaged that Retro fleet? I shot people myself. I think about that all the time. What makes you think we're any better than the Retros?"

"This is crazy. We're talking about the difference between a few people and a few billion. This is war, Tori. People die. We didn't start it. We're just protecting ourselves. You should know that. Of all people. You're the one whose father taught her how to shoot guns to protect herself. Why are you getting squeamish now?"

"I'm not squeamish. I'm . . . messed up. And I'm bothered by how quickly we've accepted the killing, especially if it serves our own purpose."

"It was one guy, Tori," I said.

"Okay, it was one guy. Tell me the truth. If you could press a button that would end the invasion, protect our time, and save the survivors, would you do it?"

"Of course," I replied. "Who wouldn't?"

"Even if it meant that by pressing that button you would wipe out the entire population of 2324?"

The question froze me.

"That's not fair," I said.

"Why not? I'm giving you the same choice the people of this time had. They're willing to destroy the population of an entire planet in order to save their own people. Would you do the same thing? To save your father and mother? To protect Pemberwick Island? Would you do it?"

I didn't have an answer. I had to examine my own thoughts and conscience in a way I never could have imagined a few weeks before.

Tori added, "It's a choice between survival and morality. Which is more important?"

I spoke slowly because I was forming my thoughts along with the words.

"Before any of this happened I would have said no," I answered. "But I see things differently now. If I had to choose between survival and morality, the choice is simple. It's kill or be killed. Yes. I'd push the button."

Tori gave me a sad chuckle. "That's what I thought."

"What about you?" I asked. "Wouldn't you push it?"

"No," she said quickly. "I see things a little differently too. Before any of this happened I probably would have pushed it. But now that I've seen how truly ugly people can become, I want to be better than an animal who lashes out when backed into a corner."

"So you'd sacrifice yourself, and the people you love, because you think it's immoral to fight back?"

"Oh no. I'm more than willing to fight back," she said with confidence. "You know that. What I won't sacrifice is my humanity. Without that, we're just like the animals the Retros think we are."

I wasn't sure how I should feel. Was Tori being ridiculous? The survival instinct is as basic as the need for food and water, and the strong survive. That had been true since the beginning of time. Nobody should have to apologize for protecting themselves. But did that mean anything is justified, no matter how heinous, in the name of survival? Were the Retros justified in wiping out the population of the past? The action, or lack of action through time, to prevent this disaster is what created their nightmare world. The Retros considered that to be an attack that was just as lethal as the drones they sent back to destroy the population. Were they only fighting back?

"I guess it all depends on your definition of humanity," I said. "And how badly you want to survive."

"I want to survive," she said. "But I also want to be able to live with myself."

The heavy door opened and an armed Retro soldier stepped in.

"Come with me," he ordered.

I thought of refusing but realized there wasn't any point to it.

Tori shrugged and got up. The guard led us out of the cell and motioned for us to walk along the corridor. He stayed behind us, ready to shoot if we dared to make an aggressive move. None of the doors we passed had windows so I couldn't look in to see where

Olivia and Kent were being held. At the end of the hallway was a stairway that we climbed for three stories, ending up in another nondescript corridor, this one filled with more activity. Retro soldiers hurried about, moving from room to room.

The guard directed us to a door toward the end of the corridor and motioned for us to enter. Tori and I stepped in, followed by the guard, who entered and closed the door behind us.

We were in a sparsely furnished office with a single desk. Unlike the dungeon cells, this room had a window. It looked out onto the silver dome, which was not exactly a pleasant view. The wall to our left was covered with a map of the world. The continents were barely recognizable since they had changed so much from our time.

None of those details mattered compared to what was in the center of the room. Sitting behind the desk with his feet up was Mr. Feit. Colonel Feit. Though this time he looked more like the Feit I had first met on Pemberwick Island. His hair was still short, but rather than the Retro military uniform he wore jeans and a blue T-shirt. He was reading from a handheld device and didn't look up until the door was closed.

"What's the right thing to say here?" he said with a typical smile. "We meet again! How's that?"

Tori and I stood silently.

"I've been working on this project for a long time," he said. "I guess you could say I dedicated my life to it. The planning was meticulous. Every contingency accounted for. Every detail anticipated. It was an awesome mission nearly seventy years in the making and it's gone exactly as planned except for one small, teeny little annoying problem."

He paused for effect. Or maybe he expected us to ask him what it was.

We didn't.

"You," he said. "A handful of kids. Incredible."

Feit shook his head with dismay. "None of the other regional commanders have to deal with this kind of aggravation. Why am I so lucky?"

"Blame yourself," I said. "You brought us into it. You came to me on Pemberwick Island. I didn't come looking for you."

Feit chuckled. Feit always chuckled. It was one of the many things I hated about him.

"Yeah, that was a bad move in hindsight. I shouldn't have gotten involved on that level. But I don't like to command from a distance. I like the action. Maybe I should stay behind a desk and delegate a little more. What do you think?"

"I think you should bite me," I said.

Feit gave me a long look, as if trying to understand where my head was. I wondered if he realized my overriding thoughts were about lunging across that desk and strangling him.

"You're not the same kid I met on that beach, Tucker," he said. "The scrawny little benchwarmer has turned into a real badass."

"Thanks to you," I said.

"Man, you really hate me, don't you? What about you, Tori? Do you see me as the personification of all things evil? Am I the big bad boogeyman?"

Tori didn't answer, which was her way of answering.

"Okay, I get it," Feit said. "But open your minds a little. Try to see things from my perspective."

He stood up and walked to the giant map of the world.

"This must be so alien to you," he said, referring to the map. "There are only seven countries now. Seven. That's it. The United States covers all of North America up to the old Arctic. Newchin spreads over what used to be known as Asia. They split Russia in two with Europa. Ambia used to be known as Africa. That place is a real pit. Then there's Brazilia, which controls South America and what used to be Central America. We lost that one in a war. Nasty business. Finally there's Australia and the New Arctic. Seven countries. Seven governments. That's it. Sounds all neat and tidy but the fact is we're all at war with each other. It's a constant battle for space. For water. For energy. For life. It's not about wealth or power or prestige, it's about survival."

Feit walked away from the map and stood directly in front of us, staring us both down.

"You hate us for what we've done to your world? You hate me? Think about how much hatred is coming your way from the people of my time, who look back at a society that saw the writing on the wall and did nothing about it."

"And that justifies mass murder?" Tori said.

"I could make that argument. What the people of the past did is just as heinous as what we're now doing."

"That's not true!" Tori argued. "Nobody in the past intentionally tried to trash the future."

"Maybe not," Feit shot back. "But they did it just the same. Whenever I spend time in the past I see gluttonous, selfish people who scrape more food off of their plates in a single meal than most people of my time get to eat in a week."

He pulled away from us and hurried to the window that looked over the dome, and the filthy city. He was getting worked up, which wasn't like him.

"This city was built on the recycled garbage of the past. That's all you left us and you think *we're* the villains? We suffer every day because of your shortsightedness. As a loyal citizen of the United States of America who proudly works under the orders of our commander in chief, I can say with total confidence and a clear conscience that it's now your turn."

Feit touched the pad he had been working on. A second later the wall opposite the map turned into an invisible panel, revealing the room next door. It was just like when the deck of the giant attack plane vanished when Tori and I were on board.

Beyond the unseen wall was a clean white room with two metallic silver poles that spanned from floor to ceiling, spaced six feet apart. The space between the poles glowed with a white light that seemed to be generated by them. In front was a silver chair with two Retro guards standing on either side.

Feit took a deep breath, trying to get his emotions back under check.

"I can't tell you how bummed I was to find out that Olivia Kinsey was part of this group of traitors that call themselves Sounders," Feit said. "Blew me away, to be honest."

"Yeah, well, not everybody from the future is an a-hole," I said.

Feit snickered. "We've known about these people for some time but haven't been able to root them out. They've been smart. They haven't made any blatant moves against the government or the military. We expect that to change. And soon. As much as you and your friends have caused me grief, it turns out it may have all been worthwhile."

"How do you figure that?" Tori asked.

"You're going to give us the Sounders," Feit said.

"Sorry to disappoint you," I said. "We don't know anything about them."

"Really?" Feit said, smugly. "Let's see."

He touched his pad again and a door opened in the next room. A Retro guard entered with a prisoner wearing an orange jumpsuit.

"Scottie," I said with a gasp.

"Friend of yours, right?" Feit said. "She caused the ruckus that let you slip away from me back at the camp." Feit broke into a sly grin and added, "Took a while for me to figure that one out."

Scottie looked confused and terrified. She struggled against the guards but it was useless. They forced her to sit in the silver chair and clamped her wrists to the armrests.

"Scottie!" I called out.

"She can't hear you," Feit said. "Or see us."

The door opened again and another Retro entered. It was Bova. Nothing good ever happened when that guy showed up. He walked to the invisible wall that separated the two rooms and gave a small nod.

"He knows we're watching," Feit said. "Now, tell me, what exactly is it that the Sounders are planning?"

Tori and I exchanged nervous looks.

"We don't know," I said. "Olivia didn't get the chance to tell us."

Feit stared me right in the eyes as if trying to read my mind.

"You saw how easily we obliterated Las Vegas," Feit said. "Developing weapons like the one we used there was one of the few legacies from the past that have proved useful. There was money in war back then. The technology we used against Las Vegas is the same as you see in there. So, tell me, what can we expect from the Sounders?"

Tori started to shake with growing anger. She gave a quick glance at the frightened woman strapped into the chair, then made a move toward Feit.

"You can't do this," she said as she took a step forward, but the Retro guard grabbed her and held her back. I made a move to help but the guard quickly raised his pulser toward me.

"I'd rather not harm your friend in there," Feit said calmly. "But it's up to you. Tell me what you know about the Sounders."

"Nothing," Tori cried. "We met a few of them and heard that something is going to happen but they didn't tell us what it was."

"It's true," I said quickly. "Olivia's apartment was attacked before she could tell us."

Feit lifted his pad and pressed it.

Bova nodded, turned to Scottie, lifted his leg up, and put his boot on the arm of the chair.

Scottie screamed with terror. She glanced behind her at the glowing light then back to Bova. She said something to him that we couldn't hear. It had to have been a plea for her life.

I'd never felt so helpless and frightened, even when bombs were flying around me. Scottie had helped me, twice, and now I held her life in my hands.

"Don't!" Tori begged. "This is monstrous."

"I can tell you something," I said. "Scottie has nothing to do with the Sounders. That much I know for sure."

Feit let out a bored sigh.

"This isn't about her, it's about *you*. I could have put your mother in that chair but that *really* wouldn't have been cool."

I lunged at Feit and instantly felt a sharp jolt of pain in my back that knocked me to my knees. The guard had fired a pulse of energy at me. It wasn't strong enough to injure me, but it sure hurt.

"The choice is yours," Feit said. "Tell me everything or . . ." he punctuated the statement with a shrug as if it were out of his hands.

I was near panic. We really didn't know anything, other than the name of Colonel Pike and the fact that we were supposedly the last piece in the puzzle of the Sounders' plan. Seeing Scottie's terrified face tore my heart out. Would the little information we had be enough for the Air Force to stop the Sounders' plan? If we gave up Colonel Pike, would she be the next one sitting in that chair?

"Last chance," Feit warned in a singsong voice.

Tori gave me a tortured look. She was as torn as I was.

"Please don't hurt her," I said, lamely. "I swear we don't know anything."

Feit pressed his pad.

Bova kicked the chair over.

Scottie opened her mouth to scream as the chair fell back through the curtain of energy between the silver poles. Her body was enveloped in white light. An instant later, she was gone. The chair tilted back to its upright position, empty.

Tori let out an anguished cry.

I think I did too. I can't say for sure. The agony of knowing

I was the cause of an innocent person's death, someone who had risked her own life to help me, was too much to bear. I had witnessed untold death and devastation over the last few weeks but this was personal. Nothing had compared to this.

Bova turned back to us, showing no emotion. He was as cold-blooded as Feit. The monster stood there, waiting for instructions.

"Tell me, was that worth it?" Feit asked.

"You can't justify this," I said, trying to keep from crying with anger. "You can look back in time and blame people for whatever you'd like, but you can't claim that what happened in the past is anything like cold-blooded murder."

My anguish was quickly turning to rage. I looked to Tori and said, "I would push that button. I would push it until every last one of these bastards was blown away."

Tori dropped her head in total anguish, and defeat.

"Let's continue," Feit said and pressed his pad again.

The door in the next room opened and two more Retro soldiers stepped in, headed for the death chair.

With them were Olivia and Kent.

SEVENTEEN

"Stop it, now," Tori demanded.

"No problem," Feit replied casually. "Tell me about the Sounders."

For one brief moment my mind flashed forward to what was about to happen. Who would be put in the chair first? Kent or Olivia? Probably Kent. Olivia's knowledge of the Sounders would make her too valuable to execute. What would I do? Would I give up Colonel Pike to save Kent? Would I admit that the Sounders had a plan to stop the Retros, even though I had no idea of what it was? Would that be enough to save him? Or would it just hurt the Sounders' chance of success?

I truly didn't know what to do.

Olivia and the Sounders did.

The two Retro soldiers pushed Kent and Olivia toward Bova.

As soon as they were released, the two soldiers faced us and put their hands on their hearts.

Sounders.

I shot a look to Tori.

She gave me a quick nod.

It was time to go.

I threw myself at the soldier behind us. He was so surprised that he didn't have time to defend himself. I grabbed for his pulser while pumping my legs, forcing him backward until he slammed into the wall.

Tori launched herself at Feit, who had his communicator up, probably to sound an alarm. He didn't get the chance. Tori tackled him and bent him back over the desk.

In the next room, the odds had changed dramatically. Bova and two Retro guards were fighting two more Sounders, along with Olivia and Kent. It was no contest. Surprise is a powerful weapon.

The Sounder soldiers first fired on the two Retro guards. One was hit and fell to the floor; the other was knocked into the white light and instantly vaporized. Bova ran for the door to escape but Kent tackled him.

Olivia grabbed the pulser of the downed guard, calmly aimed at the invisible wall, and fired.

The room next door was no longer silent. The ear-splitting sound of shattering glass erupted as the invisible wall between us was blown away, falling to the floor in a mass of sharp fragments.

Feit pushed Tori away and ran for the door.

Olivia quickly adjusted the power of the pulser and fired at him, knocking him off of his feet and throwing him into the map of the new world.

I continued to wrestle with the Retro guard until Olivia calmly stepped up to him, jammed the pulser into his back, and fired. The guard stiffened, let out a gasp, and fell unconscious.

In ten seconds we had gone from being at the mercy of murderers, to having two choice prisoners.

"How?" Feit moaned, barely able to lift his head.

Olivia strode over and looked down on him. "You have no idea how many Sounders there are. We're everywhere and we're coming for you."

She jammed the pulser into Feit's gut and fired.

Feit grunted, stiffened, and passed out.

I wished I had been the one to do that.

"He's not dead," Olivia said to me. "In case you were wondering."

Kent entered the room, pushing a sniveling Bova with both arms twisted behind his back.

"You will all die for this," Bova said.

"Really?" Kent replied. "Shut the hell up . . . *please*."

He punctuated this by twisting Bova's arms up further, causing the prison commander to cry out in pain.

The two Sounders stepped through the broken wall and into the office. One went directly to Kent and Bova.

"I'll take him from here," the soldier said.

Kent hesitated.

"It's okay," Olivia said calmly.

Kent gave in and allowed the soldier to take charge of Bova.

The other soldier said, "We have to move."

"You realize this place is full of Retro soldiers," I said to Olivia.

"And not all of them are loyal to the Air Force," she replied. "Besides, we've got protection."

She patted Bova on the cheek and said, "Isn't that right, you little weasel?"

"You're a traitor," Bova growled.

"I am," Olivia said with a flirty smile. "And you're a sadistic killer. I win."

"How are we going to get out of here?" I asked.

"Follow me," the first Sounder soldier said and went straight for the door.

The second soldier followed, pushing Bova along. We left Feit unconscious in the office. We didn't need the dead weight.

Kent, Tori, and I followed. The last to leave was Olivia, who had her pulser weapon poised and ready to fire.

As soon as we hit the corridor we were faced by several surprised Retro soldiers. None of them were armed. They stood still, not sure of what to do or how to react.

"Stay calm," the first Sounder announced. "Stand back."

The stunned soldiers moved out of the way, clearing a path for our desperate little group.

"Do something!" Bova screamed.

Nobody dared to make a move. They must have realized that as soon as they tried to stop us, Bova would be dead.

We made our way to the end of the corridor with Olivia to the rear, walking backward, ready to fire if anybody dared to attack.

The Sounders seemed to know exactly where they were going and pushed through doors that led to stairs.

"Move, now!" the first Sounder commanded.

He didn't have to say it twice. We all ran down the stairs as quickly as possible with Bova being dragged along.

"Is there a plan or are we just winging it?" Kent asked.

"Little of both," Olivia replied.

"Speed is our best friend," the first Sounder called back. "We've got to get out before the place is swarmed."

"I thought a lot of the soldiers were with the Sounders?" I asked.

"They are," Olivia said. "But we're still outnumbered and we don't want to get into a full-on battle. At least not yet."

"So we're just going to go outside and run down the street?" Tori asked.

"Not exactly," Olivia said. "Trust us."

"I do," Kent said. He meant it, too.

We kept descending, dropping down to a level that was significantly cooler and seemed to be below ground. When we reached the bottom, the first Sounder stopped at a double door and turned back to us.

"Head for the nearest car," he said. "Load in and hang on."

"Car?" Kent said. "We're not all going to fit in one car."

"Sure we will," Olivia said with a wink. She looked to the first Sounder and said, "Go."

He raised his pulser and pushed the door open.

We were instantly fired on from the other side with energy blasts that hit the walls all around us.

"Split up!" the first Sounder commanded.

I grabbed Tori's hand and pulled her off to our right as lethal shots of energy flew everywhere, hammering the cement walls and ceiling, blasting out chunks of material that filled the air with dust and debris. I pulled her behind a wide column for a moment of protection.

Peeking around the edge, I saw that we were in a subterranean train station, though the vehicles didn't look anything like the subway trains I was used to. They were individual, round cars about the size of an above-ground swimming pool with windows all around. A dozen were lined up next to one another with their doors open, ready for passengers.

The station looked like a shipping depot, with crates and equipment piled everywhere.

"Which one do we get on?" Tori asked.

"Wait until the Sounders choose," I said. "This is their show."

The battle continued, with Olivia and the first Sounder firing from behind stacked crates while continuing to move closer to the cars.

I didn't think there were many Retros, based on the number of shots that were being fired. That wouldn't last. More would be coming soon.

The Sounder with Bova made the first move. He boldly dragged the prison commander out from hiding and pulled him toward the cars. He must have thought the Retros wouldn't risk shooting at him.

He was wrong.

He got halfway across the floor to the train cars when he screamed and fell back, letting go of Bova. Someone had taken a very good, or very lucky, shot.

Bova took off screaming, "Shoot! Shoot them all!"

Olivia and the other Sounder went on offense. They ran out from where they were hiding, firing multiple shots at the stacks of crates the Retros were using for cover. It was a frightening barrage of energy as the crates were hit with such violence that they exploded into a cloud of debris, forcing the Retros to back off.

"Move!" the Sounder screamed back at us.

"That means us," I said and pulled Tori out from behind the pillar.

Kent appeared from the far side of the depot and we all ran for the round train cars.

On the far side of the station, more Retros came running with their pulsers drawn and ready. It was going to be close.

All around us the floor was blasted apart by stray pulses of energy. The Sounder and Olivia continued to fire at the Retros as they ran, but speed was everything. We had to get in a car and out of there before more Retros arrived.

The Sounder chose a car in the dead center and the rest of us followed him aboard. He went straight for the controls, which were on the opposite side from the door. Olivia jumped on next followed by Tori and me.

"Hang on!" the Sounder commanded.

He hit the throttle just as Kent stepped on board. The door wasn't even closed as the car shot forward.

"Hey!" Kent shouted.

I grabbed him by the shirt and held on tight or he would have fallen right back out. When I pulled him in the door slid shut and was instantly pummeled by rounds of energy being fired from the station.

"Jeez, he wasn't kidding about hanging on," Kent said, his eyes wide with exhilaration.

"What about the guy we left behind?" Tori asked, breathing hard.

"He's dead," the Sounder replied. "They were shooting to kill."

"I'm sorry," Tori said.

Olivia put her hand on the Sounder's shoulder in sympathy.

He didn't take his eyes off of the tunnel ahead but gave her a brief grateful smile.

I stood next to him to see we were flying through a dimly lit subway tunnel that wasn't much wider than the car we were on. The control panel was a large computer monitor touchscreen that the Sounder kept his fingers on. There was another monitor next to it that looked to be a map of the subway tunnels. A small moving light showed us where we were in the system.

"What kind of train is this?" I asked.

"It rides on a contained cushion of energy," Olivia said. "There are no tracks so there are multiple routes and tunnels to take."

"Yeah, well, let's take a tunnel they're not expecting because they're coming after us," Kent announced.

Behind us, the lights of another train car could be seen.

"What's your name?" Tori asked the Sounder.

"Sokol," he replied. "Captain Sokol." He looked at Tori and added, "Kenny."

He was a big guy with jet-black hair and dark eyes to match.

"How well do you know these tunnels, Captain Kenny Sokol?" Tori asked.

Sokol took his eyes off of the tunnel long enough to give Tori a wink.

"Don't worry," he said. "I'll give 'em a run."

We were flying through the tunnel. Literally. I didn't know how safe it was to be moving with such speed, but it didn't look as though we were getting any further away from the train that was chasing us.

"Hold on to something," Sokol warned.

I reached up and grabbed on to the overhead railing.

"Why?" Kent asked.

We reached a fork in the tunnel and Sokol took a sharp cut, sending us into the tunnel to the right.

Kent was the only one who hadn't grabbed the railing and was thrown to the deck.

"That's why," Sokol said.

"Jeez! A little more warning next time!" Kent shouted back.

"You okay?" Olivia asked.

Kent got to his feet, more embarrassed than hurt.

"I'll live," he said. "Won't I?" He directed that to Sokol.

"Doing my best," the Sounder replied.

Behind us, the chasing car made the same turn.

"Didn't lose them," I announced.

"We're headed for a multiple juncture," Sokol said. "Let's see how good they are."

This time Kent gripped the overhead rail.

"Never tried this before," Sokol said. "Should be okay."

"Should?'" Kent asked, nervously.

I glanced at the monitor to see a series of intersections coming up. It reminded me of something straight out of a video game. A life-or-death video game.

"Here we go," Sokol announced.

He threw the car into a quick right turn, flew forward for a few seconds, then hit another hard right turn.

"I doubt these junctures were designed to be taken at this speed," I said.

"They weren't," was Sokol's matter-of-fact reply.

Enough said. I watched our light on the map moving quickly as we approached several more intersections.

"Another one," Sokol called out.

He made a sharp left turn. Too sharp. The flying car bashed the wall, sending a shudder through the speeding vehicle. The circular car spun and for a second we were flying sideways. Sokol made a few quick adjustments and we spun back around until the controls faced forward again.

"I may puke," Kent said.

"They're still coming," I said.

I pointed to the monitor, where the image of the other car was on the map. They had followed us through every turn.

"I guess the answer is they are very good," Tori said.

"They have the same monitor," Sokol said. "They know every move I'm making."

"Eventually we're going to reach the end of the system," Olivia warned.

"We'll have to stop and make a stand," I said.

Sokol kept his eyes on the track. He no longer bothered making ridiculous turns. Instead, he increased the throttle.

"We can't outrun them," Tori said.

"I know, I just want to put a little distance between us," Sokol explained.

"Why?" Kent asked.

"We need a station," Sokol replied.

I looked at the monitor, searching for one.

"There," I said. "There's a juncture up ahead to the right. There's a long straightaway and then the tunnel widens. Is that a station?"

Sokol gave the monitor a quick glance, and smiled.

"It's perfect," he said.

"So we stop there and get out?" Kent asked.

"Something like that," Sokol replied.

We reached the juncture and Sokol made the turn. Once inside the next tunnel, he increased the throttle until we were moving with frightening speed. I figured he wanted to give us as much time as possible to get away once we stopped and jumped out.

"Did they follow us?" Sokol asked.

I glanced at the monitor. "Yup. Right behind us. A little further back, though."

"Perfect," Sokol said with a satisfied smile.

I looked to Tori, who seemed as confused as I was. But Sokol seemed to know what he was doing so none of us questioned him.

"I'm going to come to a stop in the next station," he explained. "It'll be abrupt so hold on. Once we stop moving, get out fast."

We rapidly approached the station but Sokol didn't slow down. He wanted to buy every possible second.

"Here we go," Sokol said. "Hang on. We're stopping in three . . . two . . . one."

The lights of the station flashed into view, and a second later Sokol powered down so quickly we had to hold on tight or we would have been thrown to the front of the car. It was an excruciating few seconds until the vehicle finally came to a stop.

Sokol quickly spun the vehicle until the door faced the platform.

"Go!" he yelled. "Get out."

The door slid open and we piled out onto the platform. A few people were there, staring in wonder at the fools who had flown into the station at breakneck speed. As we ran for the stairs that would lead to the street, I glanced back to see that Sokol was still at the controls.

"What is he doing?" I asked.

We all stopped to look back.

Sokol was furiously inputting commands into the control panel. Olivia laughed.

"Oh that's great," she said with a giggle.

"What's great?" Kent asked.

"Watch," Olivia said.

The car started moving again, in the opposite direction. As soon as it began moving the door started to slide closed. Sokol left the controls and sprinted for the opening, which was shrinking rapidly. He jumped out and cleared the frame just as the door sealed shut. A second later the nuclear-powered train car launched out of the station and disappeared back into the tunnel.

"Everybody out!" Sokol screamed to the people on the platform. "If you stay down here, you'll get hurt!"

"I love this guy," Kent said.

Sokol ran up to us and blew right by.

"Don't want to be here," he said as he ran past.

None of us did. We all took off running.

The few other people who had been in the station ran with us. They didn't exactly know what was happening, but they believed Sokol did and whatever was about to happen, it wouldn't be good.

We had an idea of what it would be. And it was very good.

We hit stairs that led us up and out to the surface.

Night had fallen. We found ourselves in what looked like an industrial area full of warehouses and barren lots. It was a desolate place with only a few dull streetlights that didn't do much more than create shadows. The area was essentially deserted.

"We're in luck," Captain Sokol said.

"This wasn't luck," Kent said, breathless. "This was brilliant!"

"Sending the train back was brilliant," Sokol said. "Doing it way out here was luck."

"What happens when two nuclear-powered trains collide?" I asked.

"I'm not exactly sure," Sokol said. "But we're about to find out."

Two hundred yards behind us, the ground erupted. The two trains had hit at full speed, causing an explosion that blew through the tunnel and continued on and up until it breached the surface beneath an ancient warehouse. The force of the explosion raged through the building and blasted through the roof, sending a cloud of debris into the sky that had to be seen as far back as the dome. A brilliant spray of light shot up through the hole, creating a beacon that lit up the decrepit neighborhood, making it come alive, if only for a brief moment.

"Yaaa!" Kent screamed in triumph. "I really hope Bova was on board."

"That was pretty slick, Kenny Sokol," Tori said.

"I told you I'd give 'em a run," Sokol said.

The dust and debris settled as the light dissipated and the smoke drifted away.

"So what happens now?" I asked. "Feit knows about the Sounders. He'll be out headhunting."

"Now we do what we've been planning for all along," Olivia said. "We strike back."

EIGHTEEN

We had a long way to go to get somewhere safe.

We didn't dare use Captain Sokol's communicator for fear the Air Force would zero in on it to track us down. That meant we had no way to call for a ride. Our only option was to walk.

I was exhausted and I'm sure Tori and Kent were too. To say it had been a long day was a total understatement. We didn't talk much as we trudged through the darkened streets. Talking took too much effort.

The city smelled. The streets were filthy. The air pollution burned my eyes. Scattered showers dropped burning rain at every turn. If the rest of future Earth was anything like this, I could understand the anger that led the United States government to invade its past self. They were acting out of desperation. I got that. I actually tried to convince myself that their monstrous tactics were somehow justified.

It wasn't that I wanted to let them off the hook; I was looking for a way to justify my *own* feelings.

If I could push the button that Tori asked about, I'd do it. I would wipe out the entire population of future Earth. Was I angry? Sure. Was I disgusted by the way Feit and Bova could so easily take lives? Absolutely. But it came down to a fight for survival. If the U.S. government of future Earth thought it was okay to murder billions of people in order to save their own population, why couldn't we do the exact same thing to save our own?

Throughout our ordeal I kept hanging on to the hope that we could one day return to our normal lives. I was kidding myself. Not only would that never happen, I felt certain I would never be able to return to my normal *self*. I had seen too much. You can't erase memories. I had become numb to the loss of human lives. Maybe that was a defense mechanism. Seeing Scottie's life so cruelly snuffed was the last straw. I would do whatever it took to survive, and to stop these monsters. Did that make me just as much of a monster as the Retros?

Maybe.

I didn't care.

Olivia and Sokol brought us to another large, nondescript building and walked straight for the front door. Lights shone from several windows of the surrounding structures. The first signs that this building housed something other than typical residents were the two burly, armed guards with pulsers who greeted us as we stepped through the front door.

We were in Sounder territory.

After quick greetings, Olivia took us to an elevator that brought us up to a top floor.

"It's late," she said. "We all need sleep. There's a room for each of you here. Take a shower. They'll send up some food and then we'll meet in the morning. That cool?"

We all grunted our approval. The idea of a shower, food, and sleep sounded better than perfect.

Olivia directed us each to a room. Tori took the first, I took the second, and Kent was last. If we needed each other during the night, we knew where to go.

My room was as simple as possible. There was a bed, a couple of chairs, and a bathroom. Even so, it was more than I needed. I immediately stripped down and got in the shower. It was the first normal, warm shower I had taken since Pemberwick Island. It was heaven. I stood under the powerful stream, letting the spray sting my skin and wash away the layers of filth. It was then that I realized how long my hair had gotten. It had been cut short for football season but now fell down into my eyes. At some point I would have to get it cut. But who would do it? It wasn't like there were any barbers around. Compared to all of the horror we'd seen, it was strange to be worried about something as dumb as getting a haircut. It was just one more of the thousands of ways the life I knew had changed forever.

Once my skin started to prune, I figured I'd had enough so I got out and grabbed the rough white towel that was hanging on the door. At least it was clean. I toweled off and stepped back into the main room to see Olivia sitting on the couch.

I instantly covered myself with the towel.

"Jeez, really?" I said, annoyed. "You gotta stop sneaking up on me in the shower."

Olivia laughed and covered her eyes. "Sorry. Bad habit. I brought you some food, and something to sleep in."

Next to her on the couch were gray sweats and a white T-shirt.

Olivia wore a similar set. I grabbed them and went back into the bathroom to put them on. When I came out, Olivia had set the tray of food on a low table. There was a bowl of some kind of grain, an apple, and a pitcher of water.

"Not exactly an Italian from Amato's," she said. "But it's all we've got. The apple is a delicacy."

"Thanks," I said. "I'm so hungry I could eat the table."

I sat and ate the bland-tasting gruel while Olivia watched. It was an uncomfortable moment. I didn't know what to say to her because I didn't know who she really was.

"I'm sorry, Tucker," she finally said.

"For what?" I replied. "The list of possibilities is pretty long."

"For messing with your head," she said. "For getting between you and Tori. For flirting with you. For leading both you and Kent on. It wasn't right. None of it was."

"I'll tell you what else wasn't right," I said. "You know I'm only fourteen, right? I know the rules of civilization have all gone out the window but some of the stuff you were doing was against the law. I mean, getting in the shower with me? Seriously?"

Olivia looked down, embarrassed, but she smiled. "It might not have been right but it wasn't against the law. I'm only sixteen."

That rocked me. I believed that the "old" Olivia might have been sixteen. She came across like a flirty, spoiled girl who was used to getting whatever she wanted. Especially from guys. But that was an act. She was a soldier. A rebel soldier. She handled herself like a seasoned fighter with the confidence that came from experience and training.

"You look shocked," she said.

"Well, yeah."

"Don't be. Life is much faster now. I joined the Air Force when I was fourteen. That's what happens when people only live to forty."

It was yet another example of how cruel and joyless the world had become.

"Okay, well, so it wasn't illegal," I said. "But it was still wrong. I get that you were in a bad spot and had to play a part. But that doesn't explain why you were messing with our heads."

"I know, you're right. How I acted had nothing to do with either my mission or with trying to hide my true identity. What you see here is what I was trained to become. I'm a soldier. I can survive in the desert for weeks. I can cut down an enemy with a pulser from fifty yards. I'm better at hand-to-hand combat than most guys. That's what they turned me into. When I was flirting with you and Kent, that was me being . . . me. The real me. Yeah, it was wrong and I was being a brat, but by doing all that it made me feel like I had a little bit of control. And I'll be honest, it was fun. I like you guys. Kent is full of himself, but he's totally genuine. And loyal. You, on the other hand, are a sweetheart. I loved hanging out with you all summer and going to the movies and seeing the reaction you had when I wore that bikini."

"Yeah, that was hot," I said.

"I know, right?" she said, giggling.

For a moment I felt as though I was sitting with the old Olivia.

"I'm sorry for causing you grief, but it was fun for me. I needed it. I needed to be that girl every once in a while or else I would have gone out of my mind."

"So you're saying the Olivia I knew wasn't a total act?" I asked.

She shrugged and gave me an innocent smile. "Like it or not."

"Then I forgive you, and thank you."

"For what?"

"For bringing back a little normal. Oh, and for saving my life back at Area 51. I like *that* Olivia too. And for this apple."

I took a big bite. It was delicious.

Olivia smiled, leaned forward, and gave me a kiss on the cheek.

"You're welcome. Finish eating and get some sleep. I'll come and get you first thing in the morning."

As she headed for the door she added, "Now I have to apologize to Kent and Tori."

"Be careful. With Kent, at least. He has no idea you were messing with me. He really does love you."

"I know he does, and he has no idea that I was flirting with you. I'm too good."

She gave me a sly wink and left.

Her visit made me feel better. Any small sign that the world hadn't been completely turned inside out was welcome. Learning that Olivia was a trained, competent soldier was unnerving; knowing that she was still a flirty, hot girl made me believe that there were still some things that were right about life. It was a small comfort, but I took it.

I finished the bowl of ick, downed the apple and the water, and stretched out on the bed. The sheets were clean and crisp. It was another tiny comfort that made me smile. I fell asleep trying to focus on those small bits of normalcy, and not on the reality that I knew would come roaring back in the morning.

———

"C'mon Rook," Kent said. "They're waiting for us."

I opened my eyes to see Kent and Tori standing over my bed. Both wore the same kind of gray sweats and white T-shirt that I had on.

Tori sat down on the edge of the bed.

"We have to decide something first," she said. "The three of us."

I rubbed my face with both hands and did my best to kick my brain into gear.

"Okay, what?" I said.

"Olivia said the Sounders have a plan to stop the Retros, and we're the last piece in the puzzle. They're going to ask us to do something. The question is how far are we willing to go?"

"What do you mean?" I asked.

"I mean they may ask us to do something that one of us isn't comfortable doing. For whatever reason. If that happens are we going to stick together? Or go on our own?"

Kent started to answer quickly, but stopped to give it more thought.

"I think we first have to find out what they want us to do," I said. "After that we can decide how to handle it. But I'll tell you this much, we came here to fight back. These people are giving us that chance. I can't imagine anything they could ask me to do would be so horrible that it would make me change my mind about that."

Tori thought about my answer, nodded thoughtfully, and said, "I hope you're right."

I pulled myself out of bed, put on the sneakers that were waiting for me underneath, then went to the bathroom and splashed water on my face.

"Good to go," I said as I left the bathroom.

Olivia was waiting for us outside in the hallway. When I saw her, it gave me a momentary shock. She was back to wearing the full camouflage fatigue uniform of the Air Force.

"Ready?" she asked. Her voice was all business. She had clicked back into Olivia-soldier mode.

"Where are we going?" Kent asked.

"To meet with the Sounder command," she replied. "They came here just to meet you."

"Let's hope we don't disappoint them," Tori said.

"You won't," Olivia said with confidence.

She led us down the corridor to an elevator that brought us to the basement. The place was a disastrous wreck of a building, which is probably why the Sounders picked it. Nobody would think to look for a group of people hanging out in a building better suited for rats. In another better world, the place would probably be condemned. We followed Olivia down a dimly lit subterranean corridor to the one room that had light shining from within.

"Here we go," Olivia said. "Relax and be yourselves."

"That's funny coming from you," Kent said.

Olivia ignored him and opened the door.

We stepped inside to see several people standing around, chatting. I had to catch my breath when I saw that they all wore Air

Force fatigues. There were five soldiers in all. Two I recognized: Colonel Pike and Captain Sokol. There was another younger woman and two guys who looked our way. When they saw us, they visibly deflated.

"You're joking," one of them said to nobody in particular. "They're children."

Colonel Pike ignored him and stepped up with her hand extended for us to shake.

"Welcome," she said. "It sounds like you had a bit more excitement yesterday."

"Yeah, you could say that," Tori said.

The woman shook all of our hands and looked each of us straight in the eye. Kenny Sokol did the same. We had their respect. I couldn't say the same thing about the other three Sounders, who stood back, silently appraising us. Whatever they had in mind for us to do, now that they had seen us they were having second thoughts.

"Please sit," Pike said.

There were a bunch of dirty, hard chairs scattered around that were probably made from the same recycled garbage as the rest of this sorry town. Tori, Kent, and I sat next to one another, facing the members of the Sounder command, who all stood facing us. Olivia stood behind us, a subtle statement that she was with us.

Colonel Pike looked at her people and scowled.

"You're all making me nervous," she said, half joking. "Would you mind easing up a little and planting it somewhere?"

Sokol chuckled to himself and pulled up a chair to sit. He was the least stiff of the group. The others grumbled but did the same.

"Better. Thank you." Pike then directed her attention to us. "Please forgive my associates. As you can imagine, we're a bit on edge."

"Join the club," Kent said.

Colonel Pike looked to be in her forties, which meant she was probably nearing the end of her life, based on the way things worked in the twenty-fourth century. She seemed to be in pretty good shape for an older lady. She could have passed for younger if not for her salt-and-pepper hair. When she spoke she didn't waste words. I guess that's what happens when you're a military commander. Unless you were Colonel Feit, that is. That guy loved to hear himself talk.

"Kinsey has given us a thorough briefing on you all," Pike began. "I must say, it was quite impressive."

"Who's Kinsey?" Kent asked me.

"Olivia," I replied.

"Oh, right."

"We know all about you, but you know little of us," she went on. "Let's correct that. We are all career Air Force. We love our country. We took an oath to protect our flag. But the direction the government, and by extension the military, has taken is untenable. No matter what we may feel about the choices made by those who came before us, there is no justification for genocide. It is barbaric. It is immoral. It must be stopped."

"You get no argument from us," I said.

"We have all been fulfilling our duties to support the mission to colonize the past. We are aware of every facet. I know Colonel Feit well. We went through the Academy together. He is, to use a word you might be familiar with, a 'tool.'"

I wanted to laugh, but held it in.

"But he's a smart tool," she added. "He sees this mission as some sort of game. Major Bova on the other hand is a very different kind of animal. He enjoys inflicting punishment. Frankly, if he were a bit more humane in his treatment of the native workers, the colonization camp would be complete by now. But those are only two of the officers who are directing this endeavor. It is a massive undertaking that was planned and prepped for years by both the military and the United States government. The goal is both simple and brutal. Our mission is to replace the population of the twenty-first century with the population of the twenty-fourth century. It is a crime that is beyond unfathomable."

"So then why have you been going along with it?" Tori asked.

"We could quit in protest," Sokol said. "But what good would that do? Many of us want this to end, but our numbers are relatively small. We could go public and refuse to do our duty, but the machine would continue on. Public opinion supports the invasion. We are in the minority. That's why the Sounders were born."

"It began with whispers," Pike said. "A few of us started voicing our concerns to each other. Carefully. Quietly. Eventually we found others who felt as we did. We'd meet secretly, often times right here in this basement. Over time our numbers grew along with our outrage. We created an extensive network within the Air Force. There are Sounders everywhere, both here and in the past, working right alongside those loyal to the Air Force's mission. We vowed to do whatever we could to disrupt their plans. Olivia Kinsey here is a perfect example. She was assigned by the Air Force to infiltrate Pemberwick Island. Her mission was to report back on the movements of SYLO once the invasion began."

"What I was going to do instead was just the opposite," Olivia said. "I was going to make myself known to SYLO and help them with whatever information I had about the Retros. But I never got the chance."

Pike said, "We have medical staff at the colonization base giving care to those who Bova would rather let die. There are drone pilots who deliberately passed over targets, saving the lives of thousands of people. Construction on many of the secondary domes has gone poorly because of mysterious disruptions in the process. We have quietly done what we could to help the victims of the past—"

"Except for the one thing that needed to be done," I said. "Stopping the invasion."

"We don't have the power to pull off a coup and overthrow the government," Sokol said. "It's as simple as that."

"So then what's the big plan?" Tori asked. "Olivia said you're going to try and stop the Air Force. If you don't have the numbers, how is that possible?"

Pike glanced back to the others as if looking to get their permission to continue. She was met with nods and shrugs.

"Our plan is to stage a mission that involves a rudimentary military tactic that has been used effectively since the dawn of warfare," she explained.

"Which is?" Tori asked.

"We're going to blow up the Bridge," Sokol said.

Tori and I exchanged looks.

"Cool," Kent said.

"Simple as that?" I said.

"No, it isn't," Pike replied. "Though the Bridge was created over seventy years ago, the phenomenon that created the time anomaly remains a mystery. Physicists from both times have studied the Bridge and have yet to come up with a definitive explanation as to why the atomic blast created it. The one thing they can all agree on is that the explosion propelled matter faster than the speed of light, which would mean the Bridge could only have been opened to the future."

"So there's no such thing as blasting open a doorway into the past?" I asked.

"So they say," Pike replied.

"You've seen the rigid frame that was built around the bridge in both times," Sokol said. "All that frame does is define the opening. It serves no other purpose. Our fear is that if we try to sabotage the Bridge in a conventional way, all we'd end up doing is destroying the frame. We need to be sure that the Bridge itself is sealed."

"So how do you do that?" Kent asked.

"Not all of the Sounders are military," Pike explained. "We have engaged physicists and engineers who are as appalled at the misuse of this incredible gift as we are. They have a theory, though unfortunately it is nothing more than a theory. Their thinking is that the only way to seal the Bridge is with another event that duplicates the original, only on this side of time."

The three of us sat there, stunned by her words.

The five Sounders stared back at us, waiting for our reaction.

"Do you understand what she's saying?' Olivia finally said.

"Uh, yeah," I said abruptly. "You're going to set off another atomic bomb inside the dome."

"Exactly," Pike said.

"Wait," Kent said. "You just so happen to have an atomic bomb lying around?

"Several," Sokol said with a mischievous smile.

"Wait, what?" Tori said.

"Kinsey tells us that you were at Fenway Park when that dome project was destroyed by the SYLO forces," Pike said. "That wasn't the only dome under construction in the past. There are three more going up as we speak."

"Why?" I asked.

"They are duplicates of the original dome here in the desert. As much as the government has decided that we're better off living in the past, they're hedging their bets. They plan to build several of those domes around the world, then once we have colonized the past and set the world on a new course, they would duplicate the event that created the original Bridge—"

"And blast a few more bridges to the future," I exclaimed. "But why?"

"You can't change the future," Sokol said. "This time will always be the disaster that it is now. The thinking is that once the world has been set on a more responsible course, Bridges can be opened to the future of that new and better world. Nobody here wants to live in the past forever. They want to live in a better version of their own time."

"Can they do that and move forward to this exact same time?" Tori asked.

"Doubtful," Pike said. "It isn't an exact science but that doesn't really matter. They want to leave this wretched time, go back to a more hospitable era, fix the mistakes that were made, and then reap the benefits of an improved future."

"They want to have their cake and eat it too," Kent said. "Is it possible?"

"In theory," Pike replied. "But it would mean setting off an atomic device in each of the new domes."

"So that's why the bombs exist," I said.

"You saw the heavily guarded building outside of the dome?" Sokol asked. "That's where they are. Our plan is to smuggle one of the devices into the dome, seal the door, and set the beast off. The physicists tell us the ensuing explosion stands a very good chance of sealing the Bridge. But even if it doesn't, the radiation released inside the dome will be enough to delay the invasion and colonization. Best-case scenario is we destroy the Bridge. Worse case is we buy time for SYLO to regroup and prepare a better defense. Either way, it's worth the risk."

The room fell silent as we tried to wrap our heads around the incredible plan.

"Any questions?" Pike asked.

"Yeah," Kent said. "Why are we the last pieces of the puzzle? I don't know anything about setting off atomic bombs."

The Sounders exchanged uneasy looks. I had the feeling we were about to hear something we weren't going to like.

"As we told you, the Sounders aren't a formidable military force," Pike said. "Once this mission is underway, it will be next to impossible to see it through without the Air Force trying to stop us."

"Yeah, duh," Kent said.

"We believe we have the capability of mounting an operation that will keep the military back long enough for us to place the device, seal the dome, and detonate it."

"Problem is," Sokol said. "There are two fronts to defend. Here, and in the past. There's a large Air Force presence in that colonization camp. They've got heavy artillery and they've got drones. The moment we controlled the Bridge from this side, all they'd have to do is attack us from the other side and we'd be finished."

"Yeah, your butts would be totally exposed," Kent said.

"That's one way of putting it," Pike replied.

"So for your plan to work, you've got to control the dome in the past as well," Tori said.

"Exactly," Pike replied. "But we don't have the strength or the numbers to do that."

"So your plan is worthless unless you can figure out a way to capture the dome in the past," Kent said.

"That's right," Pike said. "And we've come up with that plan."

"Wait, I thought you said you don't have the manpower," Kent said.

"We don't."

"Then who does?" he asked, exasperated.

There was a long moment of silence until the truth hit me.

"SYLO," I said softly.

All eyes shot to me.

"SYLO?" Kent repeated, incredulous.

"Who else? That's right, isn't it, Colonel?" I asked.

Colonel Pike answered with a small smile.

"Whoa, wait," Kent said. "You expect them to invade the base, fight their way through ground troops and those flying death machines, and set up around the dome to keep the Retros from rushing inside and stopping you from blowing up a bomb in the future?"

"Yeah, that's pretty much it," Sokol said.

"That's crazy!" Kent said with a laugh. "How are you going to get them to do that?"

Nobody said a word.

Kent looked to me, and then to Tori. A second later, the light bulb went on.

"Oh," he said softly. "And there's the last piece of the puzzle."

"The SYLO commanders have no idea that the Sounders exist," Pike said. "Trust me when I tell you that if events continue on this course, SYLO will be defeated and there is little we Sounders can do to prevent that. The past will be overrun and the remaining population will be eradicated. It won't matter what kind of resistance SYLO puts up. Our Air Force has limitless resources. We can keep sending death machines to the past, losing a hundred every hour, and replacing them with another two hundred the following day. SYLO will eventually be worn down and destroyed."

"Why doesn't SYLO just launch a nuke to blow up the Bridge themselves?" Kent asked.

"There's nobody left to launch them," Sokol answered. "The nuclear arsenals of your time are useless. It was one of the first targets when the invasion began. SYLO can't even replace the conventional weapons they've lost because there is no longer any manufacturing capability. It truly is only a matter of time and that time is now. The next offensive is gearing up. I've seen the plans. I know the missions. Most of the physical structures of the past were left intact when the first wave happened. That won't be the case this time. The Air Force is going scorched-earth. Entire cities will disappear. The wave after that will finish off the remaining population. It's about to happen. Sealing the Bridge is the only hope of stopping this insanity and giving the people of your time the chance to rebuild from what's left. Your world as you know it will cease to exist, unless we can convince SYLO to intervene."

"Unless *you* can convince them," Pike added.

"Why us?" Kent asked anxiously.

"They know you," Olivia said. She stepped forward to face us and spoke with passion. "Hell, your parents work for them. You know Granger, Tucker. If we tried to reach them directly do you think they'd believe us?"

"No," I said softly.

"Of course not," Olivia said. "They already know how we've infiltrated their arks. They'd interrogate us and try to figure out if there's any truth to what we're saying and while that's going on, the clock will be ticking on doomsday. Even if we eventually convinced them that there are people on this side who want to help, it will be too late because the offensive will be launched and the people of the past will be wiped out. This has to happen now.

Right now. We need SYLO's help and you guys are our best hope of getting it."

That was it. We knew what they wanted from us. The decision to help or not to help was ours to make.

I looked to Tori.

She took my hand and squeezed it.

"The killing has to stop," she said with certainty.

I looked to Kent.

"I think it's nuts," he said. "We'll have to dodge through a city of Retros who are all out looking for us, get back to the dome, sneak inside and jump through to the past, then find a way to escape from that damned work camp and make our way across miles of empty desert to try to somehow get to SYLO. Even if we did all of that, we'd still have to convince Granger to attack the base. I'm sorry, if that's the last piece of the puzzle then it's one sorry puzzle."

"So you're out?" I asked.

Kent looked to Olivia, took a deep breath to calm himself, and said, "No, I just want to make sure we all know the score. I already followed you through the gates of hell once, Tucker. There's nobody I trust more than you. If you're in, I am too."

I looked to Olivia.

"So?" she said. "What's it going to be?"

Every eye in the room was on me. Even the three skeptical Sounders seemed to have softened. Once again, I was put in the position of having to make a decision that would determine our fate. Only this time it wasn't just about us, it was about the past and the future of two entire worlds.

Unlike every other decision I had made, this one I had total confidence in.

"What do you say, Tucker?" Olivia asked.

I looked to my friends and said, "I say . . . we're going home."

NINETEEN

The orange coveralls.

It wasn't until I saw them that the reality of what we were about to do really hit me. Slipping back into that dreaded uniform brought home how I was living in a world that was not my own. The number on my back marked me as a hated enemy, though I was given a different number in case my original 0311 was on some "most wanted" alert list. To anybody who cared to take a second glance at me, I would look like any one of a thousand other detested prisoners.

What couldn't be seen were the two pulsers that were hidden in my sleeves.

"Is it wrong to think I look good?" Kent asked.

He was wearing Air Force camouflage fatigues. So was Tori.

The plan was to have them pose as soldiers who were moving me through the Bridge on the pretense that I was a prisoner being rotated back into the colonization camp. If anyone stopped to ask, that was their story. Two uniformed soldiers, Sounders, were coming along for the ride. Not only did they know procedure, their mission was to protect us and get us back through time and then out of the prison camp. If all went well, they would commandeer a vehicle to transport us through the desert and to a rendezvous with SYLO.

If things went south, they would run interference.

"You look great," I said to Kent. "Makes me want to shoot you."

"Good, that's what I was going for," he said.

"It gives me the creeps to wear this," Tori said. "Like it's Halloween and I'm dressed up as a mass murderer." She held up her own pulser and added, "But I like *this*."

We were still in the basement of the Sounders' building. Once we agreed to go through with the plan, things happened fast. While we got changed, the word went out to Sounders on both sides of the Bridge to be aware that we were coming through and to be prepared to provide whatever support they could to make sure we made it safely back to the twenty-first century and out of Bova's camp. These brave people were about to risk their lives because of their convictions. Not only were they putting themselves in danger, if the plan actually worked and the Bridge was closed, those who stayed in 2324 were sentencing themselves to live in the nightmare world of the twenty-fourth century. A ticket to life in the past must have been a huge temptation, but for these noble people it wasn't enough to justify the brutal actions of their government.

Worse, in order to secure the dome, they would have to reveal themselves as rebel Sounders. When the dust settled, they would surely be arrested. Or worse.

The word "hero" is overused. But in this case it totally fit.

Colonel Pike and Captain Sokol entered the dank basement in a hurry. It felt as though the clock was ticking—fast.

"These are communicators," Sokol said, handing one each to Kent and Tori. "Don't use them until you're through the Bridge. We can't risk the signal being picked up here. We don't have to worry about that in the past. It's set to a frequency that only our people monitor on that side."

"What are we supposed to use them for?" Tori asked.

"To let you know of our progress," Pike said. "We are set to move here. Once I give the command, many parts will be set in motion. We will breach the depot and secure one of the nuclear devices. Once we move it into position, we'll arm it and seal off the dome."

"Uh, won't the Air Force try to stop you?" Kent asked.

"Of course," Pike replied. "Surprise is key. The closer we get to detonation before the military comes down on us, the better. We're prepared to defend the dome and provide cover for the engineers but there's no telling how long we'll be able to hold out."

"This is going to happen whether or not SYLO comes on board," Sokol said. "Once we commit to grabbing one of the nuclear devices, we'll have to follow through to the end. Obviously we stand a better chance of success if SYLO can secure the Bridge from the other side."

"What makes you think they can do that?" I asked. "Even if they agree to it? They've attacked that camp a bunch of times and the Retros always turn them back. They can't compete with those drones."

"They won't have to," Sokol said. "That's my job. I'm taking a team through the Bridge to seize control of the command center.

The drones are controlled from a bunker near the dome."

"You're going to ground the drones?" Tori said, incredulous.

Sokol said, "That's what the communicators are for. I'll let you know as soon as we own the sky. Be sure to mention that to Captain Granger, would you? My guess is no military commander would stage a ground assault as long as those drones protect the dome. I'm sure it's why they haven't tried it yet. But once the drones are no longer a factor . . ." He smiled and shrugged.

"We're asking you to do a lot," Pike said. "But you can see how critical it is for SYLO to secure the dome."

"Not to put any more pressure on you," Sokol added, "but we don't have much time. The Air Force is gearing up for their next assault. It could come as early as tonight."

That news hung heavy in the air.

"We will get underway at seventeen hundred hours," Pike said. "Five o'clock. We will secure a device, move it into the dome, and detonate it at exactly eighteen hundred hours. Six o'clock."

"Nine hours from now," Kent said soberly. "That's all the time we have to get back there and convince SYLO to attack."

"No," Pike said. "Nine hours until the bomb goes off. SYLO would have to stage an attack long before that if they're going to control the dome."

"Oh, better still," Kent said sarcastically. "Wouldn't want to make it too easy."

"We have no choice but to go by that schedule," Sokol said. "Once the next Air Force campaign begins, the dome will be overrun with personnel and equipment and we won't stand a chance of getting the device inside. It's now or never."

"Six o'clock," I said, soberly. "It all works back from then."

"Set your watches," Kent said.

Two Sounders entered the room. Both were armed with pulsers.

"This is Chief Brock and Master Sergeant Sanchez," Sokol said. "They'll be your escorts."

Brock was a short guy with flaming-red hair and freckles. He looked like an overgrown kid. A big strong kid. Sanchez had dark skin and tight, curly black hair. Both of these guys looked like they could run through a brick wall.

"Whoa, what about Olivia?" Kent asked. "Isn't she coming with us?"

"That wouldn't be wise," Pike said. "She's known. The attack on her apartment proved that."

"So, she's staying here?" Kent said with growing concern. "That means when the Bridge blows she'll be stuck in the future."

"I'm sorry, Kent," Pike said with genuine sympathy. "I know you have all grown close, but we can't risk jeopardizing your mission."

Kent stared at the floor, his jaw muscles clenching. It looked like he was swaying, as if unsteady on his own two feet.

"Can we at least say goodbye to her?" I asked.

"Of course, she's right outside," Sokol said. "I'll send her in. Make it quick."

Pike, Sokol, and the two Sounders left the room.

I had no idea of what to say. I had expected Olivia to be with us. If anybody earned the right to have a shot at escaping the brutal future, it was her.

"All set?" Olivia said brightly as she stepped into the room.

"I'm not going," Kent said. "Not without you."

Olivia smiled sadly, walked to Kent, and hugged him.

Kent wrapped his arms around her and squeezed her tight.

These two really did have a connection. She might have been messing with me for fun, but it was clear her heart belonged to Kent. They stayed locked together like that for several seconds, neither wanting it to end.

"You have to go," Olivia said. "These guys need you. We all need you."

"It's not fair," Kent said, holding back tears. "You deserve to go. You earned it."

"Yeah, I did," Olivia said. "But the Retros know I'm a Sounder. It would be crazy to risk it."

She was right. We all knew it. Kent probably did too, but he didn't want to accept it.

"There has to be another way," he said with a note of desperation.

"If you've got an idea, I'm open," Olivia said.

He didn't.

Olivia pulled back and held him at arm's length. When she looked at him, I saw how much she truly loved the guy.

"It's come down to this," she said. "This is your chance. You've got to be strong and step up. Do it for your dad. And your mom. And for me too."

Kent bit his lip and nodded. This was killing him.

Olivia let him go and turned to Tori.

"When I grow up, I want to be just like you," she said.

Tori didn't know how to react so she just smiled awkwardly.

"You've been our heart from the beginning," Olivia added. "And our conscience. Please don't stop now."

Tori took a step forward and hugged Olivia. These two never got along, but in the end they developed a genuine respect for each other.

"I couldn't have done what you did," Tori said, her voice cracking. "Or what you're about to do."

"I could say the same thing about you," Olivia replied. "Good luck."

They pulled away and Olivia faced me. There were tears in her eyes.

"I think I'll miss you most, Scarecrow," she said.

"Shut up," I replied.

"C'mon, I love that movie! It was the first one you took me to. Remember?"

"Yeah, I remember. You said it was hokey."

"It was," she said. "That's why I loved it."

She stepped forward and the two of us hugged. She held tight and softly whispered, "Take care of them."

All I could do was hug her tighter.

"Time to go," Sokol said, leaning in the door.

Olivia pulled away from me and straightened up.

"I'm not going to be sitting around just watching all the fun," she said. "I'm on the nuclear team. Front-row seat. So do me a favor and cover my butt from the other side, would you?"

"Done," Kent said with total confidence.

There was an awkward moment of silence while we all stared at one another. I finally broke away from the group and headed for the door.

"I don't know about you guys, but I'm going home," I said and walked out the door without looking back at Olivia. To see her again would have torn my heart out.

Colonel Pike was outside of the room with Brock and Sanchez. I stood next to her, waiting for the others to follow.

Tori came out, followed by Sokol.

We all stood there, waiting. Wondering what Kent was going to do. It was a very long thirty seconds before he stepped out of the doorway. Alone.

"What are we standing around here for?" he declared. "We've got a war to start."

Pike led us up and out of the basement and into the early morning sun. A military transport vehicle was waiting for us on the street, its musical engine already humming. Sanchez went right for it and got behind the wheel. Brock rode shotgun.

Colonel Pike stopped next to the vehicle and pulled something out of her pocket that she handed to Kent and Tori.

"Identification badges," she explained. "Put them on now."

"Hey, that's my picture," Kent said. "How did you get these?"

Pike shot Sokol a bemused smile.

"It's good to be a Colonel," she said.

"Do whatever Brock and Sanchez tell you to," Sokol said. "Those two are the best, and just a little bit dangerous."

"I like that," Kent said.

"If all goes well, there will be a vehicle waiting for you outside the dome on the other side of the Bridge. They'll take you out of the camp and you'll be gone before any of the guards realize what happened."

"And if all doesn't go well?" Tori asked.

Sokol shrugged and said, "Then shoot your way out."

That gave us all a moment's pause.

"What happens once we're out of the camp?" I asked.

"You tell us," Sokol said. "We don't have any way to contact SYLO. That's why we need you."

I didn't point out that we didn't know how to make contact with them, either.

"Eighteen hundred hours," Pike said. "That's when the curtain goes up. If SYLO doesn't step in, it'll be a very short show."

"All we can do is try," I said.

Pike had said all she needed to say. She looked at each of us and softened a little.

"You're just kids," she said, mostly to herself.

"Badass kids," Kent said.

Sokol held back a chuckle.

"No words can say how honored I am to know you," Pike said. "Good luck."

We piled into the car. The last one in was Kent, who looked square at Sokol and said, "You better stop those damn drones."

Sokol didn't respond. He didn't need Kent to tell him what he had to do.

Kent got in the car, slammed the door, and we took off.

I looked back at the building to see Olivia appear in the doorway. She didn't wave. She just stood there with her hands on her hips, watching us. For a second I imagined her standing on the porch of the Blackbird Inn, wearing a red bikini and holding a tray of ice tea for Quinn and me.

I wished I hadn't looked back.

We drove silently through the filthy streets, each alone with our own thoughts. My mind was strangely blank. I didn't want to stress over each possible scenario because there was no way to predict what we would face. It was more about clearing my head, preparing to roll with whatever came our way, and trying not to hyperventilate.

After driving for what seemed like only a few seconds, Brock turned back to us.

"We'll park a hundred meters from the dome and walk the rest of the way on foot," he explained. "Standard escort formation around Pierce. Sleeper and I in front, Berringer and Sanchez behind. We'll go through a checkpoint where they'll scan your badges. Our orders have been input into the system. There should be no problem. Do not speak unless asked a direct question. Remember, we're escorting a prisoner to the forward camp. That's all you need to say. I'm the officer in charge of the transfer. All questions should be directed to me anyway. Understood?"

"What happens after we get through the Bridge?" I asked.

"We'll track down transport and drive out of the camp," he replied.

"Easy as that?" I asked.

"Easy as that. After that, you're on."

That was the part that worried me.

We drove through the early-morning light of the Bridge city

with no company. There were no other vehicles on the road and very few pedestrians. The city was only beginning to wake up. The dome loomed in the distance ahead of us. Less than nine hours from then an atomic bomb was going to be detonated inside of that structure that would hopefully save what was left of our world from the invasion.

I stared at the buildings as we drove by, sickened by what the world had become and amazed at the shortsightedness that allowed it to happen. As much as I didn't want to think ahead and guess what would happen as the day played out, I allowed myself to hope that we would never have to see this cursed city and time again.

We turned the final corner onto the wide street that would lead us to the dome.

"Oh crap," Kent said.

Stretched out before us was a line of attack ships that reached all the way to the dome. They weren't the small unmanned drones that had done so much damage throughout the world; these were the giant piloted planes that could wipe out an entire city on their own. It was the type of plane that Tori and I had sabotaged, which led to the destruction of the entire fleet of Retro planes at Area 51.

"I guess tonight really is the night," Sanchez said with awe.

These ships were floating in line, ready to pass through the Bridge on their way to delivering the final blow to the past. They were patiently waiting to do what they did best.

Destroy.

Sanchez turned onto a side street, pulled to the curb, and cut the engine.

"This is it," Brock announced. "Questions?"

"What are our chances?" Kent asked.

"Any other questions?" Brock said.

We climbed out and walked back to the main street where the giant planes were lined up. It was a sobering sight, made all the more so because from that moment on we were going to be in serious danger.

"Lead on," I said. "I'm the prisoner, remember?"

As instructed, Tori and Brock walked shoulder to shoulder in front of me; Kent and Sanchez were close behind. Now that we were near the heart of the city, and the dome, there were many more pedestrians. I kept my head down, fearing that someone might recognize me. Or worse, recognize Tori or Kent and wonder why they were wearing Air Force uniforms.

To anybody who took notice of us, they must have thought I was some dangerous master criminal. Why else would I be getting such treatment?

We passed by the low, rounded building with the steel doors we had seen when we first arrived. It was where the atomic devices were kept. There were armed guards in front. They had no idea of what was going to come down on top of their heads in a few hours.

As we neared the dome we entered an area separated from the street by a low metal fence. It was a chute that funneled personnel into the security check before entering the dome. I kept my hands in plain sight, folded in front of me. It gave me a feeling of security to feel the two pulsers that were hidden in my sleeves. In my mind I practiced a hundred times how I would let them slip out, ready to shoot.

Brock marched right up to the Retro soldier who was stationed in front of a metal archway that we would need to pass through before entering the dome.

"Prisoner transfer to the forward camp," Brock announced, holding his black pad device out for the security guy to see.

I kept my head down, but looked ahead, ready for any sign of trouble.

The guard looked bored. He made some entries into his own black pad, probably to confirm the transfer orders that Pike had put in.

"I'm jealous," the guard said.

"Why's that?" Brock asked.

"You're gonna be on the other side when the action starts," he said, gesturing to the line of monster planes.

"Right," Brock said. "When's kickoff?"

"Sometime after nightfall," the guard replied. "You have no idea how crazy it's going to get around here."

"Oh, I can take a good guess," Brock said. "Are we clear?"

The guard stepped aside to let us pass.

"Have a good trip," the guard said. "Light those bastards on the other side up for me."

"That's the plan," Tori said.

Brock shot her a stern look.

We passed through the checkpoint and strode toward the dome.

The giant doors were open, having been retracted into the shell of the immense structure. They would have to be closed by the Sounders or the blast wouldn't be contained and the entire city might be wiped out.

None of us said a word, but I knew that all of our hearts were beating a little faster, because mine sure was. We strode directly into the dome as if we belonged. Inside, in front of the giant frame that held the Bridge, was a hovering Retro fighter, ready to move through to the past. A few Retro soldiers stood guard around the structure, which was different than when we had arrived. I wondered if security had been tightened because of the Sounder activity over the past day. Or maybe it was because they were preparing the next wave of the invasion. Whatever the reason, it meant that the Sounders were going to have more of a challenge to bring in the bomb.

Gratefully, none of the guards looked on edge. They seemed more like bored traffic cops as they kept the flow of gear, planes, and personnel moving through the Bridge.

We were moving directly for the Bridge when a guard called out to us.

"Hey! Who's this guy?" he shouted.

We stopped as the guard strolled up, staring at me.

"Why does this scum get to go back?" he asked.

"He's infected with a virus that was eradicated two hundred years ago," Brock said without missing a beat. "It's fatal. Want to kiss him goodbye?"

The guard turned white and backed off quickly.

"Whoa, no, carry on. Good riddance."

The guard turned and hurried off.

"You thought of everything," I said softly.

"We try," Brock said. "Ready?"

We all stood there, bathed in the glow from within the frame.

"I want to go back," Tori said. "But I don't."

"Eight hours," Sanchez said.

"Let's go!" Kent exclaimed.

We had to wait a few more seconds as the black fighter disappeared into the white light of the Bridge, before stepping up to the frame for our turn.

"Stay alert," Brock warned.

"I can't be any more alert than I am right now," Kent said. "I'm ready to pee my pants."

"Don't do that," Brock said.

He stepped into the light and disappeared. Tori went directly after him and I was the next up. I didn't hesitate for a second.

The act of stepping through this impossible "Bridge" through time gave absolutely no sensation or sense of movement. It was no different than stepping through a doorway from one room to the next, only the next room was centuries in the past and was an entirely different stream of existence. I walked out of the light and into the dome of the past as easily as if I had gone through a doorway in my house.

The past dome looked no different than when we had come through the day before. Other than the black plane that had floated out of the giant doors ahead of us, there was very little activity.

"Smells much better," Kent said after he came through behind me. "Never thought I'd appreciate a place because of the way it smelled. Or didn't smell."

"Keep moving," Brock commanded.

My heart had been thumping from the moment we stepped out of the military vehicle back in the future. Now it was absolutely pounding. We were back in the camp where Tori, Kent, and I were prisoners. Known prisoners. We had already made one escape, and now we would attempt a second.

Brock and Tori led us out of the dome and into the hot, bright light of the Mojave desert. As much as I hated Bova's cruel camp, it was a welcome relief to see clear skies and an uncluttered view of the mountains. It made me even more angry to think of what the world would become.

"Now what?" Tori asked.

Brock pulled his communicator from his pocket and tapped it a few times. "Our ride should be waiting right . . . there."

He pointed to our right where a camouflage Humvee was parked.

"How did you pull this off?" Kent asked.

"You know we have people on this side," Sanchez said. "Once you all agreed to come back, we sent people through to alert them and set it all up."

The vehicle was only thirty yards away. We were one step closer to getting out of there. We all walked quickly but deliberately toward the waiting vehicle. Glancing around I saw no signs of the aerial attack that had hit the camp just the day before. Wreckage was cleared away and even the burned barracks was now just an empty patch of sand. The SYLO attack hadn't affected the camp in the slightest. I really hoped that wouldn't be the case with the next one.

With only steps to go, I allowed myself to believe that we were going to make it.

"Zero Three One One!" a woman called.

I froze. I had hoped I would never hear that number again, especially not then.

It was the commander of blue unit. She was leading her prisoners through the empty expanse in front of the dome when she spotted me.

We were stopped dead in our tracks. Even Brock seemed unsure of what to do.

The woman approached, looking confused.

"What the hell is going on?" she said. "I thought Bova and Feit had found you and—"

The words caught in her throat when she saw something that made even less sense to her: Two of her other prisoners were there as well, and they were wearing Air Force uniforms.

"Wha . . ." she gasped, then quickly pulled a communicator from her back pocket.

"Show's over," Brock announced.

He raised his pulser and fired, knocking the woman back and onto the ground.

So much for stealth.

"Let's go!" Sanchez announced and ran for the Humvee.

The rest of us were right behind him.

I slid the two pulsers out of my sleeves.

When we got to the vehicle, the two Sounders jumped in front while Tori, Kent, and I climbed in back. Sanchez fired up the gas engine and hit the accelerator. There was no time to be cautious. We had to get out of there.

"Stay down," Sanchez barked. "They're going to be coming at us from every angle."

He wasn't kidding. Before getting shot, the unit supervisor must have pushed the panic button, because Retro soldiers appeared from everywhere, trying to head us off. They had their pulsers up and started firing. Sanchez was good: He swerved at full speed, trying to make a difficult target. The Humvee was big and sturdy. A few shots of energy pounded us, rattling the heavy vehicle and knocking us around, but it didn't stop us.

"We're making it too easy for them," Tori announced. She rolled down the window and started shooting back. She aimed dead ahead and to the side, spraying our attackers. The blasts of energy forced the Retros to scatter as the buildings around them were rocked. Brock did the same from the other side. The Retros continued to fire back, but with more caution, because they now feared they would be shot themselves.

Sanchez drove with his foot to the floor, taking sharp, high-speed turns that I was sure would flip us over.

"Look out!" Kent shouted.

Another vehicle was headed directly for us. It was a game of chicken. Sanchez didn't blink. He charged straight ahead on a direct line for the oncoming car.

"Shoot him!" Kent screamed.

Brock leaned out of the window and fired.

He hit the windshield, forcing the car to swerve. That's when Sanchez made his move. He spun the wheel hard to the right, fishtailing our vehicle into a violent, skidding turn. Our back end clipped the front of the enemy's vehicle. It was a brutal jolt, but it didn't stop us.

"We're gonna make it," Kent said.

We were nearing the last of the new buildings. All around us, prisoners scattered to get out of our way as Retro soldiers fought to get a clean shot at us.

It was too late. They hadn't rallied fast enough. Sanchez didn't let off of the gas and we charged past the last of the barracks and out into the wide-open spaces of the Mojave. The camp had no fences surrounding it. Once we sped past the line of huge antiaircraft guns that protected the dome, there was nothing around us but miles of open desert.

"Yeah!" Kent screamed.

"We're not safe," I said. "They could follow."

"Or send out the drones," Tori said.

"That depends," Brock said.

"On what?"

"On how much they care," he replied. "They've got more important things to worry about than a couple of escaped prisoners. Tonight begins the second phase of the invasion. In the big picture, you aren't that important to them."

"Gee, thanks," Kent said.

"Of course if they knew who you really were . . ."

Tori twisted around to look back at the camp, which was quickly growing smaller.

"I don't see anybody coming," she said.

That didn't matter to Sanchez. He didn't let up off of the gas. We had to have been doing a hundred across the flat desert. He pressed on like that for several minutes while we all held our breath.

"I think we made it," Kent said full of nervous hope. "Right? We made it. Do you think we made it? I think we did."

Brock turned to face us. "We made it."

"Good, I thought so," Kent said quickly.

"So . . . where to?" Brock asked.

I wished I had the answer. I wanted to be able to tell them exactly where to go so we could be picked up by SYLO, but I didn't have a clue.

"Maybe back to Area 51," Tori said. "That's where they picked us up after the fleet was destroyed. It's as good a spot to start as any."

Brock lifted his communicator and said, "If I knew what frequency they were operating on I might be able to . . ."

He stopped talking and frowned. Something he saw on his device was bad news.

"What?" Tori asked.

"Repeat," Brock said into the device.

He read whatever the response was and his eyes went wide.

"Stop the vehicle!" he shouted to Sanchez.

Sanchez gave him a quick, surprised look and hit the brakes. The car skidded across the dry surface, twisting and slipping so violently that I feared we were going to roll as we went from a hundred to zero in three seconds flat.

"Get out!" Brock screamed.

"What happened?" Sanchez asked.

"They targeted our signal," Brock shouted as he desperately fumbled to open the door.

Up until that moment Brock had been the coolest guy under pressure that I had ever seen. Now he was in full-on panic.

The three of us were momentarily frozen, not sure of what to do.

Brock threw open his door and turned back to us.

"Move!" he screamed, his face red and his eyes wild.

He didn't move until he saw that Tori and I had gotten our doors open. Tori scrambled out of her side and Kent was right behind her. I threw open my door and jumped out.

"Run!" Brock yelled. "Get away from the vehicle!"

I heard a faint whistling sound that quickly became louder. It grew into a terrifying shriek that foretold the destruction about to happen.

A second later the missile, or whatever it was, hit the car. The Humvee exploded from the force of the powerful missile and the eruption of the gas tank. The concussion hit me in the back and threw me forward. I felt as though I was on fire. I hit the ground, face first, and saw stars. As I lay there, pressed against the ground, trying to catch my breath and pull my head together, I listened for another missile. There was nothing.

I slowly got to my knees and turned around to see the Humvee in flames. They didn't need another missile. One was plenty. I looked around for Sanchez, for we had both been on the same side of the vehicle.

"Man that was close," I said. "Another second and . . ."

I stopped talking because nobody was listening. Sanchez wasn't there.

I staggered to my feet and looked beyond the inferno to see Kent kneeling over Tori. Though my head was spinning and my knees were weak, I ran for them.

As Tori's head lay in Kent's lap, I flashed back to the final moments of Olivia's life. Her other life. It was a "death" she recovered from. This was different. We had no miracle medicine to cure her.

"Tori," I called while running to her. I dropped to my knees next to her and stared into her closed eyes, willing them to open.

They didn't.

Instead, she spoke.

"That hurt."

I let out a relieved laugh.

"You okay?" I asked Kent.

He nodded quickly.

Brock staggered up to us. "One of our operatives in the camp sent me the warning. He was in the command center when they fired the missile."

"He saved us," Tori said.

"Yeah, well, not all of us," Brock said solemnly.

I didn't understand what he meant at first. My thoughts were too jumbled. It wasn't until I realized he was staring at the burning wreckage that I put it together.

"Sanchez," I said.

"Oh my God," Kent said with a gasp.

He hadn't gotten out in time. Sanchez was yet another victim of the Retro invasion.

"I'm sorry," I said.

"Don't be sorry," Brock replied through gritted teeth. "Get us to SYLO."

TWENTY

"The dune buggy," I said. "We left it on the edge of Area 51."

"That's like, miles from here," Kent said. "A lot of miles."

Brock glanced at his communicator.

"Roughly sixty miles," he said. "Over open desert, and it's only going to get hotter. It'll take hours that we don't have."

"Then we better start walking," I said.

I helped Tori to her feet. She was shaken, but okay.

"Can that thing tell us the right direction?" she said.

Brock checked his device and pointed north. "Looks like there might be some rough terrain."

"Gee, big surprise," Kent said sarcastically.

We all took one last look at the burning wreck. The guy inside had sacrificed his life to try to stop the invasion and avert another massacre. No words were adequate.

"He won't be be forgotten," Brock said.

I started walking and the others followed. The sun was already heating up the desert floor. It wouldn't be long before we would be laboring in hundred-degree heat, without water.

"We find that dune buggy," Brock said. "Then what?"

"We left a car further back in the desert," I said. "If we can get there we'll have wheels that can cover a lot more ground. We can drive to Los Angeles. There's a SYLO ark on Catalina Island. Hopefully between here and there we'll get somebody's attention and they'll send a helicopter."

Nobody offered an opinion about the plan but I knew what was going through their heads. They were calculating the time it would take to do what I had just suggested. With the Sounders' mission set to roll in under eight hours, the grim reality was that even if everything worked out perfectly, we would be cutting it very close.

"Look," I said, sharply. "I never said I could get us to SYLO. This whole plan is a total long shot."

"Understood," Brock said. "We'll just do what we can."

The sun was rising higher in the sky and along with it, the temperature. After walking for nearly an hour, the odds of us making it back to Area 51 were feeling very small.

"We're in trouble," Kent said.

"You think?" Tori shot back.

"No, I mean we haven't been walking for all that long and I'm already hallucinating."

"What are you talking about?" I asked.

"I'm seeing a mirage. It's total wishful thinking because it's something I'm dying to see."

"What? A swimming pool?" Tori asked.

"No, that's number two. I see somebody driving our way."

"Shake it off," I said. "We've still got a long way to go."

"I see it too," Brock announced.

He pointed ahead to a distant dust storm that was rising from the desert floor. At first I thought it was being kicked up by the wind, which would have been a welcome relief from the heat, but as I focused I saw what was actually creating it: a speeding blue pickup truck.

"Can you share a mirage?" Kent asked, dumbfounded.

"No, it's real," Brock declared.

We started waving our arms and screaming to make sure whoever it was would see us. Nobody feared that it would be a Retro vehicle. They didn't drive beat-up old Fords. The truck definitely saw us and was headed our way, speeding across the dry lakebed.

"Why would anybody be driving around out here?" Tori asked.

"Who cares?" Kent shot back.

The pickup drove straight for us. There were two people in the cab wearing cowboy hats. The truck may have been ancient with faded paint and rusted side panels, but it was the sweetest ride I had ever seen. It drove right up to us, then turned and stopped as the driver leaned out of the window.

"No way," Kent said with a gasp.

"Never thought I'd be seeing you all again," the driver said with a smile. "Looks like you've been busy."

It was the elderly Native American man who had set us up with the dune buggies for our assault on Area 51. The Paiute tribe had been helping the survivors of Las Vegas plan the attack. They were the survivors' eyes in the desert, watching over the fleet of Retro drones.

Tori ran up to him, reached into the cab, and threw her arms around him.

"I can't believe you're here," she said.

"It was quite the show you all put on the other night," he said. "You really lit up the sky. We've been sifting through the wreckage of the base ever since, looking for survivors. We pulled a few out and got them help. Others weren't so lucky. There was no reason to watch the base anymore, so we turned our eyes to the test site. Every so often we'd pick up someone who escaped into the desert but mostly we just watched. After we saw this last explosion I decided to come see what was happening for myself."

He gave us all a quick look and added, "You join up with the other side?"

"The uniforms?" Tori said. "No, this is how we escaped."

"What's your name?" I asked.

"Foote," he replied. "Jimmy Foote. This is my nephew, David Foote."

"Foot?" Kent said. "As in running stealthily through the forest?"

"No. Foote with an 'e,' as in I'll use it to kick your ass if you make any more racist jokes."

"Noted," Kent said, chastised. "Glad to see you again, sir."

"Any chance of you giving us a lift back to our car?" I asked.

"You don't need the car," Foote said.

"But we do," Tori argued. "We have to get to Los Angeles as quickly as possible."

"That won't be a problem," Foote said. He held up a walkie-talkie and added, "As soon as I saw you I put out a call."

"Call to who?" Kent asked, skeptically. "Your tribe?"

"Yes," Foote said. "Without phones, this is the only way to

relay messages across any distance."

"You mean beating drums doesn't work?" Kent said, then quickly thought better of it and added, "Geez, sorry, that just came out."

Foote stared him down, then let out a small smile. "No. And it's been too windy for smoke signals."

Kent kept his eyes on the ground, but he was smiling.

I think those two liked jabbing at each other.

"After the base blew up, I watched as you got picked up by that military helicopter," Foote said. "You all seemed to know each other."

"The woman was my mother," I said.

Foote nodded knowingly, as if I had confirmed his opinion. "Well then, seems as though I made the right choice."

"What did you do?" Tori asked.

As if in answer, the far-off sound of an engine began to grow. It quickly transformed into a distinct thumping.

"Is that what I think it is?" Kent asked hopefully.

"Please say it is," Tori added.

"It is," Foote said.

It was the sound of helicopter rotors.

We looked to the sky to see a black speck in the distance that was approaching quickly.

"Did I do the right thing?" Foote asked.

Tori leaned into the car and hugged him again.

"You have no idea," she said.

"Sir," Brock said. "Forgive me for being dramatic, but you may have just saved the lives of millions of people."

Foote raised an eyebrow and said, "Really? I guess we redskins know a thing or two." He looked to Kent and added, "Right, Paleface?"

"Absolutely, sir," Kent replied with a big grin. "Well done."

The two shook hands.

The helicopter hovered overhead, giving us a clear view of something we had seen many times before. For the first time it was a welcome sight.

Painted on its belly was the unmistakable rising-sun logo.

SYLO had arrived.

———

The flight to Catalina Island took less than an hour, which meant we had roughly seven hours to convince the SYLO command to storm the Retro camp and secure the dome.

As we approached the island from the air, the scene reminded me of Pemberwick. The island was surrounded by Navy warships. There looked to be even more than on Pemberwick, because the entire land mass was surrounded, not just the stretch of shore between Catalina and the mainland. SYLO looked as though they weren't taking any chances here. It made me wonder what kind of shape Pemberwick Island was in.

When we circled down toward the center of the huge island, I saw that a tent city had been erected, much like SYLO had done on the golf course outside of Arbortown. Again, it was a much bigger operation than back home. This wasn't just a makeshift prison camp. This had become a full-on military base with several barracks, antiaircraft guns along the shore, and what looked to be hundreds of attack helicopters lined up on a dusty field.

There was also a herd of buffalo that bolted away from the landing pad as we came in. It was an odd touch to an already strange scene. As soon as we landed, several SYLO soldiers wearing the familiar deep-red camouflage fatigues threw open the door and motioned for us to exit.

"Good luck," I said to my friends and we all piled out of the helicopter.

Brock was immediately taken into custody by two of the soldiers.

"He's a friend," I called to them.

They didn't hear me. Or didn't care. With a soldier on each of his arms, they hurried Brock to a waiting jeep.

"Seven hours!" Brock called over his shoulder to us.

"He didn't need to say that," Kent said.

We weren't treated much better. I guess the fact that Tori and Kent were wearing Retro uniforms didn't help things much. A SYLO soldier was assigned to each of us. With other armed soldiers keeping watch, we were patted down and our pulsers taken. We were then separated and brought to individual jeeps.

"Talk fast," I called to my friends.

We were each pushed into the back of a different jeep, along with our escorts, who had yet to say a single word. The jeeps took off, kicking up dust as we sped toward the encampment. I took those few minutes to try to figure out what I was going to say to whatever SYLO officer we would see. I had to believe that they knew everything about the Bridge through time, so at least I wouldn't have to sell that part of the story. But convincing them to stage an all-out raid on the Retro base in Nevada? That was a tall order.

We bumped along the dirt road and drove straight into the base. There were no fences and no barbed wire. This wasn't a SYLO prison. SYLO soldiers were everywhere, but unlike Pemberwick Island, where they wore only fatigues, most of these soldiers also had on body armor and helmets.

Everyone carried a weapon.

This base was in war mode.

The jeeps separated, headed for different destinations. I was driven to a small wooden hut and hurried inside. There was a long table with chairs spaced along one side. Across from it was a single chair. I knew this drill. I was about to be interrogated. Again.

"Wait," was the one word the soldier said to me as he headed for the door.

He left, but then came back almost immediately with a bottle of Gatorade.

He handed it to me and said, "Welcome to Catalina."

"Thanks," I said and took the bottle, gratefully.

He left and I downed the entire bottle in seconds. I hadn't realized how thirsty I was. I could have knocked back three more. A few minutes later three people filed into the room. There were two women and a man in fatigues. Officers, probably. They showed no emotion as they filed in, sat at the table, and set up recording devices.

It was odd how nobody was talking. I could say that they were being all business, but I wished somebody would at least tell me why they were treating us like prisoners.

"State your name please," the man said.

I sat in the chair and said, "Tucker Pierce."

"We will be recording this interview as well as the interviews of the others who were brought in with you. Forgive the perfunctory treatment. We do not want to influence or guide your statements in any way. We have separated you in order to get each individual version."

"To see if we're all telling the truth," I said.

That got no reaction from the group.

"Just for the record," I added. "We're running out of time. Do whatever it is you've got to do. Ask whatever questions you want, but do it fast. Once you hear what I have to say, you'll know why."

"Understood," the man said. "There will not be many questions. We want you to do the talking. Please begin by relating the events between the time your helicopter was shot down over the Nevada Test Site, until you were picked up in the desert an hour ago."

I spent the next fifteen minutes telling the story. I needed to talk fast, but I didn't want to leave out any key details. If my words were stunning to any of them, they didn't show it. I didn't see any reaction until I dropped the bomb about why the Sounders helped us to escape from the island: We were there to convince them to invade the Retro base and capture the dome.

The three exchanged quick looks, which I'm guessing for this sober bunch was roughly the same as if they had all jumped up on to the table and shouted, "What!"

"So that's it," I said. "The Sounders will detonate the bomb in roughly six and a half hours, and three hundred some odd years from now. If the dome in this time isn't secured, there will be nothing to stop the Retro soldiers from going through the Bridge into the future and preventing the explosion. I know it's a lot to swallow. Or maybe it isn't. I'm sure you guys have known about this time travel Bridge for a long time. It's all new to me. I have nothing else to say to convince you other than to remind you that my friends and I destroyed the entire Retro fleet of drones at Area 51. That ought to give us a little credibility. Now that you know why I'm here, you know why acting fast is critical. And that's all I have to say."

The officers turned off their recording devices and stood.

"Now what?" I said.

"Obviously we will have to discuss this," one officer said. "Please remain here for the time being."

With that they headed for the door.

"Don't take your time," I said.

They opened the door to leave, and another soldier entered carrying a tray of food. I'd never met the guy, but I loved him on sight. I was starving and still beyond thirsty. He put the tray down on the table and said, "I'll be right outside. If you want anything else, call me."

"Thanks," I said and sat down to chow.

It was just like Thanksgiving dinner. Turkey and mashed potatoes and all the other goodies. I was in heaven. I also noted that they had given me a metal fork and knife. It was a small thing, but it proved they didn't consider me a threat. I ate, too fast, and loved every second of it. Once I was done I was left not knowing what to do. I didn't want to risk going outside. I didn't want to do anything that would go against what they told me to do. It was crazy, but the future of our world could very well depend on our ability to convince these people that we knew what we were talking about. That was a scary thought.

I must have waited there for an hour either nervously tapping my foot or pacing. I kept telling myself that the SYLO honchos were taking us seriously and were meeting to discuss what they were going to do. That wouldn't happen quickly. You don't launch a massive attack on a whim.

I did everything I could to burn energy and stay inside my own skin. I did push-ups and sit-ups. I counted the cracks in the floor. I licked the lunch plate a dozen times just to make sure I got every drop of gravy-goodness. Finally, when I couldn't take it anymore, I decided to go outside and ask the guard what was going on.

I had gotten halfway across the floor to the door, when it opened.

Stepping into the room was Captain Granger.

"Hello Mr. Pierce," he said, all business.

I think my draw dropped. Literally.

"You . . . you're not dead," I mumbled.

"Not yet," he said with no hint of irony.

He held an iPad that he was reading from. I assumed it showed transcripts from our interviews. He walked to one end of the long table, the end without the dirty plates, and sat.

"What happened to you?" I asked. "After the crash, I mean."

Without taking his eyes off of the iPad he said, "I was unconscious, so I can only go by what I've been told. Another

Skyhawk came in to rescue survivors. They were only on the ground for a few moments when they came under heavy fire. They only had time to pull out one survivor."

"So they chose their boss," I said.

Granger went back to his reading. I paced, desperately wanting him to say something.

"The future sucks, you know," I finally said. "They blame us. You, me, everybody who came before them. Part of me understands why they're trying to get the hell out."

"So you agree with their methods?" he asked.

"No," I said quickly. "But if I could press a button and wipe out every last one of them, I'd do it. Does that make me any different than them?"

"It makes you human," Granger said. "As for the morality of it all, that call has to be made by somebody with a much higher pay grade than me."

"How could this have happened?" I said. "The Bridge was open for decades. Why didn't anybody do something? We saw what was coming."

He finally put the iPad down and looked at me. "I'm not a politician. I'm not a sociologist or a psychologist. And I am far from a scientist. I'm a simple soldier. The circumstances that led us to this place are beyond my comprehension."

"How long have you known? About the Bridge, I mean."

"Ten years. That's about the time when the idea for SYLO was born. The way I understand it, from the very beginning there was tension between the governments of the present and the future. It made the Cold War pale by comparison. The future government pushed to have its existence revealed. They felt if the people of the past knew what they were creating, they would choose a different course. The present government resisted, for fear it would tear apart the fabric of society. The only reason they were able to keep the situation under wraps was because the Bridge was so isolated. All of those alien spaceship theories about Area 51 weren't far from wrong. They just missed it by sixty-five miles."

"So the present government ignored the truth?" I asked.

"No, but they were fighting a losing battle. Over the years only a small group of scientists were allowed to study the twenty-fourth century. The movement to develop renewable energy and to reduce greenhouse gases, even the push to recycle, began because they saw what was coming. But they couldn't battle against the tide of commerce. People complained the government was trying to rule their lives. The bottom line was the bottom line. Money. And yes, the various administrations and governments kid themselves into believing the small efforts that were being made would be enough to avoid the nightmare that the future had become. The truth is, we still don't know. We won't know until we get there."

"Because changing the past won't affect a future that already exists," I said.

"Exactly. Once that became known, the die was cast. When the future government realized that nothing we did could actually help them, they prepared to invade."

"And we knew about it?" I asked.

"No, we suspected it," Granger replied. "Every movement of our scientists in the twenty-fourth century was suddenly controlled and monitored. We witnessed signs of an immense military buildup. We asked to inspect various manufacturing areas and were refused. We were given the rationale that the United States of the future needed to build up their military in order to defend themselves against the other six countries they were at war with."

"But they were really preparing to invade the past," I said.

Granger nodded. "That's what we feared and that's why SYLO was born."

"*Sequentia yconomus libertate te ex inferis obedianter,*" I said. "These guardians obediently protect us from the gates of hell."

"Or something like that," Granger said with a dismissive huff. "I didn't come up with that. The decision was made to create smaller communities that we had a better chance of defending. Arks, if you will. Over a ten-year period we chose volunteers to populate these arks. We selected people from all walks of life with different areas of expertise. Doctors, engineers, architects, musicians, pretty much every skill and talent that needed to be preserved was represented, along with every race and religion."

"My father is a civil engineer," I said. "My mother is an accountant. Quinn's parents were doctors."

"Hundreds of people quietly volunteered to uproot their lives and move to an ark. The idea was that if the Retros ever attacked, we would need them in order to rebuild our world."

"When SYLO came to Pemberwick, you must have known the attack was imminent," I said.

"It was more than imminent," Granger said. "It was underway. The Retros finally made their move to come through the Bridge. I showed you the aftermath of that battle from the air."

"All those wrecked aircraft surrounding the dome," I said. "They were trying to keep the Retro planes from coming through."

"They failed," Granger said. "The battle lasted for over a week. Once we realized it was hopeless, we activated the arks. That's when SYLO landed on Pemberwick Island and here on Catalina and Fort Knox and a dozen other places. These arks were to be our last stand. But even that plan was flawed when we realized how many Retro spies had infiltrated them. You may have thought my methods were ruthless on Pemberwick Island, and they were, but I was doing all that I could to protect the ark."

I sat listening, letting this all sink in. Everything that Granger said fit. Every last piece of the puzzle had come together.

"And that brings us to today, and what you and your friends have learned," Granger said. "I believe I know you, Tucker Pierce. I shudder to think that I nearly caused your death."

"Yeah, about a dozen times," I said.

"What I'm saying is I believe you. I believe Sleeper and Berringer as well. Do you know for an absolute fact that the Retros are preparing a second-wave invasion?"

"I do," I said with confidence. "It could be as soon as tonight. We saw a dozen of those monster planes lined up on the other side of the bridge, ready to come through. They're going to wait for nightfall and finish the job. First the cities, then the population at large."

Granger nodded thoughtfully.

"This Major Brock who came back with you," Granger said. "He is an impressive young man."

"All the Sounders are," I said. "They formed an underground

network that is ready to fight back. Olivia Kinsey is a Sounder. You should shudder to think that you almost killed her, too."

Granger ignored that comment and said, "Do these Sounders realize that if they succeed in their plan to destroy the Bridge, they're ultimately committing suicide?"

"They do. That's how strongly they feel about stopping the invasion. They're planning to detonate an atomic device in the dome at six o'clock. Sharp. I believe they can do it, but only if the dome on this side of the Bridge is protected."

Granger stood and paced. It was the most nervous I'd ever seen him, except for maybe when he got the word at Fort Knox that an attack was imminent. Or when our helicopter was plummeting to earth.

"We've had a plan in place to stage a ground attack on the test site for years. But it was never carried about because of the drones. We simply cannot stand up to them."

"Unless the Sounders take them out of play," I said.

Granger's eyes lit up. The idea that the drones could be stopped was like an impossible dream come true.

"We didn't know about the Sounders," he said. "We had suspicions. Even hopes. But we never had conclusive evidence that there were forces within the Retros that could help us bring them down . . . until now."

"So does that mean you'll attack?" I asked.

Granger sat on the edge of the table and rubbed his face. The guy suddenly looked a hundred years old. I guess fighting a war will do that to you. He looked at me and chuckled. He actually chuckled.

"If a superior officer told me they were going to put our troops in harm's way based on information brought to him by a bunch of kids, I'd immediately call for his removal and court-martial, not to mention a psychiatric evaluation."

"But you aren't crazy," I said.

"Sometimes I wonder," he said, wistfully. "But there is one thing I do know: We're losing this war. SYLO has failed. All we've managed to do is prolong the inevitable. It won't matter if the Retros choose tonight to launch another attack or next week or next year. They hold all the cards. Two of the arks have already fallen. Three others are barely holding on. It really is only a matter of time before they take complete control and wipe out every last hint that our time, our society, ever existed."

It took everything I had not to ask him about Pemberwick Island, and my father.

Granger looked at me, as if seeing me for the first time. "You're a hell of a kid, you know that? All three of you are. I wish I could have met the Kinsey girl, knowing what I know now."

"Without shooting at her, you mean?"

We stared at each other for several seconds.

"Six o'clock just keeps on getting closer," I said.

The door to the building opened behind me. Granger looked up and did something I never expected. He stood up straight, like a soldier at attention.

I had no idea what he was doing, until I turned around to see who had walked into the room. When I saw him, I jumped up too.

It was a guy whose face I had only seen on TV. The last time was when he was explaining to the world how Pemberwick Island needed to be quarantined. It suddenly made sense why the defenses around Catalina Island were much stronger than anywhere else.

President Richard E. Neff was there.

He looked exactly as he did on TV, though maybe a little older. His short gray hair had become grayer and his eyes looked tired. He wore jeans and a windbreaker. Not exactly presidential attire.

"Relax son," he said with an easy smile. "I just wanted to meet the fella who has been causing all the stir."

He walked up to me with his hand out to shake.

"I'm Richard," he said warmly.

I shook his hand and mumbled, "I . . . I'm Tucker."

"I am very pleased to meet you, Tucker."

After shaking my hand he sat on the edge of the table and glanced at Granger's iPad.

"I've heard your story, Tucker," he said. "I've heard all of your stories. You've had quite the adventure."

"Yeah, you could say that," I said.

Neff chuckled. "That's exactly what Tori said."

That didn't surprise me.

"I have complete faith in Captain Granger and those in his command," Neff said. "But the decision about where we go from here rests with me. I need to ask you one question."

"Anything, sure," I said eagerly.

"Can the Sounders do this?"

I started to answer quickly, but stopped. This wasn't some random question that I could offer a quick opinion on. If these people believed me, if the president of the United States believed me, we would be responsible for sending an army into battle. People would die. Lots of people. These words would be the most important I had ever spoken in my life.

"I can't say that for sure, sir," I said thoughtfully. "It's not that I question them, or don't believe they have the ability, it's just that I'm not an expert. Anything can happen. But if you're asking me if I believe the Sounders are going to put their lives on the line to destroy the Bridge and take control of the drones, then my answer is yes. They'll do it, or die trying."

The president nodded thoughtfully.

"There's something else I can say for sure," I added.

"What's that?" the president asked.

"Unless you've got something brilliant up your sleeve that I don't know about, the Sounders are our only chance. Our last chance."

The president looked me square in the eye for several seconds. All I could do was hope my words had gotten through to him. In those few moments I saw the resolve and confidence of someone who had to shoulder the burden and responsibility of being the most powerful person in the world.

He abruptly stood and put his hand out to shake.

"Thank you, Tucker," he said. "From the bottom of my heart."

We shook hands.

He then turned to Granger and offered one simple yet profound command, "Go."

"Yes *sir*," Granger said with enthusiasm. It was the word he had been waiting to hear.

Neff started for the door.

"Just one thing," I said.

The president stopped and turned back. "Yes?"

"I'm going too," I said.

"Negative," Granger said quickly. "There's no place for you on this mission."

"If it weren't for me and my friends there wouldn't be a mission," I shot back. "All I'm asking is for my pulser back, and a ride in. You don't have to be responsible for me."

"Look, Pierce," Granger said. "Nobody has more respect for what you've all done than me. Not just respect, awe. But you aren't trained for a mission like this. It would be suicide."

"Why do you want to go so badly?" the president said.

"My mother's in that camp," I said.

That stopped them both. Granger opened his mouth to argue, but didn't.

"I'm going to get her out of there," I added.

"Funny thing," the president said. "Your friends both demanded to go as well."

"Seriously?" I asked. "Even Kent?"

"Oh yes, Mr. Berringer was quite insistent. Apparently you all want to be in on the endgame."

"We do," I said. "I think we earned it."

"Your friends said that as well."

The president looked to Granger and said, "They earned it."

"But Mr. President—"

"They *earned* it," Neff said, forcefully.

Granger softened and said, "Yes, they have."

"Good luck, Tucker," the president said. "Find your mother. Oh, and maybe save the rest of the world while you're at it."

"I'll see what I can do," I said.

The president of the United States stood up straight, looked Granger square in the eye, and said, "Now go take those bastards apart."

It was high noon.

Showdown time once again.

Six hours before the boom.

TWENTY-ONE

Decisions.

I can't begin to count the number of tough choices we had to make since the war began. (Yes, I can officially call it a war now.) Some of them were no-brainers, but most times it was maddeningly difficult to know the right way to go. If there's anything I'd learned since our world changed it's that life is not a series of black-and-white choices. There's usually a whole lot of gray area that has to be navigated. I'd tried to make decisions using both my head and my heart. That usually led down a path that at least seemed right.

As we prepared to make our final trip to the Mojave Desert, we were faced with another difficult decision. In this case, my heart had to battle with my head to tell me the right way to go.

"Ten minutes," the SYLO aide said to Tori, Kent, and me as he led us across a dusty field toward a large wooden building that looked as though it had been built in a hurry. The raw wood siding hadn't even been painted.

SYLO soldiers hurried all around us, scrambling to get to their stations. The camp had come alive with activity. There was a definite sense of excitement and tension. I guess that's what happens when you're preparing to go into battle.

The aide stopped at the door and said, "Be ready in ten or we're going without you."

"I'm ready now," Kent said, boldly.

The aide gave us a quick once-over and said, "Not dressed like that you're not."

He had a point. I was still wearing the orange prison jumpsuit while Kent and Tori had on the uniform of the enemy, the future United States Air Force.

"So what do we wear?" Tori asked.

The aide answered by opening the door and gesturing for us to go inside.

We stepped in to see that SYLO had already thought this through. Hanging from a rack in the middle of the floor were three uniforms.

SYLO uniforms.

"No way," I said without thinking.

The aide shrugged and said, "Your call. You're either on the team or you're not. Ten minutes."

He left and closed the door behind him.

The three of us were left alone, staring at the uniforms of the people who had invaded our home, hunted us down, and killed Tori's father.

"I know they're the good guys," Kent said. "But, I don't know. You spend so much time hating somebody it's hard to just . . . let it go."

Tori walked up to the rack and touched the deep red camouflage material as if it were more than just cloth. I knew where her head was because mine was right there with her. Our thoughts were back on Pemberwick Island, reliving the invasion where SYLO teams dropped from helicopters and landed on the beach. I flashed on memories of soldiers patrolling the streets, standing guard over us at the camp and chasing down runaways. The memory of Captain Granger shooting a runner had been playing in my head for weeks. It was right up there with the image of SYLO gunships firing down on the camp of rebels and killing Mr. Sleeper.

Tori touched the green-and-yellow rising-sun patch on the arm of the uniform, running her finger over the embroidered black letters: SYLO.

"*Sequentia yconomus libertate te ex inferis obedienter*," she said softly, thoughtfully.

"These guardians obediently protect us from the gates of hell," Kent added.

"Question is," Tori continued. "Do we see them as the force that destroyed our lives? Or our only shot at salvation?"

"I have to be honest," I said. "Granger. The killings. My head says one thing but my heart says another."

"It feels a little like making a pact with the devil," Kent said.

Tori took a deep breath, blew it out, stood up straight, and said, "Well then get over it. Both of you. Like it or not, we're the guardians now."

She pulled one of the uniforms off of the hanger and added, "And I'm not going to be left behind."

That was the kicker. We weren't going to be left behind.

Whatever we thought about the way SYLO acted on Pemberwick Island, without them the Sounders would fail.

I looked to Kent. He shrugged and said, "You heard her."

Five minutes later we were dressed in the deep red camouflage fatigues of our former enemy. As alien as it felt, there was also a sense that in some strange way, it was right. In spite of what had unfolded on Pemberwick Island, we *were* the guardians now. Kent even went for the beret.

Tori lifted her pulser to feel its weight. We each had one. None of us felt confidant carrying a standard Navy weapon. They were so . . . crude.

"At least SYLO didn't have these weapons on Pemberwick," she said. "We probably wouldn't be here if they did."

"How do I look?" Kent asked. "Like a badass?"

"No. Just a regular ass," I said. "Lose the beret."

He quickly yanked it off. "Man, pregame. The butterflies are jumping. I gotta find a can."

He rushed off deeper into the building in search of a bathroom, leaving Tori and me alone.

I stood there watching her as she laced up the low black boots. It flashed me back to the time Quinn and I watched her load up her father's pickup truck and expertly tie down the tarp to cover the day's catch of lobsters. She was an enigma to me then, and in some ways she still was. She dealt with loss by shutting herself off from people, because she felt the only person she could fully rely on was herself. Still, she opened up to me. Even the strongest of people sometimes need to know they aren't alone. If I had any regrets over anything I'd done since leaving

Pemberwick it would be for the few times I let her down.

"When this is over," I said. "Are we going to stay together?"

Tori looked at me with a mix of confusion and humor. "What are you asking, Tucker? You want to like, get married or something?"

"No! No. God no. I just meant that after all that's happened I can't imagine not being with you. And seeing as you've lost so much, well, I don't want you to think that you're going to be alone."

"So you feel sorry for me?"

"No, jeez, it's more like we're not just friends, we're family."

"So you want me to be your sister?"

"You're killing me here."

Tori laughed. She was messing with me. She stepped forward and wrapped her arms around me. I hugged her close.

"I know what you're saying," she said. "It's hard to look past today, but whatever happens, I can't imagine a future without you either. It's kind of what keeps me going."

That made me hug her even tighter.

"I don't want you to come today," I said. "I'm not so sure I'd be going myself, if not for my mother. You don't have to do this."

"Yeah I do," she said. "And so does Kent. You know as well as I do that this isn't just about finding your mom. We have to finish this."

I knew she would say that, but I had to give it a try.

"You have to promise me one thing, though," she said.

"What?"

"I know how angry you are. I'm right there with you. Whatever we have to do to survive is justified, except for one thing."

"What's that?"

"Murder."

"I'm not sure it's easy to tell the difference in the middle of a fight," I said.

"I know, but what's about to happen isn't just about fighting to stop the invasion. We have to be better than them. If we win today, a whole new world will be born. It has to be one that would never repeat what the Retros have done. We have to hold on to our humanity, or the new world will eventually end up in as much trouble as the old one."

"So what do you want me to promise?" I asked.

"That you won't do anything you'll regret," she said.

I wasn't so sure I could promise that. The Retros were mass murderers. They should be defeated and punished, no matter what the cost.

"I don't think you would have said that a few weeks ago," I said. "What changed?"

"I met the Sounders," she said. "These people are sacrificing themselves for a principle. They could just as easily have gone along with the program and started a better life here, but they saw how wrong that would be. They're not fighting for survival, they're fighting for what's right."

She pulled away from me and said, "That's what I'm going to do."

I didn't know what to say to her. I heard what she was saying, and it was incredibly noble. But once the fur started to fly, nobility would be the first casualty.

"Then let's just say we'll do what we have to do," I said.

She gave me an uncertain look. She wanted more but I couldn't bring myself to lie to her again. The truth was I wanted revenge. I'd wanted it since the moment Quinn was killed. If I had the chance, I was going to get it. The hell with humanity.

Kent hurried back from his mission, zipping up his uniform.

"Can't say that helped," he announced. "My stomach is still bouncing. But it feels good. I'm ready."

The three of us stood there, facing each other, dressed in our SYLO uniforms. It was a sight I would never have imagined could happen.

We were SYLO.

"This is our last chance," I said. "I know why I'm going. It's about my mom. I don't expect you guys to risk your lives for her."

"But we have to," Kent said. "This is the endgame, man. I'm not going to miss it. Besides, what would Olivia think if I bailed?"

Olivia would never know, but I didn't point that out to him.

"All I want is to find my mother and get her out of there," I said.

"Right there with you, Rook," Kent said. "But if we take out a few Retros along the way, all the better."

Tori didn't bother giving Kent her lecture about revenge and humanity.

"We'll find her," Tori said with confidence.

The front door opened and Granger stepped in, dressed in full combat gear complete with a vest and helmet. On his hip was a pistol in a holster.

"Ready?" he asked.

"Ready," we all responded.

"Second thoughts?" he asked.

"None," Kent replied.

"Then you'll need these," Granger said and motioned to someone outside.

The SYLO aide entered, carrying vests and helmets for us.

"Now we're talking!" Kent declared with relish.

As we geared up, Granger said, "You'll be transported to the desert with me in my chopper. Ground troops will be inserted, creating a wide perimeter around the base, beyond the sight lines of the Retros. We'll hold that position until we're confident that the Retro drones have been grounded."

"And what if we don't get that word?" I asked.

"Then we don't attack," he replied. "We'd be cut down before we got to within a half klick of the camp's perimeter."

I wanted to argue with him, but he was right. The SYLO ground forces would have no chance of securing the dome unless the drones were grounded. I sure hoped that Kenny Sokol and his commandos knew what they were doing.

"As soon as we can verify that the drones aren't flying, we'll advance to the base while dropping in commandos on zip lines ahead of us."

"Just like on Pemberwick Island," Kent said.

"No, on Pemberwick they didn't have mayhem in mind," Granger replied.

I looked at the watch that I had been given with the uniform.

"Two o'clock," I said. "The Sounders move at five. They'll get the bomb and move it into the dome. At the same time a team of commandos will move through the Bridge and take over the command center on this side. It's all been planned out but there's no telling how long it will take."

"They gave us communicators," Tori said, holding up her small black device. "We can't contact the other side of the Bridge, but they'll let us know when the command center is secured."

"Then stay by me," Granger ordered. "I'd like to be the first to know."

"You'll be the second," Kent said. "We'll be the first."

I think Granger was fighting the urge to punch Kent.

"I need you kids to understand something," Granger said. "Once I give the command to advance, you're on your own. We're not going in to rescue prisoners or to capture the enemy. There is only one goal here."

"Understood," I said. "Get to the dome and seal it off. That's the only thing that matters."

There was nothing more to be said. Granger stood there, awkwardly.

"I'm not proud of some of the things I've done during this campaign," he said. "But I always tried to do what was needed. I hope you believe that."

"No hard feelings," Kent said. "Not a lot, anyway."

Granger stayed focused on me.

"What you kids have done is just . . . damn epic. I wish I hadn't . . ."

He didn't finish the sentence. He couldn't find the right words, or maybe he didn't want to continue, because his voice was cracking. Instead, he stood up straight, lifted his right arm, and saluted us.

None of us knew what to do, so we didn't move.

Granger snapped off the salute and said, "Outside in five."

He then quickly ducked out of the door.

The three of us exchanged surprised looks.

"Well that was kinda cool," Kent said.

"Yeah," Tori said. "But it felt like he was saying goodbye."

"Wow," Kent said. "Thanks for ruining *that*."

"Are we ready?" I asked.

Kent stepped up to Tori and me and threw his arms around both of us. It was so un-Kent-like that I didn't know how to react.

"I love you guys," he said.

Tori and I joined in the hug. I didn't like Kent, but I loved him and I knew Tori did too. The three of us stayed that way for a solid thirty seconds before Kent broke it off, stepped back, and said, "Let's go kick us some Retro ass."

We stepped outside of the small building to a scene of organized chaos. Soldiers were running every which way, jeeps were flying by loaded with gear and personnel, and the steady sound of helicopter engines provided the soundtrack.

"Jeez," Kent said. "This is all because of us. I sure hope those Sounders weren't jerking us around."

Chief Brock jogged up to us, still wearing his Air Force uniform.

"Wanted to wish you guys luck," he said and shook each of our hands.

"You're not coming?" Tori asked.

"I want to. Granger nixed it. I guess he trusts me just so far. I am the enemy, after all. Do you have your communicators?"

Kent and Tori both pulled out their small devices. They looked like miniature iPhones.

"They work like walkie-talkies," Brock explained. "Don't mess with the frequency because you're locked in with Sokol and his team. You won't get voice, only text."

"So they're more like walkie-texties," Kent said.

"Texting doesn't need as much power," Brock said. "Harder to track, too. When Sokol's team has the command center secured, they'll let you know. Hopefully that will be in about . . ." he checked his watch ". . . three and a half hours. Man, it's getting close."

"Gee, thanks for that," Kent said.

"I understand your mother is being held at the camp," Brock said to me.

"That's my mission," I said. "I'm going to get her out."

"*Our* mission," Tori corrected.

"Once you get inside the base, try to find the Sounders you've already met. They might be able to help."

"We will," I said.

"Good. Nothing left to say but good luck," Brock said. "And thank you."

"No, thank *you*," Tori said. "What the Sounders are doing is amazing."

"It isn't amazing," Brock said. "It's right."

Tori gave me a quick look that I didn't return.

"Let's go!" Granger shouted from a jeep that screamed up and stopped next to us.

The three of us hopped in back and the driver took off, leaving

Brock in the camp to wait for the news of whether or not we had stopped the invasion. It must have made him crazy to be watching from the sideline.

We bounced over the bumpy dirt roads that had been created just for the camp, racing alongside several other jeeps that were headed for the same place: the wide-open field where the SYLO helicopters were parked. When we emerged from the trees into the clearing, the sight made me catch my breath.

"Uh . . . wow," was all Kent managed to say.

There had to be a hundred choppers scattered all over the field. Some were large transport helicopters, but there were plenty of smaller attack craft armed with missiles and heavy-duty guns. Rotors were already spinning on many of them. Others were just powering up. The combined sound was steadily growing into a deafening din of white noise.

Hundreds of SYLO soldiers scrambled across the field, headed for the various craft. Every last one was outfitted with body armor and carried an automatic weapon.

It was an impressive spectacle that gave me hope they might actually have a shot at taking over the dome.

But only if the attack planes were knocked out.

The driver brought us to one of the larger choppers and stopped just beyond the limit of the whirling rotors. Granger jumped out without a word, ducked low, and headed for the craft. The three of us followed right behind.

Jumping on board we saw that there were already a few dozen soldiers strapped into seats that lined the sides of the fuselage, facing center. The moment they saw us, the entire group applauded and cheered. It was totally unexpected, for as far as I knew the only people who knew about us were Granger and President Neff. I actually got a little choked up. Of course, Kent waved his arms in the air, eating it up. There were three empty seats waiting for us in the rear. As we made our way to them, we were repeatedly clapped on the back by the appreciative soldiers.

I found a seat, strapped in, and put on my headphones.

The soldier next to me held up his fist for a bump.

"I'm going to tell my kids I flew in with you," he said.

These guys really thought we were heroes. It was a strange sensation, though the overriding thought I had was I didn't care what he told his kids just as long as he got the chance to see them again.

Granger stood up in front to face the team.

"We'll land five klicks outside the border of the camp," he said through the intercom, which also carried his voice to the rest of the attack force. "I want wheels on the ground for no more than forty-five seconds. Get out fast, hit the deck, and keep your eyes on the camp."

My stomach flipped. These were professional soldiers. They had probably trained for this very mission. I hoped we wouldn't get in their way.

"We will stay there until I give the command to begin the assault. I chose the go-word moments ago and passed it on to the company commanders. Until you get that word, from me, you stay put with your eyes on the camp. Understood?"

"Yes sir!" the entire group replied as one.

"All right," Granger said. "The go-word is . . . strike. Strike. What's the word?"

"Strike!" the entire group called out in unison.

"That's it," Granger shouted. "We're on. Let's go get 'em!"

The entire squad answered with "Hoo-rah!"

The rotors whined.

Granger buckled in behind the pilots.

The chopper shuddered and we lifted off of the island, headed one last time into the Nevada desert.

I craned my neck to look out the window and caught an awesome sight. Dozens of other choppers were lifting off at the exact same time. We rose into the air for several seconds and hovered there. With a quick wave from Granger to the pilot, our chopper shot forward. From the window I saw several different types of helicopters flying alongside us in a loose formation. It was a formidable-looking attack force that was on its way into battle . . . based solely on our word.

I hoped we weren't going to be responsible for their annihilation.

The trip took a lot longer than I expected. We had flown between the Retro base in the Mojave and Catalina Island three times. Each time it had taken about an hour. When we hit the hour mark on this trip, we were still under full throttle. I kept checking my watch, expecting to hear that we would be landing at any moment. We didn't. I was getting antsy. Was something wrong? Did the Retros know we were coming? Time was moving, fast. I was getting nauseous, though I wasn't sure if it was because of nerves, or because we had been bouncing around inside of that tin can for too long.

I kept looking out of the window to try to see the other helicopters. That only made me more nauseous.

Finally, when we approached the two-hour mark, Granger made an announcement.

"We've been circling for nearly an hour," he said. "We're being cautious about inserting the teams, landing one at a time. The last thing we need is for someone to spot us from the base. We're the next and last ones in."

My nauseous stomach twisted as my anxiety level spiked. This was it. We descended, quickly. All around me the soldiers were checking their gear. I had nothing except for my pulser and there wasn't much to check. I gave a quick look to Tori and Kent. Tori gave me a thumbs-up. Kent's eyes were closed.

"Five seconds," the pilot announced.

Outside I saw the light-brown surface of the Mojave rising quickly as dust kicked up all around us. I braced myself for the inevitable jolt that would hit when we touched down.

"Contact!" the pilot shouted an instant before the helicopter landed, rattling my teeth.

"Move!" Granger demanded.

With practiced precision the soldiers unlatched their straps, stood, and hurried for the door. The copilot slid the door open and the soldiers poured out. We were last, just before Granger, who was standing at the door watching his troops depart. I hesitated for a second and looked at him.

"Keep moving!" he barked.

We weren't going to be getting any special consideration because we were untrained kids.

I jumped out of the chopper to see that the soldiers had formed a line, lying belly-down, shoulder to shoulder. I wasn't sure of what to do so I ran along the line until I got to the last soldier and lay down next to him. Tori was right behind me and Kent did the same. The last to arrive was Granger.

Behind us, the helicopter had powered up and was lifting off before Granger had even settled in.

Looking ahead, I couldn't see the Retro base. Not even the top of the dome. We were too far away. That was the idea. Though I did wonder how we were going to cover so much ground on foot.

That answer came seconds later. Far behind us, a huge helicopter landed. It was long, with twin rotors, front and back. A ramp dropped down from its belly and multiple troop-transport vehicles drove out, one after the other. It was like the helicopter was giving birth to a litter of trucks. When the last truck drove out the helicopter lifted off, only to be replaced by another chopper as the process was repeated.

The transport vehicles drove up behind us and each one stopped in turn, lining up next to one another much like the soldiers had done.

When the command came, this was how we would get to the base.

Within minutes, every last helicopter had departed and we were left lying in the sand with nothing to hear but the howling desert wind.

Granger had binoculars to his eyes and was focused straight ahead, no doubt looking to see if any Retros were coming out from the base to welcome us.

"Now what?" I asked.

"You tell me," Granger said.

"Uh, what?"

"Until those drones are grounded, this is as far as we go. You let us know when we're good."

I looked to Tori. She pulled out her communicator and stared at the blank screen.

"They'll tell us," she said, sounding unsure. "Right?"

I looked at my watch.

It was four-thirty.

Ninety minutes till the boom.

TWENTY-TWO

Most of the events that played out over the next few hours I witnessed firsthand.

The rest I was told about. Piecing together the series of events that occurred was tricky. I had to make some logical, educated guesses on some of the events, but in the end I believe I have put together a full, accurate picture of all that unfolded, both good and bad. When the history books are written, *all* the history books, I can only hope that they will be as honest about what happened as I have been.

The people who put themselves on the line, and sacrificed themselves, deserve nothing less.

———

Five kilometers further ahead of us, and three hundred years into the future, a small group of Air Force personnel made their way along the wide street that led to the dome in the Bridge city.

They walked calmly, but with purpose. There was nothing about them that stood out from any of the other military personnel on the street. They were led by Colonel Pike. With her was a young, intense Airman named Eric Lewis. The third person in uniform was Airman First Class Olivia Kinsey. The only member of the group not in uniform was a forty-year-old civilian named Liger. He stood out from the others because he wore plain gray fatigues, as opposed to camouflage. Liger was an engineer. A nuclear engineer.

The group passed by the queue of giant black planes that were lined up along the street, waiting to make the journey into the past. None of the team showed outward interest in the attack planes, but the presence of these killing machines raised both their anxiety level and their resolve.

They could not fail.

The four turned off the street when they arrived at the vast building with the curved roof that stood next to the massive dome that held the Bridge. They walked with confidence directly up to the two armed guards who stood in front of the heavy double doors.

The guards instantly came to attention and saluted Colonel Pike.

"Good afternoon, gentleman," Pike said.

"Is this a scheduled visit, ma'am?" one guard asked.

"Yes, but not one you would have known about," she replied.

Pike showed the guard her tablet and the orders that allowed her access to the nuclear depot. The orders were completely authentic, except that Pike was the only one who knew about them for she was the one who created them.

The guard read the orders and the blood drained from his face.

"Now?" he asked, incredulous. "*Right* now?"

"We need to move the device in ahead of these ships," Pike replied. "The natives are going to be in for one hell of a surprise."

She smiled and gave him a conspiratorial wink.

The guard looked at his partner for support. He was unsure of what to do with this sudden and dramatic development.

"We don't have much time," Pike added, with a touch of impatience. "You don't want to hold up the transfer of these ships."

"No ma'am," the second guard said. "Will you need assistance?"

"There's a technician inside, correct?" Pike asked.

"Yes ma'am," the first guard replied.

"Good," Pike said and walked boldly past the two guards. "Stay at your post."

The others kept their eyes on the ground and followed. Olivia didn't make eye contact with anyone, fearing they might recognize her as a traitorous Sounder.

Pike used her ID card to unlock the double doors. They slid open with a mechanical whine and the team strode inside.

The depot was nothing more than a huge warehouse under a dome that was five feet thick, in case of an unfortunate accident. Lined up in two rows of five were ten white cylinders, each six feet tall and three feet in diameter. There was nothing about them that gave a clue as to their deadly power. None of them had a nose cone or fins to provide aerodynamic capability, for they were never intended to be dropped from an aircraft. These weapons were built to the exact specifications of the device that was exploded as a test on the morning of January 24, 1952. Project Alcatraz. They were duplicates of the device that created the original Bridge and were intended to be used to blast more Bridges from the past into the future.

A technician wearing gray fatigues similar to the one the engineer was wearing sat at a desk playing a video game on his pad. When he saw the team enter he immediately snapped to attention and saluted.

"Mr. Liger," the man said, surprised. "I wasn't aware of an inspection—"

"This is no inspection, Mr. Swenor," Liger said. "We're deploying."

The technician, Swenor, looked as stunned as the guards outside.

"I . . . I had no idea. . . ."

Pike handed him the orders.

"Of course you didn't," she said. "Everyone has been on a need-to-know basis. Now you need to know."

Swenor read the orders quickly, his eyes growing wider with every second.

"Los Angeles?" he said, stunned.

"The dome in Dodger Stadium is ready," Pike said. "We will go active as soon as the eradication is complete."

"Amazing," he said with a mix of enthusiasm and fear.

"Let's get number 44-044 on a pallet. We don't have much time."

"Yes ma'am," Swenor replied and hurried off.

Liger looked to Pike and said, "That was the first honest thing you've said."

Pike shrugged.

Minutes later a floating pallet hovered into position next to the first bomb in line, number 44-044. The device was gently lowered, still upright, onto the floating platform. Built onto the platform was a cradle designed specifically for this purpose. Once loaded, the bomb and platform hovered three feet in the air, ready to go.

"This is incredibly exciting," Swenor said without trying to hide his glee.

"Isn't it?" Pike replied, and took the pallet's control device from him.

"But I should—" Swenor complained.

"These airmen will complete the transfer," Pike said. "Thank you for your help, Mr. Swenor. Go back to your duties. I promise, you'll remember this day and the part you played here for the rest of your life."

"Thank you ma'am, thank you," Swenor said with genuine excitement. He wore a proud smile as if he could already imagine his name in the history books.

Airmen Lewis was an expert with the hovering platform. With Olivia guiding it from the front, Lewis moved the heavy device carefully but quickly toward the front doors. Liger ran ahead, slid open the tall, heavy doors, and stood aside to let the monstrous weapon pass through.

The two guards outside stood back, watching in awe.

"It's really happening," the first guard said.

When the hovering bomb was clear of the building, the two doors slid back shut with a solid, satisfying thump.

"Good luck, ma'am," said the second guard.

He subtly put his hand over his heart.

"As you were," Pike ordered curtly.

The two guards returned to their post, guarding the depot against all intruders.

With two hundred yards to the dome, it was impossible for anyone on the street not to notice the hovering device as it was being moved along. Most knew what it was and watched with stunned wonder. Several applauded. They knew what it meant if one of these devices was being sent to the Bridge. At least they thought they knew. To them, it signified that the next phase of their invasion and colonization was underway. They had heard the plans and this was further proof that it was all coming true.

They cheered. Joy had finally come to the Bridge city. To 2324. The transfer had turned into a glorious parade to send a hero off to war. If there had been a marching band along the route, it would have struck up a patriotic song.

The Sounder team kept their heads down and moved quickly.

The attention was not welcome but it provided the Sounders with an unexpected bonus. With all eyes on the slowly moving procession, the cheering crowds didn't notice that several armed soldiers were slowly filtering into the area. With no fanfare or fuss they silently took up positions near the dome.

They waited in doorways.

They melted in with the crowd.

They hung behind the waiting aircraft.

Armored cars slipped into position on side streets.

The Sounders had arrived and they were ready.

While most of the eyes on the street were focused on the floating device, another team of Air Force personnel approached the security checkpoint at the dome.

There were ten in all, each armed for battle with vests, helmets, and heavy-duty pulsers.

When the security guard saw them, his eyes lit up.

"It's beginning, isn't it?" he asked.

The leader of the squad, Captain Kenny Sokol, handed the guard a pad with his orders.

"Just a precaution," Sokol said. "There are a lot of natives in that camp. Bova asked for additional security in case there was trouble when these ships start coming through."

"Smart," the security guard said. "I sure wouldn't mess with you guys."

Sokol took back his orders and gave the security guard a friendly pat on the arm.

"You're a wise man," he said and strode for the dome, followed by his dangerous-looking commando team.

The security guard watched the team move past him with a mix of pride and jealousy. These were warriors.

The group marched quickly and efficiently across the last few yards of cement and walked straight into the dome.

Once inside, Sokol quickly scanned the interior for military personnel.

There were two men near the Bridge who were working to guide a pallet loaded with supplies through to the past. Sokol motioned for his team to take up positions on either side of the giant frame. He gestured for the two smaller men who came in with him to move behind a stack of crates.

He wanted them to be protected.

Sokol held one other commando back and gestured toward the men who were working in front of the Bridge. No words were spoken. They knew what they had to do. Sokol and his partner pulled out their pulsers.

The workers had no idea what was coming. As soon as the platform they were guiding slipped through the Bridge, they turned back and were knocked out by two quick pulser shots. Sokol and the other commando caught them before they hit the deck and quickly pulled them off to the side.

Their pathway to the past was clear.

———

Outside of the dome, Pike and her team approached the security checkpoint with the floating bomb.

The security guard could barely contain himself. First a team of commandos, and now one of the top Air Force officers, was coming through his checkpoint . . . with a nuclear weapon no less.

"Colonel Pike," he said in awe. "I had no idea."

Pike handed the man her orders and said, "Surprise."

"This is going to be one of those days, isn't it?' he said.

"What do you mean?" Pike asked.

"This is the day our new future officially begins. Children will read about this day in history books."

Pike thought for a moment, then said, "You have no idea how right you are."

"Good luck, ma'am," the guard said.

He handed back her orders and gave her a smart salute.

Pike returned the salute and said, "Thank you. We'll need it."

Olivia and Lewis guided the device forward. They were only a few yards from the dome.

On the street, people cheered as they strained to get one final glimpse of the device they knew would be their ticket to a better future.

It was 5:15. Everything had gone exactly as planned.

Until it didn't.

A siren sounded.

The cheering instantly died. There were looks of confusion all around.

"Pick up the pace," Pike said calmly. "I believe we've been discovered."

Lewis pushed the hovering pallet faster. They needed to get inside.

Military vehicles appeared from everywhere, rushing to get to the dome. Ironically, the Sounders' mission was helped by all the attention the transfer of the nuclear device had caused. The street was full of bystanders, making it difficult for the Air Force security vehicles to get to the dome quickly. Those precious few moments allowed Pike's team to move the device inside.

The need for secrecy was over. The dozens of Sounders that had been quietly assembling nearby went into action. They sprinted for the dome and set up a defense in front of the colossal entrance. The armored vehicles that had been waiting on side streets jumped forward and blasted through the security checkpoint to form a barrier in front of the open door. The Sounders dropped down behind their vehicles for protection while raising their pulsers toward the street and the oncoming security force.

The Sounders were no longer hiding in the shadows.

The crowd scattered in panic. Most of the military personnel weren't armed and wanted no part of the battle that was about to take place. They ran for buildings and sprinted down side streets. None of them knew exactly what was happening but they sensed it wouldn't be pretty.

Olivia and Lewis floated the nuclear device to the center of the dome and lowered it to the deck.

Sokol ran up to them and said, "Who triggered the alarm?"

"The bogus orders must have bounced back," Pike said calmly. She then turned to Liger. "Arm it. Six o'clock."

"Throw them out of here," Sokol yelled to his men.

Two of his commandos carried the unconscious soldiers to the door and tossed them out of the dome.

Sokol looked up at the hovering bomb with awe. "You actually did it," he said with a mixture of wonder and joy. "To be honest, my confidence wasn't high."

"To be honest," Pike said. "I didn't think we'd even get it out of the depot."

"Now it's our turn."

"Yeah, you and those kids," Pike replied.

Pike and Sokol shook hands, then Sokol took a step back toward the Bridge.

"Let's move!" he bellowed.

The other nine commandos gathered around him in front of

the Bridge. Sokol took one last look back at the future, snapped a sharp salute to Colonel Pike, then turned and faced the white light.

"Be cool," Sokol said to his men. "The people on the other side have no idea what's happening here. Are we good?"

Each of the commandos gave a quick thumbs-up.

"All right then, let's do it."

They all stepped through the glowing frame and were gone.

The last sounds they heard of 2324 were the first sounds of a new battle.

———

Outside the dome in 2324, growing numbers of soldiers arrived and began moving toward the giant doors.

The Sounders had created a formidable defense. They fired their pulsers from behind the armored vehicles, spraying their attackers and forcing them back. The advancing soldiers had no plan of attack. They hadn't trained to stage an assault on their own base and didn't have the personnel or firepower to punch through the Sounder defense . . . which is exactly what Colonel Pike was counting on.

"How much longer?" Pike asked Liger as she watched him working furiously to program the bomb.

"This wasn't designed to be easy," he said. "There are safeguards."

"How much longer?" she asked again, calmly.

"Five minutes. Six if you keep talking to me."

Airman Lewis ran up to Pike and said, "If I'm not needed here, I'll go help outside."

"Thank you," Pike said, sincerely. "I hope you understand how many lives you helped save today."

"It was an honor, ma'am," Lewis said.

He saluted the Colonel, then raised his own pulser and charged out to join the fight.

The Sounders were holding the Air Force back, though they knew it wouldn't last. They fully expected the Air Force to bring in heavy artillery and that would be the end of it. Their mission wasn't to keep them away forever, just until the bomb was detonated.

The Air Force realized the attack was going nowhere and stopped firing. They were taking too many casualties for no gain. Within minutes the battle went from full-on raucous mayhem to eerie quiet.

There was no celebration on the Sounder side. They knew it was only a matter of time before the big guns were brought in. The question was, would the artillery show up before six o'clock?

"Done," Liger said. "Detonation in thirty-five minutes."

He pointed to a countdown clock that was already moving.

Olivia stepped up and asked, "Can it be stopped?"

"Only by someone with the codes."

The three of them stood there, their mission as good as complete.

"Then you should both go outside and join the others," Pike said. "Thank you. Both of you. I promise the sacrifice you made will one day be understood and celebrated."

"What about you?" Olivia asked.

"Someone has to stay behind and seal the door," Pike said.

"Without that door closed, the circumstances of the detonation won't be duplicated."

"Then you can go through the Bridge," Olivia said.

"Not if I want to make sure this bad boy detonates," Pike replied.

"But . . ." Olivia said. She didn't have to finish the thought.

"I know," Pike said. "But after what I did, do you think the Air Force would let me live? In either era? I'd rather go out in a flash of glory than be executed in the past, or spend the rest of my life in a cell. Please go. This is my decision and I'm okay with it."

The three walked slowly toward the open door. Beyond the door frame they saw the Sounders hiding behind the armored vehicles, ready for the next attack.

There were no soldiers charging at them. No push to get through to the dome. No counteroffensive. The only thing they could see was the first in the line of giant attack planes that was waiting for its turn to float into the past.

It hovered in place, its engine giving off the familiar musical sound.

It was a sound they hadn't heard from these planes until that moment.

"Oh my God," Olivia said with sudden realization.

The plane slowly spun to face forward. To face the open door.

"No!" Olivia screamed and ran for cover.

The plane fired its energy cannon at the armored vehicles that stood between it and the open door. Sounders scattered as the heavy vehicles exploded in front of them.

The Air Force had heavy artillery in place after all.

Liger ran for the door and dove outside.

Olivia jumped to the side, away from the open door.

The plane drifted closer and fired its cannon again. Another vehicle erupted and sharp pieces of molten shrapnel flew into the dome.

Colonel Pike didn't react fast enough. She was hit by the wave of debris and fell where she stood.

"Colonel!" Olivia screamed.

Pike didn't respond.

Olivia struggled to her feet and ran for the door, ready to jump outside and enter the fight.

The door.

The open door.

Olivia skidded to a stop. She knew that with the power of the attack planes, the Sounder defense couldn't hold much longer. With more than thirty minutes left before detonation there was plenty of time for someone with the right codes to simply stroll in and deactivate the bomb.

Unless she did something about it.

She looked about frantically until she saw what she needed. The dome's control panel was just inside the door frame. Olivia sprinted for it, scanned the rows of switches quickly, then slammed the Door Seal button.

A loud, jarring horn blared. Red lights flashed on either side of the door frame as the two massive sides of the door began to slide shut.

The black plane floated closer. There were no longer armored vehicles standing in its way.

Olivia pressed her back against the inside wall of the dome and prayed.

She heard the sharp sound of air being released and saw the light on the floor begin to shrink as the two doors closed toward each other. They were moving quickly, but was it quick enough?

Desperate shouts came from outside. Olivia couldn't understand what they were saying but she knew it meant the Air Force personnel were rushing for the door.

She stared at the line of disappearing light on the floor, willing it to shrink faster.

The sound of pulser fire echoed through the dome. The last of the Sounders were fighting again, desperately trying to keep the Air Force from getting to the dome before it was sealed.

Only a sliver of light remained on the floor. With a final metallic thud, the two doors met and slammed shut.

The blaring horn ceased. The red lights stopped flashing.

The dome in 2324 was sealed.

It was thirty minutes until the boom.

TWENTY-THREE

Kenny Sokol and his team of commandos strolled casually out of the Bridge into the twenty-first century. None gave any warning as to the mayhem they intended to bring to the camp.

A few Retro soldiers were in the mostly empty dome, performing guard duty they felt was a waste of time. When they saw the team of badass soldiers appear out of the light from the Bridge, they straightened up. Not to defend themselves, but to give the appearance that they too deserved to wear the uniform.

"You're early," one of the guards said.

"You're done," Sokol shot back.

He raised his pulser and knocked the guard off of his feet. The second guard wasn't standing for much longer. A commando took him out. Without a word, two of the commandos dragged the bodies to the side of the open door, out of sight from the outside.

"Thompson, Shaw, and Goodlad with me," Sokol ordered. "The rest of you stay here. Keep the doors open until 17:55. If it starts getting hairy before then, use your judgment and lock it down early. Understood?"

There were quiet nods of acknowledgment all around.

"Help may be on the way, but don't count on it," Sokol said. "Good luck."

There were no other pleasantries. They were professionals. They had a job to do. There was no room for emotion. Sokol and the three Sounders strolled to the mouth of the dome and stopped there.

"You two okay?" Sokol asked Goodlad and Thompson.

They nodded but their eyes were wide with anxiety. These two were not trained commandos. They were pilots. If the Sounders were to take control of the black drones, they needed experienced pilots who knew how the systems worked.

"Try to stay calm," Sokol said. "This isn't about us, it's about you. Stay out of harm's way. We'll get you inside."

The two pilots nodded in unison.

They were terrified.

"Here we go," Sokol said and led the group out of the dome.

Again, they did their best to appear as if nothing out of the ordinary was about to occur. Surprise was their most powerful weapon.

They walked casually but quickly to the aboveground bunker that served as the command-and-control center for the drone fleet. None of them had seen it for themselves, but they had studied the diagrams. Besides the dome, it was the only building in the camp that was built to withstand an attack.

It was also the only building that was guarded.

Outside of the bunker stood two armed guards who looked every bit as dangerous as Sokol's commandos. These were not low-level administrators. They were charged with guarding the most valuable asset the twenty-first-century Air Force had. The drones. The eradication of an entire world's population was being carried out from this bunker.

It didn't matter how casually Sokol and his men approached; the guards went on instant alert.

"Halt right there!" one guard called.

Sokol answered by raising his pulser and firing.

The camp was now on alert. They were under attack.

The shot missed the guard and he fired back, dropping Shaw. The guards went flat on their bellies to make difficult targets, but it did little good. Sokol and the pilots unloaded on them. One guard was knocked out instantly. The second guard, realizing how futile his position was, threw himself back toward the bunker and hit a control switch. The move released a steel door that closed over the regular wooden door, sealing the bunker. A second later the guard was hit by a pulser shot and slammed back against the wall. He was unconscious before he hit the ground.

Sokol didn't break stride. He reached into the cargo pocket in his pants and pulled out a black disk. He slapped the disk onto the door, then spun away to take cover.

With a quick but powerful explosion, the door blew down.

"You're on," Sokol said to the pilots.

The Sounders were in.

———

I lay in the dirt next to Tori, sweating like I was in a sauna. Between strained nerves and the heat, I thought I might pass out. I kept looking to Granger, waiting for some sign that we were going to do something other than lie there and bake.

The guy hadn't budged in forever. His eyes were glued to his binoculars, his attention riveted on the horizon and the Retro camp that was just beyond.

I looked at my watch for the millionth time.

5:25.

To say we were running out of time was an understatement.

We were surrounded by hundreds of SYLO fighters. None moved. None said a word. It was like they had become part of the terrain. The vehicles sat behind us, silently. After the incredible flurry of activity that rallied us for the attack and dropped us here in the desert, we had come to a complete stand-still.

All eyes were trained on the horizon.

All ears tuned for the go-word.

I leaned over to get a look at the communicator that Tori was clutching. The screen was blank. She gave me a nervous shrug.

The only sound was the desert wind blowing across the dry, flat terrain . . .

. . . and the faint musical notes that foreshadowed the arrival of the black drones.

They first appeared in the sky far in the distance, rising up from the Retro camp. It was followed shortly after by another. Two drones were in the sky.

"Damn!" Granger spat.

He picked up the walkie-talkie and said, "Hold your positions."

The black drones stopped rising, turned, and looked to be moving our way.

"They know we're here," Granger said to nobody, but I was sure it was directed at us.

Tori grabbed my shoulder.

"I'm sorry," was all I could say.

We both looked at her communicator, willing it to show us the news we were so desperate to see.

It didn't.

It looked as though our battle was over before it could begin.

"Look sharp," Granger spat into the walkie. "When they start shooting, scatter. Do not enter a vehicle. It'll be tougher for them to target individuals."

The two drones had gotten close enough that I could make out their stingray shape. They both dropped down low to begin their attack run.

"It can't end like this," Granger said, more to himself than anyone else.

The drones were nearly on us. I tensed up, ready for the first blast.

"Stand by to scramble," Granger ordered.

The drones were so low they were nearly on the ground. They knew exactly where we were. The sound of their musical engines was a familiar and frightening prelude.

I put my arm around Tori.

Kent pushed himself closer to her from the other side.

The drones arrived . . . and flew right over us without firing a single shot.

"What!" Kent exclaimed.

We turned and looked back to see the two dark drones continue past us.

"What'n hell?" Granger said.

Tori's communicator beeped.

Granger snapped a look to her.

We all did.

Her eyes went wide as she stared down at the device. She took a second to register the message.

"Well?" Granger said.

"Just one sentence," Tori said, her voice quivering.

"What is it?" Kent asked, impatiently.

Tori took a deep breath and said clearly and precisely, "We own the sky."

Behind us, the drones began to make wide arcs in opposite directions.

"I just got the same thing," Kent said, staring at his communicator, wide-eyed. "They're in."

"And we're on," Granger exlaimed. He lifted his walkie-talkie, keyed the mic, and shouted, "This is it! Fire it up! Strike! Strike! Strike!"

There was an instantaneous explosion of activity. The SYLO soldiers jumped to their feet. The vehicles roared to life. The stillness of only a few seconds before was shattered by the sounds of an invading army on the move.

Tori, Kent, and I stayed still, too stunned to react.

"Is that really it?" Tori asked, nervously. "Do we trust that one message?"

I looked around at the blur of activity.

"Too late now," I said. "It's on."

The three of us were still flat on our bellies when Granger strode back and stood in front of us.

"You all coming or do you prefer to stay here?" he snarled.

The three of us jumped to our feet and ran for the vehicle that was right behind us. It was an open troop carrier that offered little to no protection. It might have withstood driving over a landmine, but if we were attacked from the air, we were dead. At least twenty soldiers were already packed inside with their rifles between their knees.

We started for the back but Granger barked, "In the cab. I want to know if any more messages come through."

We all piled into the enclosed cab. It was tight but that was the least of our worries.

Granger barked into his walkie-talkie, "Move, with all possible speed."

The driver hit the gas and we charged forward. Once again we were moving over the flat, dry desert at breakneck speed. The truck wasn't built for comfort. We bounced over the rugged surface, banging our heads into the ceiling.

"There it is," Kent declared.

The peak of the dome appeared on the horizon.

Granger stayed focused ahead—not on the dome, on the sky.

On either side of us were dozens of transport trucks speeding together toward the camp. Their mission was to get there, fight their way through the Retro army, and secure the dome.

Mine was to find my mother and get her out safely. It meant I had to get my head together and figure out a plan to do it. I hadn't thought much about it until then because I didn't believe we'd get that far. But there we were, only a few miles away and closing fast.

The drones flew over us again. They had made a full arc and were headed back toward the Retro camp. Both dropped down low, speeding across the desert floor, headed in the same direction we were.

"What are they doing?" Kent asked.

Granger watched them intently, then smiled as if the answer had just come to him.

"Those boys really do know the score," he said. "We do not own the sky. Not yet. But we will."

The drones started firing. Not at us. At the ground.

"The antiaircraft guns," Kent exclaimed.

The Retro camp was surrounded by antiaircraft weapons that had been used to help repel SYLO attacks from the air.

That wouldn't last.

We were still too far away to pick out detail, but we could see the explosions erupting all around the camp as the weapons were destroyed by the attacking drones.

"Sokol's clearing the way," Tori said.

Granger got back on the walkie and shouted, "Bring 'em in. Now. Every last one."

"Bring what in?" Kent asked.

"The kitchen sink," Granger said with a smile.

Seconds later, helicopters thundered over us, headed straight for the camp. It was like watching a dense flock of migrating birds, all headed in perfect formation to a single spot.

"Now we own the sky," Granger said to us. "And soon we'll own that dome."

I glanced at my watch.

Twenty-five minutes left.

And counting.

TWENTY-FOUR

The Retro soldiers in the camp had their orders.

They had been attacked before. Only this time it was different. Their own planes had seemingly turned on them.

The result was mass confusion.

The artillery gunners fired from the desert floor, but they had lost valuable time, for they realized too late that they should have been firing at their own planes. Their hesitation doomed them. The drones swooped in and with every bit of firepower they possessed, unloaded on the big guns.

Inside the camp, most of the guards herded the entire prisoner population into the barracks and locked them inside. After so many had escaped into the desert during the last air raid, they must have changed their tactics. It was a huge mistake. If so many guards hadn't wasted their time rounding up prisoners instead of immediately joining those who rushed to defend the dome, they might have had a shot at taking it back. As it was, only a few dozen soldiers went for the dome . . .

. . . and were met by Sokol's commandos.

The Sounders who were already part of the camp knew what

was coming and they were prepared. They moved armored vehicles in front of the giant, open door to use as a barricade, as their counterparts had done in the future. Others were positioned inside the dome to either side of the door opening for protection. They were heavily armed and ready.

When the Retro soldiers rushed for the dome, they were cut down by a barrage of energy being fired from the Sounders' heavy-duty weapons. The Retros were only armed with small pulsers and were no match for the commandos' superior firepower. Making it that much more confusing was that they were being fired upon by other Air Force personnel.

They retreated quickly, taking cover behind the buildings near the dome.

For several minutes it was a standoff, until the Retros realized they had one very big advantage . . . numbers. There were dozens of them versus a handful of Sounders. The Retro commanders ordered them to advance. Reluctantly, the soldiers moved from the security of the buildings to rush the dome. Most were dropped in their tracks, but they kept coming.

They were soon joined by the guards who had been occupied with rounding up the prisoners. The Retro defense force was now fully manned. The commanders urged them forward ruthlessly, taking heavy losses in the hopes that enough would survive to make it through to recapture the dome. A few made it as far as the door, but were cut down before they could enter.

The Sounder defense was holding, but for how long?

In 2324 Olivia stood staring at the giant closed door of the dome. If the bomb was going to destroy the Bridge, that door would have to stay closed.

Her only way out was through the Bridge into the past.

She ran to Colonel Pike and dropped down on one knee next to her, hoping that she was still alive. Pike's eyes were glazed and unfocused, but she was still breathing. Barely.

"We're going through the Bridge," Olivia said. "I'll carry you."

Pike shook her head, wincing from the pain.

"Leave me," she said with a strained whisper.

"No way," Olivia replied. "You can be healed."

Olivia reached under the woman's back, but Pike screamed out in agony and Olivia had to let go. There was no way she could lift Pike alone. A quick, desperate look around the dome confirmed that she was on her own, but she spotted something that might help her save Pike.

———

Back in the twenty-first century, the personnel vehicles loaded with SYLO soldiers charged forward, growing closer to the camp. We were now close enough to see the barracks and, in front of them, the huge antiaircraft pulsers. Some were mangled wrecks. Several others pointed to the sky but it was hard to tell if they were shooting through the swirling smoke and dust. Still others were leveled straight ahead . . . at us.

Uh oh.

The ground exploded next to our truck and we were hit with a wave of dirt that blew us sideways.

Granger lifted his walkie and said, "Where are the Cobras? We're taking fire."

Another surge of energy hit the sand directly in front of us, sending out a spray of rock and gravel that pummeled our windshield. The driver swerved to avoid the crater that suddenly appeared before us and charged on.

The other vehicles were also being targeted. Explosions erupted everywhere, forcing our attack force to scatter.

There was another huge explosion, but this one was far off.

An antiaircraft pulser erupted in flames.

The Cobras had arrived.

Six SYLO attack helicopters swooped in low and unleashed their missiles, tearing into the giant pulser cannons, sending the gunners fleeing.

The drones were no longer working alone.

We definitely owned the sky, but now we needed to own the camp.

Tori's communicator beeped.

She held it up and read aloud, "Can't hold dome much longer."

"They need help," I said.

"Can you communicate back?" Granger asked.

"I don't know," Tori replied. "I can try to text. What do you want me to tell them?"

Granger thought for a moment then said, "Tell them . . . look to the sky."

———

At the dome, the Sounders and the commandoes were firing wildly at anything that moved. It would only be a matter of time before the Retros overran them and reseized the dome. Worse, three commandos had to break away from the dome to help defend the command center where Sokol and the pilots were controlling the drones. If the command center fell, the Retros would have the drones back and that would tip the balance back in their favor.

The battle was about to turn the wrong way . . .

. . . when several SYLO helicopters appeared overhead. The Retros stopped advancing and looked up in disbelief as a line of dark marauders swooped in and hovered above the dome. Side doors on each craft were thrown open and zip lines were dropped. Seconds later, heavily armed commandoes wearing dark-red camouflage uniforms hit the lines and slid to the ground.

SYLO had arrived.

The fighters dropped down all around the giant structure. They landed by the dozens and immediately made their way for the door of the dome.

The Retros snapped back into the moment and continued their assault. Several of the SYLO commandos were hit by pulser fire while still on the zip lines and fell to the ground, but most landed safely and returned fire, dropping many Retro soldiers and forcing others to take cover. SYLO's automatic attack weapons may have been centuries behind the technology of the Retros, but they weren't any less effective. The commandos moved in tight groups, travelling quickly between buildings, laying down short bursts of fire to protect each other.

The Retros weren't prepared for this sudden surge of attackers. They had no choice but to go from offense to defense. They could no longer advance toward the dome, for they had to protect themselves from the SYLO commandos who were coming at them from multiple angles.

The cavalry had definitely arrived.

"Stop right there!" one of the Sounder commandos shouted to a SYLO soldier who had slipped inside the dome.

"It's okay," another of the commandos said. "The kids did it. They're fighting for us."

The two commandos turned away from the lone SYLO soldier and focused on the Retro assault.

The SYLO soldier continued on into the dome. None of the Sounders questioned him as to why he wasn't wearing armor or a helmet. They were too busy ducking fire.

———

Olivia was able to wrestle Colonel Pike onto the floating palette that she had brought close to her fallen leader.

"Okay," she said. "No problem. We'll just float you right into the twenty-first century."

Olivia lifted the handheld controls and was about to raise the palette into the air, when Pike grabbed her arm.

"Kinsey, wait," Pike said through labored breaths. "I don't want to go."

"But you can be healed," Olivia argued.

"Status?" she asked.

Olivia took a quick look around to appraise the situation and said, "The dome is sealed. We're the only ones in here. The countdown is continuing. I think Sokol is holding the far side of the Bridge because no Air Force personnel have come through."

"So we're good?" Pike asked.

"Yeah, I think we're good."

"Then I'm okay with this. Thank you."

Pike gave one last squeeze to Olivia's arm, and her grip relaxed.

"Colonel?" Olivia cried.

Pike didn't respond.

Olivia checked her pulse but felt none.

Colonel Pike, the leader of the Sounders, was gone.

"The death of a traitor," came a voice from behind Olivia.

She spun to see a man wearing SYLO fatigues standing in front of the Bridge. He had just come through from the past, having slipped by the Sounder commandos.

"Forgive me if I don't grieve," the man said.

"Feit," was all Olivia managed to say.

————

Our vehicles finally made it to the outer edge of the camp. Now that we had reached the populated area we had to slow down and make our way more cautiously.

"It's about a half mile to the dome," I said.

Granger got on his walkie and barked, "All units hold your position."

Our driver followed orders and braked to a stop.

"From here on we travel by foot," Granger commanded into the walkie.

Our truck rumbled as the SYLO soldiers began jumping out. As we got out of the cab I saw all the other vehicles stopped and soldiers quickly unloading.

Granger surveyed his troops then turned to us.

"This is where we part," he said. "I'd tell you to stay here but I know you won't."

"Thank you," I said.

"For what?"

"For trusting us," I said.

He raised the walkie to his mouth but I stopped him.

"What about the prisoners?" I asked.

"What about 'em?"

"That nuclear blast from the future could destroy this camp and everybody in it."

"Can your people help evacuate the prisoners?" Tori asked. "If that door doesn't close, they're done."

"If that door doesn't close, we're *all* done," Granger shot back. He looked at his watch. "Seventeen forty-five. We've already been here too long."

He lifted the walkie and said, "Advance with caution."

All around us the unit leaders gave the order and hundreds of SYLO soldiers went on the move, tightening the ring around the Retro force.

"I don't mean to sound callous," Granger said to us. "I know the danger. The best way I can help them is by securing the dome."

"I get it," I said.

"I hope to see you back here," Granger said.

"If you don't hurry there may not be a back here to come to," Kent said.

Granger gave him a quick look. He wasn't a Kent fan. He motioned for the other men from our truck to move forward.

"Good luck," Granger said. "Be careful."

"Yeah," Kent said sarcastically. "Careful. That's what this is all about. Being careful. Jeez."

Granger gave him a sideways look and actually smiled.

"Well done," he said to us. "Very well done. Now go find your mother."

With that, he turned and hurried off after his men.

"You be careful now!" Kent called after him.

The three of us stood watching the line of SYLO soldiers sink deeper into the camp. It reminded me of the day they first landed on Pemberwick Island. They invaded our home and became the enemy. Now they were invading the home of the true enemy.

And we were wearing their uniform.

"Follow me," I said.

"Where are we going?" Kent asked.

"We'll start at the infirmary. There were Sounders there. Maybe they'll know where my mom is."

Tori took off on a run past me. Kent was more hesitant.

"What?" I asked.

"Nothing," he said. "Let's just make it quick."

"Why? You got somewhere else to be?"

His answer was to run after Tori.

Olivia grabbed for Pike's pulser, but Feit raised his own.

"Uh-unh," he warned.

She backed off.

"I don't get it," Feit said. "Do you actually enjoy living in this rancid world? You of all people? I saw how you took to Pemberwick Island. You were so, I don't know, cool. You could have gone back there to live, you know. You could have lived anywhere you wanted. But instead you gave up and joined these misguided traitors. What's the point? What do you get out of this?"

"I get to sleep at night."

Feit laughed. "Yeah, well, not for much longer." He checked the bomb. "Twelve minutes to be exact. I have to hand it to you guys, though. You Sounders. I like that name, by the way. Who thought that up? Was that you? Nah, you're just one of the followers. Maybe it was the Colonel here. But I doubt it. She wasn't all that creative."

"She figured out how to get this bomb here," Olivia said. "I'd call that creative."

Olivia glanced to the floor where Pike's pulser had fallen off of the palette. So close.

"Ooh, good one," Feit said. "I have to give you that. We never saw this coming. Did she really think blowing up the dome would stop the invasion?"

"It's got nothing to do with the dome," Olivia said. "This is a duplicate of the bomb that opened the Bridge. When it goes off it's going to reverse whatever physics created the damn tunnel and shut it down."

The smirk dropped from Feit's face. He looked around at the dome, as if seeing it in a whole new light.

Olivia took the chance to inch closer to Pike's pulser.

"Really? That's . . . just . . . genius!" he declared with genuine awe. "I thought this was just some crude attempt to stop the invasion, but you people actually put some thought into it. And you even got SYLO involved. Awesome. Seriously. Awesome. Nicely done."

Olivia couldn't help but smile.

"They did it," she said, more to herself than to Feit.

"They?" Feit asked.

The light bulb went on and he broke out in a big smile.

"Tucker?"

Feit clapped his hands on his legs as if he'd just heard a great joke.

"Those kids went and got SYLO, didn't they? That's incredible. You should see what's going on back there, it's a total mess. Bravo. My hat's off to you."

Olivia took the chance to inch closer to the pulser.

"I'm glad you're pleased," she said.

"Pleased? Not at all. It sucks. But I am impressed. You guys never give up. I admire that. It's futile, but I still admire it."

"It's not futile," Olivia said. "This bomb is going off. There's no way to stop it. But we don't have to die. We can step back through the Bridge and live in the twenty-first century. That's what you wanted all along, right? You can start over again. You can help mold a new world."

"Yeah, well that's where you're wrong," Feit said, his laughter dissipating.

"I'm not," Olivia argued. "In twelve minutes . . . boom."

Feit checked the device and said, "Eleven minutes, actually. But it's not going to happen."

"Yes it will. Unless you have the codes." Olivia stared right into Feit's eyes.

Feit smiled and gave an innocent shrug.

It was Olivia's turn to have the light bulb go on.

"No," she said with a gasp.

"Well, yeah," Feit said. "Surprise."

Olivia dove for the pulser. Feit fired and missed.

Olivia grabbed the pulser and did a somersault over Pike's body. Feit fired again, hitting the lifeless body of the Colonel. Olivia rolled onto her feet, raised the pulser, and fired blindly.

Feit had already moved.

The blast hit the edge of the Bridge's frame, harmlessly.

Feit fired again . . .

. . . and hit Olivia square in the chest. She flew backward, the pulser sailing out of her grip.

It clattered to the floor, harmlessly.

"Ouch. Sorry."

Feit turned for the bomb.

Less than ten minutes to go.

He had plenty of time to input the codes, stop the countdown, and pick up with the next phase of their mission, as planned. He would open the dome doors and allow the giant super-fighters to float in and travel through the Bridge. These fighters were not controlled by the tech-jockeys in the command center of Bova's camp. They had pilots on board. The arrival of just one of these planes would mean the end of the attempt by SYLO, and the traitorous Sounders, to seal the Bridge. Once these fighters entered the battle, the last resistance to the invasion and occupation would be eliminated. Vaporized, actually. It had been a surprising and somewhat annoying day for Feit, but in the end it turned out just fine because he was certain it would go down in history as the moment when the back of the resistance was broken.

Thanks to him.

With the confidence that ultimate victory was at hand, Feit stepped up to the bomb to enter the deactivation codes.

TWENTY-FIVE

Kent, Tori, and I ran for the infirmary and immediately jumped inside.

There were only a few patients in beds and one Retro soldier attending to them. It was the woman who had first given us the Sounder sign and allowed us to sleep in the bed next to Kent as he healed. She was exactly who we were looking for, but when she saw us, she backed away in fear.

"This is a hospital," she said with rising panic. "You have no business here."

The three of us hesitated, not understanding why she was reacting that way.

"It's our SYLO uniforms," Tori said. She lowered her pulser and said to the woman, "It's okay. Remember us? We were prisoners. You treated my friend here."

Kent gave her a little wave. "That would be me."

The woman was a raw nerve and too frightened to remember any individual patient. All she saw were the uniforms.

"Look," Tori said, and put her hand over her heart.

I did the same, offering her the Sounder salute. Kent joined in.

The woman softened, though I wasn't sure if it was because she finally recognized us, or was just relieved to know we might be on the same side.

"I don't understand," she said uncertainly. "What's happening out there?"

"SYLO and the Sounders are fighting the Air Force for control of the dome," Tori said.

"But we're looking for my mother," I said. "She's a prisoner."

The woman's eyes lit up with recognition.

"You're the ones Feit was looking for," she said.

"Yes!" Tori exclaimed. "Do you have any idea where she might be?"

"As soon as the attack began they locked all the prisoners up in their barracks. She must be there."

"Locked up?" I said, incredulous. "All the prisoners are locked in the barracks?"

Tori grabbed my arm and said, "If they're trapped here and the dome isn't closed—"

"Get out," I said to the woman. "Now. Get these patients out and as far away from the dome as you can. SYLO transport vehicles are scattered around the borders of the camp. Drive as far away from here as you can."

"Why?" she asked, dumbfounded.

"A very big bomb is about to go off," Kent said flatly. "Is that a good enough reason for you?"

It was. The woman immediately went to her patients and started to rouse them.

"You have less than twenty minutes," Tori said. "Hurry."

I ran out of the far side of the infirmary, headed for the barracks area. Kent and Tori ran right with me.

"We're running out of time," Tori said.

"We'll check the barracks and let the prisoners loose," I said.

"I'll give you ten minutes," Kent said.

"And then what?" I asked. "What's your deal? You got a date?"

Kent didn't answer. I was afraid he was going back to his old ways and wanted to bolt. That was his call. I had no right to stop him.

When we arrived at the first barracks I saw people at the windows, crowded together, trying to see what was happening outside. Or maybe they were just struggling to get air. I pulled out the pulser, aimed at the door, and blew off the lock. The door instantly flew open and orange-clad prisoners cautiously peeked their heads out.

"Get out of the camp," I shouted. "Run as far away from the dome as possible. There's a bomb."

The prisoners didn't question me. I think all they heard was "run" and "bomb." They quickly piled out of the building and ran for the camp border. I scanned the desperate mass of people as they flooded out of the door, straining to see if my mom was with them.

She wasn't.

"Go to the other buildings," I said to Tori and Kent. "Set them free but please, look for her."

The two ran off instantly. Moments later I heard their pulsers blowing open more doors. While one side of the camp was a battle zone, the other side was filled with the sounds of panicked people running for their lives.

My mother wasn't in the second building I set free. Nor was she in the third. There was absolute bedlam as a sea of terrified people scrambled to get away. We had quickly freed a dozen barracks, but my mother was not in any of them.

Tori and Kent rejoined me, winded from the effort.

Kent shook his head gravely.

"I'm sorry, Tucker," Tori said.

"There's still one more building," I said.

We ran for the final building, which was closest to the dome on the edge of the battle zone. From there I could see the fight. With the arrival of Granger and his SYLO ground troops, the Retros were now outnumbered. But they weren't done. More Retros continued to arrive from other parts of the camp. The battle was definitely still in doubt.

The last building was small, less than half the size of the others. As we got closer I saw no movement inside. My heart sank. This was my last chance. I walked right up to the door and shot off the lock. Throwing the door open I hoped to be flooded with escaping prisoners, but there were none. After a quick, nervous look to Tori I stepped inside.

It was like stepping into another world. This wasn't a barracks at all. We were inside an opulently decorated office, complete with overstuffed chairs, a couch, and rich wood paneling on the walls. Standing behind the large desk, frozen by our dramatic entrance, was Major Bova.

He stood staring at the door, probably expecting a contingency of SYLO soldiers to come storming in. Instead, he got us. Still, we were in SYLO uniforms and had pulsers aimed at his head so he threw his hands up in surrender. In the process he dropped a large duffel bag onto the floor.

"Don't shoot," he shouted. "I'm unarmed."

Seeing his weasel face brought back a flood of horrible memories, from the way he tortured prisoners before killing them, to parading my mother out in front of the prison population to try to lure us into surrendering.

"I guess you weren't in the train wreck," Kent said. "Too bad."

"Where is she?" I demanded while quickly closing the ground between us.

Bova backed away in fear and confusion.

"Wh . . . who?" he said, stuttering.

I shoved him against the back wall and jammed the pulser into his neck. Like most bullies, without backup he was a coward.

"My mother," I said, seething. "Don't pretend you don't know."

His eyes went wide with recognition.

"You!" he gasped, stunned. "Feit said you and your friends would hound us until you were dead. Why aren't you dead?"

I drove the pulser into the soft spot under his chin, making him gag.

"Where is she?" I asked again, with more force.

"I'll tell you," he said. "But I want something in return."

I wanted to say something cocky like, "In return I'll let you live" but that wasn't me.

"What is this?" Tori asked.

She had picked up the duffel that Bova dropped. Reaching inside, she pulled out a fistful of jewelry. There were golden bracelets, jeweled rings, and expensive-looking watches. She turned the bag over on the desk, spilling its contents. Besides a load more of jewelry, there were also thick rolls of cash.

"Wow," Kent said. "That's some serious stash."

"That belongs to me," Bova said, his voice cracking with uncertainty.

"You stole this from the prisoners, didn't you?" Tori said, disgusted.

"No!" he said quickly. "Of course not. I got those from . . . from . . ."

I rammed the pulser into his neck again.

"All right!" he squealed. "Yes, I did. And what's wrong with that? Spoils of war. It's not like they'll need any of it again."

Kent lunged forward and pulled Bova away from me. Before I had the chance to react he landed a punch square to his chin.

Bova's head snapped to the side, he stumbled back, hit the wall, and fell to the floor.

"And you call *us* animals!" Kent screamed with a fury I'd never heard from him before.

"That's exactly what you are," Bova shouted back, his arrogance returning. "Everyone from this time. You're all guilty of crimes far worse than pilfering a few pieces of jewelry."

Kent made another move for him but I held him back.

"Where is my mother?" I demanded.

Bova's confidence grew. He had something I wanted and that gave him leverage. He reached up to his desk and pulled himself into his rich leather chair.

Tori, Kent, and I stood across the desk in front of him.

"I'll tell you," he said. "All I want in return is to leave. Lower your weapons and let me walk out of that door."

I looked to Tori and Kent.

"Let him go," Kent said. "Who cares? Your mother is way more important than him."

Tori nodded in agreement.

"Once you leave this building, we can't help you," I said.

"Understood," Bova replied.

He reached forward, grabbed the duffel bag and started scooping up the jewelry to put back inside.

"Seriously?" Tori shouted. "Leave it."

Bova smirked as if to say, "Hey, it was worth a try" and dropped the bag.

"Where is she?" I asked.

"Right in there," he said, pointing to a closed door on the far wall. "Feit told me to keep her close in case we needed her as leverage against SYLO. Surprise! He was right. She's my leverage."

"Go get her, Rook," Kent said adamantly. "We're running out of time."

"You stay right there," I said to Bova.

Bova shrugged innocently.

I turned and walked quickly across the floor, headed for the door. Without waiting another second I grabbed the knob and threw it open.

At that instant, Bova made a quick move to reach under his desk.

We were all so tense that the little movement was enough of a warning.

We all dodged out of the way . . .

. . . as Bova's desk exploded.

The force came from a pulser shot that he fired from underneath that blew through the wooden desk and nailed the wall next to the closet, blasting out a huge hole. Though he didn't hit any of us, the sudden and surprising explosion had done its job. While we were trying to clear our heads, Bova bolted from behind the wreck of his shattered desk and threw himself out of a window.

"What the hell happened?" Kent muttered, dazed and angry.

I pulled my head together enough to remember what I had been doing. I looked through the doorway I had just opened, hoping to see my mother. What I saw instead was a closet. An empty closet. I shouldn't have been surprised, but it crushed me. My disappointment was quickly replaced by anger and I took off after Bova.

We all jumped out of the same window to land in an open dirt field between buildings.

The sound of a motorcycle firing to life brought our attention to Bova, who perched on a bike next to the building we had just come from. Kent sprinted for him. But Bova hit the accelerator and squirted away a second before Kent could reach him. The powerful motorcycle kicked up dirt, leaving a filthy cloud in its wake as it tore across the empty field with the murderous camp commander on board . . .

. . . along with the last hope we had of finding my mother.

But we weren't the only enemies Bova had to worry about.

As he sped toward the open space between the two newly constructed buildings, a group of orange-clad prisoners appeared between them. There were dozens of them, all with the same thing in mind: stopping Bova.

He turned hard to avoid them and sped toward another passage between buildings, but that was soon clogged with several more prisoners. Bova turned again and hit the throttle, headed back our way. Behind us, another group of prisoners had appeared. Within seconds the area was clogged with hundreds of prisoners that formed a circle around the fleeing man.

Their tormentor.

Bova had nowhere to go. As the circle of vengeful prisoners tightened in on him, he spun the motorcycle, desperately looking for an opening. Any opening.

"Why aren't they running away?" Tori asked.

"Unfinished business," I replied.

In one final, desperate move, Bova gunned the engine and sped directly for the circle, hoping to break through by mowing down a few lowly primates.

He didn't get far. The first prisoners he reached dodged away and grabbed him, sending the bike flying forward on its own.

They had their man.

Bova screamed, though I couldn't tell if it was with rage or agony. I didn't want to know. I also didn't want to know what those people would do with him. They carried him off as he squirmed and fought futilely.

"Payback's a bitch," I said, with absolutely no sympathy.

Kent laughed. I was glad that Bova had gotten what he deserved but I didn't think it deserved a laugh.

"I guess we're done here," Kent said.

"Not yet we're not," I said.

"Sorry, I can't wait anymore, guys. I'm out of here."

"Why? Where are you going?" Tori asked. "We still haven't found Mrs. Pierce."

"No?" Kent said with a smile, and pointed to our right.

"Tucker? I heard a familiar voice call. For a moment I didn't want to believe what I had heard. I didn't want my hopes to be smashed again. But in my heart, I knew it was real and I spun quickly to where Kent had pointed.

She stood there alone, looking dazed but very much alive.

"Hi Mom," was all I managed to say.

I ran to her and threw my arms around her.

She hugged back and did her best to control her tears. We both did.

"Where were you?" I asked. "We looked everywhere."

"I was in one of the barracks," she said. "The door blew open and people started flooding out and I got caught up in it and went with them until I heard that SYLO had invaded the camp. I came back with the others looking for Bova and what did I find? You."

She held her arm out for Tori, who joined us as Mom held us both close.

"I thought I'd never see you again," she said. "And here you are. In SYLO uniforms. What is going on?"

I wanted to tell her everything, but there wasn't time.

"They're going to destroy the dome," I said. "We've got to get out now."

"Who is?" she asked. "SYLO?"

"No," Tori answered. "There are rebels among the Retros

called Sounders. They've been plotting against their own people to stop the invasion and—"

"Wait!" I shouted.

I spun to look for Kent.

He was gone.

"What is with him?" Tori asked, irked.

My mind raced, calculating the possibility and realizing the truth.

"Oh man," I said.

"Tucker, what?" Tori asked.

"Mom, you've got to leave," I said. "Right now. Please don't ask questions, there isn't much time left. There are SYLO vehicles on the edges of the camp. Bring as many of the other prisoners with you as you can and drive away from here. Fast. Hit the desert and just keep going."

"I don't understand. . . ." Mom said, totally confused.

"You have to trust me. Go. Tori, please, take her out of here."

"What about you?" Tori asked.

"I've got to help Kent," I said.

"Help Kent?" Tori said, confused. "Do what?"

I hugged my mother, kissed her on the cheek, and said, "I know why you and Dad moved us to Pemberwick Island. I get it. I still wish you'd told me the truth but I understand why you didn't. I'm not angry anymore. Please tell Dad that."

"You can tell him yourself. What are you going to do?"

"I love you, Mom."

We touched fingers.

"I love you too. But—"

I turned and started running after Kent. I sprinted past Bova's building, scanning the camp for Retro enemies when . . .

"Where are you going?" Tori called.

I was stunned to see that she had caught up and was running with me.

"No!" I screamed. "Stay with my mother!"

"There's nothing I can do for her that she can't do for herself. What is going on, Tucker?" she asked.

"Please, get out of this camp," I begged.

"We are not splitting up," she said adamantly. "Not now. Where are we going?"

It was a waste of time arguing with her. It always was.

"To the dome," I admitted.

"Why?"

"I know what Kent is up to," I said. "He's going back through the Bridge."

"But why would he . . . ?" That's when Tori got it. "Olivia," she said, numbly.

It was fifteen minutes till the boom.

TWENTY-SIX

We skirted around the heart of the battle, which wasn't an easy thing to do.

Most of the fighting was centered at the open door of the dome, so we took a wide route around to try to come up to the door from behind.

The Sounder commandos and the SYLO soldiers who had zip lined in from helicopters were valiantly holding the Retros away from the dome. They were now outnumbered and the Retros had brought in superior firepower, but the smaller group fought tenaciously.

Granger and his ground troops had come up from behind, effectively trapping the Retro forces between them and those who were defending the dome.

Still, the Retros were not giving up. Though they had to fight a battle on two fronts, they had the numbers and the firepower to inflict serious damage, while still putting pressure on the commandos at the dome. Many Retro soldiers broke through and made a mad dash for the door, only to be cut down by SYLO or the Sounder commandos.

The body count was high all around. Retro soldiers lay dead or dying from conventional bullet wounds, while victims from both sides had fallen from the bursts of pulser energy.

The only thing that kept Tori and me from being targets was that we weren't firing back. The defenders weren't concerned about two people in SYLO uniforms working their way closer to the opening.

Along the way, we had to step over more bleeding bodies than I could count.

"Don't look," I said to Tori. "Keep moving."

It was a grisly scene, not like the sterile way the Retros had wiped out so much of the population. In that case, millions of people had been killed without a trace. This battle was different. The clatter of automatic assault weapons filled the air, along with the telltale explosions of energy from pulsers.

This was old-fashioned warfare at its worst.

We approached the command center and made our way along the wall, hugging close to it for safety when . . .

"Pierce!"

Tori and I froze and looked ahead to see an Air Force commando guarding the front door. I recognized him from our briefing back in the Bridge city. It was Thompson, one of Sokol's Sounders. We hurried up to him while scanning for potential threats.

"You did it," Thompson said. "You got 'em to come. Man, all hell is breaking loose."

"Thanks to you," Tori said. "If you hadn't taken control of the drones, SYLO wouldn't be here."

Thompson gave us a quick recap of how Sokol and the commandos boldly conquered the drone command center. It had gone exactly as planned with only one casualty.

"It's as good as over," he said. "So why are you still here?"

"We're looking for Kent Berrenger," I said.

"He just came through, headed for the dome," Thompson said. "What's going on?"

We didn't take the time to answer and ran off. "Hey, you shouldn't be here!" Thompson called after us.

He was absolutely right.

We finally made it to the opening of the dome and quickly slipped inside, only to come face to face with Captain Sokol.

He was charged up with the adrenaline of battle, with a wild look in his eyes that told me if we had been Retros, we would already be dead.

"No!" he shouted the moment he recognized us. "Not you too?"

"Kent came through here, didn't he?" Tori asked.

Sokol ran his hands through his sweaty hair in frustration.

"He went back for Kinsey," he said. "It's insane."

"Yeah, maybe," I said. "We're going to bring him back."

Sokol kept his frustration in check and said, "I'll tell you the same thing I told him. At 17:55 this door slams shut."

"Why haven't you closed it already?" Tori asked.

"We're using the dome for protection. As soon as we close the doors, we're exposed. They'll wipe us out and hammer away at this thing until they get it open. Our best chance is to keep it open until the very last moment. But once it's closed it won't open again until the bomb is detonated. If you're still back there, you're dead. If you're inside here, you're dead. Is that worth the risk?"

I looked to Tori. She gave me a small smile.

"We started this together," I said. "That's how we'll finish it."

"Kinsey may already be dead," he argued.

"Then we'll just bring Kent back," Tori said.

"Assuming he's still alive," Sokol cautioned.

"We're going," I said with finality. "And we're wasting time talking to you."

"17:55," he said. "I will not keep this door open a second longer."

I grabbed Tori's hand and we ran deeper into the dome, headed for the Bridge. We stopped just short of the giant glowing frame and stood there, staring into eternity.

I reached for my pulser. Tori already had hers up and ready.

"Five minutes," I said.

"Four minutes," she countered. "We've got to get back through and out of here."

"All right then," I said. "Let's go get 'em."

We each took a deep breath, and stepped into the future.

———

When Kent had gone through the Bridge minutes before, the first thing he spotted was Olivia lying on the ground, fifteen yards in front of the frame. He didn't see that Colonel Pike lay dead. He didn't notice the white cylinder positioned in front of the bridge that was quickly counting down to zero. He didn't even see Feit standing at the open control panel of the bomb, furiously trying to input the codes that would shut it down.

All he saw was the girl he loved lying unconscious.

He sprinted to her and fell to his knees at her head.

"Not again, oh God, not again," he cried.

He felt her neck for a pulse . . . and got one.

Quickly he dropped his pulser and scooped his arms under her to lift her up.

"You're okay," he said soothingly. "We'll hook you up to the IV back at the camp and it'll be like nothing ever happened."

"I think it'd be better if you both stayed right there," Feit said.

Kent stood bolt upright as if hit with an electric shock. He immediately registered the bomb with the open panel and the keypad inside, next to which was a countdown clock registering nine minutes and counting.

He also registered the pulser that Feit was pointing at him.

"It's so cool that you came back for her," Feit said, as if he genuinely meant it. "But I thought she was hot for Tucker. Guess that shows you what I know."

"Let me bring her back," Kent said. "Please."

"Oh! Sure!" Feit exclaimed. "Saying 'please' makes all the difference."

"Thank you."

Kent leaned down to pick up Olivia as Feit fired a pulser shot that whizzed past his ear.

Kent dove away in surprise.

"Idiot," Feit said. "I was being sarcastic. First off, why would I do that? She's a total traitor. When she gets to the court-martial she's going to wish she died here. If she thought living here was bad before, wait until they throw her into military prison. Second, you're not going back either. You've been almost as big a pain in my ass as Pierce and that Sleeper chick, so don't think for a second that I'm going to let you skip out. And finally, I hate to break this to you, but the bomb won't be going off. I'm shutting it down."

Kent went for his pulser but Feit fired at the ground, making him jump back.

"Oh no," Feit warned. "I wouldn't touch that, unless you'd rather join Olivia on the floor there. I wouldn't recommend that. It hurts."

Kent stood frozen, not sure of what to do.

"Now be a good little preppie-boy and hold still while I finish what I'm doing here before it's too late."

Feit turned back toward the bomb and came face-to-face . . .

. . . with me.

"It's already too late," I said.

I tackled him and knocked him away from the bomb. The surprise only allowed me to get the first shot in. He recovered quickly and tried to bring his pulser around to fire at me, point blank. I grabbed the weapon and wrestled him for it.

While we fought, Tori ran for Kent, who was struggling to lift Olivia.

"Go through," Tori commanded while helping to lift Olivia into Kent's arms. "Before they shut the dome."

Kent struggled to lift Olivia's limp body, then started for the Bridge.

Feit was on his back. I was over him. Both of us had our hands locked on the pulser.

Boom!

The dome was suddenly rocked by what felt like an explosion outside. The entire iron structure shook and the floor shifted. The violent force threw me off balance, which allowed Feit to pull himself up to get more leverage. Neither of us released our grip on the pulser.

If I let go, it would be over.

Kent lost his balance and fell to his knees. He lost his grip on Olivia and they both went tumbling. Tori hurried to help get the unconscious girl back up and into his arms.

"What was that?" Kent asked with dismay.

"They must be trying to blow the door down with the pulser cannons on the planes," Tori said. "Thank God it's not dark or they'd just vaporize it. C'mon."

She draped Olivia over Kent's shoulder while Kent struggled to stay upright and get to the Bridge.

Boom!

Another shot rocked the dome. The structure was built to withstand the explosion from an atomic bomb from within; there was no chance the energy cannons from outside would break through, but it did rock the place.

Kent staggered and fell again. Tori struggled to get him back up to his feet and moving.

"Hurry," she commanded.

"C'mon," Kent said.

"Right behind you."

Kent staggered forward with Olivia in his arms and stepped into the Bridge.

Out of there. Safe.

I wasn't as lucky.

That last shock wave threw me off balance. It was all Feit needed. The guy must have outweighed me by fifty pounds and he used every last one of them to wrench the pulser from my grip.

I lunged forward, grabbing at the weapon before he could level it at me.

He didn't even try. Instead he swung his elbow at my head, hitting me square in the temple. I saw stars and fell back, desperately trying to hold on to consciousness.

He backed away from me, headed for the bomb. His pulser was trained on my head.

"Just sit down, would you?" Feit said. "This will only take a second."

I thought we were done until, from the corner of my eye, I saw that Tori was out in front of the Bridge, down on one knee, with her pulser aimed at Feit.

"Stop right there," she commanded.

Feit stopped moving but he didn't take his own pulser off of me. It was a standoff. Feit was aimed at me. Tori was aimed at Feit.

"Seriously?" Feit said with frustration. "I cannot begin to express how sick I am of you two. Now let's see who wants it bad enough."

Without lowering his pulser, Feit reached up with his other hand and twisted the weapon. I heard an audible beep.

"This will now kill him," Feit said to Tori. "Are you willing to let him die? Do you have the guts for that, Tori?"

"Shoot him," I said to Tori.

Feit slowly backed toward the bomb.

"Look, I'm just going to stop this thing from going off," he said innocently. "How much time is left? Like, six minutes? Plenty of time. Let me just stop the clock and then we'll talk."

Tori fired her pulser behind his feet, forcing Feit to freeze in place.

Boom!

The dome shook again.

Feit spun and fired . . . at Tori.

Tori dove to her right and fired back . . . not at Feit, at the bomb.

Her aim was dead-on. The pulse of energy nailed the keypad next to the countdown clock, frying it.

Feit dropped his pulser and stood there staring, momentarily stunned.

"Wha . . . ?" He ran to the bomb to see that the keypad had become a mass of useless plastic, while the countdown continued. He clawed at the destroyed keys, as if he could somehow still input the now useless codes onto the melted surface.

He then spun toward Tori and with building rage screamed, "Do you realize what you've done? We had a chance to escape. Escape the fate that the people of your time created. Now you've doomed us a second time to exist in this hell on earth."

Tori was down on one knee with her pulser up and aimed directly at Feit.

"It's better than you deserve," she said.

Feit looked up and over her head. His eyes lit up. Suddenly, he took off running for the closed door of the dome.

"Stop!" Tori ordered.

Feit slowed momentarily and said, "Go on, shoot. What have I got to lose?"

He was headed for the panel that controlled the door. If he opened it, the conditions that created the Bridge in the first place would be altered. There would be immense destruction, but the Bridge would still exist.

"Don't do it!" Tori commanded.

Feit picked up speed.

Tori pulled the trigger . . . but her pulser misfired. She hit the trigger again and got nothing.

Feit laughed. Feit always laughed.

He changed direction and swooped down to pick up the pulser he had dropped. He grabbed it, saying, "This is really working out. I've still got time to personally finish you off."

He stood to face her but got me instead. I was holding Kent's pulser leveled at him.

"No you don't," I said.

In that brief instant I thought of the exact way I would always remember that moment: It was the look of shock on his face.

It was over.

He was done.

The Retros were done.

He knew it.

It was awesome.

I fired.

The pulse of energy made the weapon kick back in my hand. The force hit Feit dead-on, but rather than falling, it knocked him backward. He actually tried to keep his balance as he stumbled, pinwheeling his arms. I fired again. There was no way he was going to get away this time. The second jolt of energy knocked him off of his feet and he fell back, disappearing into the Bridge.

Boom!

The place was rocking, and not in a good way.

"You think they could break through?" Tori asked as she ran up to me.

"If an atomic bomb can't break down these walls, I doubt if one of those cannons can."

The countdown clock showed four minutes to go.

"And definitely not in four minutes," I added.

I gave one last quick look around the dome, and at the bomb that had the power to control the future and save the past. I saw that lying near the closed door was the body of Colonel Pike.

"A lot of people gave their lives to stop the Retros," Tori said.

"Yeah," I said. "I don't want to be one of them. Let's get out of here."

I took Tori's hand and we ran forward, out of the future, through the Bridge and into the past for the final time.

When we passed through into the dome, the first thing I saw was Kent standing in the middle of the vast, empty space with Olivia still in his arms. He stood with his legs spread apart and his back to us, staring ahead at the giant door of the dome.

The giant *closed* door.

My heart sank.

"Oh my God," Tori said, barely above a whisper.

"I'm sorry," was all I could think to say to my friends.

"Can we open it?" Kent asked, without even turning around.

I looked at my watch.

"No," I said flatly. "Even if I knew how we wouldn't be able to get it open and closed fast enough. If it isn't shut when the bomb goes off . . ."

I didn't have to explain any more than that.

There was nothing more we could do. From the time we had made the decision to escape from Pemberwick Island we had always been moving forward: always looking for an answer. Always searching for a way to make things right. As we stood there in that vast, empty space, the truth hit hard that we had finally run out of options.

"So close," Tori said. "We won't even know if it worked."

Kent gently rested Olivia on the floor.

"But we did it, right?" he said. "I mean, we helped make this happen. We'll go down in history."

Kent was finally going to be the hero he always imagined himself to be. Too bad he wouldn't be around to enjoy it.

"Yeah," I said. "But whatever is written won't even scratch the surface on what we did here."

Tori leaned in to hug me. I put my arm around her, then put my other arm around Kent. The three of us stood there holding one another, not knowing what else to do. In some strange way it felt right. They had become the most important people in the world to me. Together with Olivia and the Sounders, we had crushed the Retros.

"Man, I hope this doesn't hurt," Kent said.

"It won't," Tori said, sounding way more sure than she had the right to be. "We're at ground zero. As soon as—"

"Wait," I said.

Looking over Tori's shoulder, I saw something that I'd noticed the first time we came into this dome. It meant nothing to me then. Maybe it still meant nothing.

Or maybe not.

"What is that thing?" I asked, pointing.

It was the egg-shaped pod that was built into the wall of the dome. It looked like an old-fashioned diving bell with a heavy open hatch that showed its walls to be a couple of feet thick. The word EMERGENCY was stenciled on the outside above the open door.

"I'd call this an emergency," Kent said.

Kent and I scooped up Olivia and we quickly shuffled over to the pod. None of us would say it but we were all wondering the same thing: Was this device built as an emergency shelter in case something went wrong with the bomb test? The shape of the small room was roughly the same as the dome, and its walls looked just as thick. There was nothing high-tech or modern about it. It could definitely have been built in the 1950s when the dome was constructed.

There was no way to know if it could withstand an atomic blast that came roaring back from the future, but we had to give it a try.

We quickly carried Olivia into the small room and laid her down on the floor.

"Seal it up!" Kent commanded.

I went for the door, which was really more of a hatch, and was about to swing it shut when I spotted something back in the center of the dome, in front of the Bridge.

Feit.

He was lying there, either dead or unconscious.

"C'mon, Rook," Kent shouted. "Close us in."

We had seen so much death over the past weeks and not just at the hands of the Retros. We were in a war and in a war, people died. I had gone from fearing the handgun Tori kept in the glove box of the car to shooting a pulser at anyone who was a threat. In the heat of the moment I didn't hesitate to shoot anybody I thought was an enemy. I didn't feel guilty about it either, because we were the good guys. We didn't ask for this war. We didn't wipe out countless millions of people. Whatever the Retros got, they deserved. I had been driven by the need for revenge from the beginning. Making somebody suffer for what had happened had motivated me almost as much as my desire for the truth and to put an end to the misery. I wanted my life back, but I also wanted somebody to suffer for what they had done.

We had been fighting for our survival and the survival of a planet. If the bomb worked, we would win. We would stop the bad guys. The Retros would be trapped in the future and the world of our time could be rebuilt. But rebuilt into what? Would mankind make the same mistakes that led to the horrible future the Retros had been so desperate to escape from?

Did we have the humanity to rebuild a better world?

"What are you thinking, Tucker?" Tori asked.

"I'm thinking the killing has to stop somewhere," I said.

I stepped out of the hatch and made a run for Feit.

"Tucker!" Kent shouted. "Are you crazy?"

Tori jumped out and ran after me.

"Wha—?" Kent said with a gasp. "Seriously?"

I ran up to Feit and reached under his shoulders to lift him.

Tori joined me. "Is he alive?"

"I don't know and I'm not taking the time to check. Is this stupid?"

"No," she said. "But hurry."

Tori grabbed his legs and together we half carried/half dragged him back to the emergency pod.

"No way," Kent screamed. "I'm closing the hatch right now."

"No he isn't," I said to Tori, calmly.

Of course, he didn't.

We reached the hatch and awkwardly dragged Feit inside.

"Now! Close it!" I shouted at Kent.

Kent swung the heavy door closed. It locked into place with a solid, satisfying thump. The seal was so tight that it made my ears pop. There was a wheel on the inside that Kent spun to tighten the door into place.

A single red light bulb in the ceiling sprang to life the instant the hatch was closed. It flashed intermittently, as if it were a warning beacon.

"We can't stay in here for long," Kent said. "No air."

I looked at my watch.

"Thirty seconds," I said. "I think we can last that long. After that, it won't matter."

The three of us got on our knees, surrounding Olivia. We wrapped our arms around one another, more for support than protection.

Feit was not part of this circle.

We put our heads together and stayed that way, cheek to cheek.

"I'm glad we're together," Kent said.

I glanced at my watch.

Three seconds.

Two seconds.

One.

Ignition.

TWENTY-SEVEN

There was a mad rush of what sounded like wind blowing by our steel cocoon. Given that the walls were a few feet thick, I could only imagine what it sounded like outside in the dome.

We all tightened our grip on one another, waiting for . . . what? Instant annihilation? Or would there be an inviting bright light for us all to walk into? The thought hit me that by being inside this protected igloo we might have given up our chance at a quick and painless death. If we had been standing in front of the Bridge, once the nuclear rush came blasting through from the future we would have been vaporized in a nanosecond. Huddling inside a thick bunker could mean the end would come agonizingly slowly, as the heat and radiation gradually burned through the metal skin on its way to get us.

The wind turned into a shriek. The pod shuddered as if trying to brace itself against the ferocious onslaught.

Tori let out a small, tense whimper. It was the only sign of fear that any of us showed.

"This is it," Kent said.

As if on cue, the nuclear wind suddenly stopped. There

was a moment of calm, then it picked up again with even more bone-rattling violence. The floor beneath us vibrated and the pod shook. I couldn't imagine a force so strong that it could make such a solid structure tremble. I expected it to be torn from the floor and be tossed around inside the dome like a frantic pinball.

The red light continued flashing. We alternated between being bathed in blood-red light, to being thrown into total darkness.

I prayed that whatever was going to happen would happen fast. The waiting was torture. The pod grew hot, though I couldn't tell if that was from our own body heat or from the atomic fire burning outside.

The wind grew into a demonic shriek that tore into my brain.

Until it stopped.

Suddenly.

It didn't trail off, it simply ended. We were in silence. The only sound was the steady *click . . . click . . . click* of the red light as it flashed on and off.

We all looked up tentatively.

"Is that it?" Kent asked. "Is it over?"

"I don't know," I replied. "I've never been through an atomic blast before."

None of us moved. We had no idea of what to do because we didn't think we'd still be alive to have to worry about it. We stayed like that for I don't know how long. Five minutes? Ten?

"We can't go outside," Tori said. "The radiation will—"

The wheel to the hatch began turning with a metallic squeal.

Instantly, the red light went out and we were plunged into darkness.

I felt more intense panic in that moment than in the seconds before the bomb exploded.

"Someone's out there," Kent said, breathless. "They're opening it up!"

"No!" I screamed. "The radiation!"

I pushed my way past Tori and Kent, stumbling over them in the dark to get to the wheel to stop it from turning. We were all caught up in a jumble of hands and arms and legs as I lunged for the door.

"Stop!" Tori yelled. "Don't open it!"

"They can't hear you," Kent said. "It's too thick."

I struggled to prevent the wheel from turning but the force was too great.

"How could anyone be out there?" Kent said.

"It might be automatic," Tori said.

"I can't hold it," I said, straining, doing all I could to keep my grip.

With one final twist the wheel stopped and with a sucking sound, the door was unsealed.

I fell back into the arms of my friends.

What would happen when radiation flooded into the small chamber? Would we die instantly or was this the beginning of a slow, agonizing fall into a burning oblivion?

We all lay on the floor, looking up with wonder and fear as light appeared around the edges of the frame. The light grew as the door was slowly opened, blinding us.

There was a rush of air into the pod. Fresh, cool air. Was that what radiation felt like? I held my breath, for whatever good that would do.

"What in blazes?" someone bellowed outside of the pod.

The hatch was thrown open and once my eyes adjusted to the light I saw that several men were standing outside in the dome. None of them looked to have radiation suits on, but they were all carrying rifles. They were soldiers, but I couldn't tell if they were Retros or SYLO.

"Come out of there," the same guy said, gruffly. "Keep your hands where we can see 'em."

"There are two unconscious people in here," I said.

"Leave 'em," the guy commanded. "Put your hands on your head and step out."

"What's going on?" Kent whispered.

"You're asking me like I know?" I replied.

"Shut it!" the guy bellowed. "Hands on heads. Step out one at a time."

I went first. I put my hands on my head and cautiously moved forward, ducked down, and stepped out of the pod to face a line of armed soldiers, all pointing rifles at me.

They weren't SYLO *or* Retros. At least as far as I could tell. These guys were wearing dark-green combat uniforms and green helmets.

"Stand right there," the leader said. "Don't move."

The guy in charge was short, wide, and carried himself with confidence. Over his right breast pocket was a white patch with the name CARINO stitched in black. Over his left breast pocket was a black patch with U.S. ARMY stitched in yellow. Apparently a third branch of the United States military had joined the war. It was anybody's guess as to which side they were on.

I followed his orders and stood there while the others crawled out of the capsule. I looked around the dome, expecting to see damage caused by the rush of atomic energy, but there was nothing. It looked no different from when we had stepped into the pod . . . with one very big change.

The Bridge was gone.

The giant frame that encased the wormhole into the future was no longer there. In its place was a white cylinder that looked all too familiar. It was a bomb that looked exactly like the one that had just detonated in the future.

In front of it were several jeeps that these soldiers must have driven through the door that was now wide open.

"We're dead, right?" Kent asked as he stepped up to me. "Or it's a dream."

"I'm guessing we're dead," Tori said as she stepped up.

"Shut it!" Carino ordered. He turned to his men and said, "Get the others out of there. Be careful."

Several of his men charged into the pod and a few seconds later they came out carrying Olivia and Feit. They laid them down on the floor in front of us.

Olivia groaned. It was the first sign of life she had shown since being shot by Feit's pulser.

Kent knelt down to her but one of the soldiers stepped up and waved his rifle in his face.

"Back off, junior," the soldier ordered.

"She's hurt," Kent said. "Can't you see that?"

"I don't know what the hell I'm seeing," Carino said.

He walked to Olivia and looked down at her like she was an alien.

Olivia opened her eyes, blinked, and focused on the soldier who loomed over her.

"You're kind of cute," she said. "For a hallucination."

Carino backed off, stunned, and he looked like the kind of guy who didn't stun easily. He looked us all over, shaking his head, as if we were the ones who were hallucinations.

"Don't move, none of ya," he said and backed away toward his line of soldiers, most of whom were aiming their rifles at us.

From one he grabbed a chunky green canister that looked like a skinny shoebox with a huge antenna sticking out of one end. He stepped away from the group and talked into it.

"Carino here," he said. "We got 'em out."

"It's a walkie-talkie," Tori whispered.

"No it isn't," Kent said.

"Quiet!" a soldier commanded.

"What's going on?" Olivia said, groggy.

"Don't move," Kent said. "Everything's cool."

One of the soldiers snickered.

"What's so funny?" Kent asked.

"Everything is *not* cool," the soldier replied.

Carino walked back with the giant walkie-talkie, or whatever it was, held to his ear.

"Kids," he said into the device. "Yeah, kids. Four of 'em. And one older guy. They're wearing some kind of red uniforms, or costumes."

He listened and then said, "Roger. Will do. Carino out."

He lowered the walkie-talkie and looked at us with a mixture of confusion and fear.

"It's not my job to interrogate you," he said to us. "That's up to the brass. But I gotta know, how the hell did you get into the most heavily guarded military outpost in the world? No, better question: Why? You're wearing red. Are you Commies?"

"Commies?" Kent said. "What are Commies?"

The truth hit me with a ferocity that was roughly equal to the power of the atomic bomb blast.

"It didn't go off," I said.

"What didn't go off?" Carino asked.

"The test. It didn't go off."

"What test?" Kent asked, confused.

"Hell no it didn't," Carino said, glancing back to the white cylinder in the center of the dome. "When you sealed the hatch it set off alarms all over the place. The count was down to the last tick. Another half second and we would have had to cut you out of there from outside. We wouldn't be standing here right now, that's for sure."

"It's *the* test," Tori said, the truth dawning on her. "The bomb. The original test that created the Bridge. Project Alcatraz."

"Who *are* you people," Carino asked with genuine curiosity. "How did you know that name?"

"I think maybe we should save that for the brass," I said. "Are you going to take us to them now?"

Carino was too stunned to question us further. The fact that we had appeared inside of that emergency chamber was something he simply couldn't get his head around. He rubbed the back of his neck, squinted as if trying to think of something to say to us, then gave up and motioned to his men.

"Load 'em up," he ordered.

When his men lifted Feit, he let out a groan.

He was alive.

"Watch that guy," I said. "He's not one of the good guys."

"Oh and you are?" Carino asked.

"Yeah," I said. "We are."

One of the soldiers helped Olivia to her feet and into one of the waiting jeeps. Each of us had our own vehicle with a driver and a soldier riding shotgun with a pistol aimed at us. The engines fired up and we lurched forward, headed out of the dome.

If I had any doubt about what had actually happened, it was washed away the moment we drove out of the door and into the sunlight.

The camp was gone.

Not a single building or vehicle was in sight. There was nothing around us for miles but empty desert.

"Can I ask you one question?" I said to the guard who had a pistol pointed at my chest.

"What?"

"Is today January the twenty-fourth?"

"All day," he replied.

"What year is it?" I asked.

"That's two questions."

It didn't matter. I knew the answer.

It was 1952.

The atomic explosion that had blasted the Bridge into the twenty-third century never happened. We had stopped it. The Sounders had stopped it.

Kent, Olivia, Tori, Feit, and I were in the middle of the dramatic explosion that reversed the process and were thrown back to the moment it began.

Before it began . . .

. . . and was about to begin anew.

TWENTY-EIGHT

High school graduation.

I never thought I'd make it. The possibility of actually sitting at my graduation ceremony on the football field, next to my friends, watching my parents beam proudly as I walked up to get my diploma was an impossible dream that actually came true.

I ate up every second of it, mostly because it was all so normal.

I had started the day hours before on my porch, gazing out at the ocean from my home on Pemberwick Island. It was a spectacular view I never got tired of or took for granted. Not anymore. I had worked too hard and gone through too much to get back there. I appreciated every second I spent on Pemberwick and always would.

The surf was high that day, creating a series of deep booms that echoed across the beach as each new set came in. There looked to be a storm brewing in the distance, based on the deep gray clouds that hovered on the horizon and the hundreds of seagulls on the beach that had come ashore to avoid getting caught up in it. For a moment I feared that the storm might prevent me from getting to graduation, but I immediately dismissed the thought. There was nothing that would keep me from that ceremony.

The school's jazz ensemble played "Forever Young"; the keynote speaker was some author I'd never heard of who talked about striving for your goals and never taking "no" for an answer; and the valedictorian (for the record, not me) spoke about how we hadn't reached the end, but were embarking on a new beginning.

Truer words had never been spoken.

It was the kind of ceremony that was being repeated all over the country. Same speeches, different faces.

What made it all the more special was that three of the most important people in the world to me were also there: Tori, Kent, and Olivia. We had attended Kent's graduation ceremony two years before. (He wasn't the valedictorian either, for the record.)

When I stepped on that stage to receive my diploma and shake the hand of the headmaster, it gave me a feeling of peace and satisfaction I feared I would never achieve.

I wanted normal. This was normal.

What wasn't normal was the series of events that led us to that moment.

It was a strange chain that began on January 24, 1952, in the Mojave desert.

———

We were interrogated by the Army, separately of course. Being questioned had become old hat. We each gave our account of what happened and I didn't doubt for a second that we would all give the exact same story.

Except for Feit. There was no telling what he said. I made sure to explain to my interrogators exactly what his role was in the genocide that preceded the invasion of the past.

The interrogation process lasted for days, no big surprise. We were kept apart the whole time, probably so we wouldn't compare notes to keep our wacky stories straight. I didn't blame our U.S. Army hosts one single bit. Our story was impossible to believe. Different interrogators cycled through, trying to poke holes in our accounts and find the fatal flaw that proved we were making the whole thing up.

They didn't find any because none existed.

They brought in psychiatric experts to determine if we were out of our minds.

Of course, we weren't.

After the first week, we were allowed to see each other. All of us but Feit, that is. That was the first clue that they had accepted our story, including Feit's role in the death of millions of people. The four of us were brought to a building they called a Quonset hut, which was basically a long steel structure with a rounded roof, like an upside-down half-pipe. It was a comfortable place, complete with a few couches and stuffed chairs. It would have been nice if there had been modern air conditioning. The few table fans blowing around hot desert air didn't count.

I arrived first, followed shortly after by Tori. When I saw her we immediately ran to each other and hugged. We stayed that way for a good few minutes. It was like holding on to a lifeline in the midst of a swirling sea.

"You okay?" I finally asked.

She nodded and pulled away.

"I'm okay too," Kent said as he stepped in. "In case you were wondering."

We gave each other quick but genuine hugs.

"Hey I want some of that too," Olivia chirped as she bounced in.

It became a four-way hug-fest. I had said many times in the past (or the future, actually) that the four of us were all we had. It never felt truer than in that moment.

"Where's Feit?" Tori asked.

"Swinging from a noose," Kent said quickly. "I hope."

"That won't happen," I said.

"Why not?" Kent asked. "He was part of the biggest mass murder in history."

"Yeah," I said. "History that hasn't happened yet. There's no evidence to prove he did any of that."

"No," Tori said. "That he's *going* to do any it. You can't prosecute somebody for a crime they're going to commit fifty some odd years from now."

"Or three hundred years from now," Olivia said.

"Jeez, that makes my head hurt," Kent said. "Does anybody know how this happened? I mean, I could explain everything to those Army dudes except for why we're sitting here in nineteen freakin' fifty-two."

"I can only guess," I said. "When the bomb went off it somehow reversed the Bridge and blew us back to when it was first opened."

"Yeah, but how?" Kent asked.

"How?" I replied, laughing. "How did *any* of this happen?

Physicists are going to be trying to figure that out for years. Don't expect an answer from me."

"So why didn't they set off the bomb?" Olivia asked.

"Because we sealed that pod," Tori said. "It closed a circuit that sent an alarm to the firing room. When they realized somebody was in there, they stopped the countdown."

"So the bomb blast shot us back to the exact moment in 1952 before the original bomb was detonated," I said. "And by being here, we prevented it from going off."

"That means none of it happened!" Kent exclaimed. "The Bridge wasn't created so the Retros won't be able to go back to the past and vaporize all those people."

"No," Olivia said with authority. "It all happened."

"But I thought we stopped the Bridge from opening up!" Kent said, frustrated.

"I told you," Olivia said. "You can't change the past. Once something happens it can't un-happen. Our existence in the twenty-fourth century and yours in the twenty-first century were two different timelines that were connected by the Bridge."

"You mean like different dimensions running parallel to each other?" Tori asked.

"I guess," Olivia said. "I never really understood it all. I'm not sure anybody else did either. There were some geniuses who said they did but I think they were just blowing smoke."

"So that crappy future still exists?" Kent asked. "It's still out there . . . somewhere?"

"I think so," Olivia replied. "The only difference is they can no longer invade the twenty-first century because we closed the Bridge."

"That means all those people are still dead," Tori said.

"No!" Kent exclaimed. "Without the Bridge the Retros couldn't send those killer planes back."

"But that's not how it works," Olivia said, patiently. "I'm sorry Kent, but the people of the twenty-first century you lived in have to deal with what the Retros did and rebuild from what's left. But SYLO did exactly what they set out to do. They stopped the invasion and preserved society."

"With a lot of help from the Sounders," Tori pointed out.

"Yeah, and us," Kent added. "And speaking of us, where exactly do we fit into this fantasy?"

"I think we created another timeline," I said.

"We what?" Kent asked, incredulous.

"We were shot back to the past and stopped the bomb test from happening," I said. "But the past can't be changed. That means we've started the clock ticking on yet another timeline."

"Seriously?" Tori asked. "We're stuck here in . . . in . . . what? Another dimension?"

"That's exactly it," Olivia said. "As far as we know, there are three realities now. The twenty-fourth century when I was born. The early twenty-first century that you guys came from, and—"

"And a new timeline that began on January 24, 1952, with no Bridge to the future," I said, finishing her point. "Where we are right now. At least that means this reality won't be invaded by the Retros."

Kent rubbed his face anxiously. "Okay, let's pretend that's all true," he said, his voice cracking with nervous energy. "How do we get back to our own time? Our own reality?"

We all exchanged anxious looks. Nobody wanted to say the obvious so I took the step myself.

"We don't," I said with finality.

"That other life will go on without us," Tori said quietly. "And we have to make a new life here."

"But . . ." Kent was all set to jump in with a reason why that couldn't be true, but he didn't have one.

It was a sober moment as we let the undeniable reality sink in. We would never see our families again. We would never get back to Pemberwick Island. At least not to the Pemberwick Island we knew.

"I don't want to live in the past," Kent said, glum.

"Tell me about it," Olivia shot back quickly.

"There has to be a way," Kent added with a touch of desperation.

"Not unless they create another Bridge," I said. "But even if they did, there are no guarantees it would open up in the exact right time of our original lives. What we've got here, right now . . . this is it."

"Like it or not," Olivia said. "This reality, this time, is our home now."

"The people from home will think we were killed in the bomb blast," Tori said, soberly.

"At least we'll be remembered," Kent said. "They'll probably erect statues of us. We'll be the brave heroes who gave their lives to save the world." He sighed and added, "Nobody will know we're still alive in another freakin' dimension. Jeez."

"Remember that," I said.

"Remember what?" Kent asked.

"We're still alive."

With that understanding, our new lives began.

We spent the next year living at the military base sixty miles from where the dome was built. Area 51. Our existence was kept secret from all but a few top military types, scientists, and government officials. Oddly, most people who knew who we really were didn't want any contact with us. They didn't want to be influenced by knowing what would happen in the future. Or maybe they were just scared.

I think information leaked out that something odd was going on at Area 51 and it caused a slew of headlines. I'm not saying we were the aliens that everyone suspected were being kept hidden at the base, but we were undeniably alien to this world and we were most definitely kept hidden.

For the record, I never bumped into any other aliens at Area 51.

The government wasn't sure what to do with us. I'm happy to say that they didn't do any strange testing on us like you see in movies. They treated us like normal kids . . . who happened to be from the future.

On one hand they tried to learn as much as they could about the phenomenon that had ripped open a hole through time. We spoke with physicists from all over the country. They were the guys who had the least trouble believing us, because they always thought time travel was possible. Our existence justified their theories. But they were cautious about not asking us anything about specific events that had happened in our past, or their future. They saw it as an ethical dilemma. Why should a few people know about what the future held while most others didn't have that advantage? I got that. I didn't want to go messing with the world any more than we already had. How would things have changed if we told them that President Kennedy would be assassinated? Or that we would land on the moon? How much would that knowledge have changed the natural course of events? Probably a lot and maybe not for the better. There was no way to know for sure, so it was best left unsaid.

We did tell them as much as we could about what a mess the world would become due to the exhaustion of fossil fuels, pollution, and overpopulation. They took note, but didn't seem too worried about it. We got a little taste of what some of the people from our time experienced when trying to warn the world about the coming disaster.

———

The Army had a real dilemma. What should they do with us? We had no families. We didn't dare contact our grandparents. What would we tell them? We had no history. No birth certificates. We truly didn't exist. In the back of my head I was worried that they would keep us hidden away in the middle of the desert for the rest of our lives, but that wasn't the case.

New identities were created for each of us. Records were fabricated, complete with histories that said we were abandoned at birth and brought up in foster homes. The Army found wonderful families who were more than willing to take us in. Better still, they were all in the same area of the country. Los Angeles. It meant that even though we were being sent to different homes, we would still be close enough to see our true family: each other.

I once asked what had happened to Colonel Feit. Nobody gave me a straight answer. They would say things like, "He's been taken care of" or "It's best you forget about him." I didn't know if he was imprisoned, set free . . . or executed.

When the day came for us to leave the base, the commander of the unit gave us a final bit of advice. He asked us to do our best to forget the past, and the future, and to live our lives as normally as possible. He said that our records would be sealed and nobody would learn of our true identities. He also said that the Army would check up on us from time to time.

For the record, they never did.

When we left that base for the final time, it was the last contact we had with anybody who knew we had come from the future. I guess they felt it was better to pretend that we didn't exist rather than to risk the truth getting out. I think they feared that every country who developed atomic weapons would try to duplicate the Bridge, or that we'd be constantly hounded by people asking us about the future. It would have ruined any chance we had at living normal lives.

My guess is they didn't seal our records, they destroyed them.

As we were driven off through the desert in the vintage jeep, I looked back on the base for the last time and saw the final proof that the Army and the government wanted nothing to do with time travel.

The dome was being dismantled. There would be no above-ground atomic test. Project Alcatraz was scrapped, never to be resurrected. The secret of what had happened in another dimension and another time would die with those who we met there.

And eventually, with us.

Though we wanted nothing more than to live normal lives, making that happen wasn't easy. Forget all the time travel and the near destruction of our world; we had lost our home and our families. Somewhere in another dimension my parents were mourning the loss of their son. When I was younger they had joined SYLO and moved to Pemberwick Island to protect me. Though they couldn't know it, that was exactly what happened. If we had stayed living in Greenwich we would probably have been victims of the first Retro attack. I hoped my parents weren't feeling any guilt over the fact that they had lost me. I knew they would be proud of what I had done. The solid B-minus student who didn't apply himself at school had helped save the world. I hoped that would give them some consolation.

I missed them, and always would.

Tori, Kent, and Olivia were set adrift much the same way. Though we were all fostered by wonderful people, none of us felt truly complete unless we were with each other.

Living in the 1950s was a challenge. It was an age before digital technology. There were no computers or smart phones. Theaters only showed one movie at a time. The black-and-white television only received four channels. Without my iPod, I had to listen to music using plastic discs that spun on turntables.

For the record, they're called records.

Regressing technologically was annoying, but expected. There were plenty of other things I didn't expect, like not being able to wear jeans to school. I also had to keep my hair cut short because if your hair fell over your ears, they called you a girl. And most everybody smoked cigarettes. That took some getting used to.

It was also tough making new friends because I had to be careful about everything I said. I couldn't tell them that Neil Armstrong would be the first man to walk on the moon or that the Beatles were about to rock the planet or that the World Trade Center would be attacked by terrorists. I couldn't even tell them that there would *be* a World Trade Center. It was a huge pain, not only because it kept us from fully connecting with the people of that time, but because there were so many horrific events that we had the power to prevent, but couldn't. We had to let history play out naturally.

I lived for the weekends. That's when the four of us got together, usually at the beach, where nobody could hear us and we could be ourselves. We'd talk about our true pasts and the people we cared about. It relieved the pressure and helped keep me sane. But as time went on and all of our stories had been told more than once, we found ourselves talking less about the past and more about the future. Not the future we knew, the future that had yet to be written.

It was on a beautiful, warm day in Manhattan Beach, sitting on a blanket by the edge of the surf, that our lives were changed once again.

"We can't ignore it anymore," Tori said. "History is repeating itself."

"Isn't that the point?" Kent asked.

"But that means this world is on a path to the same disaster scenario that led to Olivia's world in the twenty-fourth century. Only a handful of people know what's coming and they're pretending like they don't. I'm not even convinced they truly believed we were from the future."

"So the only people who understand what's going to happen are us," Olivia said.

"Who cares?" Kent exclaimed. "Those people from the twenty-fourth century are killers. They deserve whatever they get."

"But they became killers because of what they got," Tori said. "I'm not saying what they did was justified, but they were desperate. The same thing is going to happen again."

"So what do you want to do about it?" Kent asked. "Go public? The Army will say they never heard of us and they'll put us in a zoo. Or a loony bin. There's no point. Nothing we say will make any difference because people are going to do what they're going to do."

"So we don't tell them," I said. "We change them."

I had everyone's attention.

"Uh . . . what?" Kent said.

"I've been thinking a lot about Quinn," I said. "Maybe I spend too much brain time on Pemberwick Island but I can't help it. Quinn had plans. He wanted to leave that island and make a difference. I didn't understand that. For me, living quietly on a beautiful island was all I needed. Neither of us got what we wanted and now we're in the exact same spot, living on our own little island, hiding from the world. The difference is we have the knowledge that could change the future. We can make a difference."

"We can't tell people what we know, Rook," Kent said. "They'll treat us like freaks. Hell, we *are* freaks."

"It's worse than that," Olivia said. "If we start monkeying with things there's no guarantee it won't lead to something even worse."

"You might be right," I said. "But I can't imagine anything worse than what we saw in 2324. We risked our lives to save the world once. Do you really want to sit around and watch it fall apart again?"

They all exchanged nervous glances. I had hit a nerve.

"What is it you want to do, Tucker?" Tori asked.

I smiled and said, "I want to cheat."

I had been forming the plan for months, trying to think of every possible scenario and pitfall. When I laid it out to the others, they quickly embraced it. Even Kent. They each may have had different reasons for agreeing to my vision, but the main thing was that they were with me. I knew they would be. It was the right thing to do. The only thing.

We had saved the world once. We were going to try to do it again.

The plan started with school. From that moment on we became the most dedicated students imaginable. Even me. It was all geared toward getting us into college, where the real work began. Kent took business courses. Olivia studied marketing. Tori took a double major in physics and chemistry. I studied political science and went to law school. We all received advance degrees to prepare us for the most important step.

We were going to cheat the system.

The four of us formed a company. At first, it was all about investment. That's where the cheating came in. We knew where the money was going to be, eventually. IBM, Xerox, Microsoft, Apple, Walmart, Intel. In the '60s the phrase "Made in Japan" had a negative connotation, but we knew that wouldn't last. Sony, Toyota, Datsun (that became Nissan) were all companies we knew were going to be major players. We even invested in ExxonMobil (though it was called Esso back then).

There was no guarantee that any of those companies would develop the exact same way they had back in our other world, but it was a safe bet because we knew that no matter what happened, there would be a need for the products they created. We didn't interfere, we invested. Quietly. What began with money we earned from after-school jobs slowly grew into a fortune.

An immense freakin' fortune.

With that kind of money we had the freedom to use it for whatever we wanted, and what we wanted was the Holy Grail. Our main goal was to find an energy source to replace fossil fuels. We hired visionaries: physicists, chemists, biologists, and even sociologists. They worked for decades trying to find the practical alternative to fossil fuels and nuclear energy.

They struck gold with hydrogen. It is one of nature's simplest elements. Our "H" team worked for decades to find a way to create a hydrogen fuel that didn't require the use of fossil fuels or nuclear power to produce. It was clean, it reduced the world's reliance on fossil fuels, and it only took a few billion dollars of our not-so-hard-earned cash to create.

It was a patented process that ended up making us even more

money than all of our cheating did. Though making money was never the point. Most everything we earned was plowed right back into research and development. Once we got to the point where we could no longer predict future investments it didn't matter, for we had hundreds of our own patents in place and it kept our production humming. Soon, over half the world's cars ran on hydrogen fuel, as well as the power plants that provided electricity throughout the grid.

Simply put, we had done it.

We made a difference.

The ultimate result of what we achieved won't be known for centuries, and since we didn't have a Bridge to the future, we could only speculate. But all signs pointed to the fact that we had cracked the nut. We had set the world on a better course than the one that led to the horror of Olivia's time.

Of course it wasn't all work. We had lives to live.

Kent and Olivia got married.

Not to each other.

As much as they loved each other, I think they were too much alike. They both had big personalities and loved living the life of people who had fame and money. Oh yes, creating a revolutionary new source of power brought us fame. Kent had more girlfriends than I could count, but he finally married a girl who both fed his ego and kept him in line. Not an easy task.

Olivia married an Olympic skier. They travelled the world together and were on the cover of every sports and style magazine that existed. They had two kids who were both as beautiful and athletic as their parents.

Tori and I got married too.

To each other.

I think I fell in love with her the moment I first saw her on Pemberwick Island with her long curly hair and her University of Southern Maine baseball cap. She wasn't like the other girls. Getting her to talk was next to impossible and I think that was because she actually had more to say than the other kids and knew they wouldn't understand. But I did. I often wonder if we would have ended up together if not for the Retro invasion. It's odd to find a silver lining in the nightmare we lived through, but if there was one, that was it.

Tori and I had a beautiful daughter who knows she will always be able to rely on us and trust us. It was everything to Tori that our little girl knew she had two parents who would always be there to love her. I couldn't be prouder. Of both of them.

I'm not exactly sure what happened to Mr. Feit. He dropped off the face of the earth. Part of me wondered if the Army had him executed, or locked away for life, but that didn't seem right. They had no evidence of the part he played in the atrocities. In fact, those atrocities never actually happened. Not in this world.

It was more likely that Feit had simply been released and forgotten, just as they had done with us. I'd often scour the newspapers and later the Internet, searching for signs of anybody who was having as much success in the stock market as we were. That would have been the tipoff. I didn't find a thing. If he was still alive it meant he wasn't as smart as I thought he was, or way smarter than I could have imagined.

There was one day, however, when at the beach in Santa Monica I saw a group of old-guy surfers with longboards headed for their cars. One of them was a dead ringer for Feit, right down to the long blond hair and the earring. He was older too, which fit. His hair had as much gray in it as blond. But since many older surfer dudes looked exactly like that I figured I was jumping to conclusions. The guy handed his board off to a friend and jumped behind the wheel of a sweet Maserati. He fired up the powerful engine and tore out of the parking spot with his wheels screeching.

As he flashed by where I was standing, we made eye contact. He smiled and gave me a small salute. As he sped off, I heard him laugh.

I try not to let the memory haunt me.

As much as Kent, Olivia, Tori, and I had our own lives, we never spent much time apart. We were joined together not only by our energy company, but by the bond that we had formed many years before. We were family. We had a goal. We weren't going to let the world crumble and I believe in our own small way, we succeeded.

Quinn would have been proud.

It was the common desire to fulfill this goal that brought us all to my high school graduation. Or more specifically, the high school graduation of my younger self. The guy who was born in this dimension and had barely squeaked through Greenwich High School.

In this reality, my parents hadn't moved to Pemberwick Island. There was no need because there was no Bridge to the future, no threat, no Retros. Dad kept his job with the town and my mom started her own accounting firm. They were pretty successful, too. I threw Mom a lot of work through one of our subsidiary companies. She had no idea that if she followed the money it would lead to me. Even if she had, there was no way she would have known that I was an older version of her own son, from a different time and place.

It was my bittersweet secret.

Through the years I kept tabs on young Tucker. He was pretty much the same underachieving, happy kid that I was, no big surprise. He had no idea that he was going to live a life that would make a difference.

He wouldn't get a hint of that until the day of his graduation.

The day began at our home on Pemberwick Island. Tori and I had purchased the remote property on the north side of the island known as Chinicook. It was the spot where, in another life and time, her father died trying to protect his beloved island from the invaders that had taken over our world. We built a seaside home and kept the rest of Chinicook as an unspoiled nature preserve, in honor of Mr. Sleeper.

Hours later, Tori, Kent, Olivia, and I sat by ourselves to the far side of the football stands in Cardinal Stadium. Anyone looking at us would think we were the grandparents of a graduate. Or maybe some proud aunts and uncles. They wouldn't have seen the helicopter that dropped us off behind the school an hour before the ceremony, or the bodyguards who were never far away. You can't be too careful.

We had done the same thing two years earlier for Kent's graduation from Arbortown High. We had also been to Arbortown the week before to celebrate the graduation of Tori Sleeper and Quinn Carr. It was both a satisfying and somewhat sad experience for all of us. But we weren't there just to revel in our own successes.

We were also there on business.

When young Tucker stepped up onto the stage to receive his diploma, Tori squeezed my arm and said, "I wasn't so sure you could do it."

I gave her a playful shove and said, "Hey, that kid has potential."

"I'm counting on it," she said with a sly smile.

When the ceremony was over, as the beaming parents mingled with the excited graduates, I made my way through the crowd to find Mom, Dad, and Tucker. Though I had seen them from afar many times, I never approached them. Seeing my mom and dad together gave me a mixed feeling of joy and despair. It was wonderful to see them, but I missed them terribly.

"Excuse me, Mr. and Mrs. Pierce," I said. "Congratulations."

They looked at me with big, genuine smiles that also had a touch of uncertainty. I guarantee they weren't so sure about Tucker graduating either, so the day was as much a relief as anything. Or when they saw me, was there some vague sense of recognition?

"Thanks," Dad said as his smile dropped into a look of confusion.

"Hey, aren't you—?"

"I am," I said.

Of course they'd recognize me. Not as the grown version of their own son, but as one of the most powerful people in the world, whose company invented the "H-fuel" that created a new industrial revolution. Together, we had been given more media coverage than most presidents combined.

Mom and Dad looked at me like I was an alien, and in some ways I probably was.

"What can we do for you?" Dad asked.

"I'd like a moment to speak with your son, the graduate," I said.

"Tucker?" Mom asked, incredulous.

"Do you have another son?" I asked, playfully.

"Uh, yeah, sure. I mean, no. Of course you can talk with him." She called out, "Tuck! Tucker! C'mere. Somebody wants to talk to you."

Young Tucker Pierce came bounding over, all smiles and enthusiasm. He walked right up to me and looked me right in the eye.

"Hey, I know you," he said.

"I'm not surprised," I replied.

Tucker stuck out his hand and shook mine with a strong, confident grip. With that simple act I had connected with my younger self. It was a good start. Strange, but good.

"Can I have a quiet word with you?" I asked.

"Uh, yeah, sure," Tucker said.

He gave Mom and Dad a curious look and followed me off.

I led him to the side of the football stands. On our way I saw Kent give me a big smile and a thumbs-up. Tori stood next to him with her arm draped through his. They both looked as proud as if their own kid had just graduated. Or maybe they were just enjoying the odd scene, as I had enjoyed it when they had done the same thing with their younger selves.

When we got to the side of the stands, Tucker stopped and faced me with confidence.

"What's this about?" he asked.

"What are your college plans?" I asked.

For the first time, Tucker looked unsure.

"I got accepted to a few schools," he said with a dismissive shrug. "Not sure why, my grades aren't the best. But I'm planning to go to community college. It's a whole lot cheaper."

"You've heard of my company, right?" I asked.

Tucker laughed. "Uh, yeah. I'm not from Mars."

"Well we offer scholarships to students we feel deserve encouragement and support," I said. "Full ride to the school of your choice. Including grad school."

Tucker's eyes grew wide. "And you're telling me this because . . . ?"

"We've been watching you, Tucker, and we think you have a promising future."

Tucker blinked, he smiled, he frowned, he chuckled nervously, and then he looked around as if there might be a hidden camera somewhere.

"Are you sure you've got the right guy?" he asked. "Tucker Pierce?"

"We've got the right guy," I said.

"What's the catch?" he asked.

"No catch," I replied. "The only thing we ask is that after graduation, you give serious consideration to joining us. We have offices all over the world and a wide variety of opportunities for someone who—"

"Yes," Tucker said with total conviction. "You're offering me a free ride to college and all I have to do is *consider* working for the most important people who ever existed? Why would I turn that down?"

I shrugged and said, "I don't know. You could be an idiot."

We both laughed at that. Of course we did. We had the same sense of humor.

"This isn't a joke?" he asked.

"Talk to your parents about it. Someone will be in contact with you tomorrow to outline the program. I truly hope you'll take us up on this offer. I think you would be a very valuable asset."

Tucker stuck out his hand to shake. "I'll do exactly that," he said. "But I'm pretty sure I know what's going to happen."

"Do you?" I asked. "It's not easy predicting the future."

"Oh I think this one isn't so hard. Thank you. Thank you very much."

Tucker turned and ran off, melting into the crowd, probably to find Mom and Dad.

We had had similar conversations with young Kent, Tori . . . and Quinn. Young Kent was in his second year at Cornell. Quinn had been accepted early admittance to MIT and Tori was all about going to the city. She wanted to attend NYU.

Young Tucker was right. Sometimes you *can* predict the future. If events played out the way we expected, one day these five young people would form the nucleus of the next generation of visionaries who would run our company. We needed young people with new ideas. People who thought like us. Who better to choose than . . .

us?

Olivia stepped up to me and put her arm through mine. "What did he say?"

"He'll accept," I said. "He's a smart kid, though he doesn't know it yet."

Olivia gave me a kiss on the cheek and said, "Oh he knows it. He just doesn't like to brag."

"Hey, get your hands off my man," Tori said with a smile as she walked up with Kent.

"He's my man too," Olivia said, chuckling.

"What about me?" Kent said.

"You, I have doubts about," Olivia said. "But I'll keep you around if I have to."

"How do you feel?" Tori asked me.

"I feel old," I said. "And incredibly alive."

Kent scanned the field that was still swarming with students and said, "I guess our work here is done."

"Nah," I said. "We're just getting started. Let's go home."

We turned toward the helicopter that would take us back to Pemberwick Island, away from our past, and straight into our future.

"Sir?" came an excited voice.

We all looked back to see Young Tucker running up to us.

"Change your mind already?" I asked.

"No, I just wanted to make sure. I mean. In case we don't get a call tomorrow. Do you have a business card or something?"

Kent, Tori, and Olivia laughed.

I dug into my pocket and handed my younger self a card.

"What's the matter?" I asked. "Don't you trust me?"

"For the record," Tucker said. "Not really."

That got another laugh.

"Smart," I said. "I promise we'll be in touch."

The four of us strode away from the field and the helicopter that was powering up.

I took one last look at the stadium to see that Tucker hadn't moved. He stood alone, staring at my business card as if it were some rare treasure that might disappear if he took his eyes off of it.

It was a simple card with only a few words.

SYLO

Today. Tomorrow. Forever.

Sequentia yconomus libertate te ex inferis obedianter.

We were the guardians.

We were SYLO.

THE END